HR: BEHIND CLOSED DOORS

BOOK 1

TERRY ECKSTEIN

HR: Behind Closed Doors
by Terry Eckstein

Copyright © 2024 Terry Eckstein
Mantorville Farms LLC
60779 231st Ave
Mantorville, MN 55955
507-635-5882

All rights reserved. No portion of this book may be reproduced in any form without permission from the publisher, except as permitted by US copyright law.

ISBN: 978-1-943501-02-1 US trade paperback
          978-1-943501-04-5 hardcover
          978-1-943501-03-8 e-book

Acknowledgements

I have so many people to thank for providing me with support and encouragement while I wrote this novel. The following people were closest to the project:

Kim Kaiser and Anne Granle spent many hours reviewing my weekly progress. Their changes, additions and deletions kept me focused on the story. Special thanks to Kim for allowing her image to be used on the cover.

The following people and their companies had a profound impact on the final story:

Jeffry Swertfeger, House of Phoenixx, LLC
Claudette Cruz, The Editing Sweetheart
Cheryl Murphy Lowrance, Ink Slinger Editorial Services
S Designs

A sincere thank you to three friends that had to endure my constant conversations regarding the book whenever we had dinner together:

Carla, Mary Ann and Barbara

A loving thank you to my children. They had to deal with a father that shut down parts of his life in order to stay focused on the book.

I must also mention Zeus. A loyal friend that was by my side while most of the writing took place.

Contents

Acknowledgements	5
Foreword	11
Active Shooter	13
Hangman's Noose	30
VTM	36
Interns	43
Guns at Work	52
Jeans Day	61
Help Wanted: Hot Women	65
Production Problem	68
Free Drinks	73
The Termination	88
The Letter	96
The Librarian	108
Visiting the Seagulls	133
Lactating in a Milk Truck	170
Debra	183
Grandma	197
Goat Rescue	204
The Covert Hire	211
I Got Caught	218
Molly's Bikinis	227
Curvy Women	235
Sympathy Sex	239
Adultery Defined	249

Conference Table Routine	256
Cats and Racist Dogs	262
Baseball	268
The Overnighter	274
Des Moines	292
I Should Have Listened to the Angel	313
Hickeys	322
The Video	332
Dinger	337
The Jail	346
Paul	358
Cellmate	370
Paul's Surprise	377
Bail	388
Three Years Later	397
The Eve of the Trial	400
Day 1	402
Day 2	405
Day 3	409
Day 4	427
Day 5	434
I Listened to the Angel	440
About the Author	445

Foreword

This is a work of fiction, inspired by true events the author experienced during his fifty-year career in human resources. To preserve the privacy of those who inspired the story, all names, job titles, companies, and most geographic locations where events actually occurred have been changed.

Most of this story is set in and around Mantorville, Minnesota, a community the author has come to love and cherish.

All of the characters are composites, creations combining characteristics of multiple real people with those from the author's imagination. Any resemblance to actual people, living or dead, is entirely coincidental.

Readers who have experienced harassment, abuse, and/or discrimination are cautioned that events depicted are graphic and could trigger harmful past experiences. *HR Behind Closed Doors* is suitable only for adult readers. The story contains sex, profanity, and minor violence—the things Human Resources departments don't talk about.

This novel is the first in a series that the author plans to write.

Active Shooter

Chapter 1

JIM WALKED INTO MY OFFICE with a gun in his shaking hand. I stood behind my desk. For a moment, I considered wrestling the gun from him, but Jim was much taller than me and in better shape. I looked into his bloodshot eyes and slowly asked, "What are you going to do with that gun, Jim?"

"I'm not going to hurt anybody," he replied. "I just came here because I don't want to die alone."

"Oh, Jim," I said sadly, "that'd hurt the people who love you. Your kids would be devastated. You don't want to do that."

"I've lost my family. I hurt Marjorie," said Jim. "They're much better off without me."

Three minutes earlier

Jim Rollins slammed the door of the car he'd borrowed from a friend. He was angry, venting his rage at anything close by. He'd parked in this lot many times over his last ten years working here. But this was the first time he'd chosen the front row, usually designated for visitors, and just a few steps from the main entrance to the administration building for Milk Trucks, Inc. He was supposed to be here to get his termination paperwork from the HR department.

The previous day he'd been fired by me, Connor Stone, director of human resources for MTI. Jim was a production supervisor, a position normally discharged by the director of operations. But I'd wanted to do the termination myself because I knew Jim and his family quite well. We attended the same church; I'd taught Jim's daughters in my Sunday School class. Two weeks ago, Jim was arrested and charged with felony domestic assault after he hit his wife, Marjorie, so hard that she'd needed medical treatment. He spent two days in jail before being released with a restraining order preventing him from seeing his wife or children. This past week he pleaded guilty to the charge and was awaiting his sentencing hearing.

Jim's problems were related to his alcoholism. I'd terminated Jim because of his attendance. Prior to missing four days in the past two weeks, Jim had been given three warnings over the previous year. He'd gotten more chances than most employees would've because when he wasn't drinking, he was the best supervisor the company had. His employees were loyal to him and covered for him many times.

But yesterday, his loyal friends couldn't help him. Jim had come to work late, drunk, and making a scene in his department. He was so drunk we couldn't even talk to him yesterday; I could've subjected him to a "for cause" drug test, but he'd been too difficult to work with, and I already had plenty of documentation to justify a termination. With his driver's license revoked, he'd had taken a cab to work that day, so I had one of our security officers take him back to the friend's house where he had been staying.

Today, Jim furtively looked around to make sure no one else

was in the area, then popped open the trunk of the car. He reached in and pulled out a handgun. Lifting the back of his jacket, he quickly shoved the gun between his belt and his trembling body. Jim was not here today to take care of his paperwork; he was here to take his life.

As he entered the lobby, Jim stopped at the reception desk, "Hello, Gloria."

She smiled. "Hi, Jim."

I'd let Gloria know that Jim was coming in, so she wasn't surprised to see him. I didn't tell her that Jim's employment had been terminated. I didn't have to. That news traveled fast through the informal network, surprising no one. His alcohol problem was well known, but Jim was still well-liked, and people were feeling his pain. Gloria was one of them; she'd asked if we could get Jim in a rehab program. I told her we'd tried, but that Jim had wanted no part in a program.

Now, with slurred speech, Jim told Gloria, "I'm here to see Connor for my final paperwork."

"I'll buzz you through," she replied kindly.

Jim walked to the hallway and, as the security buzzer sounded, opened the glass door to continue down the hall. As he started toward the executive suites, he reached back, pulling the gun out from under his jacket.

Gloria saw the gun and reacted quickly, activating the fire alarm. She punched the public address code into her phone to announce: "Active shooter in the building. This is not a drill. Active shooter in the building. This is not a drill." Finally, she dialed 911 to report an active shooter before joining the other employees running out of the MTI admin building.

Just then, Jim Rollins walked into my office.

Standing face-to-face with Jim and a gun, I quietly listened to him, trying to think what I should do. When he said everyone would be better off without him, I replied, "That's not what Marjorie told me."

"You talked to Marjorie?" Jim asked.

"Yes, Marjorie called me about an hour ago, pleading with me to give your job back."

"She did?"

"Marjorie said you're a good man, Jim, but that when you drink, you change."

A desperate look crossed Jim's face, and he began to howl. He raised the gun to his head and the howling got worse. He was shaking so badly, he put his left hand around his right wrist to try steadying the gun.

I hollered, "No, Jim!"

Then he fired the gun.

Five shots. Into the filing cabinet in my office.

Employees still in the hallway began screaming. I started around my desk to reach Jim, who stood with the gun still in his hand but now at his side. As I rounded the desk, I tripped over a box of employee files and fell, hitting my head on the corner of the cabinet he'd just shot full of holes. Dazed, with blood all over my face, I lay still on the floor.

Jane from Accounting was in the bathroom when this all began. She'd heard the fire alarm, but thought it was a drill—until she heard the gunshots. Now, running past my office, she saw Jim with the gun and me on the floor. She kept running, bursting through the exit doors, into the arms of a security guard, screaming, "He shot Connor! Connor's dead!"

Hank, my cousin and MTI's controller, was emergency manager for the admin building. He ran to Jane, asking "Did you see Connor?"

"Yes, I ran past his office. He's dead on the floor. Blood all over his head. Jim was there with a gun in his hand!"

"Did Jim try to hurt you?" he asked.

"No. He looked at me. He was crying. When he looked

down at Connor, I screamed and ran."

Back inside my office, Jim was helping me to sit up. "The box," I explained, "I forgot it was there."

Jim shook his head. "I just keep hurting people no matter what I do."

My phone rang, showing "Hank Thorson" on the display. I picked up as Hank blurted, "We thought you were dead."

"I tripped over a box and hit my head on the file cabinet," I told him. "Hank, I'll call you back in a minute, need to take care of a few things." I was still dizzy, but I needed to take care of Jim. I hung up and asked Jim to help me stand. Keeping one hand on my desk for balance, I asked, "Is that the only gun you have with you?"

"Yes," he replied.

"Any knives or other weapons?"

"No."

I told him to put the gun in the cabinet's top drawer and had him push the button to lock it. Jim had stopped crying, and he followed my instructions without saying a word. Then, I told him to remove his jacket and shirt and throw both behind my desk.

"If a SWAT team comes running in here," I told him, "I want them to know as soon as they see you that you're not armed." Jim removed his jacket and shirt, carefully setting them on the floor behind my desk.

I called Hank, who said Sherriff Schultz had just arrived. Hank handed him the phone.

I told the sheriff that Jim had only one weapon, which was now locked in my cabinet. I reported that Jim had removed his jacket and shirt and would be on his knees on the floor in front of me. "I'll be the guy standing—make that leaning—on my desk," I said, still dizzy.

Hearing what I said to the sheriff, Jim got down on his

knees in the middle of the office. My office was intentionally built like an exposed fishbowl; three of the four walls were made of glass and each had its own door—two led to hallways, the third into the office of the president's executive assistant.

We heard footsteps running down the hall before officers entered simultaneously from both hallway doors, shouting: "Hands in the air! Hands in the air!" Jim complied, his whole body shaking as all guns pointed at him.

The officer in charge demanded, "Where's your shirt?"

Jim responded, "On the floor behind the desk." They let him stand to put on his shirt, then handcuffed him, starting to lead him out. Jim spoke: "Wait."

Everyone stopped as he slowly turned. He looked at me and said simply, "Thank you."

I acknowledged him with a single nod.

"Tell Marjorie and the girls I love them!" he requested.

"I will," I said, then added, "I'm going to help you, Jim. It may take a day or two, but I will come visit you."

As soon as the officers left with Jim, paramedics ran into my office. I sat on my desk as they examined me and pronounced I'd need a few stitches.

With a paramedic on each side of me, I could stand with no problems, but after a few steps, I was dizzy and started to collapse. They caught me, and in moments, I was lying on a stretcher with my arms and legs strapped down. I complained about being confined and they said they'd unbuckle the straps once I was in the ambulance. As we prepared to leave, a deputy was putting up police tape to keep people out of my office.

I was rolled into the hall and out the front door. Flashing red lights all around us, we made our way to the ambulance across the parking lot, and I saw employees returning to the building. But seeing me, many of them started to cry. Others just held their hands to their face in shock.

One of the paramedics noted, "Your friends think you're dead."

"What?" I asked, confused.

The paramedic explained that a woman had come running out of the building saying I'd been shot dead. He added, "You are a sorry sight, lying there with your head covered in blood."

"Please wheel me back there and loosen these straps. I need to show them I'm alive."

The crowd was closer now but stopped their advance when they saw me. The paramedics helped me sit up, and I started waving. A surprised cheer erupted from the group as they all started to clap.

"OK, time to get you to the hospital," said another paramedic, who strapped me back down before loading me into the ambulance.

The MTI campus is located just outside the northern city limits of Rochester, Minnesota. That's why, instead of the Rochester City Police Department, the county sheriff's department answered the call. We were only ten minutes from the Saint Mary's campus of the Mayo Clinic, the world's largest hospital. I was hoping to quickly get my stitches and get home for some rest, knowing my cousin Hank would soon arrive to give me a ride.

But as I was rolled from the ambulance into the ER, I could see a large staff was waiting. They'd heard there was an active shooter at MTI and that there was a fatality, so everyone assumed I was just the first of several gunshot victims and that I'd been shot in the head. Upon learning my actual status, the crew quickly dispersed to take care of others.

My sister-in-law, Dakotah, worked as a nurse there, but

I doubted she was on shift then. ER staff worked quickly to triage me and check for concussion. After the nurse had cleaned the wound and much of the blood from my head, the doctor sutured me with eleven stitches. The nurse told me to rest until my release and I fell asleep almost immediately, only to be awakened after twenty minutes by the familiar voices of my mother and grandmother standing next to my bed. At least I was more presentable, now that all the blood had been washed off.

I should point out here that although Hank and I were born cousins, we're legally brothers. Hank's birth mother, Olive Thorson, adopted me in third grade, after my parents died in a car accident. When she insisted I keep Stone as my last name, Hank teased that she didn't want to tarnish the Thorson name. But Olive—Mom—said she wanted to let me keep my identity, keeping the Stone name alive. She raised Hank, me, Hank's biological brother James, and Moses, another son she'd adopted from Rwanda. She raised all four of us boys as a single mother. I never met her husband; my uncle died young.

My grandma is Augusta Thorson. Hank's kids refer to their great-grandma as "Grandma Gustie" but everyone around Mantorville calls her Grandma Thorson. Hank, Olive, and my Grandma (Gustie) all live in separate farmsteads near Mantorville, a few miles west of Rochester. I live near Mantorville's Zumbro Valley Golf Club, located along the Zumbro River. Mantorville is a village with just over a thousand people. It's known for its many historic buildings constructed in the 1850s of limestone blocks mined from a quarry that still operates in Mantorville today.

In the ER, the nurse directed Mom and Grandma to wait in

the lobby. As they left me, Grandma assured me that she'd continue to pray for me. She didn't need to say it; Grandma Gustie was always praying for something. While I was growing up, I'm sure she prayed just for me as much as for my three brothers combined. I always managed to get in trouble when I was younger.

James, Moses, and I were the same age, but Hank was two years older. James and Moses, who'd always followed Hank's lead, were always getting praised whereas I always got into trouble. James had been awarded for bravery when he died in combat, and he'd left three beautiful daughters to his widow; Dakotah and James met when they both served in the navy. James had made the navy his career. Dakotah left the navy but continued in the US Navy Reserve when she and James started having children. Grandma Olive takes care of the girls whenever Dakotah gets called to active duty. Dakotah is part Native American. All her daughters have her same Native American features, including her long black hair. Dakotah had just gotten promoted in her job as a nurse at Mayo Clinic.

Moses always excelled. He returned to Rwanda after receiving his master's degree; he's currently in a government job and even thinking about running for office. I thought about how today was a good example of how things usually went with us. If Hank, James, or Moses had been there instead of me, sure, they would've talked Jim out of shooting himself, just like I did. But they would not have tripped over the box and hurt themselves.

Mom and Grandma Gustie went back to Mantorville with plans for me to spend the night at Hank's place. He'd take me to work in the morning, since my vehicle was still at MTI. Hank's a widower. He lives alone now that his three kids—Jessica, Aaron, and Jacob—are scattered across the country, teaching at different universities, following in their late mother's footsteps. He'll admit she's gone, but in his heart, Hank still believes his wife is alive. He even has private investigators looking for Faith, who disappeared when she and Hank were on a cruise. I admit I still grieved for him, not really knowing what he must feel. I'd never had kids and was still good friends and stayed in touch with my ex-wife, Jami, who thrived at her job in Chicago.

I was released without restrictions and instructed to get a good night's rest. Per MTI company policy, I got a doctor's note with a full release before Hank picked me up and we headed to his house. Mom and Grandma had been busy preparing dinner in Hank's kitchen. Mom wanted to know more about the shooting, so I took a few minutes to describe what transpired while they filled the kitchen table with enough food to feed way more than four people.

We took our seats and everyone stopped talking, not knowing who'd pray. When we were younger, Grandma would call on one of us boys. Tonight, the silence was broken by Grandma. "Dear Lord, we thank you for watching over Connor today. Please continue to take care of our family, wherever we may be, throughout this world. Please bless this meal, and we thank you for providing it. Amen."

The rest of us all said together, "Amen."

I began to relax in the coziness of Hank's kitchen. Although it was mid-May, it was still cold outside. There was a wood-burning fireplace along one wall; Hank had started a fire while I was talking. We sat at a large, old, oak table at one end of the kitchen, eating church hotdish, my favorite since childhood. I knew Mom had made tonight's hotdish because it had tater tots; Grandma made hers with wild rice instead of potatoes.

Grandma was the first to speak. "I was at church yesterday and spoke with Marjorie about Jim. She talked to Pastor about getting help for Jim. She knows Jim loves her, but he's a different person when he drinks."

"It's going to be a lot harder to get him help now," I said.

"What do you think will happen to him?" Mom asked.

"Jim never threatened anyone," I told her, "But he drove without a license, carried a gun without a permit, and discharged the gun in public. Plus, he already pled guilty to assault for hitting Marjorie. He'll get some jail time, but I don't know if it'll be months or years. I'll make sure he gets into AA as soon as he's out of jail."

"That'll be good," said Grandma. "AA helps a lot of people, both Christians and non-Christians. Will Jim get his job back?"

"No," I said, "Jim has a record, so won't be eligible for rehire."

We spent the rest of supper chatting about other things before we started getting tired.

Grandma's final words that evening were about her angel. She often talked about the angel living with her. Folks in Mantorville didn't believe her, of course, but people still respected her. Even she had never seen her angel, but she told everyone about her evidence—that Jacob's dog, Thomas, can see her angel. And I'm pretty sure he can. Whenever Thomas visits Grandma Gustie, he goes from room to room looking for something and, when he finds it, he starts barking at it. To us, he's barking at an empty wall. After his initial bark-greeting, Thomas stays in the room with the angel. Thomas always prefers to be with people, except at Grandma Gustie's. There, he stays for hours in a room, presumably because he's with the angel. I actually saw the angel once when I was fourteen, but I was too ashamed to tell anyone because of what I was doing at the time.

Grandma Gustie is known as a prayer warrior in the community, with many victories she's helped win through prayer. Her husband was the first Hank Thorson, Hank's father was the second, and my brother Hank was the third. My grandfather and uncle died at young ages due to heart problems. Grandma Gustie had just turned forty when she was widowed. She and Grandpa were successful farmers, so she could've rented out her land and lived comfortably for the rest of her life. Instead, she became a missionary, working for twenty-five years across many African countries. Now, aged ninety-two, she remained the Thorson family matriarch.

"My angel never left my house today," said Grandma, adding, "so the Lord obviously knew that Connor wouldn't need the angel's help."

"I wish your angel would've been there today—to prevent me from hitting my head."

It was getting late, and I had to get to bed. Grandma and Mom left together. Hank assigned me to Jacob's bedroom and then handed me a bag Mom and Grandma had filled with overnight supplies.

As I lay in bed, I started to question why Grandma's angel didn't prevent me from tripping over the box today. I thought back to a time we'd all gathered around Jacob's bed, where he was recovering in the hospital after accidentally shooting himself in the leg. Jacob had just finished telling us how his vision got blurry every time a coyote approached him while he was lying injured in the woods. Grandma had looked at Jacob and said, "Your vision wasn't blurred when you looked at coyotes; you were seeing what was actually taking place. The same thing happened to me many years ago when I was working in Africa." This had gotten everyone's attention because we thought we'd heard all Grandma Gustie's stories about Africa, but blurred vision was not a story any of us recalled.

She continued, "I'd been in Africa about ten years when I was asked to start a new mission in an area that'd never seen any Christian missionaries. I had plenty of support from back home; so, we had the resources to construct a good-sized building to house a church, a school, and some living quarters. Things were going well. Perhaps too well, because the local leaders resented the fact that so many people in the area were becoming Christians.

"After a few months, I was warned by some of the mission's supporters; one of the workers living in the building told me an opposition group planned to burn it all. The group had secretly told the workers to leave the building that night or die in the fire. Learning this, I made everyone leave and asked them to pray for me because I was going to stay. They pleaded for me to come with them, but I decided I was going to do everything I could to save the mission."

Pausing for breath, Grandma Gustie continued, "The local people knew I had a rifle; they'd helped me hunt. I heard later that many men were reluctant to join the opposition group because they knew I had this weapon, rare in that area at that time. I never even considered using my gun; I was there to save souls, not kill people. But the opposition group never got more than twenty men because of it.

"That night, at about ten, I saw the group approaching about a half-mile away. Most of them were carrying torches, making it easy to spot them. I sat by the front window, watching them get closer and closer. I had decided that when they were near the building, I'd go out on the porch and try to talk to them. I considered bringing the rifle with me but knew that would've sent the wrong message.

"I stood up and looked out the window and my vision suddenly blurred. Just then, all the men turned and ran back to the edge of the yard. I thought maybe I'd scared them when I stood up; maybe they thought I was going to start shooting. I crossed the room to look through another window's shutters in a position where I could see them, but they couldn't see me."

"After half an hour, they started moving toward the house again. Some of the torches had burned out, but many were still brightly lit. When they got close, the same thing happened again. My vision got blurry, and the men retreated. As they turned away, my vision became clear. Then one of the men looked right at me; I could see terror in his eyes. They were all very afraid of something.

"This blurred vision and the group running away in fear repeated two more times. Then their strategy changed. They surrounded the building, splitting up to approach from multiple directions. I watched from different windows, and the same thing kept happening: my vision would become blurred, and the men would turn and run.

"Finally, they decided to stay farther away but close enough to throw their torches onto the building. But as hard as they tried, these strong men's torches never went far enough to reach the building. Sometimes, I was sure the torch would hit, but my vision would blur, and the torch would fall back into the yard. I knew the blurring was tied to what was taking place, but I didn't understand how. As morning approached, they didn't have any lit torches left, so they went back to their homes.

"News spread quickly throughout the region that the mission could not be burned down. Attendance at our church services started growing, along with school enrollments. I wrote home to the churches supporting the mission and received the funds we needed to build a larger church and school. After a while, many parents wanted to send their children to our schools, but they lived too far away to travel every day, so we built a large dormitory for those students. We eventually added an orphanage and a clinic to the mission—all because of the events on my night of 'blurred vision'."

"Did you ever figure out what caused the blurring?" Jacob had asked her.

"Yes. About a month after the eventful night, I was talking to a recent convert who asked me what had happened to the big men in white robes. I told him I didn't know what he was talking about, and he told me that he was one of the men who'd attacked the mission that night. He said that every time they got close to the building, a big man wearing a white robe and holding a shiny sword would appear and chase them back away from the building.

"He said that as the night went on, more men in white robes appeared on all sides of the building. When the group started to throw their torches at the building, the men in the white robes would use their swords to lazily swat down the torches before they reached the building. It was then that I realized what happened. God answered my prayers by sending angels to protect the mission. Whenever it made itself visible to those men, I was looking through the angel, which made my vision blurry. Apparently, when angels make themselves visible to someone, other people are unable to see clearly through the angel."

Grandma Gustie walked to the side of the bed, holding Jacob's hand in her own small hands. "You see, Jacob, each time your vision was blurred today, an angel was standing between you and the coyote, and the coyote could see the angel."

After a prolonged silence, Aaron had asked, "Why didn't God just have the angels bring Jake to the ER then? Or why didn't an angel prevent Jake from getting shot in the first place?"

Grandma Gustie replied, "I don't know. Maybe when we're with Him in heaven, we'll understand why God does specific things. But I've come to learn there's a reason for everything He does. We have to remember that we don't always do what God wants us to do. When we take actions that are not in His will, we set in motion a chain of events God never wanted us to experience."

I'd learned a lot about angels when Grandma had told us her story that night.

Still lying in bed at Hank's house, I now thought back to the day I saw an angel, almost forty years ago. I'd been looking at hunting knives in the local hardware store. The knife I wanted was seventeen dollars, but I only had fourteen on me. I picked it up, held it in my hand. I wanted it so badly. I was ready to put the sheathed knife into my pocket, to walk out of the store. Nobody would notice. Plus, I'd justified to myself that I'd mail the money to the store once I had it; I wasn't stealing, just borrowing the knife until I could afford to pay for it.

Still holding the knife, I'd looked around and seen no one in the area. Then, suddenly, a tall man stood in front of me. He wore regular clothes, but as I'd looked up to his face, his clothes changed to a shiny white robe. He didn't have a sword, but I was still terrified, speechless. The man/angel spoke to me without moving his lips. Just like you'd hear a regular person's speech, I'd heard the angel unmovingly say, don't do it.

I didn't speak, but I thought, Do what?

The angel ignored my feigned ignorance: If you do it, you'll change the course of your life.

At that moment, the hunting knife was no longer important to me. I thought, Are you my grandma's angel?

Yes.

Then, while still standing in front of me, the angel disappeared. I put the knife and sheath back in their box and left the store. So far, I'd never since been tempted to steal something that wasn't mine. And I never told anyone about the angel because I didn't want to admit that I almost broke the commandment Thou shalt not steal.

I fell asleep in Jacob's old bed that night, wishing that Grandma's angel would've intervened at work today, to prevent me from getting hurt.

Hangman's Noose

CHAPTER 2

THE NEXT MORNING, HANK AND I got to MTI at six thirty. Main offices opened at seven, but most managers arrived early. Do Not Enter tape remained over all three of my office doors.

I greeted Brian Schmidt, director of security and safety, who told me all sales managers were traveling, so I could use one of their offices, then, "Boss, I'm gonna need to see you in a couple hours. I'm in the middle of an investigation but should be done in an hour or two."

He'd worked for me over twelve years, and we had a good relationship, yet Brian always called me "Boss" and it'd become his fond nickname for me.

"What kind of investigation?" I asked.

Brian replied, "Harassment, but not sexual."

"Okay, let me know when you're ready."

Brian was a highly skilled police investigator. Both the safety manager and a security manager reported to him. His team got involved with investigations for our HR department. When it was serious, Brian personally handled the investigation himself.

I got settled in my temporary office, as my boss and the MTI president, Marvin Peterson, walked in. "Welcome back,

Connor. Things could've been a lot worse yesterday. You did a good job of managing a chaotic situation."

"Thank you," I said.

Marvin asked me to walk through all the buildings on campus this morning. He wanted everyone to see I was back at work. I told him that was a good idea and that I'd start my tour as soon as we opened. When Marvin left, I stepped into the bathroom to look in the mirror. I looked worse than I felt, so I put two Band-Aids from the first aid kit over my stitches.

The tour went well; I was warmly greeted by everyone. Yesterday's events were on the evening news, so when I walked into Jim Rollins's department, I received a standing ovation from everyone there. Some had been mad at me back when I'd terminated Jim, but after hearing how Jim's suicide was thwarted, everyone was now appreciative. I headed back to the temporary office after my ninety-minute walking tour and, as I approached, I saw Brian waiting for me in the glass-walled office.

"Boss, this is a bad one."

"Let's have it," I said.

He began, "Jevonte Harris came to work this morning and found a hangman's noose on top of the keyboard at his workstation. As you know, Jevonte is the only Black employee working in engineering's drafting and design group. He was the only person to receive a noose."

"Jevonte was on the front page of the last newsletter," I noted. "I wonder if that has anything to do with it."

"We can find out when we talk to the man who did it," Brian told me.

"You already know who it is?"

"Yes. Most employees know we have hidden and visible cameras, but not this guy. The first shows him throwing someone's jacket over a visible camera. A second shows him putting the noose on Jevonte's desk and taking the trophy Jevonte received as engineering's employee of the year. The newsletter article had a picture of Jevonte with his trophy."

"Who was it?" I asked.

Brian paused for effect, then smiled, "Buddy Jay Houston."

"Oh geez, go get him and bring him up here."

Brian smiled again as he left to get Buddy. I called Debra and asked her to prepare a termination packet for Buddy Jay Houston. Debra eagerly responded, "Really?"

"Yes," I said, "his day has come."

Buddy Jay was an HR nightmare, always complaining about something and constantly irritating his coworkers. His job performance was satisfactory, and the one time he got in serious trouble, he'd taken immediate corrective action to keep his job. Nevertheless, he still hurt the ongoing performance of his coworkers. We'd all been waiting for a reason to let him go.

A few minutes after Debra gave me the paperwork, Brian entered with Buddy Jay. They each took a chair in front of my desk. Workers in the area began staring through the glass wall at us; everyone knew that if Brian and I met together with an employee, they were most likely getting terminated.

I got up to close the door. Buddy Jay spoke first. "What's up?"

"We have a serious problem," I told him.

Buddy Jay sat up straight in his chair, "It's because of my NRA tattoo, right?"

"This has nothing to do with your NRA tattoo," I said.

Hearing this was not the issue, Buddy Jay still pulled up his sleeve to display the NRA logo on his upper arm, "I figured you were upset with me because of this. I heard you and Hank quit the NRA, so I figured you were upset about my tat.

Why'd you quit, anyway?"

As he clearly expected a response to this tangential question, I said, "Hank and I were members for over thirty years. When we first joined, they supported shooting sports, with rifles and pistols. We wanted to protect our right to arms for hunting. Our problem for us is that NRA's goal today seems to be putting guns in the hands of every mentally disturbed person in our country."

"Are you saying I'm mentally disturbed!?" Buddy Jay accused.

"No. We're here to talk about why you put a hangman's noose on Jevonte Harris's desk."

Buddy Jay looked to Brian, then at me. "That wasn't me."

"Buddy Jay, do you remember last year when I asked you to stop flying Confederate flags from your pickup truck when you were on MTI property?" I asked.

"You wouldn't let me express my Southern roots," Buddy replied.

"Don't give me that 'Southern roots' bull; we've been through this before. You have three generations before you from Wisconsin that were born and raised there. You were born and raised in Minnesota. And last year you admitted the farthest south you've ever been is Iowa. You have no Southern roots. I told you last year that flying the Confederate flag 'had the same effect as displaying a hangman's noose' and more than twenty African American MTI employees were personally offended by your display. So, you took the flags down, but now you go and put a hangman's noose on Jevonte's desk."

"Why do you think it was me?" asked Buddy Jay.

"You obviously don't know that for every camera you see at MTI, there are two hidden ones."

Buddy Jay slouched in his chair, head down.

I continued, "We have video of you throwing a uniform jacket over the visible camera, and video of you placing the noose on Jevonte's desk and taking his trophy."

Buddy Jay looked up at me, "Are you firing me?"

"Yes. You are no longer an employee of MTI."

"It's just not fair," he whined, "The black guys get all the breaks. He got a thousand-dollar bonus, and his family gets to have dinner at the Hubbell House for free. That's not fair."

"Buddy Jay, Jevonte was named the engineering employee of the year based on his coworkers' votes for most productive employee. Do I need to point out that the vast majority of coworkers are White?"

"They voted for him because his son's so popular on the football team," Buddy Jay argued. "My son should've had that running back position, but the coach wanted a black kid in the position."

I countered, "The coach most likely felt that Jevonte's son was the best qualified for the position."

"The kid is fast, but all Blacks are fast," he continued. "It goes back to when they had to run in the jungles. My son's a true American and should've had the position."

"Jevonte was born and raised in Illinois," I sighed, exasperated. "He got his college degree in Illinois. His kids were born in Illinois and have been growing up in Minnesota since we hired him. He and his family are true Americans."

Buddy Jay spewed, "Say what you want, but this company always rewards the jungle bunnies and screws the White guys."

I leaned forward. "Buddy Jay, you asked me if I thought you were mentally disturbed. I don't think you're mentally disturbed, but I can see that you are racist. I'm not going to let an overt racist work at MTI."

I handed the termination paperwork to Buddy Jay. "These

forms explain when your different benefits end and what you need to do to continue any of them. If you have any questions after you leave, you can call me or Debra. Brian will escort you to your locker to get any personal things you have there. Once you leave, you cannot return to MTI property unless you have permission from me in advance. Also, we do not tolerate any retaliation against our employees. If I hear you've caused any further trouble for Jevonte Harris, I'll report you to the sheriff. Understand?"

Buddy Jay acknowledged with his eyes and then stood up.

Brian also stood. "Let's go," he said. As the two of them walked out of my office, I called Debra to process the termination.

VTM

CHAPTER 3

IT WAS MIDMORNING, AND I hadn't checked my emails yet, but before I could open my laptop, Debra buzzed to tell me Merlot was on the line and didn't sound happy. Merlot was actually Ronald Herbst, Chief Human Resources Officer at Vocational Truck Manufacturing Company in Des Moines, Iowa. VTM was MTI's parent company since they purchased MTI five years ago. I reported directly to Marvin, the MTI president in Rochester, but on the org chart, I had a dotted line connecting me to Ronald Herbst in Des Moines.

I nicknamed him "Merlot" after an incident a few years ago. Whenever a corporate officer flew in from Des Moines to visit us, it was common practice for the MTI host to take them out to dinner after work. I chose a popular barbeque restaurant for our first outing and thought the evening went fine. But after he got back to Des Moines, he did nothing but complain to his staff about the place I'd taken him. One of his assistants, in an effort to help me, told me that in the future I should only take him to restaurants with a good wine list. The barbeque place we went to didn't even have wine. It was at that point that I gave him the name Merlot.

The nickname became even more applicable a couple months later when he and I traveled to MTI's branch in San Francisco. We'd visited the branch in the morning and on the way back to the airport, we stopped at a place Merlot knew had a good wine list. The restaurant offered a wine he'd tried a few years ago, and he couldn't stop talking about it. When the waiter informed us Merlot's special wine selection was only available by the bottle, Merlot was disappointed, so I offered to share the bottle with him.

We'd finished the whole bottle, along with our lunch, when the waiter brought our check. Company travel policy required that the highest-ranking employee at a lunch or dinner pay for the meal and report it on their expense report, but as Merlot looked over the bill, he got a strange look on his face. "The bottle of wine was $190, and with our lunch, the total is $290 before the tip."

I could see this really bothered him. He obviously didn't want to explain the three-hundred-dollar lunch to his boss. I, on the other hand, knew I could explain it to Marvin, so I said, "Let me pay for it." Merlot was relieved. I paid for lunch, and we went to the airport. I did get asked about the lunch when Marvin was approving my expense report and I told him exactly what happened. Marvin and Merlot were equals on the org chart, and Marvin wasn't going to stir up trouble over a bottle of wine.

Today, I answered his call, "Hello, Ronald."

Merlot shouted, "Why didn't you call me? I had to hear about the shooting from our CEO!"

"After Jim Rollins was arrested, I was strapped to a stretcher and ambulanced to the ER," I explained. "By the time I was able to call, I figured you'd already heard, so I didn't contact you."

"I thought he shot a file cabinet. Why did you have to go to the hospital? Did you have post-traumatic-stress issues?" he asked sarcastically.

I felt like telling Merlot he was a jerk, but instead gave him the details of the incident. After I finished, he gave me a short lecture. "I'm the CHRO; I need to know about these types of incidents right away. I don't want to hear about them from my boss. Understand?"

"Yes," I said.

Merlot abruptly hung up on me just as three women from accounting, the department headed by my brother Hank, walked into my temporary office. Mary, Pat, and Jennifer had worked at MTI for a while. Mary, the senior member of the group, having been here over twenty years, spoke first. "Can we talk to you?"

"Sure, have a chair."

They all sat down, and Mary started, "We've talked to Hank—"

"And he referred us to you because our issue involves someone from another department."

"What's the problem?" I asked.

"When Mr. Olson owned the company, men and women couldn't sit at the same table for lunch," Mary said. "The three of us have had lunch together for years. We're sometimes joined by other women, but only recently has a man begun sitting at our table. It seems that all the rules and traditions that Mr. Olson established have been done away with."

I said, "So you prefer to have a women-only table at lunch?"

Jennifer replied, "When it's just us girls, we can speak more freely and talk about women's issues. So yes, we'd like a women's table."

"Mr. Olson had a number of rules and policies that were not written or a part of the employee handbook," I said.

"Most employees appreciate the fact that we no longer have unwritten rules to follow. None of you complained when we started allowing coffee in the office."

Pat asked, "So you're not going to let us have a women's lunch table?"

I shook my head. "We're not going to create a women's lunch table, but if you tell me the name of the man who has lunch at your table, I can ask him to have lunch at a different table."

Mary spoke up. "Buddy Jay Houston."

Keeping my face straight, I looked at each woman. "I promise each of you that beginning today, Buddy Jay Houston will no longer be having lunch at your table." They all smiled and stood to shake my hand, each thanking me for solving their problem.

As they left, I thought about some of the other changes since George Olson sold the company to VTM. He actually had a rule banning men and women from traveling together. Shortly after VTM purchased our company, a female corporate VP in their HR department asked to travel with me to Texas to observe my civility training presentation. The first time I'd met her in-person, she'd made me nervous because she was so attractive. On the phone, I'd felt uncomfortable at her travel request and didn't respond right away. "Is something wrong?" she asked.

I told her, "Our previous owner didn't allow men and women to travel together, so you just caught me off guard."

"I'm a trans woman, if that helps."

I went silent again, not knowing how to respond.

She broke the silence again. "Just kidding. Actually, I'm gay, so I will not be making a move on you."

I responded, "I think we're going to get along just fine."

And we did. Julia was the closest friend I had at corporate. We didn't see each other often, but when we did, we were intimate. We cared a lot about each other, but Julia had always been clear that she planned to be with a woman. We really got to know each other well a few years ago when we went on a recruiting trip together in New England. On that trip, Julia initiated a sexual relationship with me. Our week together turned into a training week with Julia teaching me sexual things I'd never been exposed to before.

I'd always believed that by growing up in Mantorville, I was a man of the world. Mayo Clinic hired people from around the world, and many of them lived in Mantorville, so I went to school with kids from other countries and I learned about their cultural traditions. But when it came to sex, Julia exposed me to the fact that I'd lived a sheltered life in Mantorville. I was in my late forties when I met Julia and she was only the second woman I'd been naked with in my life. But I wasn't the only person at MTI getting exposed to more sex.

In my two prior decades at MTI, Mr. Olson had never tolerated sexual harassment. Recently, I'd become concerned about the notable increase in sexual harassment complaints after we transitioned from Mr. Olson's ownership to VTM. Mr. Olson's company had twelve branches with 250 employees spread throughout the USA, another 200 employees at manufacturing plants in Wisconsin, plus the main plant and headquarters in Rochester with 800 employees. Since VTM took over, we added two of their branches and hired another 50 employees in those locations. In Rochester, we added over 100 employees, mostly administrative. So, MTI's total employment went up twelve percent, from 1,250 to 1,400.

During the first year of VTM ownership, we had fifteen sexual harassment complaints, versus just one complaint every three to four years when Mr. Olson owned the company.

It was clear the huge increase in complaints wasn't due to a twelve-percent increase in employees; it was caused by a change in behavior.

The situation reminded me of being in college. I'd gone to the University of North Dakota, which had students from all kinds of sheltered backgrounds. I was there on a hockey scholarship, so couldn't really act up much, but other freshmen, especially those who came from strict families, had trouble controlling their new freedom living in the dorms. They went wild, acting like adolescents. In Mr. Olson's company culture, men and women couldn't go to lunch together and were discouraged from meeting after work. Now, after selling to VTM, many employees felt free to go wild, even making sexual advances to each other at work. Only once did a man complain about sexual advances from a woman; the rest of the complaints were from women reporting men who'd crossed the line.

The rest of my day was routine. I left early and stopped by the Rochester County jail to see Jim Rollins. He'd already pled guilty to the new charges and was waiting to be sentenced. Jim's plea agreement called for a six-month sentence for the domestic assault charge and three-months for the shooting at MTI. The sentences would be served concurrently at a state prison. So, if the judge approved the deal, Jim could be out in six months.

Jim actually looked pretty good. We could only visit for a few minutes through a window in the visitors' room. I was surprised at how positive he was. He said our pastor had visited him earlier in the day. Marjorie couldn't visit because of the restraining order, but Pastor had brought messages from Marjorie and the girls.

I smiled at him. "You sure look good today, Jim."

"I feel a lot better. Marjorie still loves me and will give me another chance. While I'm in jail, I can't drink, so I hope to be able to stay sober when I get out. And Pastor convinced me to join AA and start meetings while I'm in prison."

"That's great," I said. "We have a number of AA members at MTI. The people who stay in the program do very well."

Jim asked, "Who's in it at MTI?"

"I can only give you one name, because I don't have permission from the others. Hank has been going to meetings for over thirty years."

"Really? Hank told me he was an alcoholic, but I didn't know he still went to AA meetings."

Hank was a recovering alcoholic and hadn't had a drink for more than thirty years. He found out at an early age that he couldn't handle alcohol. He never drank every day, but when he did, he couldn't stop. Grandma Gustie led a family intervention that had hit Hank hard; he hadn't realized how he hurt people when he was drunk. He hadn't had a drink since then.

My time with Jim was up and I told him I was glad he was making plans to start life anew. An officer came to the door on my side of the glass and escorted me out.

Interns

CHAPTER 4

It was Thursday in early June. Our summer interns had started that Monday, and today I was hosting a lunch for them in the company Event Center.

Each summer, we had over thirty college juniors as interns, so every major department got at least one and some had up to six. We got the interns together for lunch every other week while they were here so that they got to know each other; I also liked to answer their questions in a group setting. By the end of summer, they understood MTI better than some long-term employees. During their senior year, ninety percent of them would receive job offers from MTI. Almost all would accept the offer; those who didn't accept were usually going on to grad school. This was their first week at work and our first group lunch went well.

After lunch, they dispersed back to their departments. As I headed back to my office, one of the interns stopped me, saying he'd like to talk about his medical exam.

I was confused. "What medical exam?"

"That's the problem I have," he said. "I talked to some of the other interns, and I seem to be the only one who had a medical exam."

"When did you have it?"

"This morning, in the Medical Center."

I pointed across the campus to a small building. "That office?"

"Yes."

Now I was concerned. Our nurse and her assistant worked at our Wisconsin plants on Thursdays. There should've been no one in that building this morning. I asked, "What time was the exam?"

"I heard the announcement a few minutes after ten."

"Announcement?"

"Yes," he said. "There was an announcement over the PA system saying I was to report to the medical center."

"Your name is Jonathon, right?"

"Yes."

As we made the block-long walk to the medical center, I called Brian. "I need you to meet me at the medical center right now. Also, can we view surveillance from the computer kiosk in the Medical Center?"

Brian responded, "Sure, Boss. As long as I log into our network, I can bring up any of the cameras. What's going on?"

"We need to investigate a complaint from one of our interns. He'll be with me when you get to the medical center."

Brian responded, "Be there shortly."

As I put my phone back in my pocket, Jonathon said, "I'm sorry for the trouble."

I clarified, "You're not causing any trouble, we just need to learn more about this medical exam."

Brian was nearby and got to the Medical Center just as Jonathon and I arrived. Brian used his master key, and the three of us entered the lobby, the first of the building's five rooms. We passed the admin assistant's large desk, several waiting-room chairs, and a computer kiosk for employee use.

The hallway held doors to four more rooms: the nurse's private office, two examination rooms, and a bathroom.

Brian asked, "What video do you need?"

"We need to see who entered this building around ten this morning," I told him.

We started reviewing the entrance-camera's video.

"Here we go," said Brian as we watched two men approach the entrance. Brian slowed the video so Jonathon could get a good look. We saw a company security guard from Brian's staff and our bottled-water vendor's deliveryman, who we subsequently named Waterman. The guard unlocked the door and held it open for Waterman to push his full cart into the lobby. The guard and Waterman waved at each other as the guard walked away, and Waterman closed the door.

Jonathon pointed, "It's the guy with the cart, except when I was with him, he was wearing a white lab coat." The large window out front allowed us to see the lobby, where we watched Waterman switch out bottles on the fountain before pushing the cart into the corner. He then walked down the hall toward the other rooms.

He was now out of our sight, so Brian explained, "The nurse's office is locked, but the two exam rooms are kept unlocked, so they're available to first responders." In less than a minute, Waterman returned to the lobby wearing a white lab coat. He then used the phone on the assistant's desk, most likely making the announcement for Jonathon to come to the Medical Center. A few minutes later, we saw Jonathon enter the lobby, where he was greeted by Waterman, who pointed down the hallway, where Jonathon receded out of our view. Brian zoomed in on the front door; the deadbolt's status indicator turned from green to red. Waterman was now alone with Jonathon in the locked building.

Jonathon told us, "The guy told me to go to the last room

and take off my shirt. It's like a typical clinic exam room and I hung my shirt in the corner area there. He came in and told me to hop up on the bench. He used a stethoscope from one of the cabinets to listen to my heart, then said he had to check my feet and do a prostate exam. He told me to get totally naked and to put on backward a lab coat he got from the cabinet.

"I went into the corner changing area, closed the curtain, and took off everything and put on the lab coat. When I opened the curtain, he was putting on rubber gloves. He told me that before we went ahead, he wanted to make sure I didn't have a hernia, so he lifted the front of the coat and did the hernia check. I've had lotsa physicals for football and hockey, so I know what to expect. But after he had me cough both ways; he did something weird."

At this point, Jonathon stopped talking. I looked at Brian, who just shrugged his shoulders.

So, I asked, "What did he do?"

"He wrapped his hand around my penis and squeezed it a couple times. Then he knelt down to look straight at my genitals and said he had to examine me. It seemed like forever, but he probably touched me for about thirty seconds before he stood up and told me to turn around so he could check my prostate. I saw him finger some Vaseline out of a jar, then he told me to bend over the table. He said to keep looking straight ahead, that if I moved my head or neck, it'd make it more difficult for him to find my prostate.

"I felt his finger slide up my butt and pull out. He said that was to distribute the lubricant and that now he was going to examine my prostate gland. I was waiting for him to stick his finger in again when he said the angle was wrong. He told me to keep looking ahead as he lowered the table. His finger was moving around a lot, thrusting in and out; he said he was having trouble finding the gland. When I heard him make a weird noise, I asked if he had found it. He said he had, that everything was good, and to stay in position while he cleaned me up. When I straightened up, I noticed him putting his phone back in his lab coat pocket. I think he took a picture of my bare ass so I was super uncomfortable, but then he told me I could get dressed. When I came back out to the lobby, I didn't see anyone in the medical center, so I returned to my department."

We'd been standing in the lobby while Jonathon described his experience. I suggested we take a look at the exam room. Jonathon started walking ahead of us to the room and I glanced at Brian; I could tell we were both thinking the same thing.

In the exam room, I started, "Jonathon, you mentioned a few things you didn't feel were appropriate for a medical exam."

"Yeah, the way he touched my genitals and took the picture, if he did take a picture. Oh, and I just realized, he never examined my feet."

Brian excused himself to check on something and I asked Jonathon, "Was this your first prostate exam?"

"Yes," he said, "but I knew that the doctor had to stick his finger up my butt."

I asked him if he'd ever seen Waterman before; he hadn't. I wondered how Waterman picked him out, how he knew Jonathon's name to page him to the Medical Center. Then I remembered we had posters all over campus picturing the interns with their names and departments.

Brian walked back in as I was telling Jonathon, "I've had a few prostate exams over the years, and at each exam, the doctor only stuck his finger in me one time, and there was no thrusting."

Brian told us, "The reason I excused myself was to check the dumpster behind the building." He pointed to the empty garbage can in the corner of the room. "I thought it was strange there was no plastic bag in the garbage, so I checked the closest dumpster and found this." Brian held up a clear plastic bag containing only a used condom. Brian insensitively remarked, "That wasn't his finger he was thrusting up your butt."

Jonathon held his hands to his face, almost crying. "Oh my God, he butt-fucked me. I want to kill him!"

"It's OK to feel that way after what you have been through," I said, "but let's do this the right way and send him to prison for many years."

Jonathan was silent for a while before he asked, "Do you really think he'd be found guilty and sent to prison?"

Brian quickly told him, "There's no question he'll be convicted. Sent away for years. We have the video. We have your description of the assault in this room. And we have his DNA. This is a slam dunk case."

Jonathan said he had to go to the bathroom.

"You can use that bathroom here, but just pee," Brian told him. "You can't take a shit or clean up your ass until the investigator decides what to do."

"What do you mean?" Jonathon pleaded.

Brian told us he'd called the sheriff before coming back from the dumpster. "The chief investigator's on his way. After he hears you describe the assault, he may want to send you to the ER so they can process a rape kit."

"Oh God," Jonathon fled to use the bathroom.

After he left, Brian asked me in a soft voice, "Which department is he from?"

"Engineering."

"That figures," Brian said.

"What do you mean?"

Brian, ever blunt, replied "Only an engineer could get butt-fucked and not know what happened."

I asked Brian to wait there with Jonathon to deal with the investigator; I needed to report this incident to Marvin and Merlot.

Brian confirmed, "Yes, Boss. And I'll go with him to the ER if that's required." When Jonathon returned to the room, I explained that Brian would remain with him the rest of the day.

I looked at Jonathon, "This day could go beyond your quitting time, and I'll make sure you're paid the overtime. Also, if you need to come in late tomorrow or if you want to take off the entire day, it'll be with pay. I also want you to know that we understand you've been through a seriously traumatic event. Here's my card with my cell number on it; you can call twenty-four seven. We also have professional counselors available if you'd like to talk to one."

Jonathon mumbled, "Okay." I held out my hand, Jonathon shook it, and I left the crime scene.

I didn't know how to start the conversation in Marvin's office. Whenever I'd brought a unique issue to him in the past, Marvin usually had a profound way of summarizing the situation and giving me advice on how to handle things in the future.

Seeing my silence, Marvin started, "Let's have it, I can tell you have something serious to tell me."

"I certainly do. An employee was sexually assaulted by a vendor in our medical center this morning."

"Who was the employee?"

"Jonathon Kochinski."

"A man?" Marvin asked.

"Yes. Jonathon is an intern who just started yesterday. We

recruited him because he's intelligent and talented. But he doesn't have much worldly knowledge. He only told me about the 'medical exam' he received because he suspected that the man doing it took a picture of his bare ass. It wasn't until Brian and I finished investigating that Jonathon realized he'd been assaulted."

Marvin asked me to give him the details. He listened intently, making some facial expressions as I described the 'prostate exam' to him. When I got to the part about Waterman thrusting, Marvin interrupted, "Stop, you're telling me the kid didn't suspect something when this guy said to 'look straight ahead,' so he could 'find the prostate gland'? What about when he lowered the table to get a better angle? And now you're telling me when Waterman started thrusting, the kid thought that was normal for a prostate exam?"

I said, "Yes, Jonathon didn't realize it wasn't a finger until Brian found a used condom in a garbage bag in the dumpster next to the medical center. When Brian held up the clear bag with the condom inside, it dawned on Jonathon he'd been raped."

Marvin asked, "What did the kid say when he saw the condom?"

"'Oh my God, he butt-fucked me.'" I told Marvin.

Marvin stared at me for a moment, then rested his arms on his desk and lowered his head onto his arms, looking into his desktop. After a long moment, he looked up at me and said, "I'll bet the kid is an engineering intern, isn't he?"

"Yes."

Marvin reacted, "Only an engineer could get butt-fucked and not know what happened."

"That seems to be the consensus," I said.

"What do you mean, consensus?"

"Brian said the same thing about engineers." I stood up.

"I need to go. I gotta call Merlot and let him know about the assault."

Marvin stood up. "You do that. I'll wait a few minutes before I call Nathan." I walked toward the door, turning back when Marvin started talking again, "Connor, let this be a lesson to you. The next time someone lubricates your ass and says they're going to stick their finger in you, make sure you're with a real doctor, in a real clinic, and by all means, don't look straight ahead." I smiled awkwardly and left.

Walking back to my temporary office, I passed my actual office and saw it'd been released for me to use again, but the blood stain was still there, too difficult to remove. Carpet layers would install a new carpet soon. I looked forward to moving back in tomorrow.

Guns at Work

CHAPTER 5

BACK AT MY TEMPORARY OFFICE, I could see that Todd Lukens, MTI's director of operations, was sitting on a guest chair waiting for me.

Todd stood up. "Hi, Connor. I need to talk to you about some rumors going around the plant. I normally don't react to rumors, but after recent events, I think we need to check them out."

"What are the rumors?" I asked.

"That two employees are carrying concealed guns at work."

"Who?"

"Jeremy Houndsworth is one of my welders. I know him pretty well and don't believe he'd carry a gun at work. The other is a new employee working in the warehouse, Ajla Grbic."

"You're right, we need to check this out right now," I told him.

"I know Jeremy. Let me talk to him," Todd requested.

"OK, you talk to Jeremy, and I'll talk to Ajla." We left the office; Todd headed to the plant and I went the opposite direction to the warehouse. As I walked to the warehouse, I called Brian to let him know about the rumors. He was still with the sheriff's investigator but said he'd send security guards to the two areas to help out. I told him he could send one to help Todd, but I'd just have the warehouse supervisor accompany me. Our security guards didn't have weapons anyway, so I figured it wouldn't matter who helped me.

Before I left the admin building, I stopped by Marvin's office to update him, but he was on the phone. Jacquelyn, his executive assistant, said he was talking to Nathan, who was VTM's CEO. That reminded me I hadn't yet called Merlot regarding the sexual assault. But I needed to take care of this gun rumor first, so I headed for the warehouse.

On my way, I thought about how Jacquelyn would not have told anyone else who Marvin was talking to, but she and I had developed quite a bit of respect for each other over the years and frequently shared confidential information. Jacquelyn was the most happily married woman I knew. She was also extremely attractive and had told me how she'd had to put a few of our managers in their place when they made advances on her, especially since VTM took over. High profile guests who were there to visit Marvin would frequently ask her out to dinner. Her standard response was that she would love to have dinner with them as long as she could bring her husband.

She had only been to dinner once, and that was because when asked to dine out, she didn't mention her husband, and that was because the person asking was a woman executive from one of the insurance companies that we did business with. They had dinner at the woman's hotel. During the dinner, Jacquelyn learned that the woman was a lesbian, and she wanted Jacquelyn to come to her room after dinner, which was when Jacquelyn learned that she was attractive to both sexes, and for the first time in her life turned down an offer to have sex with a woman.

In the warehouse office, I asked the manager, Dean Atkinson, to take a walk with me. His staff looked concerned, wondering what the HR director wanted with their boss.

After his office door shut behind us, Dean asked, "What's going on?"

"There's a rumor one of your workers is carrying a gun here at work."

"Who?"

"Ajla Grbic."

"No way," Dean declared. "Ajla has been here three weeks, and he's a good worker."

"How's his English?" I inquired.

"Pretty good. He's been in the country a couple years, and I think he knew English before he left Bosnia."

A text from Todd alerted me that the rumor about Jeremy was just that; there was no gun.

We found Ajla near the end of the second warehouse aisle. There were other employees in the area, so I suggested we walk to the end of the long aisle, where I asked Ajla, "How long have you worked here?"

"Three weeks," he said in a strong Eastern European accent I could understand clearly.

"Can you understand me when I speak?" I asked.

"Yes."

"Are you carrying a gun?"

"Yes," he said, pulling a revolver from his front pocket, causing Dean's mouth to drop open.

"Please put the gun back in your pocket," I asked of him.

He pocketed the gun, looking worried.

I asked Ajla, "Why do you have a gun with you?"

"For protection," he replied.

"During your safety training, we talked about different rules. One of those rules is that guns are not allowed in MTI buildings or parking lots. Do you remember hearing about this rule?"

"No, no, I don't know this rule," Ajla shook his head emphatically.

"Do you understand now that you're not allowed to bring guns to work?"

"Yes, I understand. No guns."

"Do you drive your own car to work?" I asked Ajla.

"Yes. It is in the parking lot."

"Good, let's go lock the gun in your car." Ajla and I walked side by side with Dean behind us. I told Ajla that starting tomorrow, he had to leave the gun at home, but for the rest of the day, he could keep the gun locked in his car. I then said, "Do you understand that you have to keep the gun at home?"

"Yes, keep gun at home. No gun at work." Dean and I watched Ajla place the gun in the glove compartment and lock his car doors. As the three of us walked back into the warehouse, I noticed there were no company policies posted on the doors. I shook Ajla's hand and thanked him for understanding the rule and for locking up his gun. Ajla kept apologizing, promising he'd never bring the gun to work again. I headed straight for Marvin's office.

After I finished describing the event, Marvin looked at me. "I thought we had a no-tolerance gun policy. Why is he still working here?"

"I had two reasons," I replied. "He's only been here three weeks, so his employee orientation and safety training were completed recently. Orientation does a good job explaining our active-shooter procedures, but it doesn't thoroughly describe our gun-ban policy. My other reason for not firing him was that the employee entrance he uses doesn't have the gun policy posted. Both those entrance doors were replaced over a month ago and the required signs and posters weren't rehung. I'm correcting these issues, so we'll be okay going forward."

Marvin agreed with my decision to not terminate Ajla's employment.

Just then, Jacquelyn stepped into the office. "Nathan is on the phone."

Marvin gave me a look as I got up from my chair. "Close the door on your way out." This was at least his second call today with our CEO, and I still hadn't called Merlot about the sexual assault or the gun.

At her large U-shaped desk just outside Marvin's office, Jacquelyn was the gatekeeper to the executive suite. I told her about the gun and was starting to leave when Howard Olson approached me in front of Jacquelyn's desk.

Howard, a distant relative of MTI's founder, was a legend in the milk-truck industry. He'd personally sold more milk trucks than any other person in the world. Over the years, he'd risen in the ranks and currently commanded a sales force of nineteen sales managers, who in turn each had two or three sales reps working for them.

Howard was excited. "Connor, you need to quit hiring these nineteen- and twenty-year-old girls as Welcome Center front desk receptionists."

"Oh?" I asked. "Explain."

"They're not ugly, but they're only average-looking. I need some really hot babes welcoming customers to MTI. The other problem is maturity," Howard continued unironically. "When they get hit on by a customer, they need to take it as a compliment and not actually accept the offer to meet at a hotel. The redhead you had working the front desk last month caused a problem with one of my biggest customers."

"Tell me what you're talking about."

Howard sighed. "The owner of Sunny Hill Dairy was here last month and asked the redhead back to his hotel room. I didn't think she was that attractive, but she had a good body and he liked her. He said she was a good fuck. His words, not mine. I don't talk like that," Howard said pointedly to me and Jacquelyn. "The point is that when he came here last week, he was expecting another good fuck, compliments of MTI, but the redhead had quit, so she wasn't here to service him."

"Maybe that's why she quit," I said.

"Nevertheless, the customer is unhappy and not in the mood to buy trucks. We need hot women who know how to politely turn down a customer. Once they start fucking the customer, MTI gets fucked, if you know what I mean."

"So, what would you like me to do?" I asked.

"I want you to replace the two girls at the front desk with two women. Hot blondes in their thirties or forties, good bodies, no muffin tops, and the maturity to accept compliments from customers without jumping into bed with them."

"What's a muffin top?" I asked.

"You know, love handles. The fat that pops up above their waistband," Howard explained.

"How about computer skills?"

"I don't care if they're on Facebook all day, as long as they can flirt with the customers without fucking them," Howard said.

"OK," I ended the conversation.

Howard returned to his office. I looked at Jacquelyn, who smiled sympathetically. We both knew nothing could be done about Howard. I headed back to my temporary office to call Merlot, considering how I'd react if another VP approached me the way Howard had just done. I would've put the guy in his place. I'd lecture him on how to talk and how MTI hires. But I couldn't do that with Howard; he was a company rock star who created so much profit for the company, he could say and do whatever he wanted. A few months ago, I'd complained to Marvin about Howard. Marvin had listened and then told me to leave Howard alone as long as he kept selling trucks.

Back in my temp-office, the phone rang. It was Debra, telling me Merlot had left me a voicemail. I was looking forward to tomorrow when I could work in my own office and monitor my voicemail myself. On his message, Merlot was definitely mad; he was so loud I had to hold the handset away from my ear: "Why do you do everything you can to piss me off? My boss had to tell me about the sexual assault and the gun in the warehouse! What the fuck are you doing, allowing the gun-toting immigrant to keep his job? You don't make the rules and policies and you sure as hell don't follow them! I want that man terminated today. Fuck! I can't believe you! I'm sure you get up every morning and think about what you can do to piss me off. Call me as soon as you complete the termination. Today!"

Instead of calling, I decided to email him so I'd have a written record:

Hello, Ronald,

I received your voice mail instructing me to terminate Ajla Grbic, the employee in possession of a gun while working in our warehouse. I discussed the incident with Marvin, and we decided to allow Ajla to continue working at MTI. We do not feel he was properly instructed on our gun policy. Also, the policy posters were not posted in Ajla's work area, so he had no way of knowing about the gun-ban policy. I'm in the process of correcting the circumstances that precipitated this situation. Ajla now understands the policy and will not bring a gun to work in the future.

It has been a busy day here; otherwise, I would have contacted you earlier.

Sincerely,

Connor Stone

Director of Human Resources

Milk Trucks, Inc.

Less than a minute after I hit send, Merlot called me. "Who do you think you are? When I give you an order, you better follow it! You report to me and don't forget it."

"I actually report to Marvin," I said. "I have reporting responsibilities to you. I give you reports, I don't report to you."

"Fuck you," Merlot said and hung up.

I finally began answering the many emails I'd received that morning, but after about ten minutes, Jacquelyn called to say Marvin wanted to see me. I expected this; Merlot wasn't going to accept my response.

The second I walked into his office, Marvin barked, "Close the door and sit down."

"You heard from Ronald Herbst?" I asked.

"I don't have time for this shit. Do you understand how big a hornet's nest you stirred up? As usual, you are correct; you report to me, not him. But the way you communicated that message really pissed him off. He was already campaigning to get you fired. Now it's his sole purpose in life."

"I felt I needed to draw a line in the sand. He was giving me orders, and I only take orders from you."

"Well, he complained to Nathan. So now you have the CEO of a Fortune 500 company dealing with complaints about a divisional HR director."

"What did Nathan say?" I asked.

"Nathan likes you. He said he told Ronald to let it go, and he told me to tell you to quit poking Merlot."

"Nathan actually said 'Merlot'?"

"Connor, everyone knows the nickname you gave Herbst.

Just do as Nathan says and 'quit poking Merlot.' Now, get out of here. Hank and I have a conference call in a few minutes. We're going to try and sell some trucks; that's what we're supposed to do around here."

Heading back to my temp-office, I looked at the progress in my office, one I'd occupied more than twenty years. The new carpet was already installed, and my furniture was being brought back in. I was looking forward to starting fresh tomorrow.

On the drive home, I remembered tomorrow wasn't only Friday; it was also our first office "jeans day" in company history. MTI traditionally held to a business-casual dress code. A few weeks ago, I talked Marvin into trying a casual day. If it worked out, we'd make every Friday a casual jeans day. I called Hank to remind him to wear jeans tomorrow.

After I hung up, I thought about when Hank and I played hockey in college. Since he was two years older than me, Hank's last two years at the University of Minnesota were my first two years at the University of North Dakota. Back then, Hank and I both wore the same size jeans. But now, while Hank still wore the same size jeans we wore when we played hockey, I had gained a lot of weight and now wore larger jeans.

Jeans Day

CHAPTER 6

I PULLED INTO AN ALMOST-FULL lot at six thirty Friday morning; everybody got to work a little early on Fridays because we ended the day an hour early. I parked my F-150 pickup next to Hank's F-250. They were both company vehicles, but most employees thought we owned them personally and teased us about the similarity.

Having a company vehicle was a benefit carried over from Mr. Olson. He always provided vehicles for his direct reports and allowed each person to drive whatever vehicle they wanted, provided it accommodated at least four people. The company paid all the expenses, and we could use the vehicles for both business and personal purposes. If you wanted to drive to Florida for a vacation, the company paid for the fuel, parking, and tolls. At the end of the year, the benefit amount was added to our W-2s, and we paid income taxes on the benefit amount, but the company paid us a stipend to cover the taxes and the stipend was grossed up. It was a great benefit, and all of Marvin's direct reports still drove company vehicles.

Everyone arriving for the day was wearing jeans and I was thrilled to see we were getting good participation in this event. Things were going great. Everyone inside was smiling and full of energy. Another thing I noticed was that I was noticing women's butts. Most of the women's jeans were tight.

Jacquelyn welcomed me back to the office I hadn't used in over two weeks, "Marvin would like to see you." I could tell by her tone that Marvin was not happy. I walked into his office and sat down in front of his desk. He hadn't asked me to close the door, so I figured he wasn't terribly upset.

Marvin started, "This jeans day was a good idea. You can go ahead and do it every Friday. You also did a good job making sure everyone knew not to wear jeans with holes. But you didn't do a good job explaining what types of shirts could be worn. There's a young woman in your HR department wearing a top that isn't appropriate for the office."

"Is it too low cut?"

"No, just the opposite. The bottom isn't low enough. I don't like looking at a woman's belly button in the office. Otherwise, everything else is fine. Correct the shirt problem and we can do this every Friday."

I told him I'd address the problem right away.

As I left Marvin's office, Jacquelyn handed me a note with a name on it. Alice. I stopped in my office to answer the phone, but I couldn't concentrate on what the caller was saying because from my desk, I could see through my glass walls into the HR offices. Alice was sitting at her desk with her back facing me. There were at least twelve inches of bare skin from the bottom of her shirt to the top of her low-rise jeans. Men walking down the hallway were actually stopping to stare. Alice had a good body and kept it obviously tanned. I saw one of the men point at her butt. Looking closer, I saw what got their attention. Alice was wearing a red thong.

On the phone, Ben Walker was complaining about tools taken from the training center. I told him I'd be there in an hour. Then, I called Alice to come to my office. I motioned through the glass for Jacquelyn and asked her to sit in on the conversation with Alice. Jacquelyn was accustomed to being a witness to my conversations with employees.

A moment later, Alice entered, and I asked her to take a seat.

She sat while noting, "I must've done something pretty bad if I'm meeting with both of you."

"You haven't done anything bad," I said. "I just want to talk to you about how you're dressed today." To my surprise, she started crying. I got up to close the two doors still open, relieved Jacquelyn was with me. Alice was bawling so hard. People frequently cried at my conference table, so I keep a box of tissues in the center of the table. I slid the box over to Alice, who wiped her tears and blew her nose.

Then she said, "I should've listened to my boyfriend this morning. He saw how I was dressed, and said I used to look good when I wore this shirt, but since I got love handles, I look gross." She started crying again.

I glanced over at Jacquelyn before reassuring the crying girl in front of me, "Alice, you don't have love handles. Believe me, every man who walked by has checked you out. The problem is not your imaginary love handles. The problem is that you're extremely attractive and the way you're dressed draws a lot of attention. So much attention that you're disrupting the workforce."

"Really?" she asked.

"Yes, really. The reason I'm talking to you is because we've decided to make every Friday a jeans day. I just want to make sure that in the future, you don't wear midriff-revealing shirts."

Alice said, "Should I go home and change?"

Before I could answer, Jacquelyn spoke, "We're about the same size. Why don't you wear my blazer the rest of the day?"

Alice said, "That'd be wonderful, thank you." All three

of us stood as Jacquelyn held up her blazer for Alice to slip into. Alice thanked Jacquelyn again and turned to leave, but stopped, turned around, and held the blazer open so I could see her body.

Alice looked at me and said, "Are you being honest? You really don't see any love handles?"

I looked at her up and down. "Alice, you have a perfect figure. What you need is a new boyfriend." Jacquelyn nodded her head in agreement with me. Alice smiled at both of us before returning to her office.

Before Jacquelyn returned to her office, I asked and she confirmed that Marvin was still planning to be gone for the next two weeks, taking PTO starting Monday.

"Would you be able to help Debra and me interview candidates for the customer center's 'babe positions'?"

She agreed and I told her to join Debra in my office in a few minutes.

"Does Debra know about this project?" she asked.

"No, but I'll tell her all about it when we meet."

I reviewed emails for the next few minutes and thought about what a good employee Debra, our lead HR assistant, had been the eight years she'd worked here. She was a forty-four-year-old single mother with a son and daughter both in college. She was also one of those rare people who got more beautiful as she got older.

Help Wanted: Hot Women

Chapter 7

Debra entered and stood between me and the doorway to Jacquelyn's office. This was the first time I'd seen her today and I blatantly checked her out a little too long before I looked her in the eyes. Her face showed her discomfort. I'd never lusted at her like that before, and it bothered both of us.

I said, "Debra, I've never seen you dress like this before. You have a very nice body. You're over forty, and you don't even have a muffin top. You're so hot; I bet you get hit on a lot. You're also very intelligent, so if a man asks you to his hotel room, you know how to politely turn him down."

"Are you hitting on me!?" she squeaked.

Jacquelyn had been standing behind Debra the whole time I was talking and now she spoke, "He's not hitting on you. He's prepping you for our meeting."

We all sat down at my table. It was a round conference table that comfortably sat five or six people. I liked getting out from behind my desk; since I started using the round table, I'd found that people were much more relaxed and talked more freely.

I started by telling Debra to post an ad for receptionists,

two to replace the ones currently working at the customer Welcome Center. "You can list the Welcome Center in the ad, because this afternoon we'll take care of the two being replaced."

"Who'll cover the positions if we terminate the two currently there?"

"We'll only terminate one, who's received about two warnings per week for multiple reasons. The other one is very good and we'll keep her as the receptionist until we find her replacement. She has a two-year accounting degree, and Hank wants her for Accounting's open clerk position."

Debra said, "Well, it sounds like the accountant will get a better position and a nice pay increase, but I'm curious why we're removing her from the customer center."

"She can't stay in the Welcome Center because she isn't hot enough."

"This sounds like something that Howard Olson would do," Debra frowned.

Jacquelyn agreed, "You've got that right."

"Debra," I said, "I need you to schedule interviews for anyone who satisfies the requirements for the receptionist job description. We'll be interviewing a lot of people, so both of you will be doing interviews, separately. When you come across one who meets the requirements and is hot, let me interview her. If they're not hot, just give them a cursory interview and send them on their way."

"How do you define hot?" Debra asked.

"Howard," I emphasized, "defines hot as blonde, attractive, good body with no muffin top and in their thirties or forties. Also, he wants them to flirt well enough to get the customer to ask them for sex, but smart enough to politely turn down the offer without getting the customer upset. My official instructions to you are to try meeting Howard's definition, but I want you to consider women of any hair color, any race, and I don't care if they have a muffin top."

"What do I use as the official reason for not hiring someone if the real reason is they're not hot enough?"

"The reason would be that other applicants are better qualified."

Then she asked, "What if a man applies and he has experience, has the required skills, and he's blond and in good shape?"

I said, "Give him a cursory interview." Debra just stared at me, slightly aghast.

Breaking an uncomfortable silence, Jacquelyn told her, "Debra, Connor feels the same way you do. He's just trying to comply with the instructions given by a high-profile manager while at the same time keeping the company out of trouble."

"I know," Debra said, "but I don't like it when the best person for the job doesn't get the job because of looks. It happened to me right out of college. I interviewed with a small company and thought I'd nailed it. They wanted someone to do accounting and HR; that was my double major. I waited for the offer and finally called the owner to find out he gave it to someone else. My friend who worked there told me that the person they hired didn't even have a degree. She just had larger breasts than me."

"Did you take any action?" I asked.

"Yes, I got implants."

I creepily thought about complimenting Debra on how good her breasts looked but decided to stay silent.

Debra stood. "Okay, we better get to work on this."

Everything concluded, I was off to visit Ben Walker.

Production Problem

CHAPTER 8

BEN MET ME AT THE entrance to the Training Center and took me to the tool rack. There were several empty hooks that should've had expensive tools hanging from them. I told him, "The entire training center is under video surveillance. We should be able to find out who took them."

"I already know who took the tools," he said. "Brian sent me the videos and tracked the tools after they left the center."

"Then we'll just terminate them for theft of company property."

"The problem," Ben explained, "is that the tools were taken from Training, but they weren't stolen from the company. The videos show a few different line leads from the night shift coming in and taking the tools to their work areas for employees to use."

"Well, that is a problem, and I'm sure it's happening because the tool crib is locked up at night when there's no one on staff to issue tools." I told Ben I'd ask Todd Lukens to get a key to our night shift manager to issue tools from the crib as needed.

Before I could leave, though, a day shift lead person headed toward us, "You guys need to do something about Molly

Dew." Molly was one of Ben's training instructors. Since Ben reported to me, I thought I better stay to see what the issue was.

Ben told him, "She's just talking to one person at a time so she can schedule them for training next week."

The lead replied, "She may be talking to one person at a time, but there are twenty men watching her as she moves up the line. Molly looks pretty good in the jeans she has on, and she's getting a lot of attention. We're supposed to complete twenty-four trucks today, but we'll be lucky to get twenty-two trucks, and that's assuming you take her off the production floor now."

I told the lead, "Give us five minutes and the problem will be resolved."

As the lead left, I instructed Ben to have a male from his department finish the scheduling. I also told him we needed to keep her off the production floor every day. "I've seen Molly dressed in some eye-catching outfits in the past," I said. "The clothes she wears are fine for the office, but not the production floor."

"I don't feel comfortable talking to her about how she looks. Especially after the incident at the mall."

"What incident?"

"My wife and I ran into Molly at the mall. I introduced the two of them and thought everything was fine. But on the way home, my wife preached at me, reminding me that I was married and had no business having such an attractive young woman working for me. She even said Molly used a fake Southern accent."

I told Ben, "Send Molly to my office, and I'll talk to her."

"Thanks, I'll go get her right now."

I was back at my desk for a couple minutes when Molly Dew knocked. I was extremely uncomfortable, checking her out as she entered. I was concerned about my lustful reaction and wanted a witness to the forthcoming discussion. Jacquelyn was on the phone, so I told Molly, "Debra's going to join us, let me see how long she's going to be." As I walked to get Debra, I tried to figure out why Molly had such an effect on me. I was surrounded by beautiful women at work every day. Why was I nervous about being alone with Molly in my office?

Debra was in her office; I explained that I needed her to witness a conversation. She grabbed a notepad and pen. Jacquelyn and Debra always took notes when they witnessed a discussion in my office. The notes ended up in the employee's file.

Back in my office, I told Molly, "Debra's going to take notes of our discussion and the notes will go in your personnel file."

"Am I in trouble?" Molly asked.

"No, you're not in trouble. We need to make a change to the way you do your job. The note will document the change."

Molly asked, "Will I get to see the note?"

"Yes, you can review your file at any time." I continued, "We had a problem on the production floor this morning. Production slowed to the point that we'll only build twenty-two trucks today instead of the twenty-four trucks in our plan."

Molly said, "I was just on the production floor, and everything seemed fine. Everyone was very friendly and easy to work with."

"The reason production slowed down is that as you walked up and down each line, twenty or so male employees watched you. They can't do their work if they're watching you. So, although you didn't do anything wrong, we have to deal with the fact that you're an attractive woman and men can't help staring at you."

Molly started to blush and then said with a sweet Southern accent, "Oh Lord, I didn't realize I had that effect on ya'll." This was the first time since the conversation started that she'd used this twang. Ben's wife was probably right about it being fake.

"Nevertheless, I'm asking you to do your job without going on the production floor again."

"That's fine. Most of my time's spent in the Training Center or my office," she said, notably without an accent.

"Okay, then we're done here," I said. Debra headed to her office. Molly took her time getting up and then held her hand out for me to shake. Debra was already out of my office, and I started to get that nervous feeling again.

As I shook her hand, Molly said with a sugary Southern accent, "I appreciate ya bein' honest with me about the effect I have on ya'll. I'm gonna hafta find a way to deal with this. Would it be possible for you and me to have further discussions? I think you could help me deal with this properly." The entire time she was talking, she held onto my hand.

With my hand still held by her, I said "I'm always available to help an employee."

Molly let go of my hand. "Thank you." Before she got to the door, she quickly turned and caught me checking her out. As my eyes went from her butt to her face, she gave a big, saccharine smile that said caught you. She left my office, and I sat down behind my desk.

I thought, what kind of power does this woman have over me? She has a nice body, but I work with many women who have nice bodies. The other women don't make me feel the way Molly makes me feel. I just don't get it.

I reviewed emails until Debra returned to my office for me to sign the discussion note.

Before she left, she said, "I hope you didn't fall for that act."

"You mean the fake Southern accent?"

Debra mimicked a thick drawl, "'Oh Lord, I didn't realize I had that effect on ya'll.' Gimme a break." She continued, "I checked her background when I got back to my office. She grew up in Alaska, graduated from the University of Washington in Seattle. She never lived in the South."

I told Debra, "After you left my office, she held my hand and asked if we could have further discussions so I could help her to deal with the revelation that she has an effect on men."

"Connor, you be careful. I've seen women like her before. She's going to use her sweet, sexy voice to get control of you."

"I appreciate the advice. I'll be careful."

"You'd better."

Free Drinks

CHAPTER 9

AFTER WORK, I DROVE TO the Hubbell House in Mantorville to meet Hank at the Stagecoach Bar. There was no on-street parking left, so I headed for the back lot and parked along the woods, the area where Roy Rogers would tie up Trigger when he dined there decades ago.

I walked in and saw a lot of MTI employees had gotten there before me, filling at least a third of the tables, which were piled with platters of onion rings, cheese curds, and seafood melts. As I sat at a large, empty, round table, the server brought me two Bacardi diets. I told her, "The bartender knows what I drink, but I usually have one at a time."

"The drinks are from those two tables over there." She pointed to a group of MTI men, who began waving at me. "They wanted me to tell you 'Thanks for making MTI a great place to work'." I thanked her, then grabbed one of the drinks and walked over to my fans.

I was about to ask what I'd done to deserve this when one of the guys raised his glass, "To Connor." Everyone followed in unison, "To Connor!" Another guy re-raised his glass, "To jeans day!" to which everyone toasted again.

Someone else said, "Connor, jeans day is the best thing that's ever happened at MTI. I worked hard to complete my orders early so I could spend some time walking around the offices, admiring all the beautiful women we work with. Today, they really stood out."

I told them all, "I'm glad you guys enjoyed the day, because Marvin decided to make every Friday a jeans day." The tables erupted with cheers, hollering, and high fives. MTI employees at the other MTI tables had been listening and now they joined the revelry. Most were men, but many women were just as excited.

I saw Hank enter and motioned for him to join me at my original table. Hank ordered his usual strawberry lemonade, and I explained what was going on. He looked at the dance floor and mentioned, "Alice sure looks happy." I looked up to see Alice dancing, putting on a show for her table. She'd ditched the blazer, and her low-rise jeans were now even lower than this morning. You could clearly see the red waiststring of her thong a couple inches above her jeans and her shirt had shimmied up even higher, showing a tremendous amount of her bare abdomen and her hips. She quickly became the center of attention for all the patrons in the bar.

I said to Hank, "I think she's looking for a new boyfriend."

"I don't think she'll have any trouble," he replied.

The server brought Hank's strawberry lemonade and two more Bacardi diets for me. I gave another thank-you wave to the tables who'd sent the drinks. Alice finished her dance and walked directly to our table. She stood between Hank and me, facing Hank. She started talking to Hank, but I wasn't listening too closely. Alice's jeans were so low, the top of her butt crack was in plain site. I was captivated by the droplets of sweat slowly gliding down her bare back. I watched to see if any of the droplets would glide into Alice's crack, but before that happened, she backed into me and said to Hank, "Please look and tell me if you can see any love handles. I already asked Connor this morning, but I want another opinion. Look closely."

Hank took a very brief glance at Alice's body and quickly proclaimed, "No love handles."

Alice jumped into Hank's lap and gave him a big hug before saying, "Do you guys want to go bar hopping tonight?"

Hank replied, "Not tonight. Connor and I have to get up early tomorrow. Our grandma has chores for us." She accepted this, but kissed Hank on the cheek and then danced back to her table. After Alice left, Hank told me we really did have chores tomorrow. "Grandma's ready to start another crop."

Most people, including Alice, knew that Grandma Gustie grew marijuana for others' use. It's still not legal in Minnesota, but Grandma said she'd break man's law if it helped God's children. Grandma didn't use it or sell it; she just gave it away to people suffering from cancer and other diseases. Many nurses and physicians at Mayo, including my sister-in-law Dakotah, even "referred" their patients to her, though Grandma usually had to show them how to roll their first joint. The cashier at the local grocery store must've thought I smoked a lot of weed because I was always buying Zig-Zag papers for Grandma's patients.

We decided to order some seafood melts and while the waitress took our order, Howard Olson, Tim Horn, and Flash Jenkins sat down at our table and each ordered different draft beers. Tim was the director of customer service and reported to Howard. Flash—his real first name—was Howard's best sales manager. All three men were built like me, so I wasn't surprised when, just as the beers arrived, Howard ordered a large platter of cheese curds and onion rings.

Next, all the men in the room focused their attention on

three women that had just entered the bar: nurses from Mayo, still in their scrubs. As the ladies walked by our table, Flash said, "I like the one with the long black hair."

Tim agreed, saying "She has the looks and the body."

Hank said, "Be careful what you say, you're talking about Connor's and my sister-in-law."

As Dakotah was getting ready to sit down, she saw Hank and me. She walked over to our table to greet us. "Well Connor, are you ready for chores tomorrow morning?"

"Yes, Hank already briefed me on Grandma's plans."

Dakotah was staring at the four drink glasses in front of me when she asked if I was driving. I looked at Hank and he said he would get me home. Dakotah said goodbye to us and said she would see us at Grandma's in the morning. As she walked back to her table, Flash, Tim and Howard were staring at Dakotah's ass. I said, "Stop it, that's my sister-in-law."

Howard changed the subject and said, "Marvin told me that every Friday was going to be a jeans day."

"That's correct," I told them all.

Flash grinned creepily, "Connor, this jeans day thing is the best idea you ever had. The scenery around the office is so much better. I spent the day coming up with reasons to call different women into my office just so I could watch them leave."

Tim agreed with Flash, then said he realized today that he needed a new assistant.

Hank said to Tim, "I thought Joan was a pretty good worker?"

"Joan's work isn't the problem. When it comes to work, she's the best I've ever had."

Hank looked concerned. "Then why do you want to replace her?"

Tim leered around the table. "Having a baby ruined Joan.

I used to enjoy her coming and going. She had perfectly shaped, firm breasts and a curvy, firm ass. She was so hot and always wore tight shirts and pants. When she returned to work after the baby, she wore everything loose, so I didn't see what she was like underneath until today. Now, her jeans are tight in the wrong way. She bulges out in all the wrong places. It was difficult for me to look at her body."

The server brought our cheese curds, onion rings, and seafood melts, but we ignored the food as the bar hushed when four MTI women walked into the bar: Debra, Jennifer from Accounting, Ruth from IT, and Joan. All eyes were on this new group of prey, but everyone at our table focused on Joan as the ladies walked by.

Howard spoke first. "I don't think she's that bad."

Tim said, "The dim lights in here help her out. She's maybe an eight now, but she was a ten before the baby. It's such a tragedy."

"So," Hank asked, "how is Joan with Excel?"

"Who gives a shit about Excel?" Tim said. "My ten has gone to an eight and you're talking about Excel."

Hank replied, "Just tell me how she is with Excel."

Tim said, "Joan is a fucking Excel wizard. She's the go-to person in our department whenever someone has an Excel or Word issue."

Hank told him, "Maybe I can help you out. Pat, my admin assistant, is having a baby, and she's already decided to be a stay-at-home mom. I'd like to talk to Joan about coming to work for me."

"Go for it," Tim scoffed.

Hank looked at me and asked, "Connor, are you okay with me talking to Joan?"

"Yes, go for it," I told him sincerely.

Hank looked back at Tim and asserted, "Okay, this is how

it's gonna go down. I'm going to tell Joan that you were bragging about how good she is with Excel. I'll let her know that Connor gave me permission to talk to her about replacing Pat. When she talks to you about this, you need to be surprised that she'd consider leaving your department."

"That's fine," Tim said, "but she may not want to work for you. She's pretty attached to me. I even think she has a thing for me."

"Okay, we'll play it by ear." Hank excused himself and headed for the restroom. Flash said he had to go too and followed Hank.

When they returned, Flash reached for an onion ring as Hank quickly pulled the tray away, out of Flash's reach.

Flash complained, "Hey!"

Hank said, "You go get your own tray. You didn't wash your hands in the bathroom."

"Dammit, Flash," Howard spoke, "I've told you before that if you don't wash your hands after fondling your dick, you stay away from the finger food. That means you use a fork to get your next cheese curd."

While we worked out our proper finger food etiquette, Alice ran across the room to join Debra and her group. She said, "Have you girls seen Hank in jeans?"

"Yes, that's all the women in IT talked about today," Ruth said.

Joan said, "I saw him once when he came to talk to Tim. I'd never seen him in jeans before, and I just wanted to wrap my legs around him."

"Joan!" Jennifer gasped. "You're a married woman."

"I know," said Joan. "Hank makes me forget I'm married."

Alice proudly revealed, "Before you all got here, I sat in Hank's lap and kissed him on the cheek."

"No way!" said Debra.

"Yep, I stood in front of him and asked him to check me out for love handles. He looked me up and down and said, 'no love handles.' So, I hopped in his lap and kissed him on the cheek."

Jennifer mentioned, "One night when he and I were working late together, I let him know I was available, but he wasn't interested. Besides, he's getting a little thin on top."

Joan said, "He could be as bald as a cue ball, and I'd do him."

Debra said, "Quiet, he's coming to our table."

Hank walked up to the table, "Joan." She looked up at him but couldn't speak. Hank said, "Joan, I was wondering if I could speak with you before you leave this evening?"

Joan said, "Sure. Do you want to do it right now?" The other women could barely hold back their giggles.

Hank said, "We could do it now. How about if we do it over there?" Hank pointed to a dark corner of the room. "We'll have more privacy." Hank and Joan walked to the corner as the women erupted laughing.

The server took a drink order from Joan and Hank, who looked at each other for a moment. It looked like Joan was hoping this would be a personal conversation, but when Hank started talking, she straightened her posture and looked serious. After Hank finished presumably telling her what he'd told us, we saw Joan nod her head vigorously. She was clearly eager for a change. The server brought their drinks and Hank lifted his glass to toast her new job. To reassure her, Hank had told her he'd tell Tim she'd hesitated to leave until offered a two-dollar-an-hour rate increase and Joan liked Hank's plan.

We saw them finish their drinks and stand. Hank held out his hand to shake, but Joan embraced him in a tight hug that lasted longer than was professional. Hank awkwardly backed up, clearly putting distance between them.

When Joan got back to her table, all the women leaned toward her so as not to miss a word. Alice spoke first, asking if Hank invited Joan to his house.

"He better have, based on the intimate hug you gave him," Ruth said.

"Hank wouldn't do that," Jennifer said.

"Come on, Joan, what happened?" Debra pleaded.

"Hank asked me to be his new assistant and I accepted."

Ruth asked, "What about Pat?"

"Pat isn't coming back after she has her baby," Debra informed them.

Joan got a big smile on her face, and everyone else started giggling.

Alice said, "You were over in the corner for a while, what else did you talk about?"

Joan said, "He said he'd heard good things about me and would like to work closely with me. I asked him how close, and he said very close."

"Oh, he didn't say that," said Jennifer.

Joan said, "He maybe didn't say it like that, but that's how he felt, I know it. Oh, and when I told him I'd be able to model bikinis for him in six months, he said, 'That's great'."

"You didn't really say that, did you?" Debra asked.

"Well, I told him I just started a new thyroid medication that'll allow me to lose enough weight so I can model bikinis again."

Jennifer said, "Joan, I hope you realize that Hank still thinks his wife is alive. He's not going to go out with any woman, especially a married one like you."

"I know, but I like to think about it," Joan said.

Debra said, "We all saw you lift your leg while you were

hugging him. I thought you were going to wrap it around him."

"I thought about it," said Joan.

Hank sauntered back, deciding not to tell Tim about Joan's eager acceptance of the new position. As he sat down at our table, Tim mumbled something.

"You have too many cheese curds in your mouth. I can't understand you," Hank said.

Tim swallowed and said, "What was the long hug for?"

"Joan was thanking me for the job offer," Hank said.

"Did she accept it?" asked Tim.

"It wasn't a done deal until I offered her another two dollars an hour," Hank said.

Tim got excited and said, "What the fuck, two dollars more per hour? You bribed her to get her to leave me. It takes a bribe of four grand a year to get one of my women to leave me."

Hank looked at Tim with a straight face and said, "You are a blessed man. I'm glad Joan accepted my bribe. Please go easy on Joan. She really felt bad about leaving you."

Tim said, "I bet she felt bad, but not bad enough to turn down four grand a year. She's a good person, but those little bulges of fat above her belt are unacceptable for any of my women." Already a hundred pounds overweight, Tim crammed more cheese curds into his mouth, mumbling "I have standards for my women. I don't want to see any fat above the belt, and I want to see large, firm tits."

Hank excused himself to the restroom again. I joined him and asked him on the way what'd really happened. Hank said that Joan accepted the job before she knew what the pay was. She said she was ready for a change. "Also, since you're HR, I'll let you know she said she has a thyroid problem and that she just started treatment for it. She expects to lose enough weight over the next six months to go back to her weekend job modeling swimsuits."

I said, "I can't wait to hear what Tim says when he sees Joan in six months."

After the bathroom, Hank stopped at another table to visit, and I headed back to Howard and his crew. Howard was ranting about too many women in the office having muffin tops. I thought of how my grandma always said "pot calling kettle black" but didn't say it because the guys would just turn it into something racist.

Howard, himself only five foot nine and well over three hundred pounds, was eating deep-fried onion rings faster than Tim was eating cheese curds. Howard was saying, "We need to change the jeans day dress code to require women with muffin tops to wear loose-fitting shirts. We shouldn't have to suffer the pain any man endures looking at a fat ass in tight jeans. Women like that have no sense of decency."

Tim agreed, "We should also ban fatties from wearing leggings and tight yoga pants."

Flash chimed in, "We definitely need to do something. It's so embarrassing when you're giving a customer a tour and we hafta walk by several fat-asses in tight clothes."

I told them, "I'm going to have to switch tables. The guys over there are sending me free drinks because they appreciate being able to work with so many beautiful women."

"Well, the majority of the women at the office do look good," Howard admitted, "but the few who're overweight ruin the whole environment."

"What do you think the women are saying about us?" I asked them. "When Hank's not at the table, we're a bunch of fat men. Way more overweight than any of the women we work with."

Howard scoffed as he very seriously said, "That may be so, but we're corporate executives. The women look past our physical appearance and are in awe of our status and position in the world." The server set down another platter of onion rings and cheese curds. Howard ordered another round of beers, and everyone filled their mouths. That particular conversation ended.

When Hank returned to our executive table, Flash looked across the room. "What's going on with Freddy and Jeanette?" We all looked to see Jeanette trying to get out of the booth they both occupied. As she stood up, she turned to face Freddy, who was sitting at the booth's edge. He wrapped his arms around Jeanette's hips and started grabbing and squeezing her butt. She slapped one of his hands away, accidentally knocking over his drink.

I stood up. "I'm going to break this up." Freddy and Jeanette were both married, but not to each other. Jeanette worked for Freddy in our Marketing department. As I was getting up, Jeanette ran by our table toward the restrooms. I looked over at Freddy, who was ordering another drink while the spilled drink was being cleaned up. "I guess there's nothing to break up. I'll go talk to Jeanette."

I entered the hallway and saw Jeanette walk past the restrooms, toward the front door. I caught up with her outside. "Jeanette, can I talk to you?" She was crying.

"Let's sit down on this bench," I suggested. We both sat.

Jeanette stopped crying and said, "I never should've said I'd have a drink after work. I actually said no, but he left me no choice."

"What do you mean?" I said.

"It all started this morning when I first got to work. Freddy started following me around and when we were alone in his office, he closed the door, walked up really close to me and said, 'I want some of this.' Then he wrapped his arms around me like for a hug, but instead grabbed my butt. Both hands. Pulled me close against him. Then he said, 'I definitely want some of this. Your ass feels so good'."

I asked, "Had Freddy done anything inappropriate prior to today?"

"Today's the first day he got physical. Prior to today, he frequently asked me out for drinks after work and would say things to me."

"What did he say?"

"He'd say things like, 'You should wear lower-cut tops because you've got pretty nice breasts'."

"Is this the first time you went out for drinks with Freddy?" I asked.

"Yes," Jeanette responded.

"What did you mean when you said Freddy left you no choice?"

"I'd turned him down twice this afternoon already when he then mentioned my performance evaluation he had to submit on Monday. He said it'd be much easier for him to finish the eval if he had some time alone with me. So, I said I'd have one drink with him. I felt pretty safe in there with all my coworkers around. I wanted to sit at a table, but he insisted on a booth.

"After we started drinking, he slid closer to me, put his hand on my back, and slid his sweaty fingers into my jeans. He asked what color my 'panties' were. I didn't say anything. I had to wrestle with him to get out of the booth. When I stood up, he grabbed my butt and tried to pull me back into the booth, so I slapped his hand away and spilled his drink. I'm sure he's going to give me a bad eval now."

"Freddy already turned in your evaluation, and it was a good one," I told her.

"Really?" Jeanette was surprised.

"Yes, but we need to take care of this problem. I don't want you to come to work on Monday morning. You can come in at noon."

"Am I in trouble?"

"No, you're not in trouble. You'll get paid for a full day, but I only want you to work in the afternoon. In the morning, I'm going to terminate Freddy's employment."

"Oh no," said Jeanette, worried.

"Freddy's behavior is unacceptable. I don't want him working at MTI any longer."

Jeanette seemed slightly relieved and said softly to herself, "I can look forward to coming to work again."

"Please don't talk to anyone about Freddy's termination until after it's done," I requested.

Jeanette acknowledged that she understood.

I saw a small smile on Jeanette's face and asked her, "Are you safe to drive home?"

"Yes. I didn't finish my first drink."

"Okay," I said, "I'll see you Monday afternoon."

"See you Monday!" She walked toward the parking lot, and I returned to the bar.

I took my chair at the executive table, but before I could speak, Howard asked, "How's Jeanette?"

"She went home. She's going to be okay," I said.

"Are you going to fire the bastard, or should I just go over there and beat the shit out of him right here?" Howard asked.

"I'll address the issue with Freddy on Monday," I replied.

Howard knew me well enough, so he knew Freddy would be terminated. Howard looked around the table, then directed his voice to his direct reports, Flash and Tim. "I may look at the pussy at the office, and I may talk about the pussy at the office, but I never touch the pussy at the office. If I want to touch a woman, I go home to my wife, and she meets all my needs." Keeping intentional eye contact with Tim and Flash, Howard continued, "The same goes for you guys. You can look, and you can talk, but if you ever touch a woman you work with, I will fire you before Connor has a chance to." Tim and Flash both acknowledged Howard's statement with quick nods.

Hank looked at me, "Grandma's expecting us at seven a.m. tomorrow. We should get going."

"I'm past my limit," I told him. "Can I take you up on your offer to give me a ride?"

"I knew I'd be taking you home when I came in and you already had two on the table," Hank said.

Morning came quickly. Hank was honking his horn at six thirty, as I put my boots on. He'd stopped off at the County Seat coffeehouse so there was a hot cup of coffee waiting for me in his truck. "Get a good night's sleep?" he asked with a concerned look.

"No, I never sleep well after I drink too much."

"Maybe that's a sign you shouldn't drink so much," said Hank.

"I've been thinking the same thing," I groaned.

We pulled right up to Grandma's old dairy barn and found her inside. "Good morning, Grandma," we said in unison.

"Good morning, boys." I took a few more steps into the barn's shade, looking down long, wide, clean, concrete-trenched aisles. The entire length of the barn, Grandma had built racks to hold plant containers above each trench. Grow lights were placed above the water sprinkler system, which hung above the plants. Grandma had an exceptionally good grow operation.

Dakotah was already at work, filling containers with soil. After Hank and I greeted her, we started to fill containers as well. Once we had dirt in all the containers, we spent the rest of the morning planting seeds. Around lunchtime, Dakotah's girls came over and we all shared lunch before Hank dropped me at my truck, still at the Hubbell House.

The Termination

CHAPTER 10

I WENT INTO WORK EARLY on Monday to get ready for Freddy's termination. There were several cars in the office parking lot already, so I wasn't the only person trying to get a jump on the week. I headed to Howard's office first; Freddy reported to Jared Green, the director of marketing, and Jared reported to Howard. I had to make sure everyone in the chain of command above Freddy was ready to deal with the termination.

"Good morning, Howard," I said as I closed the door behind me.

"Should I get Jared on the speakerphone?" Howard knew the protocol, so I said yes and sat down across his desk as he punched Jared's extension into the phone.

Jared answered, "Hello, Howard."

"Jared, I have Connor Stone on the speaker. We're going to terminate Freddy this morning."

Jared responded, "I was expecting that. I talked to a couple guys over the weekend who said they saw Freddy grab Jeanette's ass and that both of you saw it as well."

I raised my voice to be heard on speaker, "Jared, when you see Brian and I enter your building, please have everyone who's working in the open office area go to the conference room until Freddy has left the building. This will only take a few minutes, and I don't want Freddy talking to anybody as we walk him out."

Jared said, "I brought donuts today, so we'll just have coffee and donuts in the conference room."

"Save a donut for me," said Howard.

Jared cautioned me, "Connor, Freddy has a pretty quick temper. Is it only going to be you and Brian in Freddy's office for the termination?"

"No. Brian will have two security guards waiting in the open office area with empty boxes for Freddy to pack his personal things. We may have you come in when Freddy's packing up. We need to make sure he only takes what belongs to him."

"Okay," said Jared, "I'll watch for you." They both hung up and Howard asked me if I needed anything else from him.

"Just a requisition for a new marketing manager," I replied.

"It'll be on your desk when you're done with Freddy."

I left Howard's and went to my office, where Debra was waiting at my conference table. "Good morning," said Debra as she handed me two envelopes, "I prepared a termination packet and severance agreement."

"How many weeks of severance?" I asked.

"Four. And the company pays the first month of COBRA."

"Good work," I told her. "It should all be over within the hour."

As Debra left, Jacquelyn came in. "Sounds like I missed a lot by not going to the Hubbell House on Friday."

I asked if the whole office was talking about it, and Jacquelyn said they were. I told her, "If Marvin calls in from his vacation, you can tell him what happened, and that Freddy has been terminated. I'll do it within the hour." She nodded before returning to her office. I called Brian, briefed him on the plan, and asked him to meet me at the north office building with two of his guards in twenty minutes. Then, I sat down at my desk to organize my thoughts about breaking another corporate policy.

The corporate HR practice was to have security bring the employee to the HR office for the termination. I didn't like that because the employee quickly figured out they were going to be terminated when security arrived to escort them to HR. The employee got all worked up before we even started the conversation. And if we terminated them in HR, we had to drive them back to their work area to get their personal things. I terminated the employee in their work area or a conference room nearby so that when we were done, the employee left the campus.

 I always prepared myself for the termination. There were situations when I didn't have much time to prepare, like when I terminated Jim Rollins or Buddy Jay, but in Freddy's case, I had plenty of time. Over the weekend, I'd thought about how I was going to present this to Freddy. I'd gone over each possible scenario and planned my response for each one.

 I always plan how I'm going to show respect for the employee during the process. Years ago, when I made my first terminations, I was nervous, which made the employee nervous. The employee would get mad at me and the company, usually making a scene before departing. These days, I stayed calm and sat down to talk things through with the employee. After I told them they no longer worked for MTI, I'd tell them about the future and what they could expect. Most people I terminated would shake my hand before leaving. When I ran into someone years after I'd terminated them, they'd often shake my hand and even sometimes buy me a drink. They'd tell me how it'd been a wake-up call for them to change how they lived and worked, and that once they got their lives straightened out, they were able to get an even better job.

Today, I felt well prepared, and I was ready to dive in headfirst to get through the process. I drove to the north office and parked next to Brian. We entered the building together, followed by the two guards. Jared saw us coming and began ushering everyone into the conference room. I could see Freddy standing in the doorway to his office, trying to figure out what Jared was doing. Then Freddy looked down the hall and saw me, Brian, and the two guards walking toward his office.

Freddy lowered his head and looked straight at the floor for several seconds. Then he looked at us one more time, as if to check we were still walking toward him. He turned to go sit behind his desk, leaving the door to his office open, which I thought was a good sign. The guards waited in the open office area as Brian and I entered Freddy's office.

Freddy obviously knew why we were there, but said, "I don't understand why you're doing this."

Brian and I sat down in the guest chairs in front of Freddy's desk. I don't like to use the word terminate so I said, "We're letting you go because of your behavior with Jeanette." Freddy abruptly stood.

"What behavior are you talking about?" he demanded.

"I'm talking about when you groped Jeanette's butt in front of thirty coworkers last Friday."

"You're a fucking asshole; you can't fire me for that," said Freddy.

"We can terminate your employment for groping a coworker. Now, let's talk about your severance agreement."

"What severance agreement?" said Freddy, sinking heavily

into his chair.

I pulled the agreement out of its envelope and laid it in front of him. "If you consent to the terms of the agreement, you'll receive four weeks of pay plus one month of medical insurance."

"What are the terms?" asked Freddy.

"If you sign the agreement, you're releasing MTI from all liability with regard to your employment."

Freddy jumped up and yelled, "This is bullshit!" The two guards began walking toward the office door, but Brian waved them off.

Freddy started pacing back and forth behind his desk. I waited almost a minute, giving him time to gather his thoughts before he finally spoke, "You both know this isn't fair. Jeanette always dresses to invite attention; she practically begs me to touch her."

"According to Jeanette, you don't like her tops," I countered. "She said you asked her to wear more revealing tops."

"That's a perfect example," Freddy insisted. "She has a fantastic body. She almost always wears tight shirts and sweaters, knowing every man in the office is going to check her out. When she walks into my office, all I see are her tits. She's a constant tease. It's not my fault."

I asked, "So why did you grab her butt on Friday? You grabbed her at work and again at the Hubbell House."

"She came to work Friday wearing my favorite tight shirt; I'm pretty sure she knows that shirt is my favorite. But Friday was the first time I'd seen her in jeans. You guys saw her. You can't take your eyes off her. I know she wanted me to touch her, and I knew I could grab her ass."

"What do you mean, you could grab her ass?" I asked.

"I read in last week's newspaper that it's perfectly legal to grab any woman's ass in Minnesota; it's not a crime, and you can't get arrested."

Freddy was talking about the state legislature's change to harassment laws made years ago. Back then, an obviously male-dominated legislature felt charging a man with a felony for grabbing or groping a woman's buttocks was too severe a penalty. But instead of reducing the penalty, they just eliminated it. For years in Minnesota, a man could grab a woman's butt, pat a woman's butt, or rub a woman's butt and not get in trouble. It was completely legal. The article Freddy read was actually about how the current legislature had put the old law back in place, making it once again a crime to grab a woman's butt. But the article also mentioned how the law didn't go into effect until next year. So, until then, woman's butts were apparently "up for grabs" with no consequences in Minnesota.

Brian and I both stood. "Freddy, you won't get arrested for grabbing Jeanette's ass, but you are losing your job."

"Fuck you!" Freddy yelled.

I turned to Brian and said, "We're done." Brian motioned to the two guards, who each came in carrying an empty box.

Freddy began screaming as he walked around the desk toward me, "You can't fire me! I can grab every ass in this building, and you can't fire me because it's legal." He was now in my face, and I could sense Brian and his men coming up behind me. I stretched out my arms to hold the three of them back. I could tell Freddy had a strange version of respect for the law and he knew if he hit me, he'd be arrested.

I told Freddy, "You didn't break the law; you broke an MTI policy. You no longer work here."

He yelled into my face, "FUCK YOU, you can't do this!" I had to wipe his spittle from my face. Things were not going the way I'd planned, so I decided to scrap the plan and go with my gut.

Without moving from my spot, I told him, "You're going to leave the campus now. You cannot come back on MTI property unless you get my permission in advance. If you contact Jeanette or try to see her, I will notify the sheriff's department, and you will be arrested."

"I never want to see that fucking slut again! She caused this trouble. I'm losing my job because of her! And fuck you, Stone! You're an asshole. Jeanette's probably fucking you on the side."

"That's enough," I said, grabbing the benefits envelope from his desk to hand to him. "Info on your options to continue some of your benefits is in that envelope. If you have questions, you can call or email Debra or me."

"Debra," Freddy sneered, "That bitch prances around like she's a queen. She's another good piece of ass you probably fuck on a regular basis. I bet that's why you're firing me. I grabbed the ass of one of your bitches."

I indicated the guards. "These men will escort you to your car and watch you leave the property. Remember, if you come back, I will call the sheriff."

Freddy looked down at his desk. "What about the severance agreement?" he asked.

I picked up the severance agreement from his desk and ripped it in half. "There is no severance agreement."

Freddy was shocked. "If I don't get a severance, I'm going to sue you and MTI for everything you've got."

"You'll never find an attorney to take the case." I looked to the guards. "Get him out of here."

"Wait, what about my personal things?"

"We'll ship them to you." The guards walked Freddy down the hall, one guard on each side of him.

Jared had heard Freddy yelling and now emerged from the conference room. I asked him to come into Freddy's office.

"Jared, can you help Brian pack up Freddy's personal items?"

"Sure. Can I let everyone out of the conference room?"

"Yes, let's get everyone back to work."

I reminded Brian to give me the shipping docs after he'd shipped all of Freddy's things. As I drove back to the main building, I thanked God for my HR staff. They all did good work and kept the department functioning while I dealt with all the weird cases that kept popping up.

I entered my office, and Debra walked in behind me. "How'd it go?"

"It didn't go well, and there will be no severance or COBRA payment. Also, why would Freddy say that you prance around like you're some queen?"

Debra laughed and said, "Probably because I put him in his place a couple months ago at a bar in Rochester. He hit on me, and I told him to go home to his wife. Did he say anything else?"

"Yes, he said that you and Jeanette were my bitches and that I was fucking both of you."

"I'm glad he's gone," she said. Debra handed me a paper. "This came in the mail today."

THE LETTER

CHAPTER 11

I STARTED TO READ THE photocopy of a handwritten letter Debra said was addressed: "Human Resources at MTI. Only Alice and I have seen it."

I'm writing to see if you can stop the woman manager from forcing the men to have sex with her. A few times a week she walks out to where the men work and points to the one she's going to take to the office for sex. I don't like it when she takes my husband. He's getting older and can only come about twice a week, so when she has sex with him, he has to wait a few days before he can come with me. This isn't a nice thing to do to a married man. Please make her stop.

I looked questioningly at Debra. "Anonymous. Postmarked in Rochester," she told me.

"Any idea what's really happening?" I asked.

"No."

"Get Brian in my office when he's done packing up Freddy's things."

An hour later, Debra, Jacquelyn, Brian, and I sat around my conference table, each with our own copy of the anonymous letter. I started, "In the past, we've had anonymous letters accusing employees of using drugs, of being undocumented, of having a sexual affair, and of stealing from the company."

Brian confirmed, "This is the first time a manager's been accused of forcing sex on an employee."

"Not just a manager," said Debra, "We're talking about a woman forcing sex on multiple men."

Jacquelyn speculated, "There's more to this. The male victim isn't telling his wife everything."

I asked, "Where do we have a female manager with access to a private room where she can take men to have sex?" No one could think of anything, so I ended our meeting.

I thought about calling Merlot to report Freddy's termination but decided to let it go, since Marvin was on vacation. I didn't want to tell Merlot that I did the termination outside the HR office or that I didn't get Freddy's signed release.

Just then, Gloria buzzed me with a collect call from Jim Rollins.

"Hi, Connor, this is Jim. I'm glad that Gloria accepted the charges. You gave me your cell number, but I can't make calls to cellphones from prison."

"That's okay," I said, "you can call collect here anytime."

A month ago, I'd tried to visit Jim at the state prison in Stillwater, where I found out I had to preregister for authorization to visit a prisoner in a state penitentiary. "I've got good news," I told him. "I received my visitor authorization, and I'm planning to visit you this Saturday."

"That's perfect. Marjorie is visiting me on Sunday."

"Do you still need reading material?" I asked.

"Yes. Marjorie's bringing me magazines, but I could use some books."

"Hank just published another dog story," I told him. "I'll bring you a copy."

Jim said, "Be sure to tape a note to the book with my name on it. They won't let you bring anything into the visitors' room, but you can leave the book with an officer out front, and I'll get it after it's inspected."

"Sounds good," I said.

"I better let you get off this collect call. I'll see you Saturday," he said.

I'd finished dinner and was watching TV at home that night when I solved the anonymous-letter mystery. I put on my boots and headed back to the office. On the way, I called Brian. "Night shift," he answered my call. Clearly, he'd already figured it out, too.

There were two women in lead positions on the night shift who basically operated as managers. Plus, at night, most of the offices were empty, so it was possible one of those could be used for sex.

I met Brian at the west entrance of the main plant building. "This is the most likely place for it," he said. "The two female leads work near this building's main office."

The office he referred to consisted of one large, open room filled with cubicles and many private offices on the perimeter. We agreed to enter quietly and position ourselves in the cubicles, where we'd wait to see if anyone entered one of the private offices. But as we walked down the dark hallway by the supply closet, we heard a man moan. The light in the closet was on. Brian quickly pulled out his master key and, in a single motion, unlocked and yanked open the door. Everyone was shocked. Inside the room, Santiago Fernández was removing a used condom from his penis. Sheryl Betz, one of the leads, was kneeling down next to Santiago, holding cash in her hand. Brian quickly took a picture of them for the record.

Sheryl took a plastic bag from her jacket pocket and gave it to Santiago, who put his used condom in the bag and held onto it as Sheryl pocketed the cash. Brian knew what to do; he summoned a security guard to our location. We needed to split up Sheryl and Santiago before we questioned them, and I wasn't about to be alone in a room with a woman who appeared to have just given a blow job to one of our employees.

When the guard arrived, Brian had the guard take Santiago to the break room, while Brian and I stayed there with Sheryl. "What's going on?" I asked her.

"I'm just trying to make some extra cash. I only do it when the guys are on their meal break. I charge 'em forty bucks."

"So, the men have time for their meal and a blow job within the break time?" I asked.

"Yes, I'm very good at it. Most come within two minutes."

Brian and I were silent.

After a moment, Sheryl begged, "If you forget about tonight, I'll do both of you every night for a month, no-charge."

"That's not going to happen," I told her.

Sheryl looked stricken. "Are you going to fire me?"

"Most likely," I said. "But as of right now, we're suspending you. Brian and I will complete the investigation and make a decision on your job tomorrow. Let's go out to the shop and get your personal things, and then Brian and I will walk you out."

On the way to her car, I asked Sheryl, "How long have you been selling oral sex?"

"About three years."

"How much do you earn?"

"A little over ten thousand a year, tax free."

"Do you force the men to do business with you?" I asked her.

Sheryl stopped walking and looked hard at me. "I don't force them to do anything. They fight over who gets one each night. Like I said before, I only do it on mealtime, when we're all punched out. So, I can only fit in one a night."

"How many different men are you doing?"

We started walking again, and Sheryl said, "There are about ten or twelve who I do on a regular basis. And then there are the parties."

"The parties?"

"Yeah, like last month, Santiago's friend got married. I did everyone at the bachelor party."

We got to Sheryl's car and I told her I'd call her in the morning. On the verge of tears, she made one last appeal for her job, but I repeated that she'd get my decision in the morning.

Brian and I watched her weeping as she drove away. As we walked back to the building, Brian said, "Boss, I don't appreciate you making decisions for me."

"What do you mean?" I said, confused.

Brian replied, "You gave up a blow job every night for a month for free." We laughed crudely as we returned to the break room to interview Santiago.

Santiago confirmed everything Sheryl told us; I told him to finish his shift and that we'd get back to him tomorrow.

I contacted the night manager to let him know that Sheryl had to leave early.

Now free to return home, Brian and I walked to our vehicles. On the way, Brian asked, "Well, Boss, what're you going to do?"

"I don't know. Everything happened on their own time."

Brian said, "I agree. It's like reading a book during your break."

"It's not like reading a book," I said as we both smiled.

The next morning, Brian was waiting in my office. I called

Jacquelyn and Debra to join us before Brian and I told the story together. Brian ended his part typically blunt: "If you know anyone getting married, she does bachelor parties."

I ended our description by saying, "Sheryl is quite the entrepreneur."

The women were shocked. The four of us had encountered many unusual things together throughout the years, but this was by far the most bizarre situation we'd worked on.

Debra asked, "What're you going to do?"

I said, "I'm not sure."

Jacquelyn stated, "You have no choice. You have to terminate them."

"Which ones?" I asked her.

"All of them. Sheryl and all the men she had oral sex with."

I told her, "It'd be hard on the company to let that many people go from the same department."

Debra grabbed the box of Kleenex from the center of the table and started crying. We all looked at her. "I didn't know," she said through tears, "I didn't know she was selling herself." Debra blew her nose as the rest of us waited to hear more. Debra started to talk, but she was having trouble. I'd never seen her so upset.

Then she continued, "Sheryl and her husband and daughter were in a car accident four years ago. Her husband died at the scene. Her daughter got a traumatic brain injury and was paralyzed below the waist. She can't walk. Sheryl can't make it financially. I took her to the food shelf that I volunteer at and got her set up there. Sheryl works the night shift because she can't afford daycare. When she works at night, a neighbor takes care of Samantha and sleeps at their apartment. She pays the neighbor kid about two hundred bucks per week. Sheryl told me she was working on the side for cash, but I had no idea she was giving blow jobs to take care of her daughter."

"I don't understand," I said. "Sheryl's in a lead position. She should be earning more than fifty thousand a year."

Debra looked at me with fire in her eyes and said fiercely, "Her earnings aren't the problem; it's our shitty medical insurance. We charge employees very little for the insurance, so if you're healthy, the plan is cheap and you're happy. But if you have medical issues, the deductible and copays are huge. The out-of-pocket limit is the highest I've ever seen. And Sheryl doesn't earn as much as she should because she has to stay home on the nights her daughter has problems.

"Every year, she starts by using up her PTO to take care of her daughter. When vacation time runs out, she uses intermittent FMLA for the time off, but that's unpaid. When I helped Sheryl last year, her W-2 wages were forty-eight thousand and her take-home pay was thirty-eight thousand. After she pays out-of-pocket for medical, she has twenty thousand left for her and her daughter to live on. She must be using the blow-job cash to pay the babysitter."

Brian and I sat there stunned. Jacquelyn took a tissue to wipe her eyes, then looked at me and said, "I don't think you should terminate anyone; you should fix the problem. I didn't realize how bad our insurance was; I'm on my husband's plan."

Debra told Jacquelyn, "You're not the only one. Over sixty percent of our employees are on their spouse's medical plan."

After another moment of silence, I'd decided. "I'm going to take some time to work on this. Let's plan on having lunch here at noon. Jacquelyn, can you make the arrangements?" She nodded.

Brian reminded me, "You told Sheryl and Santiago you'd get back to them this morning."

I told Debra to call Santiago. "Tell him to report for his shift as usual and that I'll talk to him later tonight. Then call

HR: Behind Closed Doors

Sheryl and tell her she's not losing her job. When she comes to work tonight, have her come to the HR office to meet with you and me."

Debra said, "I will, but what are you going to do?"

"I'm going to fix the problem. Everyone meet back here at noon."

I went to find Todd Lukens, director of operations and the manager dealing with Sheryl's frequent absences. Todd explained he had another employee on Sheryl's team who backed her up whenever she needed to stay home. Then, he started to explain Sheryl's situation to me. It was clear he felt fatherly toward Sheryl and sincerely cared about her well-being.

I asked Todd, "Did you know that Sheryl has a second job where she gets paid in cash?"

"She mentioned it," he said, "but I didn't ask any questions because if she's paid in cash, it's probably illegal."

"It is illegal. Sheryl is giving forty-dollar blow jobs to the men on her team."

Todd had just taken a drink, and he spit coffee all over his desk. "What?!" he sputtered.

I told him what Brian and I had discovered the night before.

Todd looked so sad. "I don't understand why she would do that."

I explained how the company's insurance plan didn't pay well, so Sheryl had to pay out eighteen thousand each year before she had full coverage.

Accusingly, Todd said, "You're telling me that one of our employees has to stick a man's cock in her mouth every night in order to pay her daughter's medical bills?"

"Yes, that is what I'm telling you."

"What are we going to do about it?" he asked.

"We can't change the insurance plan because it's controlled by VTM, but we can make some changes to help Sheryl. We need to get her to day shift; if she stays on nights, she'll be tempted to sell herself again."

Todd suggested, "I can move some people around so that Sheryl can have the lead position in the same department, just on day shift. But she can't afford day care?"

"I'll work that out. It could take a couple of days, so I'll get back to you." We stood up, shook hands, and I returned to my office.

On the way back, I told Debra we were moving Sheryl to day shift.

"That's good, but she can't afford the day care."

I asked, "When does Sheryl's daughter start public school kindergarten?"

"Not for eighteen months."

"Okay, I have some more work to do." I went to my office to start making phone calls. I asked Jacquelyn to invite Todd Lukens to lunch. I called several private preschools in Rochester, then I called my mother, followed by Hank.

At noon, Jacquelyn, Debra, Todd Lukens, Brian, Hank, and I met for lunch at my conference table. I began, "Thanks to Todd, Sheryl will be able to transfer to day shift and keep her lead position in her same department."

"That's wonderful," said Jacquelyn.

Brian agreed.

Todd asked, "What about day care?"

I told them, "Sheryl's daughter, Samantha, will attend Med City Academy. It has a handicap-accessible bus that picks up students in the morning. My mother organized some volunteers from our church to stay with Samantha at home until the bus arrives each morning. Sheryl can leave early enough for the day shift. The academy has an after-school daycare for students until six p.m. After her shift, Sheryl will be able to pick Samantha up well before six."

Debra said, "That all sounds good, but there's no way Sheryl can afford the tuition at Med City. It's the most expensive preschool in Rochester. Kids from rich families go there."

"Samantha has a scholarship," I said.

Debra replied, "That academy doesn't have scholarships. I know because I've checked." There was a long silence as everyone stopped eating. Debra looked at me, "You're paying her tuition, aren't you?"

I admitted, "Hank and I are splitting the cost of Samantha's tuition. In eighteen months, Samantha will be in the public school system, and Hank and I will no longer make payments. Sheryl will no longer be paying ten thousand a year for the overnight babysitter, so she won't need the cash she was earning at night. She'll also pick up another four thousand a year because she won't have to take so much time off work. The school has a nurse to take care of any problems Samantha has during the day, and Sheryl will be home to take care of Samantha at night."

Todd spoke up. "This is really good. Sheryl has a four-year degree and will have lots of opportunities to get promoted on day shift."

I asked Todd, "Do you want to join Debra and me when we talk to Sheryl?"

"I'd like that," Todd said.

We finished lunch, and everyone dispersed to their work areas.

Four o'clock came quickly. Sheryl and Todd appeared at my door, followed by Debra with her notepad. I started, "Sheryl, we're going to make some changes to help you out." She smiled. "Todd, why don't you explain how Sheryl's job is going to change."

When Todd told Sheryl she'd move to the day shift and retain her lead position in the same department, Sheryl looked worried.

I told Sheryl about Med City Academy and the scholarship, how my mother or her friends would stay with Samantha each morning and get her on the bus. Debra clarified, "Connor's mom and the other ladies aren't charging you; it's a church project."

Todd said, "The school has a nurse to take care of Samantha, so you won't miss too much work and you'll be eligible for promotions."

The three of us looked at Sheryl, waiting for a response. After several seconds, Sheryl broke into a huge smile, then burst into tears as she repeated, "Thank you, thank you, thank you."

I told her, "Go home now and get some sleep tonight. Tomorrow, you need to take Samantha to the academy to enroll her in preschool. You start working your new day-shift job the day after. I adjusted your hours for last night; you'll get full pay for last night, tonight, and tomorrow."

Sheryl asked me, "Does your mother know where I live?"

"I'll give you my mom's number. She'd like you to call her after you and Samantha finish at the school tomorrow. She'll come to your apartment with her friends so they can all meet you and Samantha."

"That'll be good," said Sheryl.

Todd instructed, "You'll replace Rod Riverton; he's the current day-shift lead. He's being promoted, so everybody's coming out ahead with these changes."

I handed her a brochure from the school. "So, you can

show Samantha. I think she'll like the pictures of the playground. There are a number of students in wheelchairs, so they get their own playground. Any more questions?"

"No," Sheryl said. "I just—thank you so much."

After Todd and Sheryl left for the parking lot, Debra gave me a huge hug that lasted longer than I thought it should have. Still standing very close to me, she said, "Thank you for making this all work out. I'm very proud of you." For several seconds we stood there, very close, looking into each other's eyes until we heard Jacquelyn speak, "How did it go?"

"I'm sorry, did I interrupt you?" Jacquelyn asked.

"I was just leaving," Debra said. "Connor will fill you in on the details. It went well."

The Librarian

CHAPTER 12

THE NEXT TWO MONTHS WERE uneventful; only normal HR stuff. Prison visits to see Jim Rollins every other Saturday had become routine. Debra and I didn't have any more close encounters, but I did catch myself looking at her a lot. But whenever she caught me looking, it was always respectfully, at her as a person. She'd give me a polite smile and go about her work. I knew she felt comfortable with me because one day when we were standing in my office talking, she just grabbed a bra strap to adjust in front of me. Then one morning, Debra marched into my office, closed all three doors, and said, "We need to talk."

"Should we sit down?"

"No." We stood facing each other. I waited for Debra to say she had feelings for me, but instead she spit out, "I just witnessed Rachel showing her ass to Flash and his minions."

As a sales manager, Flash had two sales representatives and an administrative assistant, Rachel. Robert Pensla and Benny West were the sales reps.

I asked Debra to explain.

"For some time, I've noticed Flash doesn't include Rachel in his weekly staff meetings. The other sales managers include their admins, so it bothered me that Rachel wasn't included. Each week, I'd see Flash, Robert, and Benny sitting at the table, but not Rachel. Then I noticed she's never at her desk during their meetings, so today, I asked Jackie where she was. Jackie said she was in the staff meeting, just at the far end of the room."

Flash's office walls weren't glass like mine, but he had a small window through which you could see his desk and half of his long conference table.

Debra went on, "I thought it odd to see three guys sitting close together, all at one end of the table, staring at the other end. So, I quietly went in. The guys saw me right away and got nervous. I saw Rachel at the other end, moving a book around on the shelf tops. And every time she moved, her dress went up and down—up to her upper back so you could see everything! I shouted, 'Rachel!' and she dropped her dress down, turning. I just glared at the guys and came right here."

"Wait here," I told Debra. "I'm getting Rachel." I marched to Flash's office. He was sitting at the conference table with Rachel. I knew he was coaching her because when I told her to come with me, she looked to Flash for permission.

He said, "Connor. We just need a few minutes to finish this up."

"I can terminate both of you right now," I told him. "Or Rachel can come back to my office with me." Rachel looked to Flash, and he nodded, giving her permission to leave.

When we got to my office, Rachel was clearly embarrassed to see Debra.

We all sat down; Rachel faced me, her back to my front glass wall, so she didn't see Flash pass by on his way to Howard Olson's office. I began, "What's going on?"

Rachel looked down at the table, then at Debra, and then at me as she finally began, "It's been this way for months. I don't want to lose my job. I was just doing what they wanted. A few months back, Flash asked me to reshelve a bunch of books. I noticed him watching me do it. I know he's married, but it still made me feel good. When I lifted the last book up, I shifted my shoulders so my dress went up really high, showing all my legs and the bottom of my butt. I turned around and Flash was looking right at me. We stared at each other for a while, and then he said, 'nice panties.' The day after that, I came to work and saw all the same books back on his table. After that, I started shelving books three or four days a week."

I asked Rachel, "When did Flash invite Robert and Benny to start watching the show?"

"That was after the agreement."

"Tell me about the agreement," I said.

"Well, after a few months shelving books, I asked him to promote me from Admin I to Admin II. And I asked him to raise my pay three dollars an hour. He said he could probably get me to Admin II but couldn't raise my pay that much. So, I told him that if he got me the three dollars, I'd change the way I shelve books. I said I'd start wearing thongs instead of bikinis, and that once a week, I'd wear nothing—just the dress—and let him see it all."

Debra interrupted, "But Flash must've gone to Howard, because it was Howard who insisted you get a three-dollar raise."

I asked Rachel, "Has Howard ever watched you shelve books?"

"No, just Flash, Robert, and Benny."

"Did any of the men ever touch you?" I asked her.

"No, but the first time I shelved books with Benny and Robert there, Benny got up from his chair and started walking toward me. I looked to Flash, and he made Benny sit back down."

I asked for clarification, "Did Flash, Robert, or Benny ever do anything other than watch you shelve books?"

"Well, Benny keeps asking me to go out, but I always tell him I don't date married men." Then she asked, "Am I going to lose my job?"

"As long as you're truthful—tell me everything—you'll most likely keep your job."

"Everything?" Rachel asked.

"Everything. When did Benny and Robert start watching?"

"The first time was a few days after I got promoted. After a few days of seeing me in a thong, Flash called me to his office. He said he needed my help to reach the quarter's sales goal. We needed to give Benny and Robert an incentive like watching me shelve books. And he wanted them to see me that afternoon, so they'd know what they'd get a couple times a week if they made their goal. I was fine with that as long as Flash got me to the Vegas show next year. Everyone says how much fun Milk Truck Expo is, and I know only two admins get to go each year." She paused. "He immediately agreed on the condition that I end with a 'shelving finale'—thong on the table, legs spread." Silence.

Debra spoke next, "What'd you tell Flash?"

"I told him I wouldn't. I'm not gonna spread my legs for three guys at work." She looked sheepish and continued, "But I agreed to do it just for him, right then. So, he locked his door and put his phone to his ear to make it look like he was on a call. I walked to the other end of the table and did it, slowing down each time he told me to…it's just that he makes me feel so good. When he told me, 'I want to fuck you', I told him I did too, but that I don't fuck married men. He got out of his chair and started walking toward me. He was staring at my pussy. I had shaved that morning, and my lips always react to the cream that I use, so they were bright pink, almost red. He kept staring at me, actually at my pink lips. The fingers on his right hand were shaking, and I could tell he wanted to finger me, and I wanted him to do it.

"He asked if I was wet, and I told him I was always wet when I was alone with him. Then he asked me to get one of my fingers wet because he wanted to see my V-juice. I stuck a finger in my vagina and got it really wet before pulling it out and showing it to Flash. I could tell he wanted to suck my finger, so I held it out toward him, but for some reason, he didn't want to touch me. Then he asked me to lick the juice off my finger. 'Lick it very slowly,' he said. I licked my finger real slow, and Flash started to moan. Then we looked into each other's eyes and that's when I realized I was sitting naked on his table. At work. With tons of people a thin wall away. It was crazy.

"As I was getting off the table, I noticed many drops of my juice where my pussy had touched the table. I grabbed my thong and was about to wipe up the drops, when Flash said, 'No, don't wipe it up.' We both stood there, looking at the drops as they pooled together into a little puddle."

Rachel looked at Debra and then me but didn't say anything. I said, "So what happened next?"

"Later that day, when Robert and Benny were supposed to join us, it's almost like he wanted to remind me of what I did, because he put an upside-down mug over the area I'd gotten wet when I'd sat naked. The next day, the mug was gone, but there was a stain on the table where the juice had dried up. Flash would leave a note on the table each night, telling the cleaners not to clean the table. Even later, the area almost became like a shrine to commemorate our moment together, but after a few weeks, a new cleaner was assigned to Flash's office. She didn't read English well and thought the note said to clean the table.

"Flash walked in the next morning and realized the table had been cleaned. He called me to his office and told me what happened. Instead of being mad, he was pleased. Cleaning the table removed the residue from the original puddle, but the stain discoloring the table's surface was still there. Flash says he'll never forget that day. He says I'm special and he always thinks about me and our special day."

I finally spoke, "Okay, Rachel, go back to work. But you will not, for any reason, 'shelve books' again, understand?"

"Do I still have my job?" she asked.

"Yes, but nothing's final until I complete the investigation."

After the door closed behind Rachel, Debra said, "Some women are so lucky."

"What do you mean?" I said.

Debra replied, "I have had to use a lubricant for the last ten years, but Rachel leaves puddles on the table."

I didn't know how to respond to Debra. I thought about asking, "So you have an active sex life?" But instead, I remained silent for a bit and then got up and said, "I'm going to talk to Howard and Flash."

I walked across the hall to Howard's office, where Flash had gone. Howard immediately told Flash, "Give Connor and me some time to talk. We'll get back to you." Flash got up and left.

Howard immediately asserted, "He never touched her."

"That's true," I replied, "but he did many other inappropriate things with her."

"What do you mean?"

"Well, there's the three dollars for the thongs, which you approved."

"Wait a minute," said Howard, "I don't know anything about three-dollar thongs."

"You insisted on a three-dollar-per-hour pay increase for

Rachel, and in exchange, they agreed she'd wear—and remove—thongs for her striptease presentations."

Howard looked worried, "Flash didn't tell me that. When he asked to give her the rate increase, he said she was a superstar who we'd lose if we didn't do the three dollars. And what the hell are you talking about? Striptease presentations?"

Clearly, Flash had spared Howard the full story, so I said, "Flash obviously left out a lot of information when he just talked to you. Let me start at the beginning."

I went on to tell Howard everything that Rachel had just told me. When I told him about the stain on the table, Howard said, "I asked Flash about the stain when I first saw it and he said that he had spilled some really hot coffee on the table and didn't wipe it up right away."

I said, "Well, things were pretty hot in there, but I believe Rachel when she says the stain was from her V-juice."

"What do you mean, V-juice?"

I replied, "Vagina juice."

Howard stared at me for several seconds and then looked down and stared at the top of his desk for several more seconds before looking up and saying to me, "You know, every time I go to meet with Flash in his office lately, he insists we sit at the far end of his table. The whole time we are talking, he's rubbing the stain with his fingers. Now, I understand why."

I informed him, "You know that with Flash's authority over Rachel, we can't fire her without letting Flash go too."

Howard was desperate, "Let's talk to Marvin."

We both knew our boss would favor sales over HR.

As we sat in Marvin's office, I asked if Jacquelyn could join us to take notes.

Howard said, "I prefer there be no notes of this meeting."

Marvin agreed with Howard.

I started at the beginning, telling Marvin everything I'd just explained to Howard. I hadn't explained what V-juice was, so when I first used the term, Marvin asked about it, just like Howard had done.

Marvin said, "So you are telling me that the stain I see on Flash's table was created by Rachel's pussy dribbling on Flash's table?"

I said, "Yes."

Then Marvin questioned, "V-juice?"

I replied, "That's how Flash described the liquid from Rachel's vagina."

Then Marvin spoke the words Howard wanted to hear: "Connor, I hold you responsible for any problems caused by sexual activity in the office. You need to quit hiring all these attractive women to work here. Replace Rachel with an ugly, fat bitch. Then we'll see if Flash gets her to put another stain on his table."

"Members of the sales department have told me more than once to hire hot women only," I told him.

"Not any longer," Marvin directed.

I asked, "How do we justify letting Rachel go but keep Flash?"

Marvin said, "Six million dollars. Flash's team profits us that much each year. Rachel's a temptress who'll take down every man in this company if we give her a chance. She's a six-million-dollar threat. I want her out of here today."

"Rachel earns about forty thousand a year," I told him. "That's my limit on a severance agreement. She loves her job, and she's paid above average. She won't get a job making that much anywhere else."

Marvin replied, "I don't have a limit. Do what it takes to get rid of her! Today!"

Then, Marvin told Howard, "You need to come down hard on Flash. His sales-incentive concept was good; they're the only team to exceed their goal last quarter. But they spent too much time watching Rachel undress."

Howard agreed and said, "I'm also going to have some words with him about being honest with me. He misled me on this one."

Marvin looked back at me, "Replace Flash's conference table."

I said, "His table will cost at least ten thousand dollars and two weeks to replace."

"I don't care. I want his table out of his office today. Put a card table in there for now. We need to send Flash a message. I don't want him looking at her cunt juice stain, thinking about her. I want him thinking about the next sale."

Marvin leaned back in his chair and looked at me and said, "Good salesmen are always tempted by a good-looking woman. You need to make sure there is no one to tempt them." Marvin paused and then questioned, "V-juice?" Then Marvin said to me, "Get out of here and fix this."

I got up to leave, and Marvin looked at me and smiled. "Connor, I hope you have learned from this. The next time I hear about a stain on company furniture, it better be from G-juice." I gave Marvin a questioning look. He replied, "Grape juice. Now get out of here."

I left and called Debra, telling her to prepare a severance agreement for Rachel for forty thousand dollars.

She replied, "What about Flash?"

"Nothing for Flash." Debra hung up on me and, seconds later, marched through my door.

She closed the door and stood next to me. I was still sitting on my chair, looking up at her. Debra was all worked up and looked extremely attractive. I felt I knew her well enough, especially since she had shared her lubrication issue with me, to say, "You're sure beautiful when you're worked up."

"Don't try to change the subject. Why are we letting Rachel go but not Flash?" she demanded.

"Six million dollars."

"What?" she asked.

"Flash and his team profit MTI six million each year. Rachel's a 'temptress' threatening the continued existence of Flash's team."

"That's not fair. The men were in this with her."

"That's true, but we need to protect the people making six million a year for MTI."

Debra asked, "How quick will this happen?"

"As soon as you bring me the agreement." Then I added, "I'm not going to use Brian as a witness. I'd prefer you sit in with me."

As Debra left, I called Brian and asked him to have a crew remove the conference table from Flash's office after work this evening. Brian asked, "Where should I put the table, Boss?"

I said, "Put it in storage with the other excess office furniture. Also, send someone to Walmart to buy a card table and have it set up in Flash's office by morning."

"Flash isn't going to like that," said Brian.

"That's okay. Flash will understand before he comes in tomorrow."

As I hung up my phone, Howard stuck his head in, "Connor, can you talk to Flash for me? I have a personal emergency to take care of."

"I can talk to Flash," I said. "Can I help with the emergency?"

Howard said, "I can handle it. My goats are out again.

And oh, don't talk to Flash about his lying to me. I'll deal with that tomorrow."

"Okay," I said. "See you tomorrow."

When I called Debra, she answered, "Almost done, and I already warned IT."

"Good," I said. "I'm going to talk to Flash to wrap up the investigation before I bring Rachel to my office. Have them remove her access the next time I call you."

"Do you need a witness when you talk to Flash?"

"No," I said. "He'll talk more freely if he's alone with me."

Before I could close the investigation, I had to talk to Flash, so it worked out that Howard asked me to talk to him. As I approached his office, I saw Rachel and Flash at the conference table. I opened the door, "Now I need to speak to you, Flash." Rachel got up and left. "Do you realize how much liability you've subjected MTI to?" I asked him.

Flash responded, "What are you talking about?"

"You know very well what I'm talking about. You had a woman under your authority frequently strip her clothes off for your team. You paid her off with a six-thousand-dollar pay increase and the promise of a week in Vegas."

Flash said, "You make it sound so bad."

"It is bad. You're a married man with two kids. Instead of being loyal to your family, you have your assistant naked, spreading her legs on your conference table."

Flash lowered his head, "I didn't think she'd tell you. I told her not to."

"Well, now it's over. When I leave here, I'm going to terminate Rachel."

"No," Flash said. "She does good work!" Then, as an afterthought, "And she loves her job."

"You should've thought about that a long time ago. We're

going to walk her out in a few minutes. Do not warn her when I leave your office. In fact, take a walk through the plant while we exit Rachel. I don't want her to have contact with you as we take her out."

"Is she getting a good severance?"

"I can't talk about that. You need to start thinking about your future. I'd normally say that you're to have no communication with her, but I'll let you have phone calls with her. No meetings. But you can use the phone calls to let her down easy. I hope you realize she's in love with you. If you don't let her down easy, she's going to show up at your house and talk to your wife."

"Oh shit," Flash said, "I didn't even think about that."

"I've seen it happen before. Rachel says she doesn't fuck married men, so she'll try to make you a single man."

For the first time, Flash looked very worried, "I love my wife and kids. I was just having fun with Rachel."

"You were smart enough not to touch her. Now you need to be careful not to meet with her. Don't tell her your travel plans or what restaurant you and your family go to. If she knows where you're going, she'll be there."

I stood up to leave, looking back, "Your table's being replaced tonight with a small card table. In a few weeks you'll have a nice, wooden table again."

"No way," Flash said. "I'm going to talk to Howard about the table."

I said, "The order to replace your table came from Marvin, and he's not going to change his mind."

"Marvin knows about this?" Flash looked surprised.

"Yes. Marvin said he wants you thinking about the next sale rather than the cunt-juice stain on your table."

"Marvin said that?"

I told him, "Marvin also said to replace Rachel with an

ugly, fat bitch and to make sure she doesn't put a stain on your new table."

Flash protested, "This has gotten out of hand."

"Yes, it has," I agreed, "and now it's time for you to take that walk through the plant."

As Flash walked toward the plant, I went the other direction toward Rachel's cubicle. I'm doing the termination in my office because it is closer to Rachel than any of the conference rooms.

Rachel had her back to me as I walked up to her.

"Hello Rachel," I said. She turned to look at me and I said, "I need to talk to you again."

Rachel said, "I'm almost done entering this order, can I finish it first?"

"How long will it take," I asked?

"Just a couple minutes,"

I replied, "Okay, come see me when you are done."

Debra saw me walk into my office alone and called me to see what was going on.

I said, "Rachel is going to finish entering an order, when you see her come into my office, call IT and then get in here."

"Okay," she said and then hung up. I remembered that I had not seen the severance agreement, so I walked over to Debra's office to review it.

Debra handed me the agreement. "Forty thousand and six months of COBRA," she said. I skimmed through the pages and verified the release of liability and nondisclosure agreement. I looked up to see Rachel in the hallway by my office.

I told Debra, "Make the call and then join me in my office."

"Well, Rachel," I greeted her in my office, "Let's sit down." Debra joined us and I said, "Things didn't go the way I anticipated. The company has decided to let you go."

"What? You told me that if I told you everything, I'd keep my job."

I said, "I told you that you'd most likely keep your job. Nevertheless, the company has decided to let you go, and I want to discuss options for you and the company going forward."

"What options?" Rachel said.

I set the agreement in front of her and outlined the basics. Rachel just kept staring at the document but not reading it.

Finally, she looked at me, "Do I have to sign this right now?"

"No," I said. "It actually states in the agreement that you should take time to consider the terms and consult with an attorney if you so desire."

"An attorney?"

"Yes," I said. "The agreement requires you to keep its terms confidential, and the primary term is that you agree you have no claims against the company. That means you can't sue the company." The three of us sat in awkward silence for almost a minute.

Rachel kept staring at the document until she finally looked up at Debra and then at me. "I don't know what to do," she said. "Is there any way I can keep my job?"

This frequently happened when the employee I was terminating trusted me; they looked to me for advice. This put a lot of pressure on me. I was supposed to represent the company and get the best deal I could for MTI, despite my desire to practice what I knew was right.

"There is no way to keep your job," I told her. "What I

think you should do is go home and review the agreement. If you feel you need an attorney to help you decide, then you should get one. If you feel you understand the agreement and just want more money, then call me and tell me how much."

"Okay," Rachel said. "I'll go home and think about it. Do I need to leave right now?"

"Yes, Debra will go with you to your desk to get your personal items. She'll watch you go to your car and leave the property. You are not to come back on the MTI campus unless you get permission from me in advance." More silence, before we all stood, and Rachel and I shook hands.

She told me, "I will call you." Then Rachel and Debra walked out my back door.

A few minutes later, Debra returned to my office and gave me a quick hug. I looked around to see if anyone was watching before I said, "What was that for?" I looked into her beautiful eyes and wanted so much to kiss her.

Debra spoke, "I was so upset with you for letting the company screw Rachel and letting the guys off with no consequences. But you redeemed yourself when you gave her advice. You essentially told her to ask for more money."

"I know, but I had a hard time balancing the company's interests against being fair to Rachel." Just then, Jacquelyn opened the door behind Debra.

"Connor," Jacquelyn said, "Marvin wants to see you."

In Marvin's office, I closed the door before being asked, "Is she gone?"

"Yes," I said. "Debra and I met with her, and Debra walked her out."

"Good," Marvin said. "How much is this going to cost us?"

I thought for a moment. "We offered forty thousand, but

she'd rather keep her job. I don't think she'll get an attorney, but if she does, we're looking at over a million."

"A million?" Marvin asked, agitated.

"Yes," I said. "If she tells her story to a jury, we're screwed."

Marvin said, "I suppose if she starts talking about her boss making her spread naked on a table, and lick her own juice, a jury will punish us. Connor, you need to stop her from getting an attorney. We need to settle out of court. Lock her down with the NDA."

"I agree," I told him. "How high can I go?"

"As high as you have to go, but if it goes over a quarter million, I want to get involved again."

"Okay," I stood to leave.

Marvin said, "You better brief Hank on this. Both he and I will need to sign the check request."

"I'll talk to Hank right now. Should I inform Merlot?"

"No," said Marvin. "I don't want you reporting anything to corporate until this is a done deal. Corporate getting involved will only make things worse. They already think we're a bunch of out-of-control lumberjacks. The only reason we get away with this stuff is that we're the most profitable VTM company. Oh, that's another reason to wrap this up quick. We're having a particularly good month. If we can cut the check to her this month, the payout won't even be noticed."

"Understood," I said, leaving for Hank's office.

Hank hated settlements, especially for sexual harassment. I'd have to listen to his standard lecture telling me I had to change our company culture. This was the third sexual harassment settlement this year; he'd remind me that Mr. Olson never had these problems.

As I walked into his office, Hank asked, "How much?"

"How do you know I need money?"

"The tone of your voice changes when you need money. I

also noticed you in Marvin's office earlier, and it didn't look good."

"It's another sexual harassment settlement."

"Oh geez," Hank said. "I'm not even wasting my time telling you what I think. Who was it this time?"

"Flash and his team. With Rachel, over a period of months."

"I knew Flash was cheating on his wife, but I didn't think he was doing it with MTI women."

"What do you mean 'cheating on his wife'?"

Hank told me, "Several months ago, Flash stopped by my office and asked if I wanted to join him in the Cities for some strange pussy, which is apparently anyone not his wife. He said a man needs some variety in his life."

"No one was having sex with Rachel," I said. "But they were making her take her clothes off during sales meetings."

Hank repeated, "How much?"

"Over forty thousand but less than two-fifty."

"Oh geez," Hank said. "This'll be the largest settlement this year."

"It'll be even worse if she lawyers up. We should have an amount in a few days, then you and Marvin sign off."

"Does corporate know?"

"No, and Marvin wants it handled within MTI."

Hank said, "Then you better settle fast. I must report potential litigation at the end of the quarter. If you settle, there'll be nothing to report."

A couple days later, I received a call from Rachel.

"Hello, Connor."

"Hello, Rachel, how are you doing?"

"I'm not doing well. I miss my job and the people at work, but I made a decision about the agreement. I do want more money."

"OK, what amount did you decide on?"

"Well, I started looking for jobs and couldn't find any that'd pay me what I was making at MTI. It's going to take several years in a new job to get back to my MTI pay rate. So, to make up the difference for those years, I think I'll need at least seventy thousand dollars, but then I thought it would be really nice to get a check for one hundred thousand dollars."

I thought about what Rachel had just said. I was glad she hadn't mentioned an attorney. I also thought about Flash and his family and wanted to make sure Rachel was so happy with the settlement that she'd focus on some extra cash instead of thinking about Flash.

"Rachel," I started, "I need to point out that in the agreement, it says that any amount you receive is subject to payroll and withholding taxes, so to get a check for one hundred thousand, you'd need to ask for more than that."

"How much more?"

I decided to be generous with the calculation, so she'd also get a large tax refund for the year. "If you ask for two hundred thousand, the company will withhold one hundred thousand for taxes, and you'd receive a check for one hundred thousand."

"Will one hundred thousand dollars cover all the taxes?"

"Yes, and then some. You'll get a nice refund when you file your tax return."

"Let's do it," she said. "Let's make it two hundred thousand dollars."

"Okay, I'll get the check and then let's meet at the County Seat in Mantorville at ten tomorrow morning. Debra will be with me to sign as a witness to our signatures." I reminded her to bring both copies of the agreement. "We'll both sign each copy so you and the company each have one with original signatures."

Rachel confirmed and we ended the call.

I walked across the hall to Marvin's office. "Connor," he said, "you should never play poker. I can tell you have something good to tell me."

"You're correct, I just talked to Rachel. She didn't get an attorney, and she agreed to settle for two hundred thousand dollars."

"That's great," said Marvin. "Excellent job, Connor. Two hundred thousand won't be noticed this month. I assume you can get it done in the next three days?"

"Debra and I will meet with Rachel tomorrow morning. I'll have the check request to you and Hank within the hour."

I stood up to leave, as Marvin said, "Connor, this could've been a lot worse. You do good work."

The next morning, on our way to the County Seat coffeehouse, I reminded Debra that while Rachel and I were talking, she'd need to review both copies of the agreement to make sure there were no alterations.

We entered the coffeehouse and greeted Rachel, who was seated in a far corner. She was in good spirits; she had a job interview that afternoon and was looking forward to working again. While Debra reviewed the documents, Rachel told me she'd decided to quit talking to Flash. I asked her why.

"The last time I called Flash, he was driving his kids to soccer practice. I could hear their little voices in the background. I realized that if I got Flash to leave his wife, I'd be hurting his children."

"You are a wise and understanding woman, Rachel." I asked her, "Does Flash know how you feel?"

"No. Would you please tell him? He keeps calling me. I even changed his name on my phone to 'Children's Voices' to remind me he's got a family to take care of. I'm worried hearing his voice will set off my feelings for him and I'll do the wrong thing."

"I'll talk to Flash. You're doing what's best for you and Flash."

She thanked me again.

Debra had finished and handed one agreement each to Rachel and me. "OK, I drew a line through the amount of '$40,000' and filled it in with '$200,000' on each document."

After Rachel and I initialed the amount changes, we signed off on both copies, Debra notarized each one. "This is your copy," she told Rachel. "Remember it's a confidential agreement, because whoever does your taxes will be shocked by the amount of your refund. You can't tell them why MTI paid you so much this year."

"That's not a problem. I use Turbo Tax and do it myself."

"That's good," said Debra.

After a moment of quiet, I said to Debra, "We should get back to the office."

Rachel said, "I'm going to stay here a while and look at my hundred-thousand-dollar check."

Debra and I smiled, then started to walk away, but Rachel said, "Wait!" She gave Debra a warm hug before doing the same with me, saying "Remember to talk to Flash."

"I will, as soon as I get back to the office."

On the way back, I was relaxed now that we'd just settled this major issue. I started to think about Debra: she was intelligent and beautiful, and we were alone in the truck, driving down Highway 14. I felt a sudden urge to take advantage of the moment, to let her know how I felt.

I spoke, "I like you."

She smiled. "I like you too."

"No, you don't understand. I really, really like you." Debra's face lit up, and she gave me the most beautiful smile I'd ever seen. She didn't say anything, but she didn't have to.

We drove in silence for a while before I asked if she'd mind me stopping to run the pickup through the car wash. She didn't mind, so I exited at Byron for the car wash. There was no one in line behind us, so no one could see us. I decided to make my move. I asked her, "Can I kiss you?"

She looked at me and said, "Don't ask. Just do it and we'll see what happens." I released my seatbelt, leaned over, and kissed her. She released her seatbelt and leaned over and kissed me and we didn't stop. She made my whole-body tingle. Only two women had ever made me feel this way before and I didn't want the feeling to stop. But then the noise of the final car wash fans brought us back to reality. We both buckled up, as I headed back to the highway.

After about five minutes of silence, I asked her, "What's next?"

"That's what I'm thinking about. I don't know."

I told her, "I'll be in Des Moines tomorrow, but I'll be back Friday afternoon. How about dinner at the Hubbell House on Friday evening?"

"No. If we're seen together in a Hubbell House dining room, rumors will start."

"How about if we grill steaks at my house?"

"I'll bring the salad," she smiled at me. Then, "A lot of MTI people live near you. Why don't you leave a garage door up, so I can park without anyone seeing my car?"

"I can do that, or you could get an Uber to my house so you're not worried about driving home after too much wine?"

"Who said I was going home? I plan to drink a lot of wine and spend the night."

I parked the truck at MTI with a big grin on my face. Debra was grinning as well.

As we entered the building, I told her, "I'm going to Marvin's office. Let's meet in my office after you scan the agreement. Oh, and make sure I talk to Flash."

"Why don't you talk to Flash when you finish with Marvin?" she said.

"Good idea. I'll meet you after I'm done with Flash."

Marvin looked up from his desk. "Connor, how did it go?"

"It's done. Debra is scanning the signed agreement into our system as we speak."

"Great." Marvin punched Hank's number into his phone. "Hank, I'm with Connor. He just returned with the signed agreement, so there's no MTI litigation to report, other than the product liability claims."

"Got it," said Hank.

Marvin hung up and I asked, "Do you want me to report anything to Merlot or Corporate HR?"

"No, I'll tell Nathan at the appropriate time." Marvin saw I was troubled. "Are you OK with that?"

"Well, I was thinking about the policy that requires I report all sexual harassment complaints to corporate HR, but technically this wasn't a sexual harassment complaint. Rachel never complained to anyone. We caught four employees taking part in consensual inappropriate behavior and we stopped the behavior."

"That's a good response," Marvin said. "I'll use that language when I tell Nathan about Flash's sales incentive program." Marvin and I nodded before I left for Flash's office.

I closed the door behind me and sat down in front of Flash's desk. He closed his laptop, asking "What's up?"

"We reached an agreement with Rachel. She received a severance payment and agreed not to sue MTI. Rachel asked me to give you a message. She told me that the last time she talked to you on the phone, she heard your children in the background. She's not going to call you anymore, and she'd like you to stop calling her."

Flash just stared at me before he said, "I'd hoped Rachel and I could remain friends."

"Rachel knows she's either all in or all out. She's wisely chosen to be out of your life, which will protect you and your family. You need to honor her request. She told me to tell you this and to ask you to quit calling her."

"I don't like this, but if she wants me to forget about her, I will."

"Thank you." I got up and left to meet Debra in my office.

Debra and I entered separate doors to my office, at the same time. Walking toward each other, we stopped awfully close. We were staring into each other's eyes with such intensity that we didn't notice Jacquelyn standing in the doorway until she said, "Get a hotel room."

Debra and I stepped apart as Jacquelyn said, "This is the third time I've walked in on you two standing so close and looking at each other with bedroom eyes."

"It's that obvious?" I asked.

Jacquelyn said, "It is very obvious."

Debra asked her, "Do you think anyone else has noticed?"

"Not that I'm aware of, but it won't be long before the two of you are seen as a couple," Jacquelyn told us.

"That's not good," Debra replied. "I report to Connor; I can't have a relationship with him."

I said to Debra, "You better be careful, or someone will report you to HR."

"Funny," Debra said, sticking her tongue out at me just as two employees walked by my office and saw her do it.

"Both of you are playing with fire," Jacquelyn said.

I looked at Jacquelyn. "If Debra marries me, I'll quit my job and stay at home."

Debra said, "Don't rush things, Connor. I accepted your invite for dinner, not marriage."

Jacquelyn stated, "Oh, so you've already started dating. I'm obligated to report this to Marvin." We both looked at Jacquelyn. "Just kidding," she said. "I'm happy for you both. You make a good couple. Just be careful around the office."

Debra said, "We will."

"Jacquelyn, you're right, as usual. Now it's time for me to prep for tomorrow. I have meetings in Des Moines all day tomorrow and most of Friday."

"OK," Jacquelyn said. "Let's get back to work."

I sat down at my desk to review emails, but after a few minutes, I heard yelling coming from Alice's office. I looked across the hall to see Ralph McCarthy standing in front of Alice's desk, repeatedly shouting, "My name is Ralph, and I'm a man!"

I walked to Alice's office and heard her explaining to Ralph, "Every employee has to choose their pronouns, and I'm contacting everyone who hasn't yet made their selection."

Ralph stared angrily at her, "This is bullshit! Ralph's a man's name. I don't know any women named Ralph!"

"We need to know how you want to be addressed. People won't know what to call you if you don't select your pronouns," said Alice.

"They can call me Ralph."

Then he noticed me. "Connor, this pronoun stuff is bullshit. Do you know any women named Ralph?"

I replied, "Ralph, you can go back to work. You don't have to select your pronouns."

"Thank you," Ralph said and returned to his work area.

Alice just looked at me angrily until I asked her, "Why are

you requiring employees to select their pronouns?"

"Because corporate HR told me it was mandatory for every employee to choose their pronouns."

"Who at corporate HR?" I asked.

"Betty Harmoning, the new director of diversity."

"From now on, don't follow any instructions from corporate until you clear them with me."

"Okay, but Connor, why don't you want everyone to select pronouns?"

"Because Ralph's right, it's bullshit."

"But just last week you disciplined two employees because they were harassing Bryce over his pronouns. I thought you agreed with pronoun selection."

"I agree with protecting employees from harassment. Last week I protected Bryce because he got harassed after he announced he was transitioning from male to female. As of next month, he wants people to call him by his new first name, which will be Britney, and he'll go by female pronouns. We have an obligation to accept Bryce's decision and to make sure he's not mistreated for it." I paused. "But selecting pronouns is voluntary."

Alice said, "Okay, I understand what you want, but what do I tell the director of diversity when she asks me why we have so many employees who haven't selected their pronouns?"

"Tell her Connor Stone said that selection was voluntary. If she has a problem with that, she can talk to me."

"Okay," she said, and I walked back to my office to work on emails for the rest of the day.

Visiting the Seagulls

Chapter 13

On Thursday, I left home at four thirty a.m. My first meeting of the day at corporate headquarters in Des Moines was at eight o'clock and it would take me three hours of driving and another thirty minutes to park and get to the HR meeting room in the opulent VTM building.

As I drove, I thought about all the times I had to host corporate managers at MTI. Most MTI managers despised people from corporate. We wined and dined them, always on our most formal behavior. The MTI people called them "seagulls" because, as Todd Lukens once explained to me, "They fly in, eat our food, crap all over, and then fly out."

I'm sure corporate had names for divisional managers like me when we visited their headquarters. I only went to corporate a few times a year but managed to get in trouble every visit. They must've had at least one good name for me. I'd have to ask Julia. As corporate HR VP, she'd know, and she'd freely tell me; I felt we were soul mates who could talk to each other about anything. But I didn't want to think about Julia now. If I was going to think about a gorgeous woman, I'd think about Debra. Even though Julia and I had been sexually intimate, I hadn't considered falling in love with her because she'd made it clear she was looking for the right woman. But with Debra, I could fall in love.

At six thirty a.m., my phone rang. I answered from my truck, "Good morning, Brian."

"Hello, Boss. I got a call from a friend at the courthouse in Rochester late yesterday. Remember Waterman?"

"The guy that assaulted our intern?"

"That's the guy. He pleaded guilty yesterday and was sentenced to fifteen years plus lifetime registration as a sex offender."

"That's good. Please call the intern and let him know."

"He was probably already informed, but I'll contact him right now to make sure," Brian confirmed before hanging up.

The rest of the drive went fast; I was preoccupied thinking about Debra and tomorrow night. My truck rolled into VTM and I parked as close to the visitor entrance as I could. I grabbed my case and headed in.

The corporate people seemed to fear someone was out to get them; they had elaborate security throughout the campus. To get into each building, you had to show an armed guard your ID and stand there while they did a long visual observation of how you were dressed. The first year I came here, it was a quicker process: a quick ID comparison to the computer screen before getting buzzed in.

Today, the guard couldn't find my name on his computer. When he looked at my boots, he freaked out. "Those aren't dress shoes," he said.

"No, they aren't," I said, "they're work boots, and I have permission to wear them here."

"OK," the guard said. "Stand back, sir, I need to call for support." He was acting afraid of me.

Then I heard a familiar voice behind me. "John don't call for support. This man is with me; he's one of us." I turned to see Julia standing behind me.

"Hi, Julia," the guard replied. "But this man is not on my screen, and he's wearing work boots."

Julia instructed him, "Scroll all the way down to the difficult-visitor section."

"Difficult visitor?" I asked.

Julia looked at me wryly, "It's just what we call people who need special consideration."

The guard looked up. "Found him, and I see the dress shoe waiver for his deformed feet."

I looked at Julia again. "Deformed feet?"

The gate buzzed, and Julia and I walked through. Away from the guard, Julia said, "I had to say you had deformed feet in order to get you the waiver."

"I don't understand why there's a dress shoe requirement anyway. I wear high-quality Red Wing boots because they're so comfortable. I can't stand dress shoes."

"You didn't hear it from me, but the logic behind the dress shoe policy is crazy. Our chief of security went to a seminar with a session about shoe bombs. He was told that domestic terrorists could start using shoe bombs in buildings and he apparently heard bombs would only be in boots because you can't get enough explosive material into a dress shoe. Now we require all men to wear dress shoes."

"What about women?"

"There is no policy for women; I wear my thigh-high boots all the time and no one tries to stop me."

I told her, "They don't stop you in thigh-high boots because the guard's thinking about what's above the boots."

Julia smiled at me. "Are we getting together tonight?" she asked.

"I'd like that. But you can't get naked with me this time."

"Oh, I was looking forward to that."

"Believe me," I said. "I'd love to repeat your training sessions, but I may be getting serious about someone. We have our first date tomorrow night, so I wouldn't feel right."

"I understand why you don't want to get sexual, but can we at least reminisce?"

"Yes," I said. "We can talk all you want."

We reached our meeting room. Whenever I walked into a room with Julia, everyone in the room looked at her, even the women. That's how beautiful she was. Add to that her wonderful heart and spirit, and I could so easily fall in love with her. But she just wasn't interested.

The room was filled with fourteen other divisional HR directors and a few corporate people. I began greeting my peers while Julia worked the room, welcoming people to Des Moines.

Dwight Benson, corporate Senior VP of HR, asked everyone to sit. Dwight stood behind a podium at the front of the room, flanked by a large screen on one side and on the other, a head table where three corporate HR VPs who reported to Dwight sat facing the group.

The rest of us took seats at the tables configured in a U-shape facing the front. Julia sat next to me, like she did at many meetings. No one in the room suspected we had anything going on, and to Julia, I was just one of the girls. I wondered why she wasn't sitting up front with her peers today. but I left that thought as Julia leaned back in her chair. I could see that her skirt rode up high on her thighs when she was sitting. All I could think about was seeing her naked in thigh-high boots. I no longer cared why she was sitting next to me.

I was glad we were sitting at the bottom of the U, opposite of the podium at tables fitted with skirts along the inside of the U. With a wall to our backs, there was no one behind us to see how much of Julia I was seeing. The table skirts prevented anyone in front of us from seeing Julia's legs. There was one security camera in the room, and it was focused on the entrance to the room, so Julia and I were not in the camera's line of sight. I didn't have to worry about hidden cameras because the Des Moines employee union negotiated a contract that banned hidden cameras from the campus.

On the screen at the front, Dwight began showing charts reviewing twenty-five different key performance indicators by division. The metrics compared each division to its peers. MTI was usually near the top and was the best in three distinct categories: Sales per Employee, Profit per Employee, and Employee Turnover. But MTI was the worst in one category: Affirmative-Action Compliance. This was because I refused to take the time to keep affirmative-action records. Dwight was frequently upset with me about this; he'd complained to Marvin and Nathan about it on several occasions.

I took the position that MTI didn't have to have an affirmative-action plan because MTI didn't do any business with government entities. Even though VTM made sales to governments and VTM owned MTI, I argued that MTI was an autonomous division managed independently of VTM. My actions were proof that MTI was autonomous, because I still worked here after I refused to have an affirmative-action plan, despite Dwight's demanding it.

What Dwight didn't know was that before I'd taken a stand on the issue, I'd lobbied Marvin to back me and to suggest that we seek a determination on MTI's mandatory compliance from the Office of Federal Contract Compliance Programs, the federal agency requiring all companies with federal contracts to have an affirmative-action plan and to comply with all EEOC regulations. We'd hired a good law firm in Des Moines to represent us before the OFCCP and were waiting for a determination within the next few months.

At MTI, we had the raw data for EEOC compliance, and we filed the mandatory EEO-1 report and the Vets-100 report form each year. We just didn't do the time-consuming Affirmative Action Plan. By asking for a determination from OFCCP, I was also buying time to fix a couple problems. After reviewing MTI's raw data, I saw that in Rochester, Minnesota, where most of our employees worked, we'd exceed the expectations of an AAP. However, in two branches, we had problems. I noticed that in Birmingham, Alabama, we only had two Black employees out of sixty-three total employees. That meant our employee population in Birmingham was three percent Black in a city with a seventy percent Black population.

I'd given Kendall Young, our manager in Birmingham, a call to ask how he recruited new employees. He'd told me that when a position opened, he usually called his pastor to see who at his Baptist church was looking for a job. It was a big church, so he almost always found someone qualified and interested in working for MTI. When I'd asked about how many Black families were in his church, he'd just said, "We had a Black family visit last Sunday." That was all I'd needed to hear. I'd put Debra to work with Kendall to set up a proper hiring process, instructing them to make sure most hires over the next five years were Black.

The other branch with a problem was Austin, Texas. They were hiring legally, but they weren't hiring properly. When I reviewed the Austin branch data, I'd found it odd that almost all the employees' last names started with letters from the first half of the alphabet. I'd had Daniel West, our branch manager in Austin, investigate the situation and he'd told me, "Connor, you're not gonna believe this. I talked to Sylvia, who schedules the interviews. She said she prints out all the apps for a position, sorts them alphabetically, and then starts with 'A' to set up interviews, she keeps scheduling interviews until someone's hired." Daniel had apologized for not realizing it; he'd thought the supervisors were selecting the interview candidates. He immediately changed the process so now the most qualified applicants were the first scheduled for interviews.

If the OFCCP determination forced us to do an AAP, we'd still have several months to do it and could then show some progress in Birmingham. Austin wouldn't cause any problems, and Rochester would shine. The other branches and plant sites may have some small problems, but nothing I was worried about.

Dwight finished his presentation explaining the affirmative-action plan controversy at MTI. He looked right at me as he told everyone that I was subjecting the company to severe penalties and fines.

One of the newer HR directors in the group asked Dwight why I was allowed to defy his orders. I was going to stand up and tell the group that we didn't report to Dwight; we reported to our presidents. But Julia stopped me. She sensed my tension and placed her hand on my thigh. That took my attention away from the discussion. Dwight just ignored the question about his authority by saying the company had retained a law firm to sort things out.

As we all broke up for a break, Dwight motioned me to the front.

As I approached him, he explained, "Connor, I didn't intend my criticism to be directly at you. I should've made it clear I was frustrated with the leadership at MTI."

"Not a problem, I can handle it."

Then he said, "I'd like to talk with you this evening. Perhaps we can meet in the lounge at the restaurant tonight. After dinner, but before we go to the team-building event."

"That works for me. Just let me know when you're ready to talk."

"Thank you," he ended our chat.

I acknowledged with a nod.

As I headed for the bathroom, I thought about how Dwight and I could be friendly, despite our polar-opposite management styles. Dwight was a former Eagle Scout. I don't believe he'd ever committed a sin, let alone broken a company policy. Before becoming an HR professional, he'd been a Catholic priest. He and another priest left the order together over forty years ago; when laws changed recently, they married. Dwight was getting close to seventy years old, had exceptionally long white hair, and was always clean shaven.

Dwight was relatively new to VTM and was trying to prove his worth. Every time a new VP was hired, they started changing things to justify their existence; Dwight was trying to fix things that weren't broken. Apparently, I earned more than Dwight, so that only made matters worse. I found out about our salaries when Marvin tried to give me an extra-large bonus. Nathan had told Marvin I already had a higher base and higher annual bonus than Dwight got, and Nathan didn't want the difference to get even larger.

As I left the restroom, Julia was waiting for me in the hallway. She was hanging around me more than usual this visit. I walked up and asked her, "Are you falling in love with me?"

"That's not going to happen. I just like being around you."

"I like being around you as well." We both smiled at our inside secret; we knew we were both lusting as we walked back to the meeting room.

HR: Behind Closed Doors

The second half of the morning was a payroll discussion. Several divisions, like MTI, paid their employees on a weekly basis. VTM processed all payrolls in Des Moines, and they were going to change from weekly to biweekly paydays. I didn't like it, but most of the employers in the Rochester area were already biweekly. Then, as an accountant explained the planned transition steps, I became upset by some of the steps. I was getting ready to stand up when Julia stopped me again. This time, she put her hand on my thigh and, hidden from view by the long tablecloths, she slowly moved her hand up my leg. Julia knew I had erectile dysfunction, so she knew I wouldn't get hard, but she also knew from experience that I was enjoying the attention.

I just sat still for the next few minutes, letting her proceed. Most people think men who use Viagra can't come without it. That's not true. I easily came when aroused; I just couldn't get an erection. Julia understood this, so she smiled with satisfaction as she privately continued. I eventually made her stop so I wouldn't ejaculate in a room full of people. The payroll discussion ended, and we all broke for a quick lunch break.

The first session after lunch was the presentation of next year's medical insurance plan. This was the session I'd been waiting for. After dealing with Sheryl's insurance issues, I wanted VTM to reduce out-of-pocket maximums. Halfway through the session, the VP making the presentation said that MTI's out-of-pocket max was getting raised by fifteen hundred dollars more per year. She said this was necessary to bring some equity between MTI and the other divisions.

I had had enough. I pushed my chair back to stand, and Julia put her hand on my groin to try calming me again. I stood up anyway and all the VPs, including Dwight, saw Julia quickly retract her hand from my private area.

I demanded, "What do you mean 'equity between MTI and the other divisions'? MTI's out-of-pocket maximum is already ten thousand dollars higher than the other divisions."

The VP responded, "MTI employees have higher pay and larger bonuses than the employees of the other divisions. The easiest way to get equity is to make the MTI employees pay more for their insurance."

"You are so shortsighted," I said. "MTI employees have higher pay and larger bonuses because they're more productive than employees in other divisions. That's why MTI has the highest profit per employee."

"You MTI people think you're better than everyone else."

"Think we're better? We are better."

"We just want MTI to be like the other divisions," she tried explaining.

"So, you want MTI to have lower sales and lower profits, like the other divisions."

"That's enough," Dwight said. I sat down and he continued, "Connor, you need to go back to MTI and spin this in a positive direction."

"How am I going to do that?"

"The fifteen-hundred-dollar increase in deductibles and copays will be printed in the plan description. You don't need to talk about it. Instead, talk about the fact that payroll deductions for medical insurance are not going up."

"That's not spin, that's misleading."

"If you're not up to it, I can send someone over to MTI to do your work for you."

"I'd actually appreciate that, Dwight. If we're going to screw over the employees and mislead them about it, I prefer that someone else does it."

Dwight stared at me, thinking. "OK, let's take a break before our last session. When we come back, we'll go over the new applicant tracking system." Then, "Connor, I'd like a word with you."

I didn't say anything, just walked up to Dwight, as he asked, "Are you OK?"

"I'm OK. Just frustrated by the way MTI employees are treated."

"Well, your production workers do make five to fifteen thousand a year more than those at the other divisions."

"That's not a fair comparison. MTI's production workers get lower hourly rates than other divisions. But other divisions have a bunch of clock-watchers who go home after forty hours a week. MTI's workers are required to work at least forty-five hours per week, and over half of them work fifty to fifty-five per week."

"This is a debate we can have later. I also want to know if you're OK with Julia sitting by you. I asked her to try keeping you from interrupting the meeting so often, but I didn't mean for her to get so physical."

"Yeah, when she grabbed my balls, I almost screamed in pain, but I didn't want to distract from what I was going to say, so I endured the pain."

Dwight said, "Should I move her up front with the other VPs?"

I said, "No, but I'm going to tell her that if she grabs my balls again, I'm going to grab her breasts."

"I'll talk to her," Dwight promised.

I headed to the restroom as Julia was coming back in. I told her that Dwight wanted to talk to her.

When I returned to the meeting room, Julia was in her chair next to me. As I sat down, Julia made movements like she was pulling her skirt down toward her knees, but she actually pulled it up as far as she could without showing me her panties. Then I remembered that Julia didn't always wear panties; she either wore a thong or nothing at all. I'd had this happen before with other women. They did this to distract me so that they could get the advantage in the conversation they were about to start. It always worked. Julia started to talk, but all I was thinking about right now was whether she was wearing a thong or going commando.

Julia said, "Why did you tell Dwight that I grabbed your testicles?"

"I didn't. I said you grabbed my balls."

"Dwight used the word testicles." She just stared at me, waiting for me to explain why I complained to Dwight.

I told her, "When I realized he'd instructed you to keep me quiet, I took advantage of the situation to make him think that both of you had gone too far in your efforts to silence me."

"I barely touched you."

"I know, but I wanted to make Dwight feel bad. I could've told him I was going to press charges for sexual assault, and he would've believed me."

"He was really upset with me. He instructed me to still verbally persuade you to keep quiet, but not to get physical."

I half-joked, "Just wait until they start the next session. I'm going to complain about applicant tracking every few minutes."

"Please don't. I have my seven-year review next week. I'm in enough trouble. What can I say to keep you quiet?"

"You don't have to say anything," I winked at her. "If you spread your legs so I can see more and if you finger yourself and show me a very wet finger, I won't say a word the rest of the day."

"It's a deal."

HR: Behind Closed Doors

As the VP in charge of recruiting started his presentation, Julia spread her legs wider than I expected. I got nervous and looked around the room to see if anyone was watching. They were focused on the speaker. Besides, they couldn't see anything under the table anyway.

I managed to look up at the speaker every now and then, but I was focused on Julia's activity, her very active fingers working on herself so only I could see. After a while, she quietly leaned back to relax. I looked down as she was pulling her finger out. She was literally drenched. I now knew how Flash had felt and I started to think about how I was as terrible as him. But then I weakly justified myself: I was doing this with a woman who outranked me on the org chart, she and I were both single, and I hadn't started anything with Debra.

I was still looking at her wet finger under the table when Julia whispered, "Want a lick?" She looked at me and could tell that I wanted to but couldn't.

She responded by leaning over, cupping a hand in front of both our mouths so it looked like she was talking to me and didn't want others to hear. Then, still hidden from others' view, she placed her wet middle finger into my mouth. Julia removed her hands and leaned back to her chair. I looked up to see Dwight looking right at me. He smiled and gave both me and Julia a thumbs-up, thinking she'd just verbally convinced me to remain silent. We both smiled and sat quietly while the VP wrapped up his presentation. Dwight closed the session by reminding us of the schedule for dinner and laser tag team-building that night, and for tomorrow's morning meeting.

It was only four o'clock, so I planned to check into the hotel now, rather than after dinner. Most directors had flown in last night and already had their rooms.

As Julia and I neared her car, she said, "Why don't you

pick me up at my house, just like last time?"

"You're still worried about someone seeing your car at the hotel overnight?" I asked.

"Yes, which is also why I don't want to leave it here."

I followed her home, where she parked her car, grabbed her overnight bag and threw it into my truck. She hopped into the pickup and said, "I love men in trucks." Climbing into the truck caused her skirt to ride up her legs, just like at the seminar. Julia saw me looking and said, "You like my legs, don't you?"

As we drove, I said, "Yes. I really like looking at your legs and at you."

"That's sweet," she said.

We arrived at the hotel. I realized this would be the tenth time Julia would spend the night with me in a Des Moines hotel room. I remembered every time we'd been together and what we did each time. We followed our established routine. I hung Julia's bag from the handle of my roller bag and headed for the front desk. She waited for me in the lounge as I checked in as one person, put our bags in the room, and then met her at the hotel bar. She'd already ordered a diet cola for me; she knew I didn't drink any alcohol until the official events were completed. After dinner and the team-building event, we'd meet up here with others and I'd relax with a few drinks, knowing the workday was over and I wouldn't be driving.

Julia asked, "Are you changing clothes for dinner?"

"No, I'm wearing this same shirt with the dress slacks and work boots."

"I'm changing, but I'm not sure what I'm going to wear," Julia said.

"What are the options?"

"I have a very sexy low-cut top, but I don't know if I should wear it with a miniskirt or extremely tight leggings."

I gave her one of the room keys and said, "I would like to see you in the miniskirt later tonight, but for dinner, I think you should wear the leggings."

Julia stood up and said, "Aren't you coming? I like it when you watch me change clothes." I got up and we started walking toward the room. On the way, Julia asked, "Do you have jeans with you?"

"Yes."

Julia said, "I like you in jeans, why don't you change?"

"I can do that."

We got into the room, and the first thing Julia did was take all her clothes off, then she unpacked her bag and laid her clothing options on the bed. I had booked a king suite, so there was plenty of room on the bed for her things and room for me to sit on the edge of the bed. I got excited when she pulled out a pair of black, thigh-high boots and set them on the bed next to me.

I picked up one of the boots and said, "I have been fantasizing all day about you naked, except that you were wearing these boots."

Julia put the boots on and stood in front of me. "Am I as good as your fantasy?"

I said, "No. You're much better in person." She hadn't shaved recently, so there were short blond hairs around her pussy. I hadn't noticed the hairs earlier today—of course, then I was focused on her lips. I reached out and ran my fingers over the little hairs.

"I usually shave before I see you, but I ran out of time this morning."

I said, "I'm glad you didn't shave. I like the way you look and feel right now." Julia stepped closer to me and put one of her breasts on my face. I licked the nipple and then sucked on the nipple of her other breast. When I quit sucking, I said, "Let me see you walk in those boots."

I watched as each of her butt cheeks took turns moving up and down. Julia was so beautiful, whether she was facing me or walking away from me, naked or fully clothed, she was just so beautiful. I genuinely thanked God for the life I was leading before it occurred to me that most people would say I had a life of lust and fornication—not something for which I should be thanking God.

Julia interrupted my less-than-wholesome thoughts, "What do you think?"

"I'm speechless. I don't understand why such a beautiful young woman is in this room with me. You seem to enjoy your time with me, and it doesn't make sense. I'm much older than you, I'm overweight and almost bald. It doesn't make sense that you and I can be so intimate. I can't even get hard for you."

Julia walked toward me, looking determined, and started in a profoundly serious tone. "I don't want to ever hear you question why I'm attracted to you again. Got it?"

"Got it."

Julia went on, "If you were a woman, I'd marry you. I'm attracted to your heart and soul. You have such an exciting spirit. We don't have to make love; we already have so much love between us. When we get physical, it's not just sex—we're expressing the love we have for each other. And, about your erections, since I taught you how to use your fingers and tongue, you've been better than any man I've been with."

"Thank you," I said. "It makes me feel good, the way you explained our relationship." When my five-thirty alarm went off, I told her, "You need to get dressed and I need to change into my jeans. We have thirty minutes to get to the restaurant for dinner."

We arrived at the restaurant right at six o'clock. Everyone else was already seated, and the only two seats open were at opposite ends of the table. Dwight was at the head of the table, with an open seat to his right. I asked Julia to sit there and she didn't object. As she walked to her seat, I couldn't believe how obviously every man at the table was checking her out. Some of the women were uncomfortable, watching the men staring at Julia's ass. I didn't stare—I knew I'd get the chance for more than that later tonight.

I took the remaining seat between two other directors I didn't know very well. I liked getting to know everybody, so I was looking forward to the dinner. I was glad I wasn't sitting by any of the corporate HR people, especially Dwight. I was not in the mood for a disagreement, especially since I was meeting him after dinner.

Dinner was uneventful. Several people had wine and were letting their guard down, having fun. Everyone started leaving for the laser tag event and Julia told me she'd get a ride with someone else, since I had to meet with Dwight.

Dwight said, "There's an empty room next to us, let's step in there." We sat. "Connor, I want to thank you for holding back and not interrupting today's seminar as much as you usually do."

"Well, it was hard to say anything with your bouncer sitting next to me."

"I chose Julia to sit next to you because I know the two of you are close. She's always defending you when I get the corporate group together. In fact, sometimes I think the two of you have too cozy a relationship. Should I be concerned?"

"No need for concern," I said. "Julia prefers women. I'm more like a best friend to her."

"Good, that's good," he said. "The reason I wanted to talk

to you tonight is to officially put you on notice that I plan to replace you. Your management style is at odds with my style. I like the shepherd management style—where I'm the shepherd and the HR directors are my sheep. You're like a wolf, always disrupting my flock."

"I disagree. I think I'm more like a German Shepherd, not a wolf."

"What do you mean?"

"I'm like my German Shepherd, Zeus. He does everything I ask him to do, unless he disagrees with me and then, he's usually right. It's like the time Zeus and I were at Hank's hunting cabin in northern Minnesota. I came out of the cabin and told Zeus we were going for a walk. We set out on a well-traveled path, but about a hundred yards into the woods, Zeus stopped and refused to go any farther, no matter how many times I commanded him. I walked back to drag him forward when I saw his eyes shift from me to look further down the path. I turned and saw a mother bear and two cubs crossing the path. Zeus had just saved my life.

"I'm the German Shepherd trying to prevent you from leading your sheep down the wrong path. I'll never be one of your sheep, but I could be your loyal German Shepherd, keeping you out of trouble."

We sat there looking at each other before Dwight spoke, "I don't need you to keep me out of trouble. You're always in trouble. I'm getting rid of you so I can keep my flock together and bring some equality to the divisions."

"What you call equality is really forced socialism. You want to pay all the employees the same, regardless of how hard each works. That's the downside of socialism. When Mr. Olson established MTI, he set it up so the workers who made the most effort got the greatest reward. If you and your flock get your way, you'll ruin MTI."

"If I get my way," Dwight replied, "you won't be around much longer, so you better start looking for a job."

"I'll tell you the same thing I told Merlot. I don't report to you. I report to Marvin, and he's the only person who can terminate me."

"Ronald doesn't like the name you've given him; you should stop using it," Dwight said.

"You can tell Merlot that his name isn't changing. He earned it."

Dwight pulled back from the conversation, sensing he was making no headway. "I think we've talked enough. Let's go to the team-building event. This event is going to send you a message."

"I can hardly wait," I said. We each went to our cars and drove across the highway to the laser tag event.

I entered the facility and joined the group. Dwight and the VPs stood behind a table full of shirts as Dwight addressed the group, "We've done this before, so you know how it works. If you get shot, you're dead and you need to leave the laser room and come back here to wait. The last person alive wins. OK, let's get your shirts." The VPs started calling names, handing each person a shirt with their name and division logo already printed on it.

When all the shirts were gone, Julia looked at me and then asked, "Don't we have a shirt for Connor?"

One of the VPs who despised me said, "Yes, we do. I have Connor's shirt." She held up a white shirt with a large red target printed on the front and back.

"Are you serious?" I looked to Dwight, who nodded. The VP threw the shirt to me, and I put it on. No one laughed; they just looked at me with pity.

Dwight announced, "Since Connor has the least chance

of surviving, we'll let him enter the maze first."

I walked over to Dwight and whispered, "Tonight I'll become the wolf who takes out your entire flock." Dwight looked worried as I turned and walked into the maze.

Growing up, my grandma often told me and my brothers to respond to something unexpected in life with something equally unexpected, so I walked through the maze until I found a blind corner. I removed the shirt and hung it over the opposite wall; the first thing anyone coming around the blind corner would see was the target, lit up by the black lights in the room. I took a position sitting on the floor, facing the corner so I could shoot anyone who paused to shoot the target. I wouldn't have to shoot everyone, because many would shoot each other.

The buzzer signaled the game's beginning. Things went as planned: every thirty to sixty seconds, someone came around the corner and shot the target while I shot them. I knew I'd taken out two-thirds of the flock but didn't know if there were any sheep left. After a few minutes of silence, Julia walked around the corner. She wasn't wearing her gear, meaning she'd already been shot.

"Time to come out," Julia said with a wry smile, "you won." I grabbed the shirt and put it back on. "I didn't know about the shirt, Connor," she said with an embarrassed look on her face.

"I didn't think you did; you looked pretty surprised when you saw it." As Julia and I emerged from the maze, I received a round of applause from those who liked me; the others looked disappointed, sullen. The longest face in the room Dwight's as he realized his demonstration crashed and burned, failing to deliver the team-building message he'd intended.

He addressed the group but didn't acknowledge my win.

"I know that most of you plan to get together at the hotel lounge tonight, but I'm going to go home and get some sleep. See you all in the morning." Dwight headed for the exit, and I caught up to walk with him. This surprised him, "Connor, you win a laser tag game, and you think you're the man, but you're not, as you'll soon see."

"Yes, we'll soon see, Dwight. I just wanted to let you know that if you take me down, I'm going to take you and all of VTM down."

"Yeah, as if you have that much power," Dwight said.

"Yes, Dwight, I do. I know where the bodies are buried."

Dwight was puzzled, "Bodies?"

"Yep. And I know where all of them are buried."

As I returned to the group, all talking stopped. I noted, "You must be talking about me." They all laughed, so I offered, "I'm ready to start drinking!" Everyone agreed and we walked to our vehicles. Julia was walking with me when I asked, "What was the topic of the conversation I broke up?"

"Everyone, including me, is trying to figure out what is going on between you and Dwight."

There were people near us, so I said, "I'll tell you in the truck." I opened Julia's door, and she jumped in. I walked around the front and then got in.

"I've decided to come out again tonight," she said.

"What does that mean?"

"I'm going to be myself and have fun tonight. I'll wear my miniskirt and boots to the lounge, I'll drink a lot, and I'll have a lot of fun. When people ask if I need a ride, I'll say I'm spending the night with you."

"Do you really think that's wise?" I asked her.

"If people question it, I'll tell them I stay with you all the time. I'm also going to tell them that you're gay and that when

I stay with you, it's like staying with my gay father."

"Oh my God, this will get back to MTI."

"It's the perfect cover for our relationship. I'll tell people your wife divorced you because she caught you with another man," Julia said.

Neither of us talked for a bit. Then I said, "You know, Julia, it just might work."

"Does anybody at work know you're going to start dating?" she asked me.

"Just two, Jacquelyn and Debra."

"That Debra is so hot," she said. "I'd really like to get with her."

"Debra is the woman I'm dating," I told Julia, who smiled before offering, "Maybe she's bisexual."

I laughed. "I doubt it. But you know, saying I'm gay could help me at MTI. If people start seeing me with Debra, then they'll just think she's out with her gay friend."

At the hotel, I helped her out of the truck and told her, "Let's go with your story; it can only help me when Dwight tries to fire me."

"Is that what you two were talking about?"

"Yes, he told me tonight that he was going to replace me and that I should start looking for another job. I told him he didn't have the authority—that only Marvin can terminate me."

"It bothers me the way you two talk to each other," she said. "But let's not talk about it now."

I unlocked the door to our room, and Julia walked in, peeling her clothes off as I blatantly admired her body. Then she picked up a black leather vest from the bed and put it on. Most of her breasts were exposed, and the leather covering her nipples was so thin that her hard nipples were sticking way out. Then she picked the little black leather skirt from the bed and pulled it on. The skirt was so low on her hips, it reminded me of Alice on jeans day.

When Julia turned around, I could see her butt crack, just like Alice. A good amount of her midriff was bare between the bottom of the vest and the top of her skirt. Then she grabbed one of the boots and leaned over to pull it on. She was facing away from me, and the short skirt did not cover her butt when she bent over. I said, "You better be careful not to bend over like that in the lounge. I can see everything."

She said, "I will be careful, but I'm proud of my body, and I'm going to flaunt it tonight."

"I'm concerned for you."

"What are you concerned about?" Julia asked seriously.

"You're an intelligent, attractive woman with an MBA from Yale and an excellent job record. You're very promotable. But if you're just known for dressing sexy, you're not going to get the promotions."

"I appreciate your concern," she told me, "And you're right. That's why I always wear business suits when I work with anyone higher than me on the org chart, not counting Dwight."

"That's good," I said.

Julia went on, "I do need to get longer skirts, though. Last week, I flew on the company jet to San Francisco with Merlot and a couple other VPs. The entire flight, I kept catching Merlot staring at my legs. And it's not like when you look at my legs. Merlot is creepy."

"I should rename him 'Creepy Merlot.'"

Julia stepped in front of me, she is so beautiful and so sexy. Then she said, "Would you like me to go down on you right now?"

I said, "I would, but let's wait until we're back here for the night. I like it when you blow me, and we cuddle afterwards.

I like to whisper what I'm thinking about in your ear."

She said, "I love it when we cuddle, and you whisper." I stood up and we left the room.

About eighteen MTI people were already mingling around the dimly lit lounge when we got there. As Julia walked in, there were catcalls and whistles. She walked right into the crowd so they could get a good look at her. One of the guys walked up to me and said, "How do you score with such a hot woman? You have to be the luckiest man on earth." I was glad that Julia and I had agreed to 'come out' tonight so I could reply, "We stay in the same room, but no one scores."

"Yeah, right," he said. "There's no way a man could sleep with Julia and not tap that."

"A gay man could; you put a gay man in the same bed with a lesbian and all they're gonna do is sleep."

"Man, I didn't know," he said, walking away appalled.

I began to think this gay thing would work out just fine.

I caught the attention of our waiter and said, "Do you see the young woman in the black leather over there?"

"Everybody sees her."

"I'm buying her drinks tonight," I said. "She and I both drink Maker's Mark."

"How do you like it?" the waiter asked.

"We both like it neat. Also, neither of us are driving tonight, so keep pouring until we say stop." I gave him my room number for the charges and a short while later, watched him bring Julia her drink. She turned to me from across the room and gave me the sexiest smile I'd ever seen.

Julia and I stayed apart for the first three rounds. We made eye contact now and then but spent our time getting to know the other directors. I discovered over half the group admired me for standing up to Dwight; a minority of the directors thought I was disruptive, and they supported Dwight.

Julia and I had each ordered our fourth round when Julia and Melanie, one of the few female directors, started walking out to the restroom in the lobby. As they passed the bar, a drunk man in a disheveled business suit stepped away from the bar to block their path. He slurred at Julia, "Let's go to my room, baby." I started toward the man, but as I reached him, he grabbed the front of Julia's shirt, yanking it down to expose a breast. As Julia repositioned her top, I grabbed the guy by the shoulders and kneed him in the groin. He cried out in pain and crumpled to the floor. Julia turned toward me, crying onto my shoulder as we embraced.

She whispered to me, "Should I go change my clothes?"

"No," I said. "You're not the problem, the drunk on the floor is the problem." I walked with Julia and Melanie toward the restroom entrance. The bartender had already called hotel security, who were hauling the drunk out. Julia clung to my arm as the three of us walked to the restroom.

When they re-emerged, Julia was calmer, but still wanted to hold my arm. As the three of us returned to our group, everyone gathered around to give Julia their support. The waiter brought our ordered round, saying it was on the house. Julia took her drink but kept one arm intertwined with mine for the rest of the evening. Every now and then, she'd looked at me with eyes shining with love. I returned the look.

We ordered a fifth round and told the waiter to close us out. Julia and I were the only ones from our group that were left in the bar. We went into a booth in a corner at the back of the room. Julia slid into the booth. Actually, she had to use her hands to lift her body and scoot into the booth because her bare butt would not slide on the booth's upholstery. I slid in behind her. We were facing a wall, and Julia was on my right. The booth had a tall back, so no one could see us in the corner. As soon as our drinks were delivered, Julia placed my right hand on her bare thigh. She put her left hand on my right shoulder and snuggled up really close to me. I slowly moved my hand back and forth on her thigh.

She said, "Connor, you are my hero. I feel so safe and so loved when I'm around you."

I looked at her and smiled before asking, "Should we finish our drinks in our room?"

Julia said, "No, I'm in the mood now. You do me here and I will do you in the room." I immediately moved my hand down to start pleasuring her. She was moaning pretty loud, but I didn't care. Then the waiter came over, starting, "And how are we doin—" He stopped, took one look, "It looks like you're doing fine."

Julia didn't care what was going on around us and she didn't care when several minutes later, she caught her breath and asked, "Was I too loud?"

"Loud enough for everyone in the bar to hear you," I told her. "Let's take a few minutes to finish our drinks and then leave. I'm concerned that if we leave right now, everyone still here will want your autograph." She just smiled.

This corner of the room was so dimly lit, I wasn't worried about anyone seeing us. We finished our drinks and worked our way out of the booth. When we got out in the hall, we smiled at each other before Julia gave me a big hug. It wasn't a sensual hug; it was more of an I love you hug. Then she held my arm as we walked back to our room.

We had our door routine down. I unlocked the door, and Julia opened it and walked in. I liked following her into the room because she had a sexy walk as she entered a hotel room.

Julia asked, "Should I get naked?"

I said, "Only if you want to sixty-nine. Otherwise, I would

love to have you blow me while you are wearing your outfit."

"I can still feel your finger in me. I can't deal with your tongue right now."

I said, "OK. My only special request is that you unzip the vest while you do me." Julia unzipped the vest. I liked watching her breasts erupt out of the vest. I pulled the sheet and comforter back on the bed, then got undressed and rolled into the middle of the bed, lying on my back with no covers. We would cover up when we cuddled.

Julia was standing on the side of the bed, looking down at my body. "How much weight have you lost since our New England trip?"

"Seventy pounds lost with some more to go."

She said, "You're looking good."

I put a pillow under my head to make it easier to see Julia. She pulled her skirt up a little so I could see more of her legs. She was now standing at the end of the bed. I could see the tops of her tall boots; she looked so sexy in those boots. Then I focused on her beautifully shaped legs, looking at the naked portion of her legs between the bottom of her short leather skirt and the top of her leather boots.

Julia moved toward me with a slow, sexy crawl across the bed. The open vest allowed her breasts to hang down, and I thought about how every part of her body turned me on. Julia pleasured me beyond belief. Then she crawled up the bed to where I was and lay on her back as she removed all her leather clothing. After she threw the leathers off the bed and to the floor, I reached down and pulled the covers up over us. I turned to my left side as she turned onto her right; now we were facing each other as Julia pushed her left leg between my legs, making me feel so close to her. I slid my left arm under her body, allowing me to put my hands on her bare butt cheeks. I grabbed her and pulled her closer to me.

I started to whisper in her ear and said, "You are the most beautiful creature that God has created. I never thought I could fall in love with a lesbian, but I am so in love with you."

Julia whispered back, "I can feel your love. I actually feel how much you care about me. I never thought I could fall in love with a man again. You are the first man I have been with since college, and I am definitely in love with you."

I whispered, "Where is our relationship going?"

Julia said, softer than a whisper, "I don't know."

I started to whisper again but realized that Julia was asleep. I knew from experience that it wasn't comfortable for her to be lying on my left arm, so I pulled it back to my chest and held her left breast in my left hand. I really liked it when our naked bodies were so close. I let go of her breast and could then feel both of her breasts against my chest as I fell asleep.

When Julia's alarm went off at five a.m., we woke up facing each other. It felt so good to wake up with her still so close to me. She rolled over to the edge of the bed and grabbed her phone to silence the alarm. I asked why we were getting up so early.

Julia said, "I have a meeting with Nathan and Merlot after the seminar ends this morning. I want to shower and dress at home because I want to wear a suit today, especially after you advised me on how to dress at work. Just get dressed and pack up. We can shower together at my house and then you can help me pick out clothes to wear?"

We dressed and packed our things. I picked up the invoice that'd been slipped under the door and stuffed it in my bag. I put her bag on top of mine, and we rolled it to the pickup.

On the drive to her place, I said, "I've been meaning to ask you what names corporate people have for MTI visitors when they visit Des Moines. We call the corporate visitors to Minnesota 'Seagulls'."

"In general, visitors from MTI are called 'lumberjacks' but they have a special name for you that I don't understand."

"What's the name?"

"Babe."

I started laughing and explained, "Minnesota's most famous lumberjack was the mythical Paul Bunyan. Paul had a blue ox named Babe."

"That makes sense," said Julia. "Some people call you 'the ox'."

It was only a few minutes to Julia's house. I parked in the driveway behind her car and grabbed our bags from the backseat. We had two hours before we had to leave for VTM.

Julia had a large bedroom and bathroom. As soon as we got to her bedroom, she got naked, grabbed her cosmetic bag and headed for the bathroom.

She hollered back to me, "Get your clothes off and get in here. I want to brush teeth together in the nude."

I quickly got undressed and brought my travel kit into the bathroom. Julia was on the toilet, peeing. I was going to walk out, but she started talking to me, so I stayed.

"You're so comfortable around me," I said. "You get naked a lot, and you have no problem peeing in front of me." She wiped herself and flushed the toilet.

While she washed her hands, she looked at me in the mirror and replied, "I'm amazingly comfortable around you. It's difficult to explain, but I feel so close, there's no reason to hide anything from you." We grabbed our toothbrushes and put toothpaste on them, as Julia said, "I just think this is so cool. Standing naked in front of a mirror, brushing our teeth together."

I looked at her in the mirror, "I think it's cool, too, but I'm getting the better part of the deal."

Next, we got in the shower together. It was a large shower with 2 shower heads. We both lathered up with shampoo. It doesn't take long for me to shampoo my hair, but Julia, on the other hand, has exceptionally long blond hair. I just let the warm water spray on my back as I watched Julia wash her hair. The stream of suds rolled down her body, navigating her many curves.

As we showered together, I couldn't help but feel that I should spend the rest of my life with Julia. I'd seldom thought about Debra since I arrived in Des Moines.

"Do I have to get a vagina in order to marry you?" I asked.

"I was thinking about that," she replied.

"Me getting a vagina?"

"No, marrying you."

I started thinking about all the things I got to do with Julia. I wondered if I'd be able to do this

much with Debra. We finished showering and she handed me a towel.

I asked her, "Why are you meeting with Nathan and Merlot without Dwight?"

"I don't know. I received the invite during dinner last night."

"When a boss is left out of a meeting like this, it usually means that the boss is the issue. Does Dwight know about the meeting?"

"Dwight doesn't know."

"How can you be sure?"

Julia dried her body then reached for her hair dryer. "Nathan said the meeting's confidential; he specifically said not to tell Dwight. He said the only person I can talk to about the meeting, prior to and after, is you."

"Me? That's strange. I can't wait for you to have this meeting."

Julia turned the hair dryer on and mouthed over the noise, "We need to get moving!"

I got dressed in her bedroom and then went to her closet. I picked a trim-fitting suit for her to wear. When she came in, I told her, "All your skirts are too short for this meeting. I selected this suit because the slacks are a little tighter through the hips. You can dress conservatively and still show off your body. You have a good ass, so use it to your advantage." I paused. "You need to change your bra. I've seen you in bras that hold your breasts higher so that you look larger, and it gives you more authority. Don't wear a low-cut top. When women as attractive as you wear a low-cut top, the men start thinking about sex. Today, you want to be attractive and serious."

"How do you know so much about women's clothes?"

"My first major in college was fashion merchandising, and I look at a lot of women," I said. "I've also done some informal surveys," I only half-joked, "but we don't have time to talk." Julia finished dressing, I finished packing, and we left in our separate vehicles.

With Julia there, we breezed through VTM security and arrived at our seminar room ten minutes before eight. The room was buzzing with people talking about the night before. Some of the group had left the bar before Julia's attack by the drunk, so that story was being retold over and over.

Dwight walked in right at eight o'clock and asked us to take our seats. Everyone sat in the same chairs as yesterday. Dwight was introducing the last seminar topic when Nathan entered and asked Dwight if he could address the group. "Of course," Dwight said.

Nathan walked up to the podium and started by saying how good it was for us all to meet a few times a year. Then he got to his point. "I believe that all or at least most of you were at the hotel lounge last night." Julia and I were both nervous. Nathan continued, "I received a call earlier this morning from the hotel's general manager regarding the behavior of this group last night."

Julia and I were both thinking about all the noise we'd made alone in our corner booth. Then Nathan said, "The manager thanked me for VTM's patronage and wanted me to know they always like it when our groups frequent their lounge. He mentioned last night's group was livelier than normal, but that was OK because they added a lot of life to the bar. He apologized for the incident with the drunk man but said our group took care of things before security got there. He also sent me a video of the encounter, so I know the details." Then Nathan looked at Julia and said, "I'm sorry for what you went through last night. I'm glad that Connor stepped in right away and stopped the assault."

Dwight questioned, "Assault?"

Nathan explained to Dwight what had happened, and the rest of the room made approving noises and cheers. Nathan closed by saying, "I'm proud of this HR team and the good reputation you have with the hotel's management." Everyone clapped as Nathan backed away from the podium and asked Dwight, "Is it OK if I take Connor to my office for a bit? There may be some litigation as a result of last night."

"Sure, you can have him as long as you want," Dwight said.

Nathan and I walked to his office, "Connor, there's no litigation, but I needed a cover for the real reason we're meeting."

"And what's the real reason?"

"Did Julia tell you about her meeting later this morning?"

"Yes, and she explained how it had to remain confidential."

"Good," said Nathan, "You and I are going to talk about

HR: Behind Closed Doors

Julia." Almost as an afterthought, Nathan asked, "Will Dwight be upset I pulled you from the meeting?"

"No. Dwight thinks I interrupt the meeting too often."

Nathan smiled and said, "We're going to talk about that as well."

I'd never been in Nathan's office before, and I was impressed. We walked in facing a long wall of beautiful oak library shelves filled on all levels, displaying every type of truck built across VTM's various divisions. I spotted all four MTI milk truck models. To our left was Nathan's huge desk, with six guest chairs set in front of it. The credenza behind the desk was also impressive; over half the shelves displayed mementos from Nathan's career. To the right of his office entrance was a long fourteen-seat conference table, and next to that were two long sofas with a coffee table between them. Nathan motioned for me to sit on one of the sofas. We faced each other as Nathan's assistant took our beverage order. After some small talk, the assistant's assistant brought in a carafe of coffee and poured a mug for each of us. Nathan asked her to close the door as she left.

When the door closed, Nathan spoke, "There are several things I want to discuss with you. Marvin is aware of everything we're going to talk about, so you can talk to Marvin when you get back to Minnesota. But only Marvin."

"Understood."

"How much you can say to Julia will depend on how our discussion goes." Nathan said, "Marvin tells me you're just like Hank, that you won't accept a promotion if it means you'd have to relocate?"

"That's correct," I said.

"I just don't get it," Nathan said. "I've moved several times in my career to get positions with increasing responsibility. You and Hank are sacrificing career advancement in order to stay in your hometown. Marvin always takes me to the Hubbell House when I visit. What's the name of the town again?"

"Mantorville," I said.

"Oh yeah, Mantorville." Nathan took a sip of his coffee, and I did the same. "Well, I just wanted to make sure you weren't interested in a promotion that'd require you to relocate." He continued, "Dwight tells me that you and Julia are very close. I'd like to know how close."

"I think it's fair to say that Julia and I are best friends. We talk or text a couple times a week, but we only see each other the four times per year when I visit Des Moines."

"Ronald and I are going to be talking to Julia about a promotion. This would be a big increase in responsibility for her, and I need to know if you think she can handle it."

"What would the new position be?" I asked.

"Julia would be the senior VP of HR for a new acquisition. She'd report to the president of the acquired company with a dotted line to Ronald."

"Just like me."

"Yes and no," said Nathan. "Julia would have the same reporting structure as you, but much more responsibility. The company we're acquiring has over five thousand employees spread out over four different locations. She'd have a VP in each of the locations reporting to her."

"That's a significant acquisition."

"Yes," Nathan said. "It'll be four times the size of MTI. The existing management team will stay on, except for the chief HR officer, who's retiring two months after the deals complete. Julia would be the new CHRO."

I asked, "Where is the headquarters?"

"Chicago. Do you think she'd like Chicago?"

"Yes, I know she will. She lived there and worked there right after she graduated from Yale."

"Can Julia handle that much responsibility?"

"Yes," I told him. "Julia is wise for her age. She likes to have fun when she's away from work, but at work, she's all business and takes her HR responsibilities very seriously."

"Does she have the respect of the people she works with?"

"Definitely," I said. "Last night, I talked with several other directors and found they feel the same way I do. Dwight has four VPs reporting to him, but Julia is the VP everyone goes to first. She never declines to help someone, and she always sees everything through to its resolution. She's also very diplomatic and enlists the help of others when needed."

"What is her greatest weakness?"

"She's very attractive," I said.

"And that's a weakness?"

"When it comes to first impressions, it can be," I said. "After people talk with her, they realize there's a brain behind the pretty face. Once they get to know her, they see her as a competent HR professional."

We spent another half hour discussing Julia before Nathan broached my relationship with Merlot and Dwight. "It's no secret that Ronald and Dwight want you terminated," he said.

"Dwight actually told me last night he was going to replace me and that I should start looking for another job."

"We both know that's Marvin's decision, not Dwight's. Marvin says you're the best HR guy he's worked with. So far, every time you've disagreed with Ronald or Dwight, you've been right. If you're ever wrong, Marvin will have a hard time defending you."

"I realize that," I replied. "I'll do my best not to put Marvin in a difficult position."

"Good. I talked to Ronald and Marvin about changing the HR org chart. The three of us came up with the following changes: You, Julia, and Dwight will be on the same level of the org chart. As I said earlier, Julia will report to her president with a dotted line to Ronald. Dwight will continue to report to Ronald, and you'll continue to report to Marvin with a dotted line to Ronald. Although you, Dwight, and Julia will be equals on the chart, Julia and Dwight will have senior VP job titles and you'll continue to have your director title. Marvin and I wanted to make you a VP, but Ronald wouldn't agree to it. You won't have the title, but you'll be treated like a VP. Also, going forward, you and Julia will not attend Dwight's meetings; you'll each designate someone from your departments to represent you at his meetings. This should make Dwight happy, because he's complained about multiple confrontations with you at the meetings." Nathan concluded, "Well, I've had you in here for almost two hours. You better get back to the seminar."

We stood and shook hands. "Julia is going to ask me what we talked about," I told him.

"Tell Julia that we talked about her and that it was all positive. Tell her I asked you to not discuss the details until after she's met with Ronald and me."

"Understood."

I walked into the meeting room just after the seminar had concluded. Dwight gave me a questioning look, but I ignored him.

Julia walked over to me, "You were gone a long time."

"Yes, I was. Let's talk while I walk to my truck?"

"Sure," she said. "Let me get my things."

Julia went back to her chair to get her bag. I watched her walk and thought about her walking naked in our room last night with all her sexy moves. This morning, she was a professional businessperson and she looked and walked like it.

On our way outside, I began "First of all, there's no litigation. Nathan doesn't want anyone to know the real reason for the discussion, except you."

"And?"

"Nathan said I could tell you that you were the topic of our conversation and that it was all positive, but I can't discuss details with you until after you meet with him and Merlot."

Julia said, "Well, that meetings in a few minutes, so I'll call you afterward and we can compare notes."

"Sounds good," I told her. She gave me a very tight, reassuring hug and I watched her walking back to the office. It dawned on me when she turned back to wave, that her new promotion would dramatically change the frequency of our visits. A flood of emotions hit me, and I started to cry. I hollered, "Julia!" and started running to her. She turned around and waited for me as I walked the last ten feet to her.

She saw that I was crying and softly asked me, "What's wrong?" I embraced her; I didn't want to let go. "What's wrong?" she repeated.

"I just want you to know that wherever your career takes you, I'll always love you."

"Now I'm scared," said Julia. "What's going to happen at my meeting?"

"If the meeting goes well, you'll be offered a tremendous opportunity. You need to accept it."

"We're going to see each other again; I'll make sure of it," she said. "I need to get to my meeting." She gave me one last hug. I just stood there, knowing she was literally walking out of our old life into a new life without me in it. It was the right move for her, but I was devastated.

I trudged back to my truck and headed for the interstate. Fifteen minutes later, I was on I-35, heading back north to Minnesota.

Lactating in a Milk Truck

CHAPTER 14

WHEN I DROVE TO DES Moines the day before, it was early in the morning, so I received very few calls. This morning was different, however—the phone kept ringing. The first call was from Brent Coggins, our branch manager in Little Rock. Brent said he had a strange request and didn't know who to call. I said, "If it is strange, you have called the right guy."

Brent reminded me that our Arkansas sales representative, Sam Sullivan, passed away last month. Brent said, "When the family read his will, they found out that Sam asked that an MTI flag be flown over his grave. The family has asked if we can fulfill Sam's wish."

"That is a strange request," I said. "This is the first time I have heard of such a request."

"I know if Mr. Olson still owned the company, we would do it. Sam was in his thirty-sixth year with MTI when he passed. He was loyal beyond belief to MTI."

I said to Brent, "Go ahead and get the pole installed, and I will send you a new MTI flag. Be sure to get lots of pictures, and we will put an article in the newsletter."

"Are we going to get in trouble?"

"You won't, but I could. I'm officially approving the request and will take full responsibility if any trouble does develop. I'm going to limit our exposure by making a statement in the article that any employee with thirty-five or more years of service can have an MTI flag fly over their grave if they request it."

"Thanks," Brent said, "I will get the pole installed."

"Sounds good. The flag is on its way."

I hung up and called Debra. "Hello, beautiful."

"I'm with an employee right now," she said.

"Okay, call me back."

"Will do."

Debra called back a few minutes later and greeted me by saying, "You should not talk like that, I could have had you on speaker."

"Sorry," I said. "I have a quick request for you. Please send a new MTI flag to Brent Coggins at the Little Rock branch."

"That's a different request. Sounds like a good story."

"It is. I will tell you about it at dinner tonight. I'm on the road and should be in the office by two o'clock. I've got another call."

"Be safe, bye."

I switched calls and said, "Hello, Julia."

"Connor, I'm so excited, and I have you to thank for it."

"Nathan asked me questions and I answered them."

"Nathan said he wasn't sure if I was ready for such a big promotion, but after talking to you, he said you convinced him I could do the job."

"I know you will be successful in this new job. I also told him you would like Chicago. Was I right?"

"Yes. Living in Chicago is even more exciting than the new job. I will be able to afford a nicer place than the last time I was there."

"Will VTM buy your Des Moines house?"

"Yes, the company will buy my current home and pay all relo expenses. My base is going up by ninety thousand a year, and my bonus increases proportionally." We paused talking for a bit, then Julia said, "I must go. Thank you so much for making this happen."

"Let's talk again on Sunday afternoon."

"I forgot this is your weekend with Debra. Give me a report on Sunday."

"Julia, you earned this promotion, so take pleasure in it. I need to go, Marvin's calling."

Julia said, "Thank you and goodbye."

I switched calls and said, "Hello, Marvin."

"Connor, when you get back, I want to talk to you about the calls I have been getting from Nathan," Marvin said gruffly.

"I met with Nathan before I left. Is there a problem?

"No, I don't think there is a problem, just a lot of shit being said about you. I don't want to get into it until you are back in the office. Right now, I need you to fix something while you are driving."

"What is it?"

"The two new VPs are starting here on Monday. Do you have their offices ready?"

I said, "Yes, the offices are ready, and IT has their laptops set up."

"You're doing better than me. I forgot to order their vehicles, and corporate is telling me it will take a week to get the capital expenditure approved and then three more weeks to get delivery from the authorized dealer. I'm calling you because you know how to cut through the crap and get me two pickups by Monday. Can you do this?"

"Yes, as long as I have your authorization to cut corners."

"Cut as many as you have to," said Marvin, "just make sure my new direct reports have pickups on Monday."

"Consider it done," I said, and Marvin hung up.

I called Jim Day, our local Ford dealer, and said, "Hello, Jim, this is Connor Stone from MTI."

"Well, Connor," said Jim, "I haven't talked to you since Mr. Olson sold the company."

I said, "That's right. After VTM took over, they made us go through corporate purchasing and buy everything in Des Moines. My problem is that I need two pickups on Monday and corporate says it will take four weeks to get them. I'm calling to see if you can help me out."

"Not a problem. We have over sixty on the lot," said Jim. "Just tell me what you want."

I said, "What I would like to do is send two new vice presidents over to your dealership on Monday. Let them pick out anything they want and then fax or email the invoices to me. I will make sure the men get a ride over, so please do what it takes so they can drive back to the office in their new trucks."

"Send them over and have them ask for me. I will send them back to you in new trucks."

"Thanks, Jim," I said, "I appreciate your help." We both hung up, and I called Marvin.

"Hello, Marvin," I said. "The VPs will be able to select their pickups from over sixty on the lot and then drive them to the office on Monday."

"That's great, how did you pay for them?"

"The dealer is sending the invoices to me, and I will add them to my weekly expense report."

"Sounds good. I have another call, bye."

I was off the phone for a little bit and started to think about how much trouble I was going to be in when someone at corporate discovered I bought two pickups and put the purchase on my weekly expense report. I normally spent a couple thousand or less a week on travel and entertainment. The weekly report with the pickups would be for over ninety thousand dollars.

The next call was from Marjorie Rollins, Jim's wife. She invited me to their home for lunch on Sunday after church. I told her I would be there.

I started getting easy-to-answer calls from around the country. That is, they were easy calls until about one thirty. That's when Debra called and asked when I was going to be in the office. I said, "I'm making good time and should be there in fifteen minutes."

Debra said, "You need to go right to your office. Rosalyn Marin will be waiting for you there."

"What's up?"

"Rosalyn has been pumping her breast milk during her breaks, but instead of going to the medical center to do it, she would climb into a milk tanker on the assembly line. Her supervisor was okay with it because it's a long walk to the medical center from final assembly."

"It may be a little odd, but I'm okay with it as well."

"Let me continue. During today's twelve thirty lunch break, Rosalyn quickly ate her lunch before she took her pump from her locker and returned to the assembly line. She climbed up a tanker and then dropped down into the tank. This was her normal process, and her supervisor saw her go into the tank.

"However, a couple minutes later, her supervisor saw Danny Jones leave the break area and return to the assembly line when there were still fifteen minutes of break time left. The supervisor walked out to the line and saw Danny climb up the tank that Rosalyn was in and drop through the hatch. The supervisor was expecting to hear a scream or some yelling, but the whole shop was quiet. The supervisor quietly climbed up the tanker and looked through the open hatch to see Danny sucking on one of Rosalyn's breasts. The supervisor's radio bumped against the tank, and the noise caused Rosalyn and Danny to look up as milk sprayed on Danny.

"The supervisor told Rosalyn to finish pumping her milk, and Danny was brought to my office. After hearing the story, I sent Danny home early and told him to report to you on Monday morning. When Rosalyn finished, she came to my office and said she wanted to talk to you because you are the only person who would understand her behavior."

I said, "I had a couple of meetings with Rosalyn and her husband before they started in vitro, but I don't know how that gives me a better understanding about sucking breast milk in a milk truck. Danny is single, but Rosalyn is married. If Danny didn't force himself on her, this is a case of adultery, and they will both be terminated."

"Do you want me to witness your conversation with Rosalyn?"

"Definitely," I said.

Debra said, "I will let Rosalyn know you will be here in a few minutes." We both said goodbye and hung up.

I called Marvin and explained what happened in final assembly. He said I could meet with Rosalyn first, but he wanted to see me today and reminded me that it was Friday and he planned to leave at three o'clock. Leaving at three was fine with me because I wanted to start my weekend with Debra.

When I walked into my office, Rosalyn and Debra were sitting at my table. I immediately sat down after greeting both of them. Then I said, "Rosalyn, Debra has told me what happened today, and she said that you wanted to talk to me."

"That's right," said Rosalyn. "Since my husband and I talked to you about having a baby, I thought that it would be easier for you to understand what happened today."

"We talked about the two of you using in vitro fertilization. I'm assuming it worked, since you have had a baby."

"Well, we did have a baby, but not through in vitro. After we talked to you, we went to the clinic for our first in vitro conference and found out we could not afford it. The deductible on our insurance is huge, and after we pay the deductible, the insurance only pays fifty percent of in vitro costs going forward."

"So how did you get pregnant?"

"Well, our problem is that my husband is shooting blanks. We talked it over and decided that we should find our own sperm donor instead of going through the clinic. And instead of in vitro, I would have sex with the donor until I got pregnant. My husband didn't like it, but it was all we could afford. He agreed to let me have sex with another man, but with several conditions."

"What were the conditions?" I asked.

"The donor's sperm had to be checked to make sure he wasn't shooting blanks too. The donor had to sign an agreement giving up rights to the child. My husband didn't want to know the donor's name. I was not allowed to kiss the donor or touch his dick. I was not allowed to have sex with the donor at my house, the donor's house, or a hotel room. The sex had to stop as soon as I tested positive for pregnancy. I followed all the conditions and got pregnant."

"Is Danny the donor?"

"Yes. I had Danny in mind from the beginning, not because I wanted to have sex with him, but because I really like him as a friend. He's smart, in good shape, and I trust him."

"Where did you have the sex, and how often?"

"We had sex in a tank, just like when we got into the tank today. We started out doing it twice a week, but we were both enjoying it and started doing it twice a day during the morning and afternoon breaks."

Debra spoke for the first time and asked, "Breaks are only fifteen minutes. I would think it would take much longer than that to take your boots and pants off, get into position on the tank floor, and then get dressed again, let alone have time to do it. How did you do this in fifteen minutes?"

Rosalyn said, "We didn't have normal sex. I wasn't up to lying on my back and spreading my legs on a tank floor. Also, if he was lying on top of me, I know I would have kissed him. So, I would just drop my pants and panties to my ankles and bend over with my hands against the tank wall. Danny has a big, long dick, so he had no trouble doing me from behind. He's so long, I could feel him way up inside of me. I figured the farther up he went, the better chance I had of getting pregnant.

"After the first time, our bodies couldn't wait to go at it. When I would see those size fourteens coming through the hatch, I would get so wet. When he dropped into the tank, he was hard before his boots hit the tank floor. Danny is in incredibly good shape, so he had no problem donating his sperm twice a day. We both enjoyed it, but we knew it would stop as soon as I got pregnant."

I said, "So, are you saying that you have not had sex with Danny since you got pregnant?"

"That's right."

I asked, "How many times has Danny sucked your breast in a tank?"

"Today was the first time. He started by asking me for a quickie, but I told him I couldn't. I wanted to, but I love my husband and was not going to cheat on him. While we were talking, Danny was watching me pump my milk. He asked if he could have some milk. He was so polite, and he had been so kind to me during my pregnancy, I felt the least I could do was let him suck on my breast for a little bit. I didn't think it would cause all this trouble."

I said, "You didn't have sex with him because you didn't want to cheat on your husband. So, why did you let him suck on your breast?"

"Sucking on my breast didn't seem like cheating. Besides, my husband just said not to touch his dick or kiss him."

I said, "You are not the only woman in the final assembly department that is pumping breast milk. Where does the other woman go to pump her milk?"

"Her name is Liz, and she goes to her car to pump her breasts. The parking lot is a lot closer than the medical center, but I know she doesn't like it when people walk by her car and look at her. We use the same refrigerator and must label our bottles when we put them in the refrigerator so we don't mix them up."

"Which refrigerator do you use?"

"The big one in the break room, so our bottles get moved around when the rest of the guys are either taking or leaving their lunch boxes. I wish there were a more private refrigerator."

I sat at the table and remained silent. I had planned to terminate both Rosalyn and Danny, but now, I didn't feel that would be right.

The silence in the room was uncomfortable until Debra said, "Connor!"

I looked at Rosalyn and said, "Next week we are going to quickly build a small room next to the break room, and this new room will only be used for pumping breast milk. There will be a refrigerator in the room, and it will only be used for breast milk. The door on the room will be locked all the time, but the women in final assembly that are pumping breast milk will each have a key to the room."

Rosalyn smiled and said, "That's great."

"I have to ask you a personal question. Are you and your husband planning to have more children?"

"Yes. In fact, my husband would like to keep having babies until we have a boy. And since it didn't cost that much to have our girl, we can afford a few more."

"Are you planning to use Danny as the sperm doner again?"

"Yes. We have already talked about it, and I have told Danny. He's ready to donate when I'm ready. To be honest, I can't wait to feel him inside of me again."

"Okay," I interrupted her, "we get the picture.'" I continued, "I'm going to meet with Danny on Monday and let him know he needs to stay away from you when you are pumping breast milk. It will take a week to build the new room, so next week you can continue to use a milk tank, but without Danny."

"Okay."

"Also, I want you to come and see me when you are ready to start receiving donations from Danny. We can't have the sperm donation take place on company property, so I will help you find a place that meets your husband's requirements."

"Okay, I will do that. Can we quit talking about Danny's donations? Cause I'm getting really wet just thinking about it, and I don't want to have to explain why my panties are wet when I get home. My husband always likes to fuck me after work on Fridays."

I said, "We're done, you can go home."

"Okay, thank you, Connor. I knew this would work out after you heard everything."

We all stood up, said our goodbyes, and Rosalyn left my office. Debra walked up to me and whispered, "I don't understand how all these women can get so wet."

I whispered back, "It's because they are around me, and I always make women wet." Debra gave me a light slap on the face just as Jacquelyn walked into my office.

Jacquelyn said, "You guys are asking for trouble."

"He deserved it," said Debra.

"I'm sure he did," said Jacquelyn. "But Marvin is getting ready to leave, and he still wants to talk to you, Connor."

Debra said, "I'm going to head to Hy-Vee and pick up some wine and what I need for the salad." Then she looked at me and said, "I will see you at your place."

Jacquelyn said, "I forgot, this is your first dinner date. Well, have fun, but don't drink too much wine. You have to drive home after dinner."

I looked at Debra, and she gave me a cute smile. Then Jacquelyn said to Debra, "You're not driving home, are you?"

Jacquelyn looked at me, and I gave her a nice smile. Then Jacquelyn said, "Like I said before, the two of you make a nice couple, just be careful."

I looked at Debra, and I said, "Jacquelyn's right, we should be careful. Why don't you pick up some condoms at the Hy-Vee pharmacy? Trojan, the extra-large size."

Debra slapped me again, but this time a little harder.

Jacquelyn threw her hands in the air and then turned and walked back into her office as she hollered back, "Marvin's waiting."

I said goodbye to Debra and headed for Marvin's office.

Marvin was standing behind his desk, ready to leave, so I didn't sit down. I remained standing behind a guest chair, looking at Marvin.

"There's a lot of talk about you in Des Moines," Marvin said. "Your Des Moines visits are about twenty-four hours, but you manage to stir up a lot of shit with each visit. I have a few questions for you now, and I want to make this quick."

"Okay," I said.

"Are you gay?"

"No."

"Is it true that you beat the shit out of a guy in a bar to protect Julia Jones's honor?"

"I protected Julia, but I only knocked the guy to the floor. I didn't beat the shit out of him."

"Did you threaten Dwight Benson and tell him you were going to bury the bodies of his HR directors?"

"I didn't just threaten, I told Dwight I would take out his flock, and I actually shot dead all of the HR directors in a laser tag game. Also, I warned Dwight that he better not get me terminated because I know where the bodies are buried. I was just putting a scare into Dwight. You are already aware of the bodies."

"When you say bodies, I assume you are talking about our practices in Venezuela and what we buried in Manitoba?"

"That's correct. I would never do anything to hurt this company. This is my life, and I care about the people that work here."

Marvin said, "I'm tired of all this crap. The new structure that Nathan mentioned to you is now in place. You no longer have anything to do with Dwight, and you will no longer attend the HR meetings in Des Moines. Ronald Herbst says that your six HR assistants are not enough to support you and that he wants to find an HR manager to report to you. I told him we would find our own HR manager, and Nathan agreed to that."

I said, "We already have our HR manager. All the HR assistants have four-year degrees, but Debra has a graduate degree and is the only assistant that is certified as an HR professional."

Marvin said, "I agree. Promote Debra on Monday and hire a new assistant. Debra will be MTI's representative at the Des Moines meetings going forward."

We were both silent until Marvin asked, "Are you fucking Julia Jones?"

"I'm not capable of fucking anybody."

Marvin said, "Good. I'm going home. Let's start the weekend."

We both walked out of the building together. As I was getting into my pickup, Marvin hollered, "Good job on the pickups." I waved to acknowledge the compliment and then headed home.

Debra

CHAPTER 15

I GOT TO MY HOUSE before Debra and left the garage door up so she could park inside. I went through the laundry room and got only a few steps into the connected kitchen, before I heard Zeus burst through the dog door in the laundry room behind me. After sleeping without me last night, Zeus was excited to see me. He got even more excited when I told him we were going to have company. Zeus, enormous even for a German Shepherd, was vicious only to strangers; he was extremely friendly to anyone he knew and fine with new people as soon as he saw I liked them.

Someone knocked at the back door and Zeus barked a warning. I walked through the laundry room and saw my neighbor, Clint Schmitz, at the door. Clint and his wife were exceptionally good neighbors. He was the chief investigator in the county sheriff's department, and Shelly was a nurse at Mayo.

Clint asked if he could use my push mower again. "Mine's still in the shop, and I'd like to finish the areas I couldn't do with my rider, before I go to work."

"No problem, you can use it anytime. The door to the garden shed is always unlocked."

"Thanks," said Clint. "It'll be good to finish before it rains tonight. I'll bring it back before I start my shift."

I asked him, "How was Zeus while I was gone?"

"As usual, no problem at all," Clint smiled. The two of them got along well. Clint and Shelly always took care of Zeus when I traveled. We said our goodbyes. Zeus had heard Clint and I talking, so after I closed the door, Zeus shot through the dog door to make sure Clint got home okay.

Debra would be here soon, so I took my bag upstairs to my bedroom and changed into my jeans.

I heard the garage door closing and Zeus was barking like crazy, wanting to get into the garage. I hollered to Debra to stand back and as I opened the door; Zeus knocked it wide open to burst into the garage. He went immediately to Debra and started smelling every part of her body. Then he jumped up and started humping her right side. I had to holler twice to get him to back off.

"That's quite a greeting," Debra said.

"Zeus is just reading my mind," I joked.

As Debra began unpacking the groceries in the kitchen, she asked, "Are you going to drink Bacardi or wine tonight?"

"I always drink Bacardi and diet unless I'm having a romantic evening with a woman, then I drink whatever she's drinking."

"So, what did you and Julia drink last night?"

"Maker's Mark."

"Did you have sex with her?"

"That's a popular question. Marvin just asked me if I was fucking Julia Jones."

"What did you tell Marvin?"

"I told Marvin that I was not capable of fucking anyone. I'll tell you that I had sex with Julia last night, but we did not have sexual intercourse. We had sexual relations."

"Well, I knew you needed Viagra because I saw the old

emails from your Canadian pharmacy back when you were still married."

"I quit using Viagra after my divorce. I'm taking five different prescriptions right now to treat my diabetes, blood pressure, and cholesterol. I don't want to add a sixth drug to the mix."

"I'm glad we're being so open with each other. And it's fine you were with Julia last night."

"I'm glad you feel that way, but mind telling me why you feel that way?"

"Because I'm currently dating two men. They know about each other, and they're dating other women. I think it'll be good for you and I to get to know each other better while we still have relations with other people."

"That makes me feel a lot better. It bothered me on the way home, having been with Julia last night and thinking about being with you tonight. I'm glad we're talking about it."

"Let's quit talking and start doing. I'll take the wine. You get the glasses and a corkscrew and meet me upstairs."

I started looking through the drawer; I hadn't opened a bottle of wine in this house since I divorced, but I found the corkscrew, grabbed a couple of wine glasses, and headed to my bedroom. I walked into the bedroom and saw Debra standing by the bed with her back to me. I watched her slide her thong down her legs and then she threw it on her jeans, which were lying at the end of the bed. She turned her head to look at me and said, "Can you unhook my bra?"

"Yes, I can." I walked over to her and quickly unhooked her bra, saying, "Can't you reach your bra?"

"Of course I can, silly," she said with a sly smile, "I just wanted you to do it."

Debra turned around, and I looked at her and kept looking at her. Her ass and breasts were larger than Julia's, and they were perfectly proportioned. I had dreamed of seeing her naked, but she was even better than I imagined.

Finally, Debra said, "Are you okay?"

I said, "Yes, I'm very okay. It's just that...that."

"What?"

"I knew you had a good body," I told her, "But I never dreamed you'd be so perfect, so beautiful."

"Thank you," she said. "Can you please open the wine before you get undressed?"

I opened the wine and poured two glasses. As I took my clothes off, I thought about how lucky I was to be having sex with two different women who knew about each other and were okay with it.

Debra said, "After we finish our first glass of wine—" She stopped with a worried look on her face. "I forgot the chocolate to go with the wine. Wait here. I'll go get it."

I watched her walk down the hall and admired how great her butt was. Julia's butt cheeks moved up and down when she walked in the nude. Debra's moved both up and down and side to side as she walked in the nude.

While Debra was downstairs, I heard a knock at the back door and saw Clint's sheriff's deputy car outside. Debra wouldn't know Clint was just there as my neighbor. She must've waited for a moment before deciding she'd better see what the officer wanted. I could barely hear their voices.

"Can I help you, Officer?"

Clint's voice: "Is Connor here?"

"Connor's home, but he can't come to the door right now because we're not dressed."

I decided to go downstairs and heard Clint tell Debra that he'd returned my lawnmower.

Debra closed the door and turned to me with a big grin, "I guess he's your neighbor?"

"That's right, and he must think I live a wild life."

"Why do you say that?"

"Because when Julia spent a weekend with me, Clint caught Julia and I naked in the laundry room just like you and me."

"So how did that come about?"

"Julia and I had sex on the living room floor, and Julia makes a lot of noise when she comes. Clint heard the screams and came over to see if everything was okay. Julia was in the kitchen, butt naked, just like you, getting a glass of water when Clint knocked at the back door. She hesitated, but when she saw the uniform, she felt she had to answer the door. She stood there with the door open just like you, assuring Clint that she was okay. I heard him ask if I was okay, so I walked into the laundry room, also naked, and told him everything was fine. Clint smiled and went home."

Debra walked to the cupboard, grabbed the chocolates she'd bought earlier, and led me upstairs.

We entered the bedroom, and I wrapped my arms around her and pulled her naked body to my naked body. I let my hands slide down her bare back until I had her butt cheeks in my hands. I had dreamed about doing this so many times in my office. I love the feel of women's bare butt cheeks in my hands. I liked it with Julia, and now, for the first time, I was feeling Debra's and really enjoying it.

Debra said, "Let's have another glass of wine." I poured two more glasses, and we sat on the bed, sipping our wine. "Let's talk shop," she told me. "I need four glasses of wine in me before I can get really frisky."

"What do you consider really frisky?"

"You'll have to wait and see. First, I need to tell you what happened today."

"I thought I already knew what happened. Was there more than the breastfeeding?"

"There was also a blow job." Debra paused to take a large gulp of wine. "Sharon Kensky came into my office this morning with a complaint. She's been working in the paint prep department for more than six months and has been passed over twice for her ninety-day reviews and pay increases. She said that when she complained to her supervisor, Justin Sullivan, he told her that no woman in his department gets a pay increase until they give him a blow job. I told Sharon I'd look into the situation and get back to her later in the day."

"What did you find out?"

"I checked the system and found out Sharon's set up for annual reviews instead of quarterly reviews, so she never even appeared on the review lists Justin's assigned. I called Justin to my office to ask him if he ever told Sharon what she'd alleged. To my surprise, he confirmed he had, but said he was just kidding; he'd planned to get the review-timing problem fixed, but had forgotten to report it to HR. I told him that Sharon believes he's serious about the blow job because she thinks she's now been 'passed over' twice. Justin told me I could talk to Ben Walker to confirm his story because Ben heard him talking to Sharon that day, and Justin said he was sure that both Ben and Sharon knew he was kidding. I told Justin not to discuss this with anyone and sent him back to the paint shop.

"Then I talked to Ben in the training office. He acknowledged hearing Justin talking to Sharon about a blow job but had thought Justin was joking and that all three of them were laughing about it after Justin said it. I called Justin and Sharon both to your office. Justin got there first, so I told him Sharon would get her missing increases, and that at the appropriate time, he needed to apologize to Sharon. He agreed. When Sharon arrived, I explained everything to her, and Justin apologized for his remark. I told her we'd increase her rate by fifty cents for three months retroactively, plus another fifty cents immediately for the second missed review, and that she'd get a written review and be eligible for another increase of up to fifty cents in three months. Sharon was happy when she left your office. Then, I told Justin he'd be issued a written warning on Monday. He understood."

I thought it was odd that Debra was telling me all this right now, but I figured she was filling time while the wine kicked in. Plus, I was flattered she wanted my reassurance, so I told her the truth: "You did a good job. I wouldn't have done anything differently."

"Thank you," she smiled. "You refill our glasses; I'll go get another bottle."

Debra returned quickly, and I offered her the full glass of wine. "Just a minute," she said and grabbed the corkscrew, deftly opening the second bottle, "We'll let this one breathe while we drink."

We leaned closer and kissed. I looked into her eyes and teased, "If you give me a blow job tonight, I'll promote you on Monday and give you a nice pay increase."

She didn't think it was funny. "You know I'm already going to do that tonight, so why would you say that?"

"I thought it was a cute way to bring up the subject of your promotion."

"What promotion?"

"Marvin and the guys in Des Moines decided I need an HR manager reporting to me. I told Marvin we didn't need to do a search because we have you. Marvin agreed and approved your promotion."

Debra spilled wine on me as she leaned closer to kiss me and say "I'm going to blow you all night." We paused to drink more wine and Debra chatted, "How was your drive home?"

"Traffic was light, but I had a lot of calls. The one I keep thinking about was from Marjorie Rollins, Jim's wife."

"Why did she call?"

"She invited me over for Sunday dinner after church. I told her I'd be there, but I know she's gonna plead with me to give Jim his job back."

"Haven't you explained to her that he would never pass a background check?"

"I have, but things changed yesterday, so I just may give Jim his job again," I said.

"What changed?"

"Dwight told everyone that because our cost to screen new hires is increasing, the company's changing background checks and drug testing to reduce costs. Effective immediately, employees re-hired within eight months of termination won't be drug tested or background checked."

"Connor, Jim hit his wife and shot up your office. It doesn't matter if the policy changes, you can't rehire him. It doesn't matter if you stay within the policy; it's just common sense to not rehire him."

"I want to do the right thing. Jim will never get a decent-paying job with his record. His family's hurting because he's making less than half of what he got at MTI. And he's changed. He doesn't drink and he goes weekly to AA. It may not make sense to rehire him, but it's the right thing to do, and I'm going to do it."

"Then you better not let Des Moines know about it."

"I agree. I won't even inform Hank or Marvin, so they'll have plausible deniability. I'll have to get Todd Lukens to agree to it, but I'm sure he'll jump at the chance to get Jim back."

Debra slid off the bed and stood. "I can see you've already

made up your mind, so let's have that fourth glass of wine and start getting frisky." She poured us each another glass. She looked thoughtful, "I'm going to assume you can't keep a condom on your limp dick?"

"Limp dick? It's never been addressed that way in the past, but to answer your question, I have never worn a condom in my life."

"So, Julia just stuck it in her mouth last night with no protection?"

"Yes, but you need to understand, I'm fifty-two years old and you're the third woman I've even been naked with in my entire life. I've only had full sexual intercourse with one woman, and I was married to her for almost twenty years. I haven't had intercourse since my divorce over twelve years ago. Julia told me she hasn't been with a man since she was in college. I don't know how many women she's been with lately, but she's incredibly careful and she's very healthy. Also, I have showered since last night."

"Well, that's a good hygiene report," said Debra. "I'm incredibly careful too. Since my divorce, every man I've had any type of sex with has worn a condom." With those necessary details out of the way, Debra seemed satisfied. We finished our wine. She set both our glasses on the nightstand, and I lay back. Then, she jumped on me. As we kissed, it occurred to me how fickle I was. Last night and this morning, I was dreaming about being married to Julia. Now I was thinking about spending the rest of my life with Debra.

We kissed for a long time before Debra slid down my body and profoundly pleased me. Then, without saying a word, she got up and grabbed the bottle of wine and took several swigs to wash out her mouth. She looked at me and said, "It's been a while, that was the real thing."

Debra got back on top of me and we switched positions.

Then I slid down her body and pleased her over and over again. Then, as I worked my way back up her body, I stopped to give each beautiful breast a kiss. I looked into Debra's eyes, and we started kissing again.

    Being with Debra was amazing. It wasn't just about sex; it was the warmth of being intimate with someone I cared about, who understood my job and its complexity, who I could talk about my entire life with, someone who radiated the same warmth back to me.

Afterward, she told me, "I really mean this: I've never felt like that before. Come here and kiss me." Neither of us wanted this to stop. Years of anticipation were being fulfilled this night. We eventually stopped kissing and just lay still, looking at each other.

    After a while, Debra said, "I'm tired. I'm going to use the bathroom, then let's get some rest."

    "I'll use the guest bathroom. Meet you back here."

    When I returned to my bedroom, Debra had pulled the comforter and sheet back. She'd also poured two more glasses of wine. Debra took a sip, but I didn't. I said, "Before we drink our wine, I would like you to do something special for me."

    "What," she asked.

    "Would you walk down the hall and back? I like watching you walk in the nude."

    Debra handed me her glass and then did her walk down the hall. I liked watching her butt's seductive moves. When she reached the end of the hall, she turned and walked back. Her breasts bounced around in a sexually arousing rhythm in sync with each step she took.

    "You are so sexy," I said.

Debra responded with the cutest smile I had ever seen her make. I took a step back and looked at her whole body. "What are you doing?" she said.

"I'm admiring you. I have always thought you were a beautiful woman, but looking at your naked body has revealed more beauty than I ever expected. You are absolutely gorgeous. So gorgeous that I feel inadequate standing here with my limp dick."

"I didn't mean for it to sound so critical when I used the word *limp*. You made me feel so good tonight, more than any other man has."

"I hope so. I try to make up for my inadequacies."

We finished the second bottle of wine and crawled into bed. "If I face you, we'll end up kissing ourselves to sleep," Debra explained as she turned from me, wiggling her butt into me. We both relaxed and fell asleep.

Neither of us had set an alarm for Saturday morning, and we slept late. Earlier, I heard Zeus enter the bedroom a couple times to see if I was awake yet. He respected my need to get rest, so he never woke me unless he saw my eyes open or if he heard Scott Simon on the kitchen radio alarm at seven o'clock on Saturday mornings. I liked listening to Scott on Minnesota Public Radio; no matter what problems there were in the world, Scott always made me feel like we'd all make it through.

I heard the kitchen radio turn on and Zeus was already bedside, licking my face to get me up. Debra rolled over, "Is there someone downstairs?"

"No, that's Scott on the radio," I told her.

"I listen to his show, too, but I listen at nine." She checked her phone and said, "We didn't grill the steaks or eat my salad."

"Do you want to spend more time here, and we can do the dinner tonight?"

"No, I have a date tonight."

"Who with?"

"The doctor. I'm going to end it with him tonight."

"Are you going to end it before or after sex?" I asked.

"I haven't decided."

"Now I just have to compete with the carpenter."

"It's not a competition. I like both of you. I don't want to talk about other men right now."

We resumed where we'd left off last night. A short while later, we both collapsed, satisfied.

"Now we must get married," I teased. "You've spoiled me, raised my expectations for sex."

"Now that we know what works, we can do this at least once a week."

"Why don't you drop the doctor tonight and then drop the carpenter tomorrow?"

"I can't do that. The doctor and I don't connect, but the carpenter and I have a great connection, just like you and me."

"So, the carpenter has good people skills; does he have anything else?"

"Yes. He has wonderful hands."

"For making things?"

"Yes, he makes nice things, but his hands also make me feel very good." Debra got up. "I'm going to take a shower."

I grabbed my travel bag and headed to the guest bathroom to do the same.

I finished first and was back in my bedroom getting dressed when Debra walked out of the bathroom in her beautiful naked body. I watched her take a thong from her bag and then put one foot at a time into it. She pulled it up her body and positioned the strap in her butt crack. Next, she grabbed a pair of socks from the bag and sat on the bed before putting the socks on. When she stood up and grabbed her jeans, I said, "Wait."

I walked over to her, reached around her, and grabbed those beautiful butt cheeks. "Do you have any idea how good your ass feels?"

"Grabbing my butt doesn't do anything for me, but if it brings pleasure to you, then go for it."

As I looked into her eyes, I continued squeezing. Then I leaned in to kiss her on the neck, but Debra jerked back and said, "You didn't shave. If you're going to kiss me on the neck, you need to be clean shaven, otherwise you will scratch my face and make it all red."

"Can I hold you in my hands and kiss you on the mouth?"

"Yes."

I grabbed her butt, and we started kissing. I didn't have a shirt on, so her large, naked breasts were pressing against my nipples. It reminded me of the times in my office when we stood so close that her breasts touched my chest. I wondered what life in the office was going to be like after today. We kissed for a couple minutes, and then Debra said she had to get going.

"We didn't eat last night. Do you want to join me for breakfast at the County Seat?" I asked.

"Sure, but we need to drive separately so people think we met there."

We left my house separately and enjoyed a comfortable breakfast together. We ate and then lingered over four cups of coffee, deciding to have a sleepover every Friday. After Debra went home, I decided to run out to Grandma's farm. Walking to my pickup, I first crossed the street to get some dark chocolate at the Chocolate Shoppe. Grandma loved their dark chocolates, made right here in Mantorville. Hank and I preferred the milk chocolates, but I had to limit my consumption because of my diabetes.

Grandma

CHAPTER 16

I WANTED TO TALK TO Grandma Gustie about Debra. I'd felt so confused and guilty as she'd driven away. Debra and Julia knew about each other, but I still felt guilty about being in love with two women at once.

I drove up her driveway and saw Grandma coming from the barn with her basket. I parked by the house and walked to meet her. She smiled at me, "Good morning, Connor."

"Good morning, Grandma. Did you get many eggs this morning?"

"Yes. It was a good morning. I got fourteen. Have you had breakfast?"

"I just came from the County Seat."

"Well, I just made some of their coffee. It should be done brewing if you want to join me for a cup."

We went into the house, and I sat at the kitchen table. I didn't need another cup of coffee, but I welcomed the chance to talk with Grandma. She set her cup on the table, got a clean one from the cupboard for me, and poured us each a full mug. I set the box of dark chocolates near her and opened it.

"You brought my favorite chocolates! I will enjoy them," she said, "but first, I can tell something's bothering you.

What is it?"

"I need some advice about women and relationships."

"You started asking me questions about girls when you were twelve years old. I didn't think we'd be talking about the same subject forty years later."

I began, "After Jami, I didn't think I'd ever have another relationship. I was happy being single, but then I became friends with a younger woman who made me feel young again. We got closer, started having sex a few times a year. It would've been more often, but she lives in Des Moines. What complicates things is that she'd prefer to marry a woman, but despite that, we're both in love with each other."

Grandma had been listening with a friendly, neutral expression on her face, but when she heard I was in love with a "lesbian" her eyes opened wide. Her face wore a serious expression, "Would this woman happen to be Julia?"

"Yes, that's her. I forgot you met her at Hank's place when she spent a weekend with me."

"She was a very nice young lady; I liked her a lot."

"The thing is, Julia just got promoted, so she's moving to Chicago, and it'll be much harder for us to see each other. But it's more complicated than that because I've fallen in love with a second woman. You know her as well—Debra, the attractive woman who works for me."

"Debra is another fine young woman," Grandma said. "And I doubt she's gay."

"Correct. She and I get closer every year we've worked together, and recently it's become romantic. She spent last night at my house, and we had sex for the first time. So, now I'm in love, and having sex, with two women."

"Do Julia and Debra know about each other?"

"Yes, they know each other, and they know I'm having sex with both of them. They're both okay with it. The three of us are consenting, single adults. Today, that's considered okay, Grandma. But you always taught me that unmarried sex is wrong. That's why I want your advice. Before Julia and Debra, I had only had sex with Jami, and she was my wife. Now I'm a 'fornicator' and I feel bad about it. But I keep thinking how there's no commandment that says 'thou shalt not fornicate' and I'm just so frustrated."

"It's complicated. The teachings are not clear."

"I know. And I'm reading my Bible, trying to separate teachings of God and Jesus from those just recording that historical period's cultural norms. I want to follow God's rules, not laws based on old men's opinions six thousand years ago. So, by definition, fornication includes adultery, prostitution, and sex between unmarried people. But adultery is the only one of those three mentioned in the commandments. I've never committed adultery or hired a prostitute, but I am lusting after and having consensual sex with unmarried women."

Grandma repositioned herself in her chair before speaking, "A few Christian faiths permit fornication between consenting, unmarried couples, but the vast majority consider any form of fornication to be a sin."

"Do you think I'm sinning when I have sex with Debra or Julia?"

"Jesus made it clear that adultery and prostitution were unacceptable, and he referred to both as sins. Most religious leaders would consider what you are doing to be a sin as well, especially lusting in general."

"But would Jesus consider what I'm doing to be a sin?"

"I'm not Jesus, but if what you're doing is not a sin, then it is certainly an abomination."

"How do you define an abomination?"

"By definition, an abomination is something offensive to God."

"Well, until recently, most religious leaders believed homosexuality was an abomination. Today, many of those same ministers welcome gay people into their congregations. So, it seems to me that things that were once considered an abomination can later in time be considered acceptable when cultural norms change."

Grandma thought for a moment. "Adultery and prostitution are both prohibited, but I feel that sex before marriage is also prohibited. You need to make the determination based on your own conscience and what you feel deep in your heart."

"Did you have sex before you were married?"

"No one has ever asked me that before." We sat in silence until Grandma continued, "In my entire life, I've only had sex with your grandfather. We started our sexual relations after we were married. It wasn't easy to wait, but your grandpa Hank and I both thought it was what God wanted."

"I understand."

We had some more silence, then Grandma took one of the chocolates from the box and bit off half of it. She chewed it slowly and gave me a closed-mouth grin as she let the chocolate melt in her mouth. She took a sip of coffee before looking into my eyes. "If you're still close to the Lord, it will be easier for you to decide. Are you still praying every day?"

"Yes, I'm praying frequently these days. I always have a formal prayer, but I also talk to God several times a day with short prayers. Sometimes, when I'm saying my formal prayer, I deviate from what I normally say and bring up other issues, so my prayers can last one or more hours. That's when I feel most refreshed, ready to take on the world."

"That's good. A person with a strong prayer life becomes a stronger person and can discern the path that God has for them."

"Well, I hope I'm taking the right path tomorrow. I'm concerned I might be getting in more trouble than I can handle when I talk to Jim and Marjorie tomorrow."

"What are you doing?"

"Marjorie invited me over for lunch after church. I told her I'd be there, and I expect them to beg for Jim's job. I'll listen to them and then tell them about my plan to rehire Jim. There's no way anyone above me at the company will approve of Jim being rehired, so I'm going to do it without telling anybody, not even Hank. Jim's boss will know, but not anyone else."

"There are so many people in your company, I don't see how you will be able to keep it a secret."

"I expect the news to eventually reach Des Moines after a month or two, but by then, Jim will have proven what a good manager he is when he isn't drinking. I'm hoping that when everyone sees how Jim's department has improved, they'll just give me a warning and let Jim keep his job."

"You need to pray about this. It sounds like you're doing the right thing, but you need to be sure."

I stood. "I will be sure, or I won't do it."

Grandma got up and gave me a hug. "Please come by more often. I like to know how you're doing."

"I will. Thank you for today's advice."

Grandma walked me to the door and thanked me for the chocolates. She gave me another hug before I left her house.

As I drove home, I reminisced about the weekend that Julia had spent in Mantorville. One evening, we played tennis. Julia beat me pretty good and I was tired. We walked off the court and started to head back to my house when we walked by a bench surrounded by bushes. It was like a little cave with a bench inside it. I took Julia's hand, led her into the cave, and said, "Let's rest here before we walk back." I sat down on the bench, but Julia stood in front of me. Then she reached behind her back and unhooked her bra, followed by some quick movements of her arms and her bra being pulled out of her left sleeve. Then she lifted up her shirt as I slid my hands under her skirt and grabbed her bare butt and pulled her closer to me. Julia didn't say anything, but she took a step back, reached under her skirt, and pulled a red thong down her legs. She tossed the thong on top of the bra, which was next to me on the bench.

This outdoor experience was the first time I brought Julia to orgasm with my tongue. Julia made a lot of noise when she came, so I quickly escorted her out of the cave before a neighbor could come to check on the noise. We had a refreshing walk home, debating how loud is too loud. Julia didn't believe she made that much noise.

The week after our event in the bushes, the *Mantorville Express*, our weekly newspaper, ran a story based on the sheriff's report from the previous week. This was the article I sent to Julia:

"Mystery in the Bushes"

> Last week's sheriff's report included the account of a 911 call and the subsequent investigation. At 8:34 p.m. last Saturday, a male jogger that was running in the area of the Mantorville tennis court called 911 to report a woman in distress somewhere in the tennis court area. The caller said he had just run by the tennis court and had not seen anyone on the court. Upon hearing the woman's screams, the man stopped running and looked back at the court but did not see anybody. A squad was dispatched to investigate the complaint. The caller said the woman screamed several times in a row and then, after

a moment of silence, the woman yelled in very slow speech, "Oh my God." Officers searched the area but found no person or persons. However, the officers did search a rest area near the court and found a woman's white bra and a red thong. Both items were bagged and placed in the county's evidence locker at the courthouse. The case remains open.

Julia was blown away and could not believe our sexual encounter made the news. She had never lived in a small town and could not believe that her bra and thong were being stored in an evidence locker at the Mantorville courthouse.

I'd gone home planning to mow my lawn, but the grass was still wet from the rain Clint had predicted last night. I decided to relax. Every so often, Hank would spend a Saturday traveling around the area, visiting thrift stores and flea markets. I sometimes accompanied him. The last time we went thrifting together, Hank encouraged me to buy a basket of Jon Hassler books. I'd started reading The Love Hunter and decided now was a good time to finish it. I skipped lunch, then mowed the lawn that afternoon. After I finished, I prepped my Sunday School lesson. Prepping only took half an hour; the church provided the lesson plan, so I just needed to get familiar with the Bible verses it was based on.

Goat Rescue

CHAPTER 17

I'D JUST FINISHED READING THE Bible when I received a desperate phone call from Robert Pensla, one of Flash's sales reps. Robert usually spoke with a strong, confident voice, but that Saturday afternoon, he was all choked up, "Connor, I think I'm going to be arrested. I don't know what to do."

"Where are you, and what happened?"

"I'm at the tire store in Rochester, the one we take all the company cars. My car was overdue for new tires, so I thought I'd have new ones installed before I went up to the Cities this afternoon. I left the car there; they call when it's ready. I walked across the street to wait at the restaurant and after a few minutes, three police cars pulled in at the tire place. That's when the store called, asking me to return because of a problem with my car. When I got there, the police started asking me questions about my goat. I guess one of the technicians thought they heard a crying woman in my trunk, so they popped it and found my goat."

"Why did you have a goat in the trunk of your company car?"

"I was taking it to my father-in-law in the Cities. He wants to butcher it for the meat. But the police want to talk to the car's owner, since it isn't my car. I explained that MTI owns the car, and now they want to talk to an official from the company. To make matters worse, someone from the store called the Humane Society and now they're asking me why I abused the goat."

"Robert, please stop answering people's questions. Let everyone know that a company representative will be there soon to clear things up. I'm only twenty minutes away."

"Okay."

"If anything else comes up before I get there, call me to give me a heads-up."

"Okay. Please hurry."

I immediately called the MTI decal shop. I told them what I needed and asked them to be ready to install it in half an hour.

I left in my pickup and called Hank. "This is Connor. Is your horse trailer still operational?"

"Yes. As a matter of fact, I washed it this morning. Why?"

"MTI has a problem with an abused goat in Rochester. I need you to run your trailer over to the decal shop to have a decal installed. Then, meet me at the tire store we use in Rochester. Robert Pensla's being held there by the police because they think he abused a goat with his company car."

"I'm sure there's a good story here, but just tell me, what does the decal say?"

"Mantorville Goat Rescue. I need you to pick up the goat and take it to your farm to live out its life."

"I'm on my way. Will you be at the tire store?" Hank asked.

"I'll be there in fifteen minutes."

Pulling up to the tire store, I saw there were now five police cars, two TV news vehicles, and a Humane Society truck. I quickly introduced myself to the officers and got permission to speak with Robert. Then, I saw the goat. It was painted green on one side and purple on the other. Two people from the society were doing something with the goat's legs. They explained to me that the people who'd abused the goat had painted it different colors and then continued the abuse. When they finished the torture and abuse, they bound the goat's legs and locked it in the dark trunk. The people from the society had freed its legs and were removing the remaining ropes while they talked to me.

I asked, "How was the goat abused?"

One of the people said, "That man over there"—pointing at Robert—"showed us a video of the abuse. The police confiscated his phone as evidence. The video shows the goat being held down against its wishes while they painted him. Then a bunch of men chased the animal around, scaring him to death."

"I see the number four painted on him. The goat must represent Brett Favre."

"Why do you say that?"

"Because Brett played for both the Vikings and the Packers. Their team colors are purple and green. Also, Brett had the number four with both teams."

"That makes sense. The abuser kept talking about 'Brett' but we thought he was talking about a human. He said that Brett liked to play football, so we thought he meant a person."

I thanked the Humane Society crew for bringing me up to speed. Then I walked over to Robert and said, "Hello, Robert, where did you get your friend Brett?"

"I'm in a touch football league, and Brett belongs to one of my teammates. I don't understand why everyone's so upset. The goat's going to have its throat cut in a couple hours and then he'll be dead. Why all the fuss because I had him in my trunk?"

"Well, being tied up and locked in a dark trunk is not the way I'd want to spend the last hours of my life."

"They keep saying I abused him because the team lets him play touch football with us. He loves to kick the ball around. They saw the video of him playing with us and they think it's abuse. Brett would kick the ball and then run after it to kick it again. The team would try to get to the ball before Brett, but those people think we were chasing Brett instead of the ball."

"Robert, today I'm going to try keeping you out of jail. On Monday, you'll be disciplined for causing all this trouble. To keep you out of jail, I'll offer to send Brett to a farm where he can live out his natural life."

"You can't do that; my father-in-law is looking forward to eating him. We planned to have a goat steak barbecue tonight."

"Robert, take a look around at what you've caused. Five police vehicles with flashing lights, a Humane Society truck, two TV crews, a Post Bulletin reporter, and at least two hundred bystanders! They all know about the MTI vehicle transporting an abused goat to slaughter. You need to decide if you want your job or if you want to eat Brett. If you don't agree to send Brett to a farm, then you'll lose your job; I'll terminate your employment right here in this parking lot."

"Okay, you can have the goat, but where are you going to find a farm to take a purple and green goat?"

"Hank's on his way here right now with a trailer to haul Brett to his farm."

I told the officer in charge that MTI was unaware of our salesman's plans to haul a goat in his company car, that he'd be reprimanded for his actions, and that the company would provide a home for the goat on a nice farm where he could live out his natural life. The officer told me Robert would be released after he was issued a citation for animal cruelty. I asked if I could take possession of the goat; the officer said it was up to the Humane Society. I thanked the officer and returned to the people taking care of Brett.

There was now a third Humane Society worker with Brett. We recognized each other because she'd helped me adopt Zeus two years ago. I told her how Zeus was thriving. Then we talked about Brett. I acknowledged that painting Brett was abusive, as was tying his legs and keeping him in the trunk. The workers re-watched the video and now agreed they could see Brett was playing and enjoying it. When I told them my brother ran a goat rescue service on his farm, they were elated and agreed to release Brett to Hank, who was just arriving with his Mantorville Goat-Rescue trailer.

A crowd formed around the trailer as the officers escorted the Humane Society workers, who escorted Brett, to the trailer. The news crews were already interviewing Hank about his farm, where Brett could roam over a hundred acres of woods, prairie, streams, and a river running through it all. Brett would be sheltered from severe weather in a barn with plenty of straw and hay.

When asked about the MTI car being used to transport Brett, Hank referred the reporters to me. I told the camera, "The management at Milk Trucks Inc. was shocked to hear that an employee used a company vehicle to transport a goat, named Brett. MTI has long supported our local Humane Society. Rochester Police have issued a citation to our employee, who will also be disciplined by MTI. We will reimburse the Humane Society for today and MTI will also cover costs of veterinary care and to board Brett on a farm for the rest of his life. This could have been a bad day for Brett, but thanks to an observant employee here at the tire center, Brett can look forward to a wonderful life."

The crowd cheered as Hank opened the trailer doors to reveal a fresh bundle of hay. Brett caught the scent and jumped into the trailer. The crowd cheered again as Brett turned, his mouth full of hay. Cameras zoomed in on Brett happily munching before Hank closed the trailer to take Brett home.

I told the tire center to replace Robert's tires; we'd pick up the car on Monday. I wanted to control the media story, so as soon as the police finished with him, I got Robert in my truck with instructions to stay quiet. Finally, I thanked the Humane Society people for their cooperation, gave them my business card, and asked them to send me a bill for their services.

I dropped Robert off at his house, and on my way back to Mantorville, called Todd Lukens.

Todd answered, "I just saw you on breaking news on one of the local stations."

"It's been an exciting afternoon," I said, "and now I need to ask you about something else that could be exciting if you want to do it."

"What do you have?"

"If I could arrange to rehire Jim Rollins, would you take him back?"

"In a heartbeat. But how are you going to get around the background check?"

"VTM just changed the rehire policy to exclude eight-month rehires. But this is still controversial, so I'm only telling you and Debra. By the time Marvin or Des Moines find out, Jim will have proved himself a valued supervisor. Also, if any problems do develop, I'll take full responsibility."

"I'm okay with Jim coming back, and I'll share responsibility with you."

"Thank you, Todd. I appreciate that. I'm having lunch with the Rollins family after church tomorrow. When can I tell Jim he can start?"

"I need a day to prep his staff. Have him start Tuesday at his regular time. Will HR see him first?"

"No. Debra will take care of the paperwork. And we're going to require Jim to stay in his department for a few weeks. I don't want him running around where everybody can see he's back."

"Connor, this will really help us. Jim will have us back to our old high-efficiency levels in no time."

"Let's meet Monday morning to work out details. I'll give Jim and Marjorie the good news."

"Sounds good. Try to stay out of trouble the rest of the weekend.".

The Covert Hire

CHAPTER 18

I HAD A GOOD NIGHT'S sleep and got up early. I prayed for an hour before I left for church. I started praying for guidance about Julia and Debra. I asked God if fornication was okay if it was between consenting, single adults. Then I thought about how God was moving Julia out of my life. I'd only be having sex with Debra. Maybe fornication was okay if I only had sex with one woman. I was so uncertain. Then I prayed about meeting with Jim and Marjorie. The Rollins girls were all in their teens, fully aware of Jim's issues. It bothered me that Jim couldn't provide for his family when he was such a capable person.

At church, I taught Sunday School and then sat through the service, not hearing a word of Pastor's sermon. My thoughts went back and forth. If I wasn't thinking about my fornication issues, I was thinking about getting fired for re-hiring Jim.

After church, I went straight to Jim and Marjorie's home; I actually got there before them. We had an enjoyable lunch and then the girls exited the house in what appeared to be a planned departure.

With just Marjorie, Jim, and I at the table, Marjorie spoke first. "Well, Connor, I'm sure you know why we asked you here."

"Yes," I said. "But before you ask, I want you to know I've got a plan to get Jim back at MTI."

They both perked up, surprised. "That's great! What's the plan?" Jim asked.

"Let me lay it out for you. VTM just changed the rehire policy so we're no longer running background checks on former employees rehired within eight months. I can rehire you without breaking the letter of the law on the written policy. But if I asked anyone for permission to rehire you, I'd be told no. I'm going to do it anyway and hope that by the time word gets out, you'll have proven you're a valuable asset to MTI."

"Are you going to get in trouble?" Jim asked.

"I'm sure I will, but I know I'm doing the right thing. You've made noticeable changes in your life. I know you'll be a good employee this time. I expect to get yelled at but not much more than that. So, it's important we bring you back without letting everyone know. Todd Lukens wants you back and tomorrow, he'll prep your department's employees for your return. We'd like you to start Tuesday at your regular time. Go straight to your department, not to HR or anywhere else. Debra knows you're returning and will reinstate your old pay rate. Please don't even use your radio; if someone calls for you on the radio, respond to them by cellphone. Outside your department, we don't want it known you're back until the people above me eventually find out."

"I understand," Jim said.

Marjorie grinned, "Connor, I don't know what to say. This is so wonderful."

"Like I said, bringing Jim back is the right thing to do."

We sat in silence for a moment before I said to Jim, "Feel free to talk to Todd, Debra, or me if you have any questions. When the other supervisors find out you're back, let them know to only contact you by cell or come to your department to talk. You can tell them your restrictions are only for a few weeks."

I smiled at Jim and his eyes started to well up with tears. Then Marjorie started to cry as Jim kept repeating, "Thank you." Marjorie and Jim hugged each other, then included me in a group hug.

"I'm going to leave so you can give the news to your girls. Be sure to explain that they need to keep this quiet for a few weeks," I told them.

They both agreed to do that, and I left.

Monday morning came quickly, and on my way to work, I called Julia to tell her about Debra's promotion. Julia asked how Debra was in bed and I said I didn't want to get into it. Julia teased me, "It looks like a woman just needs to have sex with you to get a promotion. It worked for me and now Debra."

"I didn't even think about that. I guess it's true," I kidded. "Anyway, I need something from you."

"What?"

"I need to know the salary ranges for HR managers in the company. I want to increase Debra's salary as much as possible and be able to justify it."

"No problem. I'm in the parking lot now. I'll email the info in a few minutes."

"Great, thanks, bye."

Debra waited in my office with a cheery expression on her face. I told her we'd meet about her new position in a few hours. Then I brought her up to speed on my discussions with Todd Lukens and Jim and Marjorie Rollins.

"Aren't you going to tell me about the goat?" Debra asked.

"I forgot about the goat; I'll tell you about that if you tell me about the doctor. Did you let him down easy?"

"It went well, and we didn't have sex."

"So, the doctor's out, but we still have the carpenter."

"Yes, we do, and I plan to see both of you every week."

Jacquelyn walked in, and we all sat down at the table. Then Marvin asked to join us. The women started to get up, but Marvin insisted they stay. "I'm assuming you're talking about the goat," he said. "I thought I'd save Connor some time and let him tell the story to all of us at once."

They'd all seen the breaking news on TV, so I filled in the gaps. When I finished, Marvin complimented me for turning something extremely negative into something very good. We all stood, and Marvin shook Debra's hand, congratulating her on her promotion.

Jacquelyn asked, "What promotion?"

"Debra is now our HR manager," I told her.

"Congratulations," Jacquelyn smiled.

Marvin returned to his office, and Jacquelyn asked both Debra and me, "How was Friday night?"

Debra smiled, and I said, "I'm finding it hard to get used to seeing Debra with clothes on."

"Stop talking like that!" Debra told me.

"Jacquelyn can handle it," I smiled at both of them.

Before returning to her office, Jacquelyn said, "Sounds like you two had an exciting weekend."

With the two of us alone in my office, I looked at Debra. "I'm going to kiss you right now," I said and started walking toward her.

"It's not going to happen." She turned and went to her office.

I sat down and read the info Julia had emailed. I ran the numbers by Marvin, then called Debra back to my office. I started, "After Friday night, I think about you constantly."

"I think about you, too, but when we're at work, we need to think about work."

"You're right, let's talk about your new job. As HR manager, you'll attend the quarterly HR meetings in Des Moines, representing MTI. You've already accumulated most of the manager's authority and duties over the years, but now we'll formalize it and tell all the HR assistants that they report to you. Our two admin assistants will also report to you. Set up a staff meeting, and I'll make the announcement."

"We haven't talked about what I'm giving up."

"Yes, we need to do that. Why don't you make a list of responsibilities that can be transferred to the other HR assistants. Also, enter a requisition to hire another HR assistant."

"Anything else?"

"Yes. Change Jim Rollins to active status so he can clock in tomorrow. I'm asking you to do this with the understanding that you don't agree with it. If I get in trouble, I'll make it clear that I forced you to do it and that you were firm in your objection to rehiring Jim."

"Thank you."

"Oh, I almost forgot, your base salary will increase twenty-five thousand more per year and you'll be eligible for an annual bonus worth ten percent of your salary if the company meets the annual profit goal."

Debra was speechless before she broke into a giant smile. "Now I want to kiss you," she said.

Jacquelyn interrupted to tell me the new VPs were in the lobby. I told Debra, "I still want you to handle on-boarding for officers, so wait here so I can introduce you."

I greeted the two men and brought them back to meet Debra. Then they met with Marvin for twenty minutes before I gave them a ride to the Ford dealership and told them how the vehicle program worked. They were impressed and got excited when they learned they could select any pickup on the lot. I introduced them to Jerry Day and told them I'd see them at MTI with their new trucks.

Back at the office, Debra and I met with the HR staff in the main conference room so I could announce her new position. Everyone clapped; they were sincerely happy for Debra, even when I explained some of them would pick up some of her old responsibilities. I let them know we'd hire another HR assistant to replace her. I also pointed out that they all now reported to Debra, not me.

The only thing that happened the rest of the day was our receiving an internal applicant for the open HR assistant position. It was Molly Dew. Debra said Molly had asked her about the position; Molly had wanted to know if the position would involve working directly with me. Debra had told her it would not. Then, Debra told me that as long as she was HR manager, Molly Dew would never work in HR.

Before I left for the day, I checked with Todd, who confirmed he'd talked to Jim's department. He'd also called Jim to let him know everyone there was looking forward to his return.

On my way home, I called Hank to see how things were going with his new goat-rescue business. He mentioned George Olson was going to give him a doe; George said goats didn't do well if they were alone.

When I got home, I made a sandwich for supper and spent some time with Zeus before going to bed early.

The next morning at work, I called Debra to see if Jim Rollins had clocked in. He had and was a few minutes early. I was nervous but still felt I'd made the right decision. Jim's first week went well. He kept a low profile, and there were no repercussions regarding his return. The second week, I had a few managers make comments to me, saying they were surprised he was rehired.

During his third week, I was nervous when I received a call from a corporate accountant, but she only asked about the two pickups on my expense report. I just mentioned that the division president had approved the report, and it was accepted.

Debra and I were getting closer as each week went by. She was spending Friday nights at my house, and last Friday had been our third together in a row. We spent most of our time in bed, but last Friday, we watched a movie before making love. I kept using the M word with her. She frequently said she loved me, but she didn't want to talk about marriage.

I Got Caught

CHAPTER 19

WE WERE WELL INTO THE third week of Jim's return when Jacquelyn jogged into my office and said, "Marvin needs you right away."

I walked into Marvin's office, and he said, "Close the door. I have Nathan and Ronald on the phone."

I said, "Good morning, gentlemen."

"Good morning," Nathan said.

Ronald said, "Did you rehire Jim Rollins?"

"Yes," I said.

"What the hell were you thinking?" said Ronald.

"Jim's department was performing poorly in his absence. When the company's rehire policy changed regarding background checks, I jumped at the opportunity to rehire Jim. The decision to rehire was a good one. After two weeks, the department is already back to operating with the highest efficiency in the company," I said.

Ronald replied, "We received a letter from an anonymous employee stating they were afraid to come to work because the man that shot Connor was working in the plant again."

"Well, we know I wasn't shot. Bringing Jim Rollins back was the right thing to do. He hasn't had a drink in seven months, and he goes to AA meetings every week. I visited with his family before I made the decision, and they confirmed he is staying sober and that he is a good father and husband. When Jim is sober, he is the best supervisor we have."

Ronald said, "This is unacceptable. We have no choice but to terminate your employment. You have placed the entire workforce in danger. You started by allowing immigrants to carry guns in the warehouse and now you put a suicidal drunk back in the plant."

Nathan said, "Connor, I must agree with Ronald. You have gone too far this time."

I said, "I disagree but understand your concerns. Jim is doing a good job for the company, and I am confident I made the right decision."

Ronald asked, "Who else was involved in this decision?"

"No one," I said. "I made the decision on my own and did not tell Marvin. When Debra found out about Jim coming back, she protested. She agrees with your position."

"Who is Debra?" Nathan asked.

"Debra Saint Vincent is our new HR manager; we just promoted her," said Marvin.

Nathan said, "Connor, please leave the room. We need to discuss your future."

"Yes, sir." I left and returned to my office.

After an hour, Jacquelyn called me to return to Marvin's office.

I walked into Marvin's office, and he said, "Close the door and sit down." After I sat down, he said, "You can remain an MTI employee if you accept the job that I'm going to offer you, but you will no longer be the director of human resources."

I said nothing. I just looked at Marvin.

He continued, "I'm very disappointed that you did not

come to me before you rehired Jim."

"What is going to happen to Jim?"

"Jim will keep his job. We got Todd Lukens on the conference call, and he told Nathan, Ronald, and me that he agreed with your decision when you approached him. Todd confirmed that Jim Rollins has dramatically improved the performance of his department. Todd also said that Jim is a changed man, and Todd believes he is going to stay sober."

"I'm glad that Jim will stay. I thank you for that," I said.

"Nevertheless, Ronald insisted that you be terminated for poor judgement. I agreed that not involving me with the Jim Rollins decision was poor judgement, but I also understand that you were shielding me from the controversy by not involving me. I didn't think you should be terminated for the Jim Rollins incident when you have a track record of making good decisions. In the end, Nathan decided to take you out of HR and allow you to have five areas of responsibility. One of the five will be new, but the other four areas are currently handled by you."

"So what is my new job?"

"You will continue to have employee relations, community relations, security, and training. The new area will be facilities. You have been involved in lease negotiations, new construction, and remodeling projects. You should be able to jump right in and handle facility management for MTI's North American operations. You will keep your director title. Your pay and bonus plan will not change. You will continue to report to me, and you will keep your company vehicle. You will no longer have a dotted line to Ronald or anyone else in Des Moines. So, do you want the job?"

"Yes. I look forward to the new job."

"Ronald wants you out of the executive suite, so you will move to an office in the training building. Since you are now director of facilities, you can choose your office location."

I asked, "How is HR going to be restructured?"

"Well, you pretty much set up the new structure when you told Ronald that Debra agreed with him. Ronald and Nathan have approved making Debra the interim director of HR. If she does a good job for the next six months, we will remove the *interim* from her title. I have already talked to Debra, and she is aware of everything that I have just told you. Debra now reports directly to me."

The two of us sat quietly looking at each other. Then I said, "Marvin, I want to thank you for putting this new job together for me. I realize I could be unemployed right now, but because of you, I have an excellent job with a company that I love. Thank you for taking care of me."

"Connor, you have solved many problems for me over the years, and I hope you will solve many more in the years to come. You will no longer have Ronald and Dwight looking over your shoulder. You will be able to operate with much more freedom than you have had in the past. I want you to stop by my office at least once a day to give me an update on what you are doing."

"I will look forward to that."

"Okay," said Marvin. "You need to start packing and find an office. I need to brief Jacquelyn on what we are doing and prepare an announcement." Marvin stood up, so I stood up and we shook hands before I left his office.

I went to my office and called Debra, and she came right over to see me. She walked in, closed the doors, and sat down at the table with me. I said, "I can't get over how beautiful you are."

"That's the last thing you should be thinking about. Are you going to be okay?"

"This ended good. Jim Rollins has a respectable job, and I

still have a job. I think my new job is going to be fun."

"I thought you would be more upset."

"No. I was prepared for much worse. I'm going to be fine, and you got another promotion and a bigger office."

"According to Marvin, you set me up to get your job by telling Ronald that I agreed with him."

"I knew that Ronald would jump at the chance to get someone that agreed with him in my position."

"Things are changing so fast."

"Yes, and I like change. I'm going to drive up to the training center and find an office. I will be moved by tomorrow, and you can move in here right away. This should make you happy. Now you are no longer fucking your boss."

"Stop talking like that."

"Are we still good for Friday night?"

"Yes. I have you down for every Friday night."

Jacquelyn knocked on the door and stepped in. "I'm going to prepare the announcement that Marvin just dictated to me. He would like both of you to review it before it is released. Are you going to be around the rest of the morning?"

Debra said, "Yes."

I said, "I'm going to go look for an office, but I will be back in thirty minutes."

Jacquelyn said, "Perfect," and closed the door.

I drove up to the training center and stopped in to see Ben Walker, my training manager. I told Ben about the announcement that would soon be made and why the changes were taking place. When I asked about open offices, he said there were three open offices that had outside windows and one in the center of the building, but it had no windows.

I looked at the three offices with windows, but they were too small for me to have a conference table. The office in the center of the building had a hallway on each side of it, so there were two doors to the office. This building was built after Mr. Olson sold the company. Mr. Olson always insisted on glass walls for most offices, but the offices in the training center were all solid walls with no windows. There wasn't even a window in the doors. I was used to working in a fishbowl, so this was going to be different. I selected the office in the center of the building because it had room for a conference table.

When I got back to my office, Jacquelyn and Debra were at my table, reviewing the announcement. I sat down, and Jacquelyn handed me a copy to review. Debra and I were both okay with it, so Jacquelyn returned to her office. I suggested to Debra that we both meet with Brian Schmidt to let him know what was going on and to let him know that he was now reporting to both Debra and me.

We met with Brian and explained that he reported to Debra on safety matters and to me for security matters. I told Brian that he would still be involved with some facility issues, and I asked him to find me some office furniture and to try and get everything from the items we had in storage and not to buy anything new.

In the afternoon, Brian called me to let me know that I now had a furnished office. I told him to meet me at the new office so I could look things over. As I left my old office, Debra met me in the hall and said that IT would have the phones changed around tonight so that she and I would receive our calls in our new offices tomorrow. I asked her to have one of her assistants pack everything that was currently in my file cabinets into boxes, and with that, I left.

Brian greeted me as I walked into my new office. "Have a chair," he said, and motioned to the chair behind my new desk. I sat down and started to look around. The desk was large, with a matching credenza behind it. The desk chair was comfortable and armless, the way I liked my chair. There were two matching guest chairs in front of the desk. The conference table was rectangular and exceptionally long, with twelve chairs around it. There were two large lateral file cabinets across the office, behind the far end of the conference table.

I asked, "Don't we have any round conference tables?"

"No. In fact, this is the only conference table we have."

"Oh no," I said as I walked to the end of the table. "This is Flash's old table; I can tell by the stain."

"Yes, this is Flash's table, and it was the only table in storage. Is it going to be okay?"

"It will have to do; I just need to find something to put over the stain."

"Are you ever going to tell me the story behind this table?"

"No, never," I said. "Oh, what about keys?"

Brian pulled an envelope out of his shirt pocket and handed the envelope to me and said, "There are two keys there. One will work on all the exterior doors to this building and the other will work on both doors to this office."

I said, "I think we're good here. Overnight, please have the boxes in my old office transferred here."

"Will do. And by the way, my security team issues parking tickets when someone parks in the wrong location. We have some employees that just ignore the tickets, so I would like to start issuing written warnings to some of the frequent violators. How about if I write up the warnings and you can sign off on them?"

"That will be fine," I said.

I returned to my old office for the last time. It was quitting time, so I locked the office for the last time and walked over to Debra's office and gave her the key. It was Thursday night, so I said, "I know we will be together tomorrow, but do you want to stop somewhere for a drink on the way home tonight?"

"No, I'm meeting the carpenter tonight."

"I thought you spent Saturdays with him?"

"I do, and I'm seeing him this Saturday, but he called me and said he wanted to stop by for a few minutes tonight. I didn't know you were going to ask me out, so I told him he could stop by my place this evening."

"I don't like this guy; he should be Saturdays only."

"Well, I like both of you, and he asked to see me tonight before you did. If you had asked first, I would be with you tonight."

"I don't like this arrangement. I've known you for years, how long have you known him?"

"We have been dating for six months, and I knew him casually for four months before we started dating."

"Are you going to have sex with him tonight?"

"I'm not going to start telling you every time I'm going to have sex with him."

"So you are?"

"I don't ask you when you are going to have sex with Julia."

"I will probably never have sex with Julia again."

Jacquelyn walked up behind me and said good night to both of us.

I said to Jacquelyn, "I'll walk out with you, since this is the last time that we will be leaving from the same parking lot."

I looked at Debra but didn't say anything. I turned and walked out with Jacquelyn.

I drove to Mantorville and had dinner at the Hubbell House. Throughout dinner, all I could think about was the carpenter. I wanted Debra all to myself, not just for sex, but to live with me for the rest of our lives. I needed to convince Debra that it was our destiny to be together. The carpenter was not in the picture.

After dinner, I went home and did some organizing so Henrietta could clean in the morning.

Molly's Bikinis

CHAPTER 20

I WAS UP EARLY; IT was Friday and I wanted to leave work by three today. I drove to the training center, parked in the front row, and entered my new building. I was unlocking my office door when Molly Dew greeted me in the hallway. Apparently, her office was directly across the hall from mine.

"Hello, Connor," she smiled, seductively, "I'm glad you're moving in, so close to my office! We never did have those 'counseling sessions' we talked about."

I replied, "I know you sent me a few meeting invitations I had to decline, but with my new position, I should be available, especially since we're just across the hall from each other."

"How about if I stop by later this morning?" I didn't answer right away. I was nervous being alone with her, and both Debra and Julia had warned me to be careful. She asked again, "Do you have some free time this morning?"

"I'll be unpacking boxes all morning, so stop by any time," I said.

"Can I step in right now and take a peek at your office?"

I held the door open as Molly walked by me, getting closer than she needed to. As she walked by me, I saw her ass for the first time. I couldn't believe how tight her jeans were. She did a quick turn and caught me checking her out before she said, putting on her Southern accent, "Lordy, such a large conference table."

"It was the only one available. I'm glad my office is long enough for it to fit into."

She drawled, "Well, ya know what they say about fellas with long offices."

"No, what do they say?"

"I'll explain it to you sometime."

Molly sauntered back toward her office, and I checked her out again, but this time I anticipated the turn and smiled at her as she looked at me.

I unlocked the second door and left both office doors open so people felt free to stop by and talk to me. And they did. By midmorning, I'd had over a dozen visitors. They correctly assumed that my new job was punishment for bringing Jim Rollins back to MTI. They all thought it was unfair, but they were glad that Jim was back. No one believed me when I said it, but I really was looking forward to the new job.

About ten thirty, Molly strolled into my office and casually closed and locked both doors without asking. I was sitting behind my desk and gave her a questioning look.

She explained, "I need to speak with you about something personal."

"Okay, have a chair."

"No, thank you, it'll be better if I stand."

She moved closer, standing between the guest chair and my desk. "My husband and I are planning to take our first cruise and I need to get some new bikinis. I'm hoping you can help me decide on a style." Then, Molly undid her jeans and started wiggling out of them. She hooked a finger on each side of her panties and said, "I want to know how low you think my bottoms should go." She started to pull down slowly. I just kept silently staring as she pushed her panties down to thigh-level. "How do you think I'll look on a nude beach?"

I looked up at her eyes and said, "That's enough. Get dressed and go back to your office."

"Are you mad at me?"

"No, just uncomfortable. From now on, when you come to see me, leave my office doors open."

Molly pulled her panties and jeans up and slowly walked to open each door. She smiled at me before leaving the office. I sat at my desk, trying to figure out what had just happened.

If I told Debra about the incident, she'd immediately fire Molly. I didn't want that, so I decided not to tell anyone about Molly's exhibition. I thought about tonight and watching Debra wriggle out of her jeans. Debra touched my heart. Molly was a sexual curiosity; the only feeling she created in me was discomfort. I felt a sudden urge to talk to Debra, so I left my office and drove to the admin building.

Debra was alone, so I walked into her office, closed the open doors, and sat down in front of my old desk. "What's up?" she asked.

"I unpacked all my boxes this morning and then I started thinking about you and the carpenter. I'm not going to ask if you had sex last night, but I'm curious to know why he wanted to talk to you."

"Well, I don't feel I need to explain to you, but I will say that we did not have sex last night."

"If you didn't have sex, then what he said must've been important."

"It was important. He feels the same way you do. He

doesn't want me to have sex with other men. He wants a committed relationship and eventually marriage."

Debra and I sat in our chairs in silence, just looking at each other. Then I asked, "So what are you going to do?"

"I don't know. I'm in love with two wonderful men, and they both want a one-man woman. Last night, he was so kind to me. I wanted to make love to him, but he doesn't want to make love to me until I agree to a committed relationship with him."

"Well, he's a stronger man than me. I could never turn down sex with you." More silence, then I said, "Are we still on for tonight?"

"Yes, definitely. I've been looking forward to tonight all week."

"How about we stop by the Hubbell House for half an hour on our way to my place?"

"That'd be fun, but we need to arrive and leave at different times so no one thinks we're together.

"Not a problem." Then I continued, "I was thinking we should repeat what we've been doing the last few Fridays and skip dinner, then have breakfast together the next morning."

"I like that, and I'll bring the wine again."

Jacquelyn started knocking on the side door. Debra waved her in as I stood up.

"Debra, Marvin needs to see you," she said before closing the door and returning to her office.

Debra stood up, "See you after work."

Back in my office, Molly walked in close behind me, carrying a carafe of coffee, and said, "I'm leaving at noon today. I thought it'd be nice to have coffee together before I leave. Are you game?"

"Yes, I am. I only drink coffee in the mornings, so you're

catching me just in time."

Molly had brought her mug with her and set it on the conference table with the carafe. I grabbed my mug from the desk and joined her at the conference table.

Molly filled our mugs and sat down before saying, "Do you have plans for the weekend?"

"Yes. I'm going to finish a book I'm reading, and I'm going to help Hank finish the fence on his new goat pasture." Some silence, and then I said, "Tell me about your husband's job."

"Why do you want to know about that?"

"I'm just curious. You mentioned him this morning, and I'd like to know what he does."

"He sells office equipment to large companies in the Midwest. He travels a lot, so I have many lonely nights, often three nights a week."

"What do you do to keep from getting lonely when he's gone?"

"I usually visit friends, and on Wednesday nights, I go to church."

Molly went on to talk about her family and their strong ties to their church. She said she'd been going every Sunday morning and Wednesday night for as long as she could remember. I told her that my church past was similar, but that I quit going to the Wednesday evening services after my divorce. We talked some more about church and learned we had similar faiths in different denominations. During our chat, our mugs had gotten low. Molly reached for the carafe, but I told her I needed to leave soon for a lunch meeting. She put the carafe down without filling either cup. Then she said, "I hope I didn't offend you when I asked you for advice this morning."

"I wasn't offended; I was shocked. I like talking to you, but I prefer to have a conversation with the doors open. I can't believe you showed me your pussy."

"Pussy! I don't have a pussy. A pussy is a weak man. What I showed you was my kitty."

"Kitty?"

"Yes, I prefer to call that part of my body my kitty because kitty is much more playful and feminine than pussy."

"Okay, so why did you show me your kitty?"

"I really do need advice on how low my bikinis should be. I've also found that the more of me men see, the more comfortable they are with me."

"So, do you show your kitty to a lot of men?"

"I'm very selective; I only show it to men I want to have sex with."

I was about to respond when Howard Olson texted me. "My ride for lunch is waiting outside," I told her. "We'll have to finish this conversation next week."

Molly stood up and grabbed her mug and the carafe. She smiled, "Have a nice weekend."

When I got into Howard's car, the first thing he said was, "Well, Connor, how do you like being banished from the executive suites?"

"I was prepared to lose my job, so changing jobs and moving to a different office isn't so bad."

"Did they cut your pay?"

"No, and I still report directly to Marvin. I intend to have some fun with the new job."

"Well, I'm glad they didn't cut your pay, but they shouldn't have taken HR away from you."

"Marvin didn't really have a choice. I pushed things to the limit this time. The boys in Des Moines wanted me terminated, but Marvin convinced Nathan that I should be retained in a different role, one that has nothing to do with corporate."

"Marvin told me you're the best HR guy he's ever worked with."

"Well, Marvin is the best president that I have reported to."

It took us a few minutes to get downtown, and then Howard pulled into Michael's Restaurant. Howard asked, "Does Jim Rollins know you risked your job for him?"

"I'm sure he knows by now. Bringing Jim back was the right thing to do. I'm glad Des Moines decided to let him remain in his position."

"I asked around, and everyone I talk to believes you made the right decision. They say Jim's a new man, and that he's doing an excellent job running his department." During our lunch, Howard told me he'd gotten Marvin's agreement for me to continue handling two things for him. The first was managing dealership integration. Every few years, MTI bought a milk-truck dealership who'd been selling our competitors' trucks and we converted them to MTI-owned sales branches. MTI had no dealers, only company-owned sales branches. As the integrator, I was the liaison between the acquired facility and the various departments at MTI.

My second area of continuing responsibility was managing resources and issues at the Las Vegas trade shows. I'd purchase about fifty thousand dollars in show tickets to disperse among our sales reps as they lined up customers to take to shows. I also carried about twenty thousand in cash to disburse to the reps as needed. We didn't allow the reps to charge visits to strip clubs on their company credit cards, so I provided the cash to the reps who entertained customers at the strip joints. As for resolving problems at the shows, they were different each time. I negotiated settlements and got signed releases from people and businesses harmed by our employees. In many cases, I paid bribes to get what I needed. The bribes got recorded as tips on my expense report. I never bribed police officers or government officials, but I frequently bribed hotel and casino security officers and managers.

I was glad Howard had gotten Marvin to agree to let me keep both these duties I enjoyed doing. Howard and I had a good lunch and then he dropped me off back at the training center, where the rest of the afternoon was quiet.

By three o'clock, I was on the road, headed for the Hubbell House.

Curvy Women

CHAPTER 21

I **PARKED MY TRUCK AND** headed for the entrance to the Hubbell House. Across the parking lot, I saw Debra, Jennifer, Ruth, and Joan gathered together. They must be waiting for someone before they made their grand entrance. I entered the bar and saw that Howard and his crew were already at their table. Hank had gone straight home to do his goat chores.

In addition to Tim and Flash, Howard had Steve Solomon with him. Steve was a marketing consultant that Howard brought in a few times a year. Everyone was in jeans except Steve. His company required business casual clothing at all times when with a customer.

As I sat down, the bar food was served. I was no longer getting free drinks, so I ordered a donkey, (a Moscow mule with no alcohol). I knew I would have plenty of alcohol later tonight. I said hello to Steve, and we restarted the same conversation we had three months ago. Steve despised deer hunting. He was a vegan and didn't believe that any animal should be hunted.

Steve was about six foot two and very lean. I played tennis with him the last time he was here and could not believe how good he was. He was in excellent shape and liked to show off his body. He played tennis with me at the Mantorville court. He wore tennis shorts and no shirt. Steve had no fat on his body. All he had under his skin was muscle and bone. Women hung around the tennis court, trying to compete for Steve's attention.

Tonight, we were having a good conversation about hunting when Steve quit talking while in the middle of a sentence. His jaw dropped open as everyone at our table watched Debra walk in with Jennifer, Ruth, Joan and Ruby Dillon, an IT consultant. All the men in the bar were checking out all the women as they walked to their table. That is, all the men except Steve. He was focused exclusively on Ruby.

Ruby was a substantial woman, a stunningly attractive full-figured woman. She wasn't wearing jeans; she never did. Ruby was wearing a delightful skirt with a matching blazer. She had boots instead of heels, and her blouse was cut low enough to tastefully show off her voluptuous breasts.

"Why haven't I seen her before?" Steve said.

"She's a contractor, like you. Her name is Ruby Dillon, and she is only here a few times a year," I replied.

"Who does she work for?" Steve asked.

"Ruby works for herself; she owns an IT consulting company," I said.

The five women sat at a round table. After ordering their first round, Ruby started asking questions about Steve. Ruby was just as interested in Steve as he was with her.

Back at the executive table, Flash asked Steve, "Why are you interested in Ruby? You could have any woman at that table, so why are you interested in the chubby one?"

"She's not chubby, she's a curvy woman, and she's gorgeous. For men built like me, a curvy woman provides the best sex," Steve said with a sly smile.

"Why?" Flash responded.

Steve smiled again and said, "If I'm doing it with a skinny woman, it's bone on bone, and it doesn't feel good. But with a curvy woman, there's more cushion for the pushing. And we both feel good because while I get the cushion, she gets to feel more inside her than she gets from most men."

"What do you mean by more inside her?" Flash asked.

Steve repeated the same sly smile then looked around our table and said, "You guys are all overweight. When you get between a woman's thighs, you can't penetrate as deep as I can because your fat doesn't allow you to get as close to the critical area as I can. Most curvy women know this and look forward to doing it with a lean man."

With that said, Steve stood up and proclaimed, "I have a sudden need to talk to another consultant." He stood up, turned, and started walking toward the round table.

Back at the women's table, Ruby had learned that Steve was a consultant like her. Debra explained that Connor had told Steve to stay away from MTI women, but Ruth quickly told Ruby that she was a consultant, not an MTI woman. Jennifer talked about the time she saw Steve working out at her gym in Rochester. She added, "Whenever Steve spends the weekend here, he always works out at the same gym I'm a member of in Rochester."

Jennifer was about to describe Steve's body when she looked up and said, "He's coming to our table."

Steve walked up to the table and exchanged greetings with everyone. Then he looked at Ruby and said, "I understand your name is Ruby and that you're a consultant like me."

"Yes," Ruby said. "Pleased to meet you."

"I'm pleased to meet you as well," Steve said. "I would like to talk to you. How about if we grab a table in the corner and chat some more?"

Ruby smiled at Steve before standing up. Then the two

of them walked over to a table in the corner of the bar. All the men at Howard's table and all of the women at the round table were watching Steve and Ruby. Steve did most of the talking, and Ruby smiled a lot.

After about fifteen minutes, they returned to their original tables. Ruby got to her table first and sat down without saying anything. Then Jennifer said, "Ruby, you have to tell us what you talked about."

"Okay," said Ruby. "We talked about where we live and where we travel, and then he asked about tonight."

"What about tonight?" asked Jennifer.

"It turns out that we are staying at the same hotel in Rochester. We're going to meet for dinner tonight and then have dessert in my room," replied Ruby. There were oohs and aahs from the women.

As Steve sat down with the men, he explained the evening plan for Ruby and himself. There were more oohs and aahs from the men.

"Ruby is a very lovely lady," said Steve. "I'm looking forward to getting to know her."

I looked across the room and saw Debra get up and leave. I knew she had to stop to get the wine on her way to my place, so I took a few minutes to finish my drink before I left.

Sympathy Sex

CHAPTER 22

I PULLED INTO MY GARAGE and left the door up for Debra. Clint and Shelly were out of town for the weekend, so I didn't have to worry about Clint interrupting Debra and me this time. Zeus was his typical, happy self. I told him that Debra was coming over again, and that there would be no humping her this time; for three Fridays in a row, he'd greeted her by humping her leg.

After only a couple minutes, I heard the garage door closing. Zeus ran toward the garage and greeted Debra in the hallway. She had a bag full of wine and her overnight bag. She looked at Zeus and said, "What, no special greeting this time?"

"I just told him not to."

She told Zeus, "You listen very well."

Debra took three bottles of wine out of the bag and placed them on the kitchen counter.

I was already holding the corkscrew and two glasses. Debra grabbed the three bottles, and we headed upstairs to my bedroom. She'd stripped naked before I got the cork out of the first bottle. I poured wine into our glasses, and she downed half a glass before I'd even set the bottle down.

I said, "You seem to be in a hurry."

"Just for the wine. Otherwise, I'm in the mood to take it slow tonight."

"I still find it hard to adjust to you being naked. An hour ago, we were both in our offices. Now you're standing like this in my bedroom. I can't take my eyes off you."

"Kiss me," said Debra.

I walked over to her and gave her a peck on the lips. But Debra pulled me closer and wrapped her arms around me as I did the same. After a while standing and kissing, Debra, who was still holding her glass, finished the wine and gave me the empty glass to refill. She drank another glass while I continued to work on my first glass. This was our fourth Friday night together, but the entire time, I had trouble concentrating on pleasing Debra. All I could think about was the carpenter.

I went down on Debra, repeating what made her happy on our previous night's together. I must have done okay, because she was louder than our previous Fridays. While she was climaxing for the fourth or fifth time, I kept thinking that the carpenter had it right. The relationship should be one man with one woman. I wanted the carpenter out of Debra's life.

When I had finished with Debra, we changed positions and she made me feel so good. It was different this time because she played with me more when she had me in her mouth. Each Friday with Debra was getting better.

The next morning was like previous Saturdays. At six o'clock, Zeus started checking to see if I was awake. I kept my eyes closed every time I heard him coming. It wasn't long before I heard Scott Simon in the kitchen. Seconds later, Zeus was barking at Debra and me.

Debra said, "It's impossible for us to sleep in on Saturdays."

"That's right, so we might as well get up. County Seat again?"

"Yes, and like the other times, we drive separately."

"Okay," I said, but inside I was thinking that it no longer mattered if people thought we were hooking up. Debra no longer worked for me. I was more concerned about the carpenter than I was about what other people thought.

Soon, we were in our separate vehicles, driving to the County Seat. We parked by the Opera House and started walking to the coffee shop. On the way, we ran into Darryl Dickson, the mayor of Mantorville. I introduced him to Debra as the three of us walked to the County Seat. Waiting at the entrance were our state representative and state senator. They both greeted me with "Hello, Connor," and I introduced them to Debra. We let the government officials order first, and they took their table. Debra and I ordered and took our own table in the corner. As we walked by other tables to get to our corner, everybody greeted me with "Good morning, Connor" or "Hello, Connor."

Debra and I sipped coffee for a couple minutes in silence before I asked, "What are you thinking about?"

After more silence, Debra finally looked at me and sighed, "I need to marry the carpenter."

It was like I'd just been hit by a truck. My heart had never felt so heavy. I just looked at her, saying nothing.

Debra spoke again. "He's more like me; we're both introverts. Connor, you're such an extrovert. It doesn't matter whether we're at a meeting in Rochester or together in Mantorville, everybody knows you. I really believe that a husband and wife need to be equally yoked. Not just in their beliefs and values, but in their personalities as well. You're always working the room, introducing yourself to strangers. I'm not like that. I wouldn't feel comfortable living life the way you do."

More silence, before I told her, "This is the last thing I expected to hear this morning. I understand your need to pick one man. I agree with the carpenter on that. But I thought if I was going to lose you, it'd be because of my 'limp dick'."

"Connor, let me be perfectly clear with you. Making love with you is the most wonderful thing I've ever done. My best pleasure is always from you. If my decision were based on sex, I'd be with you, but marriage is about compatibility, and I'm more compatible with the carpenter. You need to be with somebody more like you, someone like Molly Dew, not her specifically because she is married, but someone like her."

I couldn't believe what I was hearing. I wanted to marry Debra. We'd made love a few hours ago, and now I was being dumped.

I asked her, "Was last night sympathy sex?"

"Sympathy sex? No, I didn't make my decision until we sat down at this table. Sympathy sex?"

I started to speak, but our breakfast was served. We ate quickly with little conversation. As we left the coffee shop, everyone said, "Goodbye, Connor." Each time I heard my name, it was like the person was stabbing a knife into my heart.

We reached our cars, and Debra gave me a goodbye hug—an exceedingly long, goodbye-forever hug, pressing her whole body into mine. I didn't want to let go, and she must've felt the same way as she lingered. We eventually released each other and went our separate ways. Metaphorically and literally.

I drove home. As the garage door closed behind me, I broke down sobbing. When I finally got out of the car, Zeus came to me. He'd never seen me cry before, and was genuinely concerned; he started to whine, feeling sorry for me.

I sobbed off and on for over an hour. Then I had a sudden need to be with someone, so I called Julia.

"Connor, hello," she answered.

"I'm calling to see if I can come and visit you. We would have tonight and all-day Sunday together."

"Now isn't a good time."

"Why not?"

"Well, I hadn't decided how I was going to tell you this, but I think you knew it was coming. I'm in a committed relationship with the woman I told you about. I'm moving into her loft today, and we're talking about marriage." After a short silence, "Are you okay? Did something happen with Debra?"

"Debra just dumped me for her carpenter and now you tell me this. It's not a good day for me, but it's a wonderful day for the women I love."

"Oh, Connor, I'm so sorry."

I tried to pull myself together and be strong, so I asked, "Where's your new loft located?"

"I keep calling it a loft, but it's actually a penthouse in the South Loop."

"Penthouse? She must be as successful as you."

"Her name is Dianna. I told you before, she owns a firm that consults for our company."

"That's great. Julia, I want you to know that I am sincerely happy for you."

"Thank you, Connor, that means a lot to me. I hope you and I remain close friends."

"I'd like that. I'm going to need a friend I can talk to. The two women I love both left me on the same day. I saw it coming with you, but Debra really surprised me this morning."

"I'm worried about you, with what just happened to your

job and now Debra."

"I'll be fine; I just need to adjust to the changes. I'm really going to miss the intimate times we had."

"Me too. Connor, you're a wonderful man. I'm confident you'll find the right person for you."

"I know. I just don't like this uncertainty, not knowing when I'll find her. But hey, you're moving today, so I'm going to let you get back to that."

"Are you sure you don't want to talk some more?"

"I always enjoy talking to you, but right now I feel bad because I'm keeping you from what you need to get done. Please call me after you're moved in."

"Thank you, Connor. I will always love you."

"And I will always love you."

I went to my bedroom, lay down on the bed, and started to cry again. Zeus lay on the floor beside me and started to whine. I felt bad about how I was making Zeus feel and realized I needed to pull myself together or I'd be making everyone around me feel my pain.

I texted Debra that I was genuinely happy for her and wished her and the carpenter a great life together.

I felt so alone and rejected. I hadn't felt this way in so long. But I knew I needed to be alert and recognize God's direction when he gave it to me.

Monday morning, I left for work early and was the first person in the training center. I started the coffee brewing and went to my office. I answered emails for half an hour, then got up for some coffee. But as I walked toward the door with my mug, Molly walked into my office with a carafe and her mug.

"Looks like we're starting Monday the way we finished

Friday," I said.

"That's right," she grinned.

I sat down and Molly pulled a chair next to me, so we were facing each other with no table in between. She wore a cheap, short skirt, already up to her thighs. Molly didn't cross her legs and noticed me looking. We both smiled. Then Molly said, "So, where did our conversation end on Friday?"

"We were talking about showing yourself to men and why you do it."

"I like to watch how it affects men. And see? You wanna know how high my skirt's gonna go."

We heard voices in the hall; Molly pulled her skirt down and rolled her chair to the side of the table. I was adding coffee to my cup when Ben Walker greeted us, "I wondered who made the coffee. I'm usually the first one in the building."

"I couldn't sleep, so I came in early," I told him.

Ben was obviously uncomfortable seeing one of his employees, Molly, talking to his boss. "So, what are the two of you discussing?"

"We're talking about Molly's role in the training department. I'm going to meet with each member of your team to better understand their responsibilities."

"Are you making changes to how we do things?" he asked.

"I won't know until I've talked to everyone, including you."

Ben noticed Molly's short skirt as she stood and said, "I need to get going. I'm teaching an Outlook class in a few minutes."

We both watched Molly leave the room and Ben said, "If my wife saw Molly today, she'd make me quit my job."

"Yes, Molly definitely gets a man's attention. Do you want to grab your mug and join me for a few minutes?"

"I can't right now. I'm doing an orientation in the tool crib with some new employees, so I need to get going. Maybe we can talk later today?"

"Okay, sounds good," I said.

Ben left my office, and I sat alone at the table, drinking coffee, and reflected briefly on where my life was going, given the events of the last couple days. Grandma Gustie always told me to be alert for direction, but the direction I was going didn't seem right. I decided to go over to the admin building to see how things were going in the executive suite. I stopped at Jacquelyn's desk, and when Marvin saw me, he called me into his office. He started, "Howard told me that you two discussed your continuing responsibilities."

"Yes," I said. "I like handling dealer integration and the Las Vegas shows."

"You've managed both areas well, so it only makes sense that you continue to do so." He paused. "There's some chatter going around about you and Debra becoming an item. The two of you have been having breakfast every Saturday in Mantorville?"

"Debra and I have always been close, but she's involved with another man. We've been getting together on Saturday mornings for about a month now to eat and discuss the other man because she's getting profoundly serious about him. It wouldn't surprise me if she married him. Rest assured; the man is not one of our employees."

"Okay. I just wanted to make sure we don't have any conflicts. I don't want another call from Des Moines."

Marvin's door was open, so Jacquelyn heard every word between Marvin and me. As I stood to leave, I saw her wiping a tear from her eye. We smiled sadly at each other as I left for Debra's office.

I didn't close the doors as I entered Debra's office. I didn't want to call attention to my visit. "Good morning," she said.

"Good morning." I sat down and spoke softly. "Someone saw us hugging in Mantorville, and they told Marvin that we're together every Saturday morning in Mantorville."

"Oh shit."

"It'll be okay. I told Marvin we've been meeting because you're seeking my advice about a man you're getting serious about. He accepted that explanation."

"Good."

"However, Jacquelyn heard the conversation, so she knows we're no longer together."

Just then, Jacquelyn walked in and said, "I want you both to know that I never said anything to Marvin."

"I know you didn't," I told her.

Jacquelyn looked at both of us, "Is it really over?"

"Yes," I said. "We're both okay with it, and we're moving on." I looked at Debra. "Right?"

"That's right," Debra confirmed.

Jacquelyn said, "Good. I just want the best for both of you."

"Thank you," I told her.

Debra said, "Thank you, Jacquelyn, I appreciate your concern. I know you really care about both Connor and me. We've talked it through, and I believe we're doing what's best for both of us."

I didn't agree, but I remained silent.

Jacquelyn smiled at both of us before returning to her office.

Debra and I sat there looking at each other in silence before I finally spoke, "I was going to go visit Julia, but she's busy moving in with her future wife."

"You told me she was seeing someone; I didn't realize it

was that serious."

"I didn't think it was that serious either, but it is, and Julia's very happy."

"Oh, Connor, the women in your life are going different directions. How are you doing?"

"I'm trying to figure my life out. I was so close to both you and Julia, and I'm not talking about the sex. Before I got sexually intimate with either of you, we'd developed close emotional friendships and intimate relationships. Now, I don't have a close relationship with any women other than those I'm related to."

"Connor, you need to be open to meeting other women. Julia and I became friends with you because you're open and caring, and you're a particularly good listener. Once a woman sees your heart, she can't help but fall in love with you. I did and Julia did. It just wasn't right for us to take the next step. But the right woman will come along. You need to be ready for that."

"Thanks. I hope I can continue to come to you for advice?"

"Always."

I stood up to leave and asked, "Can I get a hug?"

"No," she said, then she smiled.

Adultery Defined

CHAPTER 23

I RETURNED TO MY OFFICE and spent the next few hours on emails. I didn't leave for lunch, so I helped myself to one of the leftover sandwiches from someone's lunch meeting. About midafternoon, I looked up from my computer when I heard my door close. Despite my specific request last week to keep the doors open, Molly had closed it and now stood in front of it, a harshly seductive smile on her face. But my attention quickly went from her face to the rest of her body.

At our morning coffee, I'd thought the skirt she was wearing was too short for the office, but after looking for a while as she stood in front of my door, I came to see how good she looked in it. Its tightness was somehow appropriate for her, fitting her personality. Molly watched me as I admired her. She felt comfortable enough to turn around and lock the door. "I thought I told you not to close the doors when you came into my office," I said.

Then, as she walked across the room to the other door, she uttered a cliché, "Those were your words, but your eyes say something else." I didn't say anything as Molly closed and locked the second door. She smiled as she walked behind my desk and hopped up on it. She then pushed herself further onto the desk, so her knees were at my edge of the desk. The hem of the dress was now higher on her thighs, exposing most of her legs. Molly asked, "Do you think I'm dressed OK for the office?"

"Your skirt is a little short."

"Do ya really think so?" she responded with a slight Southern twang. She kicked off her shoes, hopped off the desk, and drawled, "Does it show too much when I bend over?" I was enjoying this and knew I shouldn't. Molly had bent over so far that I could see most of her butt.

I said, "I can see you're wearing purple panties."

She stood up and yanked off her panties, crudely tossing them on the corner of my desk. She walked a few steps away, bent over, and said, "Now, what do you see?"

"I can see your pussy between your legs."

"What! I told you a pussy is a weak man. What you saw between my legs was my kitty."

"I stand corrected. I saw your kitty."

"Good. If you are nice to my kitty, I will purr for you."

She walked over to me and pulled her skirt up a little before she hopped up on the desk again, her bare ass on top of a stack of disciplinary parking-warning notices.

I'd swung my chair to the left so that my right hand was on the desk, close to her bare leg. Molly asked, "Do you like my legs?" I said nothing, but she knew what I was thinking and said, "I like how you make me feel. Move your hand up my leg." Her voice was sexy and soft; it relaxed me and at the same time filled me with excitement. I began to slowly move my hand up her thigh as she responded with a quiet purring sound to my repetitive movements as I pleasured her. I was so excited by this half-naked woman in my hands. Then, abruptly, she was done; she pushed my hand away from her and said, "Enough."

She slid off the desk with the warning notice stuck to her bare ass. I reached over to pull the paper off her and noticed something. "The word warning is in ink on your butt," I told her.

"My husband isn't home tonight. I'll clean it this evening."

She stood there in her bare feet with her panties still on my desk. Looking down at me still sitting in my chair, Molly stepped closer, "Do you want to fuck me? We can do it right now."

I suddenly became extremely uncomfortable again. "What are we doing?" I asked her, "I thought you were a Christian."

"I am," Molly said.

"What about 'Thou shalt not commit adultery'?"

"We're not committing adultery; we're just fuckin' around. We can do all sorts of sex stuff without committing adultery. It's not adultery until one or both of us fall in love. That's why I normally fuck married men. They're less likely to fall in love with me. I'm making an exception with you because I think you're emotionally strong enough to fuck me and not fall in love. Am I right?"

Confused by her flawed logic, I said "I'm still trying to figure out how a married person can justify having sex with someone not their spouse."

"Fuckin' around's like playin' golf together," Molly said. "We can fuck like animals as long as we don't fall in love. When a married person falls in love with someone else, it becomes adultery."

"Did you come up with this belief on your own?" I asked.

"No," she said. "I learned about it from my English professor in college."

"Was he married?"

"Yes," said Molly, "and before you ask, yes, I did fuck him;

I fucked him a lot."

"Does your husband know about this?" I asked.

"No," she said. "He'd never understand."

I sat on my chair, looking at this beautiful woman who wanted to have sex with me. I didn't agree with her definition of adultery, but I wanted to. I could certainly explore the thesis with her.

Molly interrupted my thoughts, "Are you used to condoms? A lotta guys I fuck had vasectomies, so they don't feel they need to wear a condom."

"I've had a vasectomy, and I've never worn a condom."

"You've never used a condom?"

"No," I replied. "I've only had sexual intercourse with one woman my entire life, and I was married to her for eighteen years."

"One woman!" Molly said, as if it were impossible. "I thought you were divorced?"

"I've been divorced for over twelve years. I've had sexual relations with women, like we just did, but because I can't get an erection without Viagra, which I haven't used in twelve years, I don't need a condom." I changed the subject and asked her age.

"Twenty-nine, and yours?" she replied.

"I'm fifty-two. You're young and beautiful. Why do you want to make love to an overweight, balding man almost twice your age?"

"First of all, we wouldn't make love, we'd fuck. I love to fuck men in authority; I don't care how old you are or what you look like as long as you fuck me with authority." She pulled her shirt over her head and threw it on the floor, followed by her bra.

I thought about how unbelievable this all was, when knock, knock, knock. Someone was at the door.

Molly calmly put her bra and shirt back on, smoothly and swiftly stepping into her shoes. This was definitely not her first time in this situation. She took a small bottle of cologne from her skirt pocket and sprayed the air twice. She explained, "The room smells like sex. I'm just getting rid of the sex odor."

She walked to the door while adjusting her skirt and then opened it to Brian standing there. Molly greeted him, said she was finished, and left. I looked to my side and saw Molly's panties still on the corner of my desk. Luckily, Brian was busy watching Molly leave, so I quickly grabbed the panties and stuffed them in my pocket. Brian sat and was starting to speak when Molly came jogging back into the office. She looked at the desktop that no longer held her panties. "I thought I left something here, but I guess not."

I told her, "Let's continue our conversation later today."

Molly turned, smiled, and slowly drawled, "I'd appreciate that."

Brian said, "She uses enough perfume."

"Yeah, it's pretty strong."

"She's in Dean Atkinson's office a lot. I can always smell her perfume in there."

"Dean Atkinson?"

"Yes."

"So, what's up?"

"Well, Boss," Brian said, "I know I don't report to you for safety anymore, but I have a real problem with Debra." I asked him what the problem was, and he said, "Do you know what a guntiino is?"

"No."

"It's the name of the long draping scarf worn by Somali women, who're now being allowed to wear their flowing dresses—the everyday ones are called baati—in the warehouses."

"Oh no," I said. "We're just inviting an accident." I had always allowed the long dresses in non-safety-sensitive departments, but not in warehouse or production areas.

Brian then said, "Molly's skirt is a safety hazard as well."

"What?" I said. Brian then went on to say that two forklifts had collided at an intersection in the warehouse this morning. Apparently, both drivers were watching Molly as she walked down the aisle.

"Was anyone hurt?" I asked.

"No," Brian said, "but we have a few thousand dollars in damages to the machines."

I then changed the subject to the Somali women and asked Brian if he'd talked with Debra about the long dresses. "Yes," Brian said, "she feels the same as you and me, but Des Moines told her we need to be more flexible and sensitive to cultural issues."

"That's bullshit," I said. "Someone's going to get hurt."

I promised Brian that I'd look into it. As he left, I called Debra.

"Brian just briefed me on the Somali women in the warehouse," I told her.

"There's not much we can do; Des Moines HR got an anonymous letter from someone claiming to be an MTI employee, saying that they're being forced to wear clothing unacceptable to their faith."

"There's going to be an accident," I said.

"I know, but Ronald told me that if I want to keep my new job, I better let the women wear their dresses in the warehouse."

"I need to find a way to let go and not care; otherwise, this is going to keep happening and it'll drive me crazy."

"I agree, let it go and worry about your own responsibilities."

"I'll try," I said. I was going to hang up when Debra spoke again.

"Connor, I have some bad news for you. We received a wage garnishment from the IRS. They say you owe over three hundred thousand dollars, and we're to start withholding immediately."

"I didn't expect the IRS to act so quickly. I received the notice of the tax lien a few months ago."

Debra asked, "Is this related to your problem with the winery?"

"Yes. The manager embezzled over seven hundred thousand from the winery, and about half of that came from federal tax deposits that he never made. Since I was the officer responsible for the winery's finances, the IRS is coming after me."

"The deduction amount is about three thousand per month. Are you going to be able to continue paying the tuition for Sheryl's daughter?"

"I'll definitely continue to pay the tuition. My mortgage payment is about three thousand per month. I've already quit paying the mortgage until I figure this out."

"Okay," said Debra. We both said goodbye and hung up.

I stood up to go to the bathroom and realized I still had Molly's panties in my pocket. I pulled them out and dropped them in the lower drawer of my desk.

Conference Table Routine

CHAPTER 24

THE REST OF THE AFTERNOON went fast. It was already after quitting time. I was at the back of my office, looking for a document in one of the filing cabinets when Molly walked in and closed and locked both doors before walking back to me.

I asked, "Here for your panties?"

"No, I'm here for another orgasm."

She bent over the table and pulled the back of her skirt above her waist, so her bare ass was facing me.

"What am I supposed to do in this position? I told you I can't get hard."

She asked, "Do you know what grinding is?"

"Yes, when a woman grinds her butt into a man's groin."

"Right, except I want you to grind me. And as you are grinding your groin into my butt, reach in front and finger me. I know you like my butt, so this should be good for both of us. You can even drop your slacks and underwear so your penis can rub against my bare cheeks."

"I'll keep my pants up."

Molly started wiggling her butt as she stuck it out toward

me. I pressed my groin against her and started grinding back and forth. Then, while I continued the grinding, I bent over, reached in front of her, and slid my middle finger into her welcoming vagina. She was hotter and wetter than the first time.

From this position, I could use my experienced moves. I must be good at this, because Molly was freaking out and making all sorts of sounds. I wasn't concerned about the noise because the building was empty except for us. She was right about this being good for both of us. I actually came but kept grinding as my finger satisfied her. About a minute later, Molly had some tremors just before her orgasm. She had been holding up her abdomen with stiff arms, but after I removed my hand, she allowed her torso to lay flat on the table and moaned for a while.

When she turned around, I leaned in to kiss her, but she stopped me and said, "No kissing." I looked at her and she explained, "If we kiss, we could fall in love. We can't fall in love; that'd be adultery. We can fuck around, but we can't kiss. Okay?"

"Okay," I said.

I didn't agree with her logic, but when she said, "We need to do this a few times a week," I rationalized it by thinking that it wasn't that much of a sin if we didn't make out and I kept my clothes on. Plus, Molly doesn't think it was a sin at all.

I said, "I look forward to seeing you more often, but."

Molly was hesitant, standing and staring at me while she breathed heavily through her nose. Then she said, "I smell cum. Did you come?"

"Yes."

"Wow, so we both came. That's great. I'll have to spray my cologne when we do it during office hours."

"No, I'm only going to come after office hours. I'm not going to walk around with sex odor coming from my boxers all day."

"So, you're going to make me wait all day?"

"No, but what we just did will only happen at the end of the day," I told her.

"That works for me. I need to clock out now, or Ben will make me explain why I stayed so late."

"That's right. By the way, I understand that your cologne can be smelled in Dean Atkinson's office quite often. Would you care to explain?"

"Dean is one of the men I fuck on a regular basis. I told you I fuck other men."

"I'm having trouble understanding how you're so casual about it."

"You'll get used to it," she replied. "Can we have coffee again tomorrow morning?"

"I don't know. It bothered Ben when he saw you in here this morning."

"Maybe I should just report directly to you, then we wouldn't have to worry about Ben."

"If you come up with a way to justify the change, I'll consider it."

"I'll have a justification by tomorrow morning."

Molly walked toward the door, and I asked, "How about a hug goodbye?"

"No hugs or kisses. Those are my rules. Everything else goes."

On the drive home, I thought about adultery; I was participating in the sin of adultery, I was stealing sex with another man's wife, and I was planning to do it again. With Debra and Julia, it was fornication, and I didn't think that was a sin. Before today, I never would've sinned intentionally. But for some reason I didn't feel bad. Molly made it so much fun, and she didn't even think we were sinning. I thought, Can two Christians have sex if one of them is married and they don't fall in love? But I'd never ask Grandma that question, because I already knew her answer. I was sinning; it didn't matter how you described it. I told myself that Molly was actually sinning more than me because she was married, and I wasn't.

After supper, I did some reading, but before bed, I went online and ordered five thongs for Molly. I picked the sexiest thongs I could find in assorted colors. I selected next-day delivery to my house.

I got to work early again and made the coffee. A little before seven, Molly walked into my office with the carafe and her mug. I grabbed my mug and joined her at the table. She was wearing leggings today, so there were no bare legs to look at.

"I've been thinking about you since I got up this morning," I told her.

"I been thinkin' too. Wanna hear my idea to report directly to you?"

"Yes, go ahead."

I leaned back in my chair to listen as Molly stood up to use the white board on the side wall. I couldn't help but stare at her. She looked so good in her leggings.

"God," Molly said, "if you're gonna stare at me like that, I can't imagine how other guys are gonna look at me today."

"You're right. If I were still HR director, I'd send you home to change. You better stay in this building today. Definitely stay out of production and warehouse buildings."

"I like it when men admire me, but I don't like it when they just keep staring."

Molly drew an org chart of the training department. I was at the top, followed by Ben. Below Ben were six trainers and an administrative assistant. Ben had seven people reporting to him. Molly labeled the six trainers with their primary areas of responsibility: four taught only production and warehouse jobs, one was part production and part computer applications, and Molly was full-time computer applications.

Molly said, "This is the current structure of the training department. I can make some adjustments and get my training hours down to twenty per week."

"How are you going to do that?"

"I can increase class sizes to have fewer classes per week. Also, I spend about ten hours a week on admin tasks the assistant can do. So, with those changes, I could work twenty hours per week for Ben as a trainer and twenty hours a week for you as a public-and employee-relations assistant."

I told her, "HR just posted a job for a part-time assistant for me."

"I know. I can assume that role and you won't have to hire anyone."

"This could work. Let me run it by Debra and Marvin. I'm sure it'll get approved."

"Also, I have an education degree with a minor in public relations. I'm currently earning nineteen dollars an hour. I believe that in this new position, I'm worth twenty-three dollars per hour."

"A four-dollar increase?"

"I assure you I'll earn it. I'm assuming my new position would require me to travel with you from time to time, so I could see to all your needs, day and night." Molly gave me her sweet smile. She knew she had me.

"I'm sure I can get the job structure changes approved right away," I told her. "But the pay increase may take a while."

"Okay, but please try to get everything approved."

Ben walked into my office and saw the whiteboard. "That's our org chart," he noted.

"Molly, I'll get back to you. I want to talk to Ben now. Have a chair, Ben."

Ben said, "Molly seems to be spending a lot of time with you. Are you okay with it?"

"Yes. She has some good ideas. She'd like to take on the part-time position I just posted to assist me in my new role. She feels she can continue to work for you and do the computer application training and work twenty hours a week for me."

"How's she going to do that?"

"That's what I asked her. She says that she can increase her class-size and she believes your assistant can take on Molly's current administrative duties."

Ben thought for a while and said, "This is a good plan. My admin's been in the job for six months now so she's ready to take on more."

"I need to get it approved by Marvin and Debra. I'll attempt that later today."

My phone rang, and I walked over to my desk to answer it. "Hello, Jacquelyn."

"Connor, Marvin would like to see you right away."

I told Ben that I needed to see Marvin and that I'd get back to him later.

Cats and Racist Dogs

CHAPTER 25

I DROVE TO THE ADMIN building and Marvin saw me in his office immediately. "Take a chair," he said. "Debra just talked to me about a serious problem we agree falls within your area of responsibility: facilities and security."

"What's the problem?"

"Cats. Our campus is on the edge of town, and we're getting an increasing number of feral cats going in and out of the plant through all the open overhead doors."

"We've had this problem ever since VTM purchased MTI from Mr. Olson. Why is it an issue now?"

"Last night, during a break, one of our employees tried to pick up one of the cats and was bitten on his finger. The cat ran off and we couldn't find it. So, out of an abundance of caution, our nurse instructed the employee to start the series of rabies shots. It's considered a work comp injury, and I want this to be the last recordable injury from a cat bite. Debra said that you'd already protested against the VTM change that brought all these cats to our property. So, give me the history of this problem."

"Sure. When Mr. Olson owned the company, we had a dog living in each of the plant and warehouse buildings that operated with overhead doors left open. If a cat entered a building, the dog would chase it away. We also had a couple yard dogs that did the same thing outside. The dogs kept the cats away until the boys in Des Moines ordered us to get rid of the dogs."

"And why did they do that?"

"Des Moines felt that one of the dogs was racist."

"Racist?"

"Yes. One of the dogs would aggressively bark at Black men. He didn't bite or attack, but he'd stand back about twenty feet and bark like he was really scared and angry. All the company dogs were rescue dogs, so we assumed this dog was previously owned by a Black man who beat him. The dog didn't have a problem with Black women, just Black men. One of our workers sent a letter to Des Moines; they investigated and determined the dog was racist and instructed us to get rid of all the dogs."

"Well then, bringing the dogs back is not an option." Marvin considered, "Say, one of our security guards is a former Marine sniper. Why don't you have him come in on a Saturday night when were shut down and have him shoot every cat he sees?"

"I don't think our friends at the Humane Society would like that. But I can collaborate with them and come up with a way to get rid of the cats."

"You're right. Take care of the problem and keep MTI out of trouble."

"I will."

I left Marvin and walked over to Debra's office. I told her I'd take care of the cats and then I told her Molly's re-organization idea. At first Debra was hesitant because it came from Molly, but after hearing that Ben agreed with the plan, she seriously considered it and approved the change, effective at once. She said we didn't have to run it by Marvin because we weren't adding an employee and my part-time-assistant position had already been approved. I was going to propose the pay increase next, but Debra beat me to it.

"Connor, I'm sure this change in responsibility is deserving of a pay increase, but I was just notified by Des Moines that they've imposed a wage freeze on all divisions. We can propose pay changes, but each must now be approved by the division president and corporate HR. How much are you proposing?"

"Molly is currently at nineteen per hour. I'm proposing taking her to twenty-four. She only asked for four dollars, but I'm asking for five because I expect corporate to lower the request."

"Can you justify five dollars?"

"Yes. Molly has a four-year degree in education, minoring in PR. You're aware of her extroversion and people skills. I'll tell her that the decision won't be made for ninety days. I'd rather wait and get what I'm asking for than push through a lower amount."

"Okay, the increase isn't so bad when you take into account that all our educators are underpaid."

Debra said, "I'll process the reporting change today so you can announce it. I'll let things settle down a bit at corporate and submit the pay-change request in a few weeks, making it effective ninety days from today."

I thanked Debra and headed back to my office. On the way, I called Brian to meet with me. Ben saw me enter the building and immediately came to my office. As he walked in, I said, "Have a chair." I did the same, joining him at my table.

"Is the plan approved?" asked Ben.

"Yes, just as we discussed."

"Is she getting a pay increase?"

"We won't know for ninety days. Des Moines just implemented a pay freeze for all divisions."

"Can I announce the change?"

"Yes, let everyone know, including Molly. Give her a couple weeks to make the adjustments so she can give me twenty hours a week."

Just then, Brian walked in, and I motioned for him to take a chair at the table. Ben started to get up, but I asked him to stay.

I said to both of them, "We had an incident last night. Brian, you're already aware of the cat bite."

I then went on to explain my discussion with Marvin. I asked Ben to update all the production-curriculum to include instructions to not feed the cats. I asked Brian to acquire enough live-cat traps to cover every overhead-door building plus some more for the yard. I also told him to contact Dr. Bruce and make arrangements for a live cat drop-off at his animal hospital, including medical care treatment, spay/neutering, and standard vaccinations prior to each healthy cat being turned over to the Humane Society. MTI would pay all the adoption fees.

Brian said, "This is going to be a costly project."

"Not as costly as a rabies death," I said.

Both men agreed and left my office.

I sat down behind my desk as Molly walked in and asked, "Did my plan get approved?"

"Yes, but don't say anything, because Ben wants to make the announcement. When that meeting's over, come back here, and we'll go over the details of your new responsibilities."

We smiled at each other as she walked toward the conference room.

I knew the meeting would be short, so I expected Molly

when she returned soon after. "Was the news well received?" I asked.

"Yes. Everyone seemed fine with it in the meeting."

"I did request your pay increase," I told her. "But I won't know if it's approved for ninety days."

"Ben told us there was a pay freeze in effect right now."

"That's correct, but there are always exceptions. The request will be considered, since it involves a change in responsibility. During these ninety days, you'll have the opportunity to prove yourself."

Molly smiled, using her drawl, "What'll ya want me to do?"

"I want you to impress my boss."

"What would you like me to do to Marvin?"

"I don't want you to do anything to Marvin. I don't want you to go near Marvin. If Marvin saw you in these leggings, he'd order me to terminate your employment today."

"So, you don't like my leggings?"

"I love your leggings. I like to look at you in your leggings, but they expose every detail. They're not appropriate for the office."

"Well, I feel uncomfortable in them because everyone's staring at me. I'll never wear them to work again. But I would like to wear them sometime when you and I are out somewhere together, maybe when we travel?"

"That opportunity is coming soon; we have a trip in three weeks."

"Really!? Where are we going? Chicago, San Francisco, or New York?"

"Des Moines," I said.

"Oh. Well, it's still a trip. Will we ever go someplace cool?"

"Probably not. Des Moines will most likely be as cool as we get for an overnight trip."

"Well, maybe I'll have time to do Ronnie when we're in Des Moines."

"Who's Ronnie?"

"Ronald Herbst. He's a corporate bigshot."

"I know who 'Merlot' is. Are you telling me you fuck Ronald Herbst!?"

"Every time he comes to Rochester."

"How did this start?"

"He sat in on one of my classes about a year ago. After class, he invited me to dinner at his hotel. After dinner, he invited me to his room for dessert, and dessert ended up being our first fuck."

"I can't believe you're fucking Ronald Herbst."

"He's a good fuck," she said coarsely. "He doesn't want to talk, just fuck. And he fucks me with authority. When I'm riding him and my boobs are bouncing up and down, he just stares and thrusts. He makes me feel so good."

"Do you realize he's the person at corporate who has to approve your pay increase?"

"You're kidding! Well, that's good; I'm sure that Ronnie'll take care of lil' ol' me."

"If Ronald asks, please don't tell him about us. He'd freak out if he knew I was doing you."

"Well, you're not doing me. We haven't fucked, kissed, or hugged. There's nothing to tell him."

"Good."

So, Molly was fucking corporate officers in addition to managers in Rochester. This was getting harder to handle. One side of me said I should stay away from this rude, vulgar woman; it was exactly what Debra warned me about. But I let the other side of me stay in control, and it said to ask her the next question.

Baseball

CHAPTER 26

"Say, Molly, are you available to go to a meeting with me tonight?"

"Yes. My husband doesn't get home until Friday. What kind of meeting?"

"It's a baseball game. The Community Chest leaders from all the large employers are getting together on the party deck at tonight's Honkers game." The Honkers were a nonaffiliated single-A baseball team with several former players who'd made it to the Big Show.

"There'll be plenty of food and beer and you'll have a chance to get to know many people we'll work with on this year's campaign," I told her.

"Oh, that sounds fun! I want to change into jeans, so why don't you pick me up at my house?"

"If we leave at our normal quitting time, we'll have time for you to change and still stop somewhere for drinks on our way to the ballpark."

"I don't drink alcohol. Instead of a bar, let's spend some time at my house. I can model some bikinis for you."

"I didn't realize you don't drink."

"My church doesn't condone alcohol. I tried it once in high school, got sick, and never took another drink."

"Good to know. Okay, let's get some work done before we

have to leave."

The end of the day came quickly. I followed Molly down Highway 52 to her home in a newer neighborhood. She parked in her garage, and I parked behind her. The house was a split-level design, so we walked in the front door and up a short flight of steps. The living room was on our right, and the kitchen was up ahead.

"Should I wait here?" I asked as we walked into the living room.

"No, let's go to the bedroom. You can watch me change clothes."

And that's exactly what we did. At first, it reminded me of being with Julia or Debra; Molly stripped naked and started laying her bikinis out on the bed. Women always got naked with me in a bedroom, probably because they knew I couldn't get hard and take it to the next level. Molly put on her first bikini and stood in front of the mirror, checking herself out from different angles. Then she tried on the other two, checking herself out with each one. While still wearing the third one, she looked at me and asked, "What do ya think?"

I was sitting on the edge of the bed where she and her husband slept, just staring at her. "I can't believe how good you look naked."

Molly walked over to me and took her top off. Next, she pulled the strings on each hip at the same time and then spread her legs, so the bikini bottom dropped to the floor. Then she leaned into me and put her left breast against my mouth, the way Julia used to do. I thought I was in heaven as I held her naked body. This was the ass that totally captivated me at work, and now I was holding a bare butt cheek in each of my hands. I moved to proceed further when Molly stopped me, "No, I want you to touch me like that at the game."

I let go of her. "That'll be difficult; we won't be sitting in the stands. We'll be on the party deck, standing and mingling with the crowd."

"Who pays for all of this? Is this where my Community Chest donation goes? Paying for beer, food, and reserved seats?"

"All the Community Chest funds are used for charitable purposes. Tonight is paid for by the large employers attending the event."

"That's good. Who am I gonna meet tonight?"

"Business leaders, business owners, bank presidents, and clinic officials."

"Wow, it sounds like I'll meet a lot of men in authority. Make sure I bring my cards with me. Oh, how many bank presidents will be there?" she crudely asked.

"There'll be six or seven bank presidents in attendance. I don't know if I like this. Every time I introduce you to a man, I'll think you're going to be doing him next week."

"We can only hope. I do like variety, and I'd love to fuck a bank president." Molly paused and then said, "We should get going. I want as much mingling time as we can get."

"Do I have to worry about you getting a ride home with someone else?"

"No, I wouldn't do that to you. What kind of lady do ya think I am? I may fuck a couple of 'em tomorrow, but tonight, I'm all yours."

Molly got dressed more conservatively than normal. She put on a white shirt that proved she had nice breasts without exposing herself too much. Instead of tight jeans, she wore a loose skirt that covered half her thighs but still showed off her long legs. She looked exceptionally good."

We got on the deck just as everyone else was arriving. We

didn't even watch the game. During the first four innings, Molly stayed by me so I could introduce her as MTI's new Community Chest campaign manager. She had no pockets, so I carried her business cards. I thought she'd hand them out when I introduced her, but no, she waited until she'd met every man there. Then she took the cards and went off on her own to chat with each man she planned to fuck. She was basically throwing herself at them, encouraging them to call her. Most of the men gave Molly their cards. She was having an exciting time.

When Molly ran out of cards, she came back to me. "How did you do?" I asked her.

"Very well. I handed out nineteen cards."

"How many will you fuck?"

"Eight for sure; they're ready to fuck me tonight. Two others are possibilities and the remaining nine are definite nos."

"Are you ready to leave?"

"Not until you get your magic finger in my kitty."

"I have looked around but didn't find a safe place."

"We don't need safe; you need to be more adventurous."

"What do you have in mind?"

"Let's go to the women's restroom, and I will sneak you into a stall."

"No way, I'm not getting caught in the women's bathroom."

"Okay, then you sneak me into the men's bathroom, and we will share a stall."

We said goodbye to several people as we left. All the men watched Molly as we made our way off the party deck. She must have known they would be watching, because she had pulled her skirt higher on her waist to expose more of her legs.

We walked into the men's restroom together. There were men at the sinks, but no one saw us enter. We went into the first open stall. Molly pulled the toilet cover down and then told me to stand in front of the toilet so it would look like I was peeing. Molly pulled her skirt up to her waist then kneeled on top of the toilet cover and stretched out her arms to lean against the wall behind the toilet. She was incredibly quiet.

Molly was wearing a thong and started to wiggle her bare butt against me. This was like our conference table position, so I reached in front and started to finger her. She was very wet and horny and came very quickly without making much noise. She stood back on the floor and whispered, "Time to leave."

I left the stall first, and she waited a few seconds before she did the same. Two men entered the restroom as I was leaving, and one of them asked Molly, "What are you doing in here?"

Molly said, "The lines for the women's restroom were too long." Both men nodded. Molly walked by them and joined me at the door. She giggled all the way to the car. We were some of the first to leave the game, so we were pretty much alone in the parking lot. Molly started walking in front of me, pulling her skirt up a little with each step she took. By the time we reached the car, she was wearing nothing below the waist except her thong and sandals.

She leaned against the car and stuck her kitty out toward me. I started to finger her again, moving slower than in the stall. I was enjoying this and naturally leaned in like I was going to kiss her but stopped before our lips touched. I stayed in this position until she came. And she came with a lot more noise this time. When she recovered, I was still close to her with our lips a few inches apart. Then, suddenly, Molly pressed her lips against mine for just a brief moment before pulling away.

Molly said, "I would really like to kiss you, but we can't

start that. I'm not going to commit adultery." I was disappointed but also happy to hear that she wanted to kiss me.

When we arrived at Molly's house, I got out and walked her to the door. She was so appreciative; I could tell she liked being treated like a lady.

I drove home, thinking about how terrible I was. When I was physically with Molly, I didn't feel bad. She made me happy, and she thought everything we did was okay. But when I was alone, I knew I was no longer just a fornicator; I'd become an adulterer.

For the next couple weeks, my job went well, and Molly and I established a pattern. Every morning, Monday through Thursday, she'd wear a skirt or dress, walk in with a coffee carafe and lock both of my office doors. I'd sit behind my desk as Molly removed her panties and set them on my desk. I'd use my hands to pleasure her, then I'd give her one of the new thongs I'd kept purchasing. Each day, I'd throw her old panties into my lower desk drawer. I told Molly I wanted to convert all her panties to thongs. After we'd finish, Molly would sit at the conference table, and I would unlock the doors while she filled our mugs. A few times a week, after work, on days when Molly and I were the only ones left in the building, we'd do more.

The Overnighter

CHAPTER 27

Three weeks after the cat bite, Brian walked into my office and said, "Connor, we hit thirty today."

"Thirty what?"

"We caught our thirtieth cat in a live trap this morning. It's on its way to Dr. Bruce right now."

"Do you know how many are still at the hospital?"

"This one will make four at the hospital. Twenty-six have been adopted."

"That's great. This project has gone very well. Thank you for getting on top of it right away."

"No problem, Boss."

Brian left as Ben walked into my office. "Good morning, Connor. According to my calendar, you and Molly are out on Thursday and Friday. Is that still the plan?"

"That's the plan."

"Are you and Molly flying or driving?"

"I always drive."

"I know you do. How come everyone in Des Moines flies here?"

"They want the airline miles. It's just over two hundred miles one way, but the airlines give them five hundred miles each way. It's ridiculous, because they fly from Des Moines to Minneapolis and then switch planes and fly back to Rochester. It takes three hours for that and longer if they have to wait for the Rochester flight. If I tried doing that, Marvin would come down hard on me. It takes me just over three hours to drive and costs a lot less than flying."

"Molly thought you were going to be flying, but I told her last week that you never fly to Des Moines. She was disappointed. I guess she hasn't flown for several years."

"I don't think Molly will be doing any flying in her new position unless something comes up that I'm not aware of."

"Well, Connor, I'm glad she's traveling with you and not me. My wife would never let me travel with Molly."

"You should be happy your wife cares about you and your marriage. I envy you."

"You're right, I should be glad she cares that much. When it comes down to it, I'm grateful."

Ben left my office, and I went to see Marvin. I reported that we'd caught thirty cats and twenty-six had already been adopted. Marvin was pleased but too busy to talk. I walked over to Debra's office and gave her the cat update.

Debra accepted the good news and then said, "I hear you're traveling with Molly this week."

"That's correct, we're in Des Moines on Thursday and Friday. Just out one night."

"If we were still together, I would not let you travel with Molly."

"If we were still together, I would respect your wishes."

"Connor, you need to be careful. If you start sleeping with her, there'll be problems."

"So, you're saying I should never sleep with someone who reports to me?"

"Stop it, you know this is different from you and me."

"I know, I'm just giving you a tough time. Anyway, how did you hear about my travel plans?"

"Molly's been bragging about traveling with you, and it got back to me."

"Bragging?"

"Yes. Everyone at MTI knows who you are, so it makes her feel good to tell people she's traveling with you. She's acting like the two of you are flying to Paris. Connor, please be careful."

"I will, and thanks for caring. I really mean that," I told her.

"Just a minute. Before you leave, why are you going to Des Moines? I thought this new job was going to keep you out of Des Moines."

"So did I, but VTM decided to really promote Community Chest participation at all divisions. They're holding meetings for all the Community Chest division leaders in Des Moines. Molly and I will participate in a day and a half of meetings."

"I thought MTI was already the top Community Chest fundraiser of all the divisions?"

"We are, but remember, corporate wants to make MTI like all the other divisions. They'll force changes on MTI, so we raise less money."

"Well, please stay out of trouble with corporate. You don't have Julia there to protect you anymore."

"Don't worry, Marvin's already given me orders to keep my mouth shut and let Molly do the talking."

"That's a good plan."

"I need to get back to my office. Molly and I don't leave until Thursday morning, so I'll still be here all day tomorrow."

On my drive back to the training center, I received a call from my neighbor Clint. He was home today because it was his week to work nights. He said that Zeus went after a woman from my mortgage company when she was trying to hang a paper on my front doorknob. Zeus came around the corner and chased her off the property. He never touched her, but he kept lunging toward her until she was outside his invisible fence. The woman was terrified and said she was going to report the incident to her boss. She said a vicious dog like Zeus should be put down. Clint told the woman he'd witnessed the whole thing; Zeus was careful not to touch her. He also told her that one of his cameras covers the front door and that he knew I had a camera in that area as well.

"Connor, these mortgage people only come around when someone's behind on their payments. Are you going to be okay?"

"I'm a few months behind, so the bank sends an inspector out each month to make sure I haven't abandoned the property."

"I thought you paid cash for the house. Why do you have a mortgage?"

"I paid cash when I bought the house ten years ago. But two years ago, I took out a three-hundred-thousand-dollar loan to invest in the Mantorville Winery."

"Oh, so you're caught up in that mess."

"Yes. Is Zeus going to be okay until I get home?"

"He calmed down as soon as the woman left."

"Good. Thanks for looking after him," I told Clint.

"Zeus is never a problem. Today, he was just doing his job."

"And remember," I reminded him, "I'm out of town on Thursday night."

"Got you covered," he confirmed. "I'll be working, but Shelly will be home."

"Okay, I'll see you when I get home."

"Bye."

I entered the training center and Molly followed me into my office, carrying a carafe of coffee. We hadn't had our morning session, but I was more anxious to have coffee with her than I was to feel her body. After having had many conversations with her, Molly was becoming more than just a sex object to me.

Molly grabbed my attention when she pulled her panties down her legs slower than normal and announced, "This is the last time." I gave her a questioning look and she said, "From now on, I'll only be wearing thongs to work. No more panties."

"So, I have all your panties?"

"Yes, and I must admit you have good taste. My husband loves the thongs you bought me."

"Has he asked why you switched to thongs?"

"Yep, and I told him the less I wear, the better I feel. He doesn't like it when I talk sexy. He's not like you."

"I think most men like it when you talk sexy. I bet your husband does, too; he just doesn't admit it."

Molly came closer, and I began the same process we did four days a week.

Neither of us spoke for a minute, and then Molly said, "Oh, I do still have my church panties. I'm keeping those. I'd never wear a thong to church."

Molly came quickly, resumed her spot at the conference table, and poured us coffee as I unlocked the doors.

After we'd talked a while, Ben walked in. I immediately noticed I'd left Molly's panties on top of my desk. Molly saw my concern and swiveled her chair toward Ben, so he'd see most of her thighs. Ben couldn't help but look at Molly, giving me enough time to grab the panties and stuff them in my pocket.

The rest of the day was uneventful until quitting time. Debra called to ask for help, "We had a sexual harassment complaint today, and I need you to finish the investigation by tomorrow morning. I have conference calls all morning."

"No problem," I said. "What are the details?"

"Iris Trudeau has made a complaint against Elwood Davenport. I already took her statement and will send it to you. I told Iris to stay home in the morning but to report to work at noon. Brian's looking for video and should have something for you in the morning. You should talk to Elwood early enough so you can suspend him and get him off the property before noon."

"No problem."

"Do you want me to send one of my assistants to your office to take notes and be your witness?"

"No, I'll use Molly."

"Molly Dew?"

"Yes. Do you have a problem with that?"

"I guess not, you just caught me off guard. I'm still getting used to the fact that Molly Dew is working with you."

"Okay, I'll review your email and the video in the morning and take care of Elwood."

"Thank you, bye."

As I hung up my phone, Molly walked into my office and closed one door before crudely asking "Are you ready to come all over my bare butt?"

"We can't do that tonight. There are several people in the conference room, and they'll be there a while. But close the other door, too. I need to talk to you about a special project."

"Ooh, it must be really special if I'm closing the doors."

"Have a chair," I instructed seriously. "Tomorrow morning, after our coffee, I'm going to question a male employee accused of sexual harassment. I need you to witness the conversation and take notes."

"Sounds like fun. I knew my job would get more interesting if I worked directly for you."

"Just remember, you can't talk or ask questions. Your job will be to witness the conversation between the man and me. And take notes."

"I understand. Can you tell me what he did?"

"He is accused of grinding his penis into a female employee's ass."

"Like you do to me?"

"Yes, but this man did not have consent, and he was hard when he did it."

"Ooh, I can't wait to hear all the details."

"Tomorrow, I need you to dress very conservatively. A loose-fitting top, not low cut, and a loose-fitting long skirt. Okay?"

"Okay, but if I come to work with a long skirt and no underwear, do you still have a thong you can give me after you finger me?"

"Yes. I have two thongs left. We'll go through our usual morning routine and then do the interview. I should have video by morning, so we'll watch that before we confront him."

"Video of the grinding?"

"Yes. If the cameras were working, we'll have it all on video."

"Ooh, I'm getting excited," she said.

"Please remember that the woman is devastated. She's afraid to be near the coworker who allegedly harassed her."

"I don't understand why women are bothered by these things. If a man at work ground his hard cock into me, I'd say 'let's get a room.' We should be able to be more physical at work."

"Can you behave tomorrow, or do I need to get someone else to be my witness?"

"I'll be an excellent witness for you, and I'll take thorough, accurate notes."

"Good. Let's get out of here. Tomorrow's our last day in the office before our trip to Des Moines."

"This is gonna be a wonderful week. I already have two guys lined up for extracurricular activities in Des Moines," Molly said with a smile and a wink.

"Is Ronald one of them?"

"Yes. I'm going to fuck Ronnie and Jared at the hotel before you and I go to dinner."

"Ronnie and Jared at the same time?"

"No. What kind of girl do ya think I am? I'll coordinate things so I can do you and them, each of you at separate times."

"Good, just make sure I'm first. I don't want sloppy seconds or thirds to Ronald Herbst."

We walked to our cars and went to our separate homes.

I had a good night's sleep and arrived at work early on Wednesday morning. I was the first one in the building, but I didn't make coffee. I wanted to see the video for the complaint investigation. Brian had emailed me two videos: one from last Friday and another from yesterday. I watched the oldest one first. Elwood and Iris both wore jeans. Iris was using the copy machine when Elwood approached, rubbing his groin against her butt as he went by. Iris immediately turned and angrily said something to Elwood, who turned and walked away.

In the video from yesterday, both Iris and Elwood were

wearing lightweight slacks. I surmised that this was why Iris had reported feeling his erection yesterday but not on the previous Friday. Elwood approached Iris just like the week before, except this time, as he slid by her, he thrust into her twice. Iris jumped back, arms in the air, visibly yelling at Elwood. He held his hands up like an "innocent man" and walked away.

As I finished the second video, Molly stuck her head through the door to say she was making coffee. I didn't see what she was wearing but hoped it was conservative. Next, I called Debra and told her what was on the videos. I suggested we terminate instead of suspend Elwood. Debra agreed and sent me a severance and release agreement along with the standard benefit documents.

A few minutes later, Molly walked in with coffee and closed both doors. I thanked her for dressing appropriately today.

"You were clear on what you wanted. I'm glad you approve. Hey, do you have the videos?"

"Yes."

"Oh, good. Let's watch them while you finger me."

"No way."

"It won't take any longer for me to come," she assured me. "I'm a woman. I can multitask."

"Okay," I stupidly agreed, and started the videos.

Molly moved closer and pulled up her long skirt. "Keep playing them over and over until I come."

During the playbacks, every time she saw Elwood thrusting, Molly would make a passionate sound and get even more excited.

After she'd finished, I opened both doors and sat down at the table with her.

Despite having just been aroused by another woman's

sexual assault, Molly said, "Iris looked pretty upset in the video. I guess if you're not into playing around, having someone thrust his hard cock into your butt could be upsetting."

I sighed, exasperated. "I was supposed to get Elwood's statement and then suspend him until the investigation is complete. But I'm not going to do that. The video is enough to allow me to immediately terminate him."

"Oh, that's too bad," Molly said as she looked at me, seeking approval to approach Elwood.

"Don't even think about him. You're going to be a witness to his termination. You can't go after him for a quick fuck."

"I understand, and I will not pursue him."

"Okay, good. Let's go over to the parts-office building. I reserved a conference room and have two people from security meeting us there." I grabbed my laptop, and we drove over in my pickup.

The two guards met us at the entrance, and we all went to the conference room. I told Molly and the guards to wait there while I got Elwood and instructed the guards to wait out in the hallway when I returned. They'd both managed several terminations before and knew the routine.

Elwood walked alongside me without speaking. I was sure he knew what was happening. When we entered the conference room, the guards left and closed the door. Elwood and I sat at the table with Molly.

Elwood began, "I suppose this is about Iris?"

"Yes, it is. Let's take a look at what happened." I opened my laptop and showed both videos to Elwood.

"I was just having some fun, but the videos make it look pretty bad."

"Yes, it is pretty bad, and that's why your employment is being terminated."

"Terminated! I was just having fun. I've done the same thing to two other women, and they just laughed it off. Besides, Iris lost her husband a month ago to a heart attack. I figured she'd be ready for some action. I was just trying to please her."

"You're disgusting," I told him. "The company is offering two weeks' severance if you sign a release agreement. If it were up to me, I wouldn't give you any severance pay."

"What's the release for?"

"If you sign, you're agreeing not to sue MTI."

"If you're only giving me two weeks' pay, I'm definitely going to sue the company."

"That would be a mistake. If you sue MTI, the county prosecutor will get the video of what you did, because I'll make sure that assault charges are filed against you; the videos will become evidence. Your face will be on local TV and on the internet." I added, "Everyone will see what a puny pecker you have."

"What do you mean, puny? I have an average-size dick."

"Maybe so, but in the video, it looks pretty small." I took a chance and said, "Molly, what did you think about Elwood's hard penis in the video?"

Molly knew what I was doing and said, "Well, I've seen a lot of men with erect penises, but the one in the video is the smallest hard dick I've ever seen, except for the little ones I see when I change babies' diapers at church."

A beautiful woman had just told him he had a baby boy dick; Elwood was humiliated.

"So, if I sign the release right now, then the video goes nowhere?"

"That is correct," I said. "The video goes into a retention file and gets destroyed in seven years. I also need to point out that you do not have to sign the release today. You can think about it a few weeks before you sign."

"That's okay, I'll sign right now. When do I get the two weeks' pay?"

"If you sign today, the check will be mailed tomorrow."

Elwood signed the release, and the guards took him to his desk and then to his car.

When Molly and I were alone in the conference room, she said, "His dick was actually average, but I knew what you wanted me to say."

"I was impressed by how you handled it."

"How did you know that insulting his dick would make him sign the release?"

"Aren't most men worried about their size? I knew he'd do anything to keep the video private."

"He looked really hurt when he left," she said.

"I know. I might've felt bad for him if he hadn't said he'd done it because Iris hadn't had sex for a month. But I have no compassion for him; targeting a recent widow he thought was vulnerable makes him a sexual predator."

Bringing it back to her own interests, Molly replied, "Yeah, by the time he left the room, I no longer had any desire to do him."

"I'll take the release agreement to Debra and then brief Marvin on tomorrow's trip."

"Okay. I'm busy until quitting time. Today I'm teaching my regular classes plus Thursday and Friday's as well. Oh, I almost forgot to ask you something. Since we didn't get to do it last night, how about we do it at your place after work tonight?"

"Sure."

"Also, I packed a bag for two nights and have it in my car. I thought I'd spend tonight at your house, so you don't have to drive to pick me up in Rochester tomorrow. Okay?"

"Yes, that makes sense."

On the way to Debra's office, I thought about how my feelings for Molly were changing. I certainly wasn't in love with her, but I was starting to like her. She was vulgar and brash, but also smart and becoming a good assistant. She was incredibly good at keeping sex non-romantic, and I was starting to enjoy sexual activities without any relational commitment. Her being married didn't bother me enough to stop, even though mentally I knew it was wrong and that I was sinning. Whenever I felt the need to talk to Grandma about it, I just reminded myself that I already knew what she'd say.

Debra waved me into her office, she pushed the mute button on her speakerphone, and asked me, "How did it go?"

"I'll give you the details later, but he's terminated. He already signed the release."

"Good work. I need to get back to this call."

I set the release on her desk as she returned to the call and I walked across the hall to meet Marvin, who waved me in. I didn't say anything about Elwood; that was Debra's job now.

Marvin told me, "I need you to behave in Des Moines and not stir up any trouble."

"That won't be a problem. I'm not meeting with any HR people."

"I meant what I said before. Let Molly do the talking. By the way, how's she doing?"

"Better than I expected. She is becoming very helpful."

Jacquelyn buzzed Marvin, who told me, "I need to take this. Safe travels."

I walked out, closing his door behind me.

"Hello, Jacquelyn."

"Hi, Connor. I hear you're going on a trip with Molly Dew."

"The word seems to be getting around."

"She's so excited to be working with you, talking about you all the time. She usually stops by here once a day and 'talks to me' until she gets an opportunity to give Marvin her smile."

"Well, if she gets to be a pest, let me know and I'll put a stop to her visits."

"Are you and Molly becoming an item?"

"No. You're the only person I can say this to, I'm still in love with Debra. I respect her decision, and I agree with it; she's definitely better off with her carpenter than she would be with me."

"Well, people are starting to talk about you and Molly."

"Molly's turning out to be a better assistant than I expected, but there's no love between us."

"Okay, just be careful. She's not like Debra," Jacquelyn cautioned me.

At four o'clock, Molly and I were separately heading to my house in Mantorville. Molly followed me and I'd told her to park next to me in the garage. When Debra stayed overnight, I didn't care if someone saw her car, but Debra did care and always parked in the garage. Molly was married, so I didn't want anyone to see her car in my driveway overnight.

Zeus would be anxious about a strange woman. It was just yesterday that he'd chased the mortgage woman away. His invisible fence prevented him from entering via the garage's overhead door, so he'd have to wait in the house until I let him into the garage. I warned Molly about Zeus's greetings and told her that he sometimes read my mind.

After Molly and I exited our vehicles, Zeus zipped by me and went straight to Molly. After smelling every part of her body, he did the same thing to her that he'd done to Debra—humped her right leg. Molly started giggling, enjoying the attention of this huge German Shepherd. I told Zeus to stop, and he reluctantly obeyed.

Molly now understood my comment and said, "Well, I hope he's reading your mind; I'd love you to do that to me."

"He is reading my mind, but remember, I'm not capable of doing it like Zeus."

As we walked into the house, Molly asked me where my bedroom was and then immediately went upstairs. She walked into my bedroom and stripped naked.

"I plan to stay naked until we leave tomorrow morning," she announced.

"I'll enjoy that, but I was planning to grill on the deck for dinner. You may want to put something on for that. The deck is private until someone decides to walk into the backyard."

"I'll take my chances. I don't mind showing off my body."

"My neighbor will be stopping by. He'll be taking care of Zeus while I'm away. But he usually goes to the laundry room door; from there, the deck's out of sight."

"That's fine. I look forward to being naked outside tonight. But right now, I want to do you like never before." Molly leaned over my bed and started wiggling her bare butt at me. "I want you to come all over my naked ass."

That was all Molly had to say. I quickly undressed as I watched Molly lean on the bed with her butt in the air, wiggling at me. As I approached her, I dripped on her thigh.

She said, "Anxious, aren't we?"

I pushed my guy into her right butt cheek and then reached around with my right hand and slid my middle finger into her kitty. Warm oil flowed out, making a damp stain on my comforter. Her kitty was hotter than normal and full of warm oil. For a moment, I thought about how jealous Debra would be. Then I focused on beautiful Molly. I was using my usual movements, but I was getting an unusual response from Molly. She was already groaning and much louder than normal. This lasted for a few minutes. Her groaning got me more excited, and I increased the intensity with which I was rubbing her. That really got her going, and her moaning turned into very loud ooooohs and ahhhhhhs. This continued for a pleasant amount of time.

Molly had never been this loud before, and she was really getting me excited. I could feel the pressure building within me, and I was feeling so good. I moved my hips back to take some pressure off my guy, and then boom! I shot semen all over Molly's butt cheek. She must have felt the semen running down her butt, because she got really excited, and her hips started shaking uncontrollably. Then she climaxed. Her whole body shook for a few seconds, followed by the loudest scream I have ever heard a woman make. When the scream stopped, her arms were frozen in position, still holding her body above the bed. I removed my hand from her kitty, and she collapsed onto the bed. She lay there still for about a minute before rolling over and looking into my eyes. Molly scooted further onto the bed and said, "Hold me."

I lay down beside her, wrapped my arms around her, and pulled her close. I leaned in to kiss her, but Molly turned her face to avoid the kiss and said, "Just hold me."

I held her close, and Molly responded by squeezing me back. After a minute, we just lay on the bed in each other's arms, looking into each other's eyes.

"Making love to you is extremely exciting" I told her. "And by the way, we didn't just fuck around; we made love. Holding you afterward was even better than coming all over you."

Molly didn't speak. Instead, she got a worried look on her face.

When I reached down to pick up my boxers, she said, "Hey, I thought we were staying naked until tomorrow."

"You're staying naked. I'm going to wear my boxers. Otherwise, I'll be dripping everywhere I walk."

"Connor, you just emptied all your cum on me. How can you still have anything to drip?"

"If I'm around your naked body, I will be dripping every few minutes."

Molly smiled and then drawled, "Lordy, I didn't know I had that effect on men." We both laughed.

Later, I grilled chicken while Molly and I shared a pitcher of ice water on the deck. It was still quite warm out, so Molly was still naked, lying on a lounge chair. I was comfortable in my boxers and T-shirt, enjoying the moment.

The doorbell rang. "I'm sure that's Clint," I said. "I'll take care of him." I walked into the house and headed for the laundry room, not knowing Clint was following the chicken smells to the backyard.

I got back to the deck just in time to see Molly stand, walk to Clint, and shake his hand. "You must be Clint," she said.

"Yes. I'm Connor's neighbor."

Clint struggled to keep his eyes focused on Molly's face. I spoke, "So, the two of you have met?"

"Yes, we have," said Molly.

Clint addressed me, "Here's a flash drive with the video of the woman and Zeus today."

I took it and thanked him.

Clint said, "I'll leave the two of you to your chicken and head home."

I said, "Why don't you leave through the house, and I will give you the salsa that Shelly had me buy?"

"Okay."

As Clint and I walked through the house to the kitchen, he said, "Connor, I don't understand how you get so many beautiful women to run around your place in the nude."

"Believe me, if I ever figure it out, I will let you know."

Clint took the salsa and went home.

Molly and I had some leftover salad with our chicken. Then we cuddled while watching a movie before going to bed early. In bed, we didn't do anything sexual. Molly was noticeably quiet. We held each other again while under the sheet. Then, after a few minutes, we separated and fell asleep.

Des Moines

CHAPTER 28

My alarm woke us at four a.m. Molly used my bathroom, and I used the guest bathroom. I was ready before Molly, so I made coffee for our travel mugs. When Molly joined me in the kitchen, I couldn't believe how professional she looked. She wore a very conservative business suit.

"Wow," I said, "you look very professional."

"Thank you. I want to make a good impression with the corporate people."

"You will."

We said goodbye to Zeus and headed for the garage. I put our bags in the backseat of my truck and held the passenger door open for Molly, who gave me a nice smile as she climbed into her seat.

We drove an hour with little conversation. I finally said, "What's bothering you?"

"You know."

"I do?"

"Yes," she said. "We're falling in love, and we can't do that. I know you don't get it, but I really love my husband. And I'm starting to get feelings for you, and that isn't right."

I told her, "I have some feelings for you, too. But I don't

know how to manage them, and we're committing adultery, which isn't right."

Molly replied, "We haven't committed adultery yet. I said I was starting to get feelings, but I'm not in love with you yet. We haven't committed adultery until one of us is in love with the other. Are you in love with me?"

"I could get there."

"But you aren't there yet. We need to fuck around without getting emotional."

There wasn't much more talk during the rest of the drive, until the last hour, when my call with a manager in Springfield, Missouri kept Molly entertained.

He started, "Connor, I know you're not HR anymore, but I'm not comfortable talking to Debra about this, so I'm calling you."

"What's the issue?"

"Ever since we started paying parts-salespeople commissions based on individual sales instead of team sales, competition between my two parts-counter people has gotten intense. They used to get along well and work as a team. Under this new individual program, Kristin is selling three times as much as Nick, and she's not being fair about it."

"What is she doing that isn't fair?"

"Kristin's an attractive woman. Under the team-commission program, she dressed very conservatively. She and Nick each made about half of the counter sales. Now, Kristin dresses very sexy and uses her breasts to get most of the male customers to go to her."

"How does she use her breasts?"

"The parts-counter is the perfect height for Kristin to rest her breasts on it, which also puts her in a position to be awfully close to the customer. My parts manager thinks it's great because our overall sales are up since she started dressing this way, but Nick's sales are down, and he's not a happy camper. Things have gotten so bad that even when Kristin has four or more customers in her line and Nick has no customers at his counter, no one will leave her line to go to Nick's. They prefer to wait so they can get a good look at her boobs."

"You know, this isn't an issue for HR. It's an issue for Howard Olson. He needs to go back to the team commission system. Let me talk with Howard."

"I did talk to Howard, and he told me to get over it. Howard said that sales are up and that's all that matters."

"I'll talk to Howard," I told him and ended the call.

Molly was giggling quietly in her seat. "You have so many interesting things to deal with in your job."

"Yes, I do. And you did an excellent job staying quiet during the call. Please do the same on the rest of the calls."

"I will," Molly replied. "This is fun."

Next, I called Howard.

"Hi, Connor. I hear you're traveling with the company babe today."

Molly had a big smile on her face. I said, "I've never heard her called a babe before."

"That woman is so hot; I get hard every time she walks by my office," Howard said, "Are you driving?"

"Yes."

"I sure hope you don't have me on speaker."

"I'm using my earbuds, so we're okay," I lied.

"So, are you fucking her?" Howard asked.

"No. You know better than that. The reason I'm calling is that I just talked with Tommy, our manager in Springfield."

"He called me earlier and I told him I wasn't going to go back to the old system. Sales are up with individual commissions. If we go back to teams, Kristin will earn less money and go back to her old way of dressing. Then our total sales will go down."

"Why don't you explain the situation to Debra," I offered. "Then you can raise Kristin's base to offset the lower commissions."

"I can raise Kristin's base as long as she keeps showing the customers her boobs."

"I didn't hear you say that, and you definitely do not want to say that to Debra."

"Okay, I need to get going. I'll talk to Debra this afternoon and see what we can work out. And thanks, Connor, you lucky son of a bitch. Have a good fuckin' time in Des Moines, or should I say, have a good time fucking in Des Moines."

"Goodbye, Howard."

I looked over at Molly, who could hardly contain herself, "I guess I should start fucking Howard."

"No, you shouldn't. You need to stay away from all the officers."

"I'm still doing Ronnie."

"And he's the only one. You can't do more officers; it will only cause trouble."

"How high up is Ronnie?"

"Ronald is the same as a division president, like Marvin."

"Wow, I didn't realize he was that high up."

The phone rang. I looked at it and said to Molly, "It's Marvin. Be very quiet." I answered.

"Hello, Connor. Do you have me on speaker?"

"Yes," I answered truthfully.

Marvin said, "Hello, Molly."

"Hello, Marvin," she said.

He began, "Connor, something's come up, and you need to meet with Nathan as soon as you get to the office."

"I can do that. I'm scheduled to give the first presentation today, but Molly's more than capable of representing MTI and doing the presentation for me."

"Sounds good. Nathan's going to need you for at least an hour."

"Okay."

"Give me a call when you're done with Nathan. Got to go. Have another call."

I said goodbye and looked at Molly.

She had an excited smile on her face as she reached over and placed her left hand on my right hand and said, "I'll make you proud. I'm going to enjoy this because I know all about it. I made your slides, I facilitated half the Community Chest small-group meetings last year, and I've fucked a good share of the local Community Chest leaders."

"Yes, you're more than qualified," I replied drolly. "I just wish I knew why Nathan wants to meet with me."

The remaining minutes of our drive went quickly as Molly, and I discussed her presentation. At VTM, we even got through security fast. I took Molly to the meeting room and introduced her to the people I knew. As I left for Nathan's office, I saw Merlot walk into the meeting room. I came to these Community Chest kick-off meetings every year, and this was the first time he'd attended.

I walked into Nathan's outer office and greeted his assistant, who escorted me to the inner office. Just like last time, Nathan motioned me to sit across from him on the couch and we ordered coffee.

"Ronald will join us in a few minutes, after he finishes making the opening remarks at the Community Chest seminar."

I asked, "What's the purpose of our meeting?"

"We're going to be talking about Julia."

"Julia?"

"Yes, but we'll wait until Ronald joins us. Right now, I'll tell you that Ronald, Marvin, and I talked with Debra this morning regarding her position as acting HR director. We originally gave her a six-month trial period, but she's been doing such an excellent job, we told her this morning that she has full position effective immediately."

"That's great. She is doing a good job."

"You know, Connor, every time I talk to Debra, she manages to credit you for her success. She claims that you trained and mentored her since she started working at MTI."

"That's nice of Debra to say that, but I've learned a lot from her as well."

Just then, Merlot walked in and sat next to Nathan. "Have you gentlemen already started?"

Nathan said, "No, we were talking about Debra. Ronald, why don't you get us started?"

"Connor, when we promoted Julia, we thought she was bisexual at worst. Now, we hear she's planning to marry another lesbo. If people find out we put a dyke in a leadership position, it'll really hurt VTM's reputation. Connor, if you knew about this, you should've told us before we promoted her."

"Your vocabulary is as old as your understanding of modern culture," I replied.

Merlot said, "We know that you and Julia spent many nights in the same hotel room whenever you were in Des Moines and when the two of you traveled together. So, we assumed Julia was either hetero or bi."

I said, "We stayed in the same room. We never had sexual intercourse."

Merlot probed, "Are you telling us that you spent that many nights with a woman as attractive as Julia and never stuck your dick in her once?"

"Yes," I said. "We spent many nights together. But I swear to both of you that my penis has never been in her vagina."

"We're getting too personal," said Nathan.

"We're not only getting too personal," I told them. "We're also ignoring a tremendous opportunity. We should promote the fact that Julia's going to marry Dianna. We should get them on the cover of a magazine as Chicago's new power couple. When VTM becomes known as a modern progressive company, we'll be able to attract a lot of new talent. We struggle to fill our open positions because we ignore an entire segment of the population. Julia's sexuality is a positive for VTM, not a negative."

Merlot said, "I don't want homos working for VTM."

"Then why'd you hire Dwight Benson for senior VP of HR?"

"Dwight slipped through the cracks," he said.

"You are so out of touch with reality," I told him.

"Connor, you want to take us in the wrong direction. We need to change our screening process to identify lesbos and fags before we hire them. We don't want those people working for us! They bring diseases with them."

I was speechless. I knew Merlot was an asshole but had no idea he was so ignorant. I looked wide-eyed at Nathan, waiting for a response. After a period of silence, Nathan said, "This discussion is over. Connor, you can join the Community Chest seminar. Ronald, you can leave too. I need some time to think."

Merlot followed me out and we went our separate ways. I stepped into the back of the seminar room for the last five minutes of Molly's presentation. I was incredibly pleased with what I heard and saw. She looked great, and not in a sexy way. She was attractive, articulate, and very professional. During the fifteen-minute break after her presentation, Molly was surrounded by people with questions. I didn't trust the privacy of a busy VTM conference room, so I headed to the parking lot to call Marvin.

"Hello, Connor" he answered. "I just got off the phone with Nathan. He says you're stirring up trouble in Des Moines again, but this time, Nathan says it's not your fault."

"Nathan must be referring to Merlot's rant," I replied. "I knew he operated by a set of 'traditional' standards, but the way he just talked about lesbians took me back at least a couple decades."

"Nathan told me he's never heard Ronald speak like that about gay people and that his 'statements reveal some deeply troubling beliefs Ronald has hidden until now'."

"Did Nathan say if he was going to do anything about it?"

"Nathan didn't say anything specific about Ronald," Marvin said. "He did say that you made some good suggestions and that he'd most likely follow your advice."

"That's good."

"Connor, I want you to be on guard while you're in Des Moines. I know how Ronald thinks; he's going to feel he's lost a battle to you, but not the war. He'll look for ways to get back at you. Be careful."

"Understood."

Marvin said, "I have to go. Will I see you in the office tomorrow?"

"No," I said. "We don't leave Des Moines until after lunch tomorrow."

"Okay, see you Monday. If we don't talk until then, have a good weekend."

We said our goodbyes. As I walked back to the building, my phone rang. It was Julia.

"Hello, Connor," she said with a voice that still made me

melt.

"I'm in Des Moines," I said.

"I know. I talked to Debra this morning. We're both worried about you. Things were easier when you were sleeping with Debra or me. One of us was always there to look after you. Now, you're traveling with a woman who can't possibly care about you the way Debra and I care about you."

"I miss those days. But we've all moved on in different directions."

"Yes, we have," she said. "But you're still looking after me. I just got off the phone with Nathan. He said you've been talking about me again. Actually, about Dianna and me."

"I have. What did Nathan say?"

"He needs pictures of Dianna and me together so VTM can do a press release to promote VTM as a progressive company, proud of their 'lesbian' senior VP. Nathan said you suggested it."

"I did, but Merlot didn't like the suggestion. He's apparently a huge homophobe. He actually thinks we need a screening process that weeds out 'lesbos and fags' before we hire them."

"Ronald said that?"

"Yes, and then Nathan had us leave his office so he could think about what to do. Sounds like he made the right decision if he's doing my suggestion. You know I've never liked Merlot, but he even caught me off guard with that nonsense. He's way worse than I thought."

"You better be careful. I'm sure he still wants to terminate you."

"I know. Marvin just warned me, too. I hate to cut this short, but I need to get back inside."

"Okay, but please be careful. Be on guard—not only for Ronald, but with your travel partner, too. Both Debra and I worry about you with her."

"I'll be careful."

We said goodbye and I went back to the Community Chest conference, where the session leader was asking everyone to sit. Molly broke away from the small group of people still asking her questions. We sat together at the back of the room, and I could see she was incredibly pleased with how the division representatives received her. After lunch, we went outside to get away from Molly's fans. I could tell that she needed a break, so we took a walk together around the campus. We walked for a few minutes without saying anything. When I told her how proud I was of her, she abruptly stopped walking and told me seriously, "I'm so thankful for what you're doing for me. I usually have to dress and be sexy to get men to notice me. Today, both the men and the women were interested in me and what I had to say. I feel so good about how things went with my presentation."

"Molly, today you didn't use sex to impress. You used your intellect and communication skills to earn the respect and admiration of your division peers. You have more than sex going for you and today you proved yourself talented and intelligent."

Molly leaned in, giving me a long, passionate kiss followed by a loving hug. We parted with uneasy smiles. We were happy, but we also knew we were in danger of falling in love, which even by Molly's definition, meant we were on the path to committing adultery.

After the seminar, we had an early dinner before going to our hotel. We had separate rooms and opened the doors adjoining them. We met in Molly's room and then she dropped the bombshell. "I'm gonna stop fucking other guys. From now on it's just you and my husband. I already called Jared and told him I wouldn't be able to meet him tonight. I couldn't get ahold of Ronnie."

Just then, there was a knock at Molly's door. "Who is it?" she asked.

"Room service." Molly and I both recognized Ronald's voice.

I turned to leave but found the adjoining door in my room had closed. With no doorknob to it on Molly's side, the only way out was through the hall. But there was no way I was going to pass by Merlot; Molly was already half naked. When I got her attention and pointed to the door, she calmly told me to hide in the closet.

I thought for a second, but realized it was the only option to avoid a confrontation with Merlot. I got in the closet. I could see through the louvers and had a perfect view of the bed. There was another knock at the door. Molly looked at me. She couldn't see me in the dark closet, but she knew I could see her. She looked good, standing there naked, but she had a worried look on her face.

There was a third knock on the door. As Molly walked to open the door, she transformed into her sexy mistress persona. I thought about Marvin's warning when it hit me: I needed to record this, so I'd have something on Merlot. Getting video through the louvered door would be difficult, but I could record the audio. I got out my phone.

She opened the door completely naked and said with her Southern accent, "Hiya, Ronnie."

He quickly stepped into the room and closed the door before saying, "I love how you walk around the room without any clothes as if that's how you always are." He removed his shoes, pants, and boxers.

"I like being naked around you, Ronnie. I like watching your dick grow big and hard." Molly had a condom in her hand. She opened the package and rolled the condom onto his penis.

"Where's your boss?"

"He's in his room down the hall," Molly told him.

"I know you fuck a lot of men, but are you fucking Connor?"

"No. I've made it clear to him that I'm willing, but he has no interest in me."

"I knew it. I'm sure he's a fag. He's like other fags I know. They hang around beautiful women, so people think they're straight, but they never fuck women."

Molly laid on the bed and said, "I wouldn't know about that. I've been thinking about you all day. I'm looking forward to the feeling I get when you slide Mr. Ronald into me."

Ronald, still wearing his shirt and socks, got on to the bed. Molly made pleasurable sounds, but I could tell she was exaggerating to make him feel good. My view was disgusting. Seeing Molly's beautiful naked body smooshing with Merlot's grotesque form made me feel terrible. I got it all on my phone. The thought of playing the recording for him later made it only slightly less horrific.

He finished quickly and, looking for a place to discard the condom, he started walking toward the closet I was in before Molly said, "There's a basket behind the desk."

He told her, "I can't believe how energized you make me feel. After I fuck you, I'm ready to take on the world. I wish you lived in Des Moines; we could get together a few times a week. You'd be great for my career. I don't have sex with my wife anymore. Having kids ruined her. She was a great mother, did an excellent job with our kids, but now they're all grown up and gone, I'm left with a dried-up old woman with a loose box I can't stick anything into." He paused a beat, then continued "I've come up with a plan. I'll get you a job with VTM, here in Des Moines. You said your husband can live anywhere in the Midwest, so there's no problem for you to move here. I'll get us an apartment to use for our rendezvous a few times per week."

"That sounds exciting," she told him, "But we've had our house less than a year. We'd lose money if we sold now. I'd still do it for you, Ronnie, but my husband wouldn't want to sell."

"You won't lose money. I'll have the company buy your house. There won't be a realtor fee, the company will pay closing costs, and I'll authorize well above the house's appraised value. VTM pays your moving costs and any closing costs on your new home in Des Moines. Plus, you'll get a nice pay increase. Instead of working by the hour for that fag, Connor, I'll put you on salary. Eighty thousand per year."

"Wow, Ronnie. You can do all that?"

"I can do all that and more. We may even start fucking in my office if you're open to doing that?"

"Oh, Ronnie. I've never fucked a man in his office before, but for you, I would. This is just so exciting."

"I'm excited, too, especially if I can fuck you in my office. I'll get started on this right away. In a couple weeks, I'll send you a written job offer."

"Ronnie, this is so great. I'm going to fuck you in your office every day!"

Merlot had been getting dressed while he talked, and now he was ready to leave, but Molly was still walking around in the nude.

"Molly, watch your email; you'll see a job offer within two weeks."

"What's my new job going to be?"

"I don't know yet. I need to move some people around to create a position for you, but I'll get it done."

With her Southern twang, Molly said, "I know ya will,

Ronnie. You always get it done."

Merlot said, "I need to go, but grab the door for me. I want to watch you walk by."

"Oh, Ronnie," she drawled, walking to the door. She opened it and stood to the side as Merlot walked by, grabbed her left butt cheek and said, "Watch your emails."

Molly closed the door behind him and immediately walked to the closet. I shut off my phone and stuck it in my pocket as the doors opened.

"Connor, are you okay?"

"I'm fine, but I hated it. Seeing you with him was disgusting."

"It was just a fuck," Molly said, "and it was the last time Ronnie will fuck me."

"That's good to hear. You made it sound like you'll go work for him."

"I went along with him, but I could never fuck him again. Did you hear the way he talked about his wife? Ronnie is a crude man."

"So, what are you going to do when you get the offer?"

"I'll ask him a few questions and then wait a couple weeks before I tell him my husband won't even consider leaving Rochester."

"Save the email he sends you," I told her. "It could come in handy down the road."

I thought about telling Molly that I recorded everything but decided against it.

Molly walked to me, wrapped her naked body around me, and gave me a strong hug. Then she stepped back and looked me in the eyes. "I meant what I said before Ronnie knocked on the door. I'm only going to have sex with you and my husband. Tonight was Ronnie's last time."

"Molly, he offered you a huge promotion with a big pay

increase. I thought you'd accept it."

"Connor, you think I use sex to get ahead. I don't. I fuck around because I like to fuck, but I'm not going to fuck my way up the org chart. I want to earn promotions, and you're helping me do that."

"The more I get to know you, the better I feel about you," I told her.

"That's good, but we need to find a way to grow closer without committing adultery. Tonight, we could try short kisses and brief hugs."

"Molly," I said. "At some point you're going to have to admit we're falling in love."

"We are not there yet!"

Molly was in complete denial. She said she loved her husband and would never leave him. "Are we sleeping in your bed or mine?" Molly asked.

"Let's sleep in my bed," I said. "That way if you get tired of me, you can move back to your room."

We went to our separate showers. When I came out, Molly was already under my sheets. I crawled in to join her as she snuggled up next to me. I started to touch her body and she said, "No, not tonight. Let's just cuddle and talk."

"I'd love that." I didn't say anything about it, but I was still seeing images of Molly and Merlot having sex. I was glad she'd showered to wash Merlot off her. I asked her if we would ever have oral sex.

"Maybe someday," she said. "It's not like I've never done it. But all the blow jobs were on men who were distant, not capable of falling in love with me. I definitely wasn't in love with them." Molly was quiet for a bit and then said, "Oral sex with you would definitely be adultery."

"You say things like you 'have feelings for me' or that 'we're emotionally close.' Why can't you just admit we're in love?"

"Because we are not in love. We're close, but we are not in love. I told you: I love my husband. I could never leave him or cheat on him by falling in love with another man."

"What is sex with your husband like?"

"The sex itself is boring, but after he comes, he really makes me feel loved. He holds me and makes me feel so wanted that I just want to have babies with him. I guess that's why I keep doing other men. If I want exciting sex, I fuck them. If I want to feel loved, I fuck my husband. My relationship with you is so odd. You take me out and let me flirt with other men, and you turn me on in public. My husband would never do anything like that. So, you excite me with sex, but I'm also starting to have those feelings for you."

I said, "Would you ever marry me?"

"I don't know. If my decision were based on sex, I'd marry you, but I want more than that."

We lay together in silence the rest of the night.

My alarm woke us at six thirty. We had to be back at VTM by eight. I shut off the alarm and turned to hold Molly in my arms. I pulled her close and looked at her beautiful face. She opened her eyes to me and smiled. Then I said the words: "I love you."

Molly jerked out of the bed and ran to her room. I waited a bit and heard her crying. I walked into her room and saw her crying into a bath towel. Molly whispered, "I can't fall in love with you. I can't."

"We can talk more on the way home," I told her. "Right now, we need to get ready for our meeting."

I went back to my room to shave and brush my teeth. Molly was quicker; I was still getting dressed when she entered my room, dressed, packed, and ready to go. We got to the meeting room ten minutes early. Neither one of us were presenting today, so it was an easy morning. During breaks, Molly was still popular, and she answered a lot of questions. After lunch, we hit the road.

On the drive home, Molly and I debated. A few months ago, I'd been concerned that relations between unmarried, consenting adults was a sin. Now, I was blatantly committing adultery, but the woman I was committing it with didn't believe we'd gone far enough to have committed the sin. I told her that her husband didn't deserve to have her sleeping around with other men. She responded that she'd only been fucking around for fun, that until she met me, she'd never had feelings for anyone but her husband. I said, "There you go again, talking about feelings without acknowledging love."

"We are not in love," Molly said. "I agree that we could be, but we're not. At least, not yet."

"At least not yet?" I asked hopefully. "So, you won't admit we're in love, but you just acknowledged that we will be."

"I said not yet. That isn't a guarantee we will be."

"We can't go on like this," I said. "You need to pick who you're going to be with. Pick your husband or pick me, but you must choose one of us."

"Why can't we just keep doing what we're doing? If we don't make out and we don't have oral sex, I don't think we're sinning. I know we probably shouldn't hug when we're naked, but I like hugging, and it is not as bad as doing things with our lips, which is just too intimate. Using lips makes it adultery."

"I don't get your logic."

"Fucking around isn't adultery. I'm getting tired of explaining this to you."

"Well, I know it's adultery, and I can't live like this. I felt guilty having sex with single women, but now I am knowingly committing adultery with you, and it's driving me crazy."

"So, what are we gonna do?" she asked.

"I'm going to give us another week. If you haven't decided to leave your husband by then, we'll have to break this off, which means you should transfer to another department."

"I can't do that; my career is taking off because of you. If you abandon me, I have to start all over. Plus, I can't leave my husband in a week."

"You don't have to leave him in a week. You just need to commit to leaving him. You can take a few months to make a plan, get your things in order, and then leave him."

"Okay, I have a week to think about it, and I will."

"Think really hard about it. Because I'm not going to keep fucking around with you, committing adultery. I want to get right with God, and I can't do that unless you get a divorce or get another job."

"Why can't we just keep working together, but quit the sexual relationship?"

"Because I'm in love with you. You've cast some kind of sexual spell on me. I want to marry you and spend the rest of my life with you. I want to fuck around with you and do all kinds of sexual things with you. I don't think you realize how much control you have over me. When I look at your bare ass, I'm ready to do anything you want me to. You have complete control over me, and I can't continue to live that way."

Molly immediately unbuckled her seatbelt and pulled her skirt above her waist and pushed her leggings down to her knees. She turned away from me to her side and started wiggling her bare butt at me. I reached over and grabbed her left butt cheek and held on to it.

I said, "This is what needs to change. It's so easy for you to use your beauty and your sexy body to get whatever you want from me."

Molly rolled back into her seat and adjusted her clothing, putting it back in place.

I said, "We won't be able to work together unless we plan to get married."

We traveled the rest of the way without phone calls, and instead of talking about our relationship, we argued about what music to listen to on my satellite radio. I preferred Tim McGraw and Molly wanted to listen to Adele. About 2:30, Marvin called.

"Hello," I answered.

"Hello, Connor, Molly," greeted Marvin.

"Hello, Marvin," said Molly.

Marvin said, "Connor, from now on I want you to always take Molly with you on your Des Moines trips. This is the first time you've been to Des Moines without getting into trouble. I haven't had any negative calls regarding you, and the calls I did get were very complimentary regarding Molly."

I said, "That's good."

"Molly, you did a great job and impressed a lot of people," said Marvin.

"Thank you," said Molly. "Connor's the best mentor I've ever had."

Marvin replied, "Connor is good at that. The two of you make a good team."

"Thanks again," said Molly.

A short while later, we pulled into my garage. Molly had gotten a text from her husband, saying he was home, so she was anxious to get going. Before she left, Molly embraced me for a much longer than normal hug when Clint's voice interrupted us, "Welcome home."

Molly greeted him, got in her car, and backed out of the

garage. Before she left, she opened her window down and said goodbye to both Clint and me.

Clint said, "She seems like a very nice person."

"Not to change the subject, but how was Zeus?" I asked him.

"Zeus has been a particularly good boy. He's sleeping in the backyard."

"He usually greets me when I get home."

"There's so much construction noise in the neighborhood, he most likely didn't hear the garage door open."

Clint and I walked to the backyard. Sure enough, Zeus was sound asleep in the middle of the yard. I called, "Zeus!" and he jumped up, barking happily as he ran to me. He almost knocked me over when he stood on his rear legs and easily put his front legs around my shoulders.

Clint said he had to start his shift soon, so he headed home to change into uniform. As usual, now that I was home, Zeus stuck to me like glue for a couple hours. After supper, I sat down to read, and Zeus went outside to patrol his territory. I went to bed early and slept until Scott Simon and Zeus woke me up the next morning.

I spent Saturday thinking a lot. I listened to Weekend Edition and drank my morning coffee with Zeus in the kitchen while I read the Post Bulletin on my laptop. Then, I decided to get ready for tomorrow; I brought my Bible to the kitchen, where I planned to read tomorrow's Sunday School lesson. But I didn't feel good as I opened my Bible. I was intentionally sinning almost every day, and here I sat with God's word, planning how I was going to tell middle school children how to be good Christians. I was glad that within a week, I'd know where my relationship with Molly was going. I quickly did my lesson prep and went for a walk around Mantorville. When I returned home, I spent the rest of the day reading.

I was up early on Sunday and had breakfast in Rochester before going to church. I felt like such a hypocrite during my class, telling the kids how important it was to follow the same ten commandments I violated several times a week. During class, God woke me up to the true extent of my sins when a small boy asked what 'covet' meant. It hit me like a ton of bricks; I wasn't just rationalizing away the sin of adultery. I was clearly coveting my neighbor's wife.

I explained it to the class, every word I uttered was like a piercing of my soul: "When we want something that isn't ours, and we want it so bad that we are ready to just take it, but we don't. That's coveting. God says it's not just a sin to steal something, but it's even a sin when we want it so bad we think about taking it."

I Should Have Listened to the Angel

CHAPTER 29

I ARRIVED AT WORK EARLY on Monday and made the coffee. Twenty minutes later, Molly walked into my office with the coffee carafe and her mug. She was bubbly and full of smiles. She closed and locked both doors and used her sexy walk to get behind my desk. She kicked her shoes off and then pulled her tight-fitting dress over her shoulders and dropped it on the floor.

"Why are you getting naked?" I asked her.

"Because you make me happy. My career is starting to advance, and it's all because of you. I'm so happy, I just want to stay naked in your office all day."

"I'd like that, but we need to get started on our work for the day. We can leave work early so you can be naked at my house after we get out of here."

Molly walked closer and said, "Naked at your house, that sounds so nice."

We went through the same, patterned motions we'd been doing for weeks. Afterward, she quickly got dressed, but only pulled her dress down to her waist. She wiggled her bare butt as she walked to the table, sat down, and poured our coffee.

"Can I open the doors?" I asked her.

"Yes, go ahead."

"Are you going to pull your dress down?"

"Do I have to?"

"Yes."

She smiled, then stood, and pulled her dress down. That smile created so much desire in me. I still hadn't decided how I could force her decision to choose me or her husband.

I spent most of that day preoccupied, thinking about different scenarios to put her in a position to choose one of us. The best I'd come up with was to send an anonymous letter to him, telling him that his wife was having an affair with Connor Stone. The problem was I couldn't control whether Molly or her husband would open the letter. Then I remembered she got emails from her husband on her laptop, which she left in her unlocked office. It would only take a minute to get on her computer and find her husband's email address. I'd use a phony email account and a library computer to send the message.

As I drove home with Molly following me, I felt confident in my email plan. Although I was confident I could do it, I was also uncomfortable sneaking around and sending it anonymously. I preferred to face things head-on, a style of confrontation that had worked well for me in the past. I wasn't sure what I was going to do, just that I needed to do it soon.

I got out of my truck and was waiting in my garage for Molly to arrive. Zeus was already barking in the house, eager to see who was in the garage. When Molly got out of her car, she was completely naked. She saw the surprised look on my face and said, "You said I could get naked at your house." Then, "I have some good news for you. I've been thinking and praying, and I've come to a decision."

"And what is the decision?" I asked, hopeful she'd chosen me over her husband.

"I've decided it's okay for us to kiss and make out."

This wasn't even the decision I expected to hear, but she was right, it was good news for me. Molly walked up to me and wrapped her naked body around me. She started to kiss me the way she'd "accidentally" kissed me on our Friday walk at VTM. When she stopped kissing, she continued to hold me. Then she started wiggling her butt into my groin. She was moving so hard and fast against me that I was concerned she was going to hurt herself.

"Excuse me," said Clint, standing in the open garage door.

Molly stopped grinding me and turned to face Clint. She smiled at him, "Well, hello, it's good to see you again."

Clint smiled back, "It's always good to see you."

Molly's smile widened, exhibiting her pride in pleasing yet another man with her naked body. Then she said, "I'm going to say hi to Zeus while you men talk." Molly took pleasure being in the nude as she walked by Clint and into the house.

Clint told me, "I always seem to come over at the right times."

"I've noticed. It seems any time a woman gets naked at my house, I can expect a visit from you."

"I can't get over how beautiful your female friends are."

"This one knows how to use her beauty to get anything she wants from me, so I've decided to marry her."

"What?"

"Yeah, I've asked Molly to marry me, but she needs to talk to her husband first."

"Husband?"

"Yes, she's married. I'm committing adultery every time I'm with her," I sighed. "That's why tonight's going to be the last time I have sex with her until she leaves her husband. I told her that by the end of the week, she needs to choose between her husband and me."

"Wow, I could never live like you."

"I can't live like this any longer. I'm living in continuous sin, committing adultery several times a week. Even in my office. And now I'm seriously thinking about stealing her away from her husband."

"Gee, Connor, I always thought you were a conservative Christian who stayed out of trouble."

"I was, until I fell for Molly. Then I started making excuses to explain my sin. Now, I want to get right with God. So tonight," I noticed myself still rationalizing the sins I had every intention of continuing to commit, "is the last night unless she decides to marry me."

"Connor, you're under a lot of pressure right now. If you need someone to talk to, I'm always available."

I thanked Clint as he headed off for home and his night shift. I closed the overhead garage door and entered the house. Molly was sitting on the couch with Zeus.

I asked her, "Do you want to run down to the Hubbell House for a bite to eat?"

"No. I'm not hungry. Let's stay here and fuck around. I only have a few hours before I need to be home in bed."

"What time's your appointment tomorrow?"

"It's at seven, so I won't be too late to work. Say, Connor, would you be a gentleman and get my thong from the car? I'm dripping all over."

"I would be honored to retrieve the thong from your car."

I went back into the garage and found Molly's thong in the backseat of her car. I handed it to her and then watched her stand up and put it on. I knew she intentionally pulled it up her legs slowly just to tease me. I asked her, "Why haven't I seen this thong before? There's hardly anything to it."

"That's because it's not a thong—it's a G-string."

"I'm going to use the guest bathroom," I told her. "You can use mine if you like. Then we can meet on my bed."

Just as I was walking away, Molly's phone rang. She said it was her husband and waved me away. The last thing I heard her say as I went up the stairs was that we were at the Hubbell House getting a bite to eat. Another lie, I thought.

After the bathroom, I took my clothes off in the guest bedroom, except for my boxers, and walked over to my bedroom, but Molly was not to be found. Then I heard someone say "Hello" in the kitchen. It was Adele, singing in the kitchen.

I went downstairs and found Molly, still in her G-string, standing by the kitchen island, looking at a magazine. I asked her why she didn't come upstairs. Molly held up the magazine and asked, "Why do you have a magazine full of bikinis?"

I said, "That's from the same company that sells me your thongs. It's their swimsuit edition."

"Come over here and look at some of these."

Molly and I stood at the island and looked at several pictures of models in bikinis. Molly wanted to know which ones would look good on her. "Finally, I said, "Molly, with your body, you're going to look good in any bikini."

"Thank you, but I need to find one that my husband will approve of."

"Well, what does your husband like?"

"My husband likes to see my boobs and my kitty all covered up. I've never told you this before, but on our honeymoon, I was wearing a bikini that showed everything. I liked it, and so did every man except my husband. He didn't like the way everyone was looking at me. He asked me to put something else on. To this day, he does not want me dressing sexy in public."

"I don't understand how you have been able to fuck around and not get caught by your husband."

"My husband has led a sheltered life. He'd never consider fucking another woman, and he doesn't even think about me fucking another man."

"How many times since you got married?"

"I quit counting at a hundred."

"Wow, that's much higher than I expected," I told her.

"Well, it wasn't that many men. I did a number of them more than once and it was just fucking. You're the first man I've had feelings for since I fell in love with my husband."

I said, "Let's go upstairs." We walked together to the stairway, but I let Molly go in front of me as we walked up the steps. I loved watching her butt move back and forth, especially when her butt cheeks were bare. As we reached the top of the stairs, I grabbed the string waistband of her G-string and let it snap back in place.

We entered my room, and Molly jumped onto the bed and didn't get under the covers. She was lying in the middle of the bed with her legs spread wide.

I looked at the small patch of fabric between her legs. "There's not much to your G-string."

"I know, but some of the guys I used to fuck liked to see me in it because it's skimpier. From now on, only you and my husband will see me in a G-string."

As Molly slipped out of her G-string, I stripped off my boxers and joined her. Molly crawled on top and started to kiss me. I couldn't believe how good she kissed; I wished we'd done this from the start. Then it hit me: I could do something tonight that would force Molly to tell her husband about us.

We made out for a long time before Molly asked, "Will

you eat me out tonight? My husband never has."

I told her I'd like that, and she said, "Wait here. I need to use the bathroom first."

As the door closed behind her, I got out of bed and was startled upright to see an angel standing there. It appeared suddenly, out of nowhere and looked like the angel from the hardware store when I was young. This time I wasn't afraid of it. It was obvious why it was there; I'd almost expected the angel to get involved. After all, adultery was a bigger sin than stealing.

I asked, "Are you my grandma's angel?"

"Yes. I watch over your grandma." We were talking the same way we did almost forty years ago. I could hear the angel, but its lips didn't move. Likewise, I didn't open my mouth, but it heard what I thought.

"Why does Grandma have her own angel?"

The angel said, "I'm not here to explain my work to you. I'm here to tell you to stop your sin and to abandon the plan you just came up with."

I said, "I need to force the issue to stop the sin."

"If you go through with your plan, it will alter the course of the rest of your life."

Just as the angel finished talking, I heard the bathroom door open. I couldn't see Molly because the angel was standing in front of her.

Molly said, "Wow. Connor, where are you? I can't see anything; it's all fuzzy in here."

I walked through the angel to Molly. It was like walking through an air curtain, but instead of air blowing over me, it felt more like a shower of static electricity. As Molly spoke, I looked back, and the angel was gone.

Molly said, "Now I can see you. For a moment, the room was a big blur. I couldn't make out anything."

I put my hands on her hips before sliding further down and grabbing her bare butt cheeks.

Molly said, "Let's get on the bed. It's been almost ten years since someone's eaten me. I wanna relax and enjoy it."

She lay on her back in the center of the bed with her head touching the pillow but not on the pillow. Then she spread her legs wide. I lay down between her legs with my head in front of her kitty. I slid my hands under her butt, Molly's ass felt so good in my hands. I was in heaven, and I could have stayed in that position all night. I started my performance and Molly was enjoying this, as evidenced by her louder and louder moans of pleasure.

Her moans grew increasingly louder. Then, she freaked out, but I kept going. She started to scream stop, stop, and so I stopped.

Molly lay back to relax. I still had my hands under her butt and didn't want to move them, so I lay my head on her kitty. That made her jerk. She was still coming down from her high.

Finally, she lay back to relax. Since this was the first time we'd had oral sex, I didn't know if she'd want to make out. But I realized that now was the time to execute my plan. I expected the angel to appear at any moment, but it didn't, so I started kissing Molly on her neck. She was still aroused as I started to kiss her neck passionately and continuously, and she began her pleasure noises anew. Then she stopped me for a moment, "Be sure you don't give me a hickey."

"I won't."

I didn't reveal that I'd already strategically placed several hickeys on both sides of her neck and a few on the back of her neck. They were good hickeys and would still be dark red when her husband got home on Thursday. I'd executed my plan and was prepared to confront her husband.

When I stopped kissing her neck, Molly started kissing me on my mouth. We made out for half an hour before Molly announced she had to leave. I prayed she wouldn't use the bathroom and see herself in the mirror, and she didn't. As we walked down the stairs, Molly stopped on the first landing, looked me in the eyes and said, "Tonight we did everything I said I'd never do with you. I just want you to know that this is the first time I ever cheated on my husband."

Molly and I walked to the garage, and I watched her stand outside her car to get dressed. Thrilled at this newfound permission to kiss, we made out for a couple more minutes before she left. I knew she was going to be mad tomorrow; I just hoped I could steer her in the right direction.

Hickeys

Chapter 30

I GOT TO WORK AND made the coffee. Molly was at her eye exam, so I drank my coffee alone.

Around nine thirty, I saw Molly enter her office, then march right back out towards me. She wore a sweater with a high collar to cover the hickeys. She closed both doors, came behind my desk and said, "Do you have my phone?" I gave her the phone she'd left at my house and reached out to touch her.

She jerked back. "Don't even think about fingering me. What am I going to tell my husband? What were you thinking?"

"Tell your husband that Connor Stone gave you the hickeys. That you're having an affair with Connor, and you want to marry him."

"I haven't made that decision. I love my husband. I want to have babies with him."

"Are you going to leave your husband?"

"No."

At this point, I knew I should've listened to the angel. The two of us stood there, staring at each other.

Molly glared at me, "So what am I supposed to do? You fucked my whole life up."

"You always said you liked to fuck around."

"Yes, but without my husband knowing. You left me no choice; I have to tell him about you. But I don't know how he'll react. He may kick me out of our house."

"You can move in with me."

"No, I want to keep my husband."

"We have a meeting in the main building in fifteen minutes," I told her. "Do you want to ride with me like normal, or do you want to drive in separate vehicles?"

"I'll ride with you, but I need a couple minutes to get ready before we leave." Molly went to her office, and I sat at my desk thinking about what everyone would say when word got out about Molly and me.

On our drive to the meeting, Molly told me she'd only tell her husband about me—not about the hundred other times she'd fucked someone else since they'd been married.

I parked my pickup in the main office lot, but before we got out, Molly said, "Last night, I told you it was the first time I cheated on my husband. That's the truth. Other than my husband, you are the only man I've loved. But that's over. I'm no longer in love with you. I need to concentrate on keeping my husband. That means no more fingering in the office or hugs or kisses. We're over."

"I wanted you to choose, and you have. I don't like your decision, but I will respect it."

"Thank you. I just wish you hadn't given me these hickeys."

"I wish I hadn't either, but at the time it seemed like the thing to do. I didn't expect you to choose your husband. You were so passionate last night, and when you said that we could kiss and make out, I thought for sure you'd choose me."

"I was in love with you last night, but I'm not anymore. When I saw the hickeys in my bathroom mirror, I immediately felt the pain my husband is gonna feel when he finds out

I had an affair with you. He's been so loyal to me, and now I'm going to hurt him."

"When are you going to tell him?"

"He gets home Thursday afternoon. I'll tell him when I get home on Thursday."

"How are you going to tell him? Are you going to show him the hickeys right away?"

"I don't know. When he called last night, I told him I was with you. He'll figure out you gave me the hickeys, so I'm just gonna tell him I made a big mistake, one I'll never make again. Then I'll ask him to forgive me."

"We need to get inside. We're already late."

The meeting went fast. Molly and I went back to our building. I sat at my desk with both office doors closed. I felt like I needed to do something, but I didn't know what. Finally, I got up and opened my doors. Molly was sitting at her desk, staring at a blank wall. I told her I'd be gone for a couple hours. She smiled goodbye but didn't say anything.

I drove to the main building and went to Hank's office.

Hank observed, "This is going to be very serious."

"It is," I said. "I need to talk to you, and I don't want to do it here. How about we take an early lunch?"

Hank, ever the understanding big brother, said, "Sure, Connor, I'll drive."

We drove downtown and parked in a ramp by one of Rochester's newer hotel restaurants. Hank said he'd been here once before and that they had a nice, quiet dining room. I hadn't said anything about Molly during our drive, but after we placed our orders, I said, "Hank, I've been having an affair with a married woman."

Hank said, "Molly Dew?"

"It's that obvious?"

"Last Friday, Howard said he was sure you were fucking

Molly in Des Moines. I was going to talk to you after work yesterday, but you left early."

"It didn't start in Des Moines; it has been going on for a while. It drove me crazy that I was committing adultery every time I was with her. I told her we couldn't keep doing this, that she had to choose her husband or me. I wanted the sinning to stop one way or another. Last night, I gave her a bunch of hickeys on her neck to force her choice; she chose her husband. She's really mad at me and plans to tell her husband she had an affair with me. So, in addition to dealing with her as an angry ex-lover, I also have to start looking over my shoulder for an angry husband."

"When are you going to tell Mom and Grandma?"

"I haven't even thought about that," I sighed. "I do need to tell them before they hear it on the street."

"Have you asked God for forgiveness?"

"I can't. I have no right to ask. I knowingly committed adultery over and over again."

"That's why Jesus died on the cross for us. It doesn't matter if it's one sin or many. If you repent and ask, you know Jesus will forgive you."

"I don't deserve forgiveness."

"I can tell you're remorseful. You need to express that to God and ask Jesus to forgive you."

"Hank, I know you're right. I just can't do it."

Our salad was served, and we quit talking for a while.

When we started our main course, I told him, "Grandma's angel tried to stop me."

"What?"

"Yes. And it wasn't the first time the angel appeared to me."

I told Hank about the angel in the hardware store when I was fourteen, how I listened in the hardware store but didn't listen to the angel last night. I gave all the details and then Hank said, almost scared for me, "I can't believe you ignored the angel's warning and then walked through it."

I replied, "The thought of having sex with Molly for the rest of my life was overwhelming. Lust controlled my mind; I coveted her so much that I tried to steal her."

"Connor," he told me firmly, "You need to get right with God."

"I know, but I don't deserve it. Every time, I did it fully aware. I knew I was sinning, and I did it anyway."

"You know," he said thoughtfully, "I don't believe you committed adultery. You certainly sinned. You're single, and she's married. Molly was the one committing the sin of adultery. Your sins were coveting her and stealing."

"I don't agree. I know many Christians agree with you, but I feel that as long as one of us in a sexual relationship is married, then both people are adulterers."

"Well, it doesn't really matter who's correct. In either case, you sinned equally, and you need to get right with God."

We finished lunch and on the way back to work, Hank continued to encourage me to repent and ask for forgiveness. I continued to resist. When we walked back into the lobby of Hank's building, Gloria told me Debra wanted to see me. I said goodbye to Hank and headed for Debra's office.

I walked into Debra's office and greeted her, and she replied by motioning me to sit at the table. Then, she got up from her desk and closed all the doors before speaking, "Molly was just in here and had quite a bit to tell me."

"And what did Molly have to say?"

"Connor, be careful how you respond to me," Debra cautioned. "Molly said that you agreed to give her a raise and help advance her career in exchange for sexual favors. She told me that she had sex with you at your house last night, and she showed me hickeys on her neck that she claims are from you."

I thought for a moment and then decided to do a Bill Clinton. So, I said, "I'm speaking to the director of human resources when I say I did not have sexual relations with that woman." Then I said, "I'm speaking to a close friend when I say that I have had consensual sexual relations with Molly Dew for a few months."

Debra replied, "Why is Molly trying to make it sound like it was not consensual?"

"Well, she told me she was going to show her husband the hickeys on Thursday when he returns home from a trip. She also told me she'd admit to our sexual relationship and ask him to forgive her. Now, it sounds like she's changed her mind, and that she's going to tell her husband I forced her to have sex with me. That way she's a victim and doesn't have to ask him for forgiveness."

"Why did you give her hickeys?"

"Because I was tired of committing adultery every time I had sex with her. I wanted to force her to confront her husband and choose between him or me. I didn't anticipate her making a complaint to HR."

"Well, you know the drill. I already sent her home for the rest of the day with pay. She'll return to work tomorrow. I'm suspending you with pay until we complete the investigation."

"Oh, Debra, come on."

"Connor, you haven't left me any options. You know that."

"I know, I just don't know how to officially respond to the complaint. If I go on the record and tell the truth, I'll immediately be terminated. You won't have any other choice."

Debra said, "You need to go to your office and get your laptop and anything else you need and then go home. You can't come back to the MTI campus until this is done."

I asked, "Have you told Marvin?"

"Not yet."

"Marvin's going to give up on me. I've caused him a lot of trouble."

"After you leave my office, I'll tell Marvin and then call Merlot. Do I have to remind you not to have any communication with Molly?"

I considered telling Debra about Molly and Merlot having sex in front of me in Des Moines but decided that now was not the time to bring it up. I told her, "I won't contact Molly and I'll go home and lay low. I will not contact anyone at MTI. If I receive a call or an email, I will handle it properly."

"Connor, I will do everything I can to help you, but we both know it's going to be hard for you to survive this."

"I know. I'm glad you're in charge. I could really use a hug right now, but I can't ask you to do that in this fishbowl."

I stood up and headed for the door.

As I put my hand on the doorknob, Debra said, "Wait."

She got up from her chair, walked to me, and embraced me with the greatest, wholly-encompassing hug I'd ever received. When she released me, she wiped tears from her eyes and said, "You need to leave."

When I returned to my office, Molly's car wasn't in the parking lot, and her office door was closed. I quickly packed my computer and placed any files on my desk into the computer bag. I didn't want to talk to anyone, so I immediately left and drove home.

I arrived home and noticed Clint outside, in his yard. I walked over to Clint's to take him up on his offer to listen.

"You're home early," he greeted me.

"Yeah. I was just suspended from MTI."

"Why?"

"Molly made a complaint against me. She told HR that I required her to have sex with me in exchange for me helping advance her career."

"Why would she say that?"

"Because the plan I executed last night backfired on me."

I went on to tell Clint everything that happened last night, minus the angel.

When I finished talking, Clint asked, "Hickeys?"

"Yeah. Things didn't work out as planned."

"Nevertheless, you're no longer committing adultery."

"That's correct, so I guess part of my plan worked."

"Well, Connor, Molly sure seemed to enjoy being naked around you whenever I saw her. I believe I only saw her once with clothes on. And last night, I couldn't believe how aggressively she was grinding her bare ass into you."

"Clint, someday I'll tell you all my Molly Dew stories, but right now, I need to come up with a way to convince MTI that Molly is lying. The hickeys are not helping me."

"What are you going to do?"

"I'm going to go in the house and pray."

"Okay. I'll see you later."

I walked into the house and said hi to Zeus. Then I went to my bedroom, knelt by my bed, folded my hands, and started praying. I prayed for different things I wanted God to do to help me, but mostly I talked with God about all the stupid things I'd done. I "apologized" for everything I'd done wrong, but I didn't ask Him to forgive my sins. After about an hour, I stood and began thinking about how I was going to tell Mom and Grandma.

I went down to the kitchen to get something to drink. I opened the fridge and grabbed a beer, but before I opened it, my phone rang. It was Ben Walker.

"Hello, Ben."

"Hello, Connor. I see that both you and Molly are gone. Are you going to be back this afternoon?"

"We're not together. Molly will be back tomorrow. I've been suspended because of a complaint made by Molly. I can't say more than that. You should talk to Debra about things going forward."

"Oh, Connor, I'm so sorry. Can I do anything to help you?"

"Thanks for the offer, but I don't need anything right now. Just keep your head low and don't get caught up in this."

"I'm fairly sure I know what this involves. I can't help thinking that my wife's warnings saved me from being the one suspended."

"When you get home tonight, give your wife a special hug. She cares about you, and she has protected you."

"I will. Take care of yourself, Connor."

"I will."

We said our goodbyes and I reached for the beer, but the phone rang again. It was Brian Schmidt.

"Hello, Brian."

"Hello, Boss. Where are you?"

"I'm at home. I was suspended today because of a complaint made by Molly Dew."

"Oh, Boss. I know you can't talk about it, but it's pretty obvious what it's about. She was all over you, but the guys never expected you to get in trouble."

"What do you mean? What guys?"

"Several guys at MTI started a pool, just like for football. We bet on which MTI man would get taken down by Molly Dew. We all knew it was just a matter of time, but nobody bet on you. Everybody thought you were too smart to fall into her trap."

"I wasn't smart enough, and I'm still in the trap."

"Let me know if I can help you with anything."

"Thanks." We said our goodbyes and I put the beer back in the fridge and called Hank. I wanted him to hear about the suspension from me.

I told Hank about the suspension, and he got really upset. Not with me, but with Molly. Hank said he'd "talk to Debra" and hung up.

About thirty minutes later, Hank called me back. He told me Debra had agreed it wasn't fair, but that I was in trouble no matter how I handled it. Repeating what Debra had told him and what I already knew, Hank re-hashed: "If you admit to having an affair with Molly, you lose your job for sleeping with an employee who happens to be married. If you continue to officially deny any sexual activity with her, then her story gets more believable because of the hickeys.

"Then Debra told me that Merlot told her to fire Connor with no severance. Marvin feels the same way as Debra, that there's no way out of this for you. She hasn't heard what Nathan thinks." Then he said, "Debra decided not to do anything until Molly talks to her husband on Thursday night. So, Friday morning, after Debra talks to Molly, she'll make a decision and run it up the flagpole."

The Video

CHAPTER 31

I GOT UP AT MY normal time on Wednesday morning. I didn't shower. I got dressed and took a one-hour walk through Mantorville. I didn't stop at the County Seat because I didn't want to answer questions about why I wasn't at work.

I called Hank and asked him to stop by so I could give him something but said I didn't want to discuss it over the phone.

A couple hours later, we were drinking coffee in my kitchen when I gave him a USB drive.

"What's this?" Hank asked.

"It's a video of Ronald Herbst fucking Molly Dew."

"How did you get this?"

I told Hank about the adjoining hotel rooms, the closed door, and me hiding in the closet. Then I said, "The video quality is poor, but the audio is good."

"How do you want me to use this?"

"I think you should call Merlot and tell him that if I'm terminated, you think I deserve a normal severance. Play parts of the audio for him to hear. Tell him that if I don't receive a good severance, the video goes online."

"Merlot will want the thumb drive."

"He's not going to get the drive. Plus, I have a copy on the cloud. Tell him I'll keep both copies and not release them as long as I'm treated fairly."

Hank held up the drive, "When I listen to this, will I just hear a bunch of sex sounds, or do they actually talk?"

"They talk a lot. There's enough on there to cause Merlot to lose his job and his marriage. He'll freak out when you play some of it for him."

Hank stood up and said, "I'm going to take care of this as soon as I get to the office."

"Thanks. Things haven't changed since we were boys. You're still getting me out of trouble."

"That's what big brothers are for." He gave me a hug and left to go back to the office.

That night, Hank called to tell me how he'd handled it. After returning to work, he'd listened to the recording right away and realized it held multiple reasons for Ronald to prevent its going public. Hank didn't waste any time taking action, hearing it made him realize Merlot could lose his job and his marriage. Then, he'd gone home to call Merlot's mobile number. Hank told him he wanted to make sure I received a fair severance payment if I got fired. When Merlot laughed, Hank told him about the video. Merlot had scoffed, "Fuck you, Hank, I've never had sex with Molly Dew, so there's no such video." Then Hank played the recording and told him I had it on thumb drive, backed up to the cloud.

Apparently, Merlot had then backtracked, "This just shows I had consensual sex with Molly. I didn't rape her like Connor did." But when Hank played the segment where he mocked his wife and offered to set up Molly in Des Moines, Merlot went silent before saying, "What does Connor want?" Hank told him I wanted a fair severance, which worked out to around sixty thousand, but that he felt I deserved more because I was basically being fired for having consensual sex, since Molly was lying.

When Merlot said that even if I hadn't raped her, I'd still had sex with a married woman who worked for me, Hank had replied, "My grandma would say that's the pot calling the kettle black." Hank told Merlot he could come up with the severance amount, as long as it was a lot higher than sixty. But when Merlot said he wanted the file destroyed, Hank told him what I'd promised—to not release it online if I was treated fairly.

After I thanked Hank, I called and asked Mom and Grandma to meet me for coffee together tomorrow morning. I told them only that I'd been suspended from my job and that I wanted to share the details with them tomorrow. They both had questions, but I told them I'd explain everything in-person.

Thursday morning, Grandma poured coffee into three cups. I began by apologizing to Grandma and Mom for the bad reputation I created for the family. Then I said, "I've been suspended from my job because I had a sexual relationship with a married woman who worked for me."

Mom said, "Oh, Connor."

Grandma said, "How could this happen?"

"After Debra and Julia broke up with me, I got close to the young woman who worked for me in my new job. We started having sexual relations on a regular basis. After a while, I asked her to leave her husband and marry me."

Mom said again, "Oh, Connor."

I continued, "When we were together this past Monday, I put a lot of hickeys on her neck, knowing they'd force her to tell her husband about me. I wanted the confrontation because I didn't want to continue committing a sin whenever I was with her. But my plan didn't go the way I wanted. She decided to stay with her husband and no longer wants a relationship with me."

Grandma asked, "Has she told her husband yet?"

"No, he's on a trip and won't be home until tonight. That's when she plans to tell him. She originally told me she'd tell her husband that she had sex with me and then ask him for forgiveness. However, yesterday she told Debra, who's now in my old position as HR director, that I forced her to have sex with me in exchange for me helping her career advance."

"Is that what she's going to tell her husband?" Mom asked.

"I don't know. She keeps changing her story."

Grandma asked, "What does Debra think?"

"Debra has no choice; she's going to have to terminate me tomorrow."

Grandma said, "Have you confessed your sins and asked for forgiveness?"

"Hank keeps telling me to do that, but I can't. I knowingly sinned over and over again. I can't ask God to forgive me. I don't deserve it."

Mom said, "I can see you regret what you did. You need to confess and ask that your sins be forgiven. Then seek the Lord's help."

Grandma said, "Connor, throughout your life you've helped many people. Now you need to help yourself by listening to your mother."

"I'm sorry, I just can't."

"Well," Grandma said, "Even though you're not ready, we can still pray for help."

Grandma and Mom prayed with me then. And I knew they wouldn't stop praying until it was all over. They both gave me warm hugs before I went home.

On my drive home, I was overwhelmed with uncertainty, so I called Debra for an update. She told me it was likely I'd be terminated tomorrow because Marvin was concerned Molly was setting the company up for a lawsuit.

Once home, I went back upstairs to keep praying. Zeus had started praying with me. While I knelt on the floor with my arms on my bed, he'd lie on the floor a few feet from me, keeping his head up and staring at me.

I prayed for over an hour before I had to stand and stretch. Since Tuesday, every time I prayed, I thanked God for everything He'd done for me. Then I asked for help to get through this. I tried not to be too specific when asking for help, because I'd learned over the years that things went better if I let God work out the details instead of me. But admittedly, I was still asking God to "fix" the problem for me so I could avoid the repercussions. Throughout the afternoon and evening, I prayed several more times. I saw no way out of my situation. I should have listened to the angel.

DINGER

CHAPTER 32

IT WAS FRIDAY MORNING AND Zeus was making his time-to-get-up noises, but I didn't sleep much last night. All I could think about was the trouble I created for my family. Molly's ass wasn't worth the embarrassment Mom and Grandma would suffer when news of my termination got out. I stayed in bed as long as I could, thinking about what I'd do for a living now that my career at MTI was over. Milk Trucks Inc. had been my life for decades. I had no desire to work somewhere else. And the way things were ending at MTI, nobody was going to want to hire me.

At ten, I got up and got dressed. Made some toast with peanut butter and ate in the living room while I watched videos on my laptop until two. Then I heated up some soup for lunch and sat in the kitchen for a while. After I finished the soup, I took a nap in the living room until four.

I was sitting at the kitchen table, thinking about my life when Zeus sensed my despair; he walked over and put his paw on my knee, trying to comfort me. He was always there for me. I started to cry, and Zeus started to whine. I got down and gave Zeus a big hug and he wrapped his front legs around me. Then the doorbell rang.

I got up and looked through the laundry room entrance

window, I saw Clint and another officer I didn't recognize.

I opened the door and Clint said, "Hello, Connor, can we come in?"

"Sure."

Clint introduced the other officer as Deputy Roy Dinger. I held out my hand to shake hands with Deputy Dinger, but he ignored my gesture and walked by me into my kitchen.

I invited both of them to sit and have some coffee.

Clint said, "Actually, I need to leave, but Officer Dinger can sit down with you."

I said, "What's going on?"

"Last night, we dispatched two deputies to a Mayo emergency room in Rochester. Molly Dew was there with her husband, claiming that she'd been raped."

"Oh God!" I exclaimed. "What happened?"

Clint responded, "She wasn't claiming that she was raped last night, she claims you raped her on Monday night."

"You've got to be kidding."

"I wish I were, but I'm not. The reason Officer Dinger is here from Yellow River County is that you know everyone in the Mantorville County sheriff's department. Our sheriff recused himself and the entire department from this investigation. In addition, the county attorney and the judge have recused themselves and won't be involved in your case.

"The sheriff over in Yellow River has agreed to do the sexual assault investigation, and he's assigned Officer Dinger to lead the effort. Mantorville County deputies will assist in the investigation, but Officer Dinger is in charge. Before the officer questions you, I need to leave because I will most likely be a witness in this case."

I just stood there, speechless. The woman I wanted to marry was now accusing me of sexually assaulting her. I should have listened to the angel.

Finally, I asked Clint, "Are you and I going to be able to talk to each other going forward?"

"We can always talk in general terms," Clint said, "just no specifics about the case. After I'm questioned by Officer Dinger, I'll tell you what I said to him."

We said goodbye and Clint left the house.

Then, Officer Dinger began, "Molly Dew claims she was in your home this past Monday."

"That's correct."

"Did you have sexual relations with Mrs. Dew that night?"

I didn't respond right away. I'd never heard anyone refer to Molly as Mrs. Dew. Then I thought about the question. At work, I officially said I didn't have sex with her. I thought I should be consistent and say the same thing here. But everyone at work knew that I really did have sex with her, and I'd already told Clint about Monday night.

"Mr. Stone," he asked again, "did you have sex with Mrs. Dew on Monday night?"

"I'm sorry, I've never heard Molly called Mrs. Dew before. But to answer your question, we did have sex on Monday night."

"In what room did the sexual activity take place?"

"In my bedroom."

"Did any sexual activity take place on the couch in the living room?"

"No, all the sex took place in my bedroom."

He asked, "Did you show any pornographic pictures to her that evening?"

"No, I've never shown her any pornographic pictures."

"Did you tell her that you were infatuated with her ass?"

"I don't recall using the word infatuated that night, but I've told her something similar on many occasions."

"Did you force her to have sex with you?"

"No."

"Did you push her down on the couch and penetrate her?"

"I didn't force her to do anything. And what do you mean when you say penetrate?" I asked him.

"Did you use your tongue to penetrate her vagina and perform oral sex on her?"

"I did use my tongue for oral sex, but that took place upstairs on my bed."

"Did you take her phone from her?"

"No."

"Did you bring her phone to work on Tuesday morning?"

"Yes, because she forgot it at my place."

"Did you prevent her from making a 911 call on Monday night?"

"No."

Dinger started to ask the next question, but I interrupted him and asked, "Do you think I should get an attorney?"

Dinger replied, "Do you think you need an attorney?"

I thought to myself for a moment and said, "We're done, I'm going to get an attorney. You can leave now."

Dinger said, "I don't think so." Then he took his cellphone from its holster and punched in a number. When he spoke, all he said was, "Send in the troops."

Over the next few minutes, four more sheriff's cars appeared in my driveway. Six more deputies, including Clint, now stood in my kitchen.

Dinger said, "Connor Stone, I have a warrant, and I'm placing you under arrest. You'll be charged with twenty-seven counts of sexual assault."

"Twenty-seven counts?"

Dinger said, "Yes, twenty-six times in your office plus last Monday. You're a sexual predator, and I'm going to put you away for the rest of your life."

"What do you mean twenty-six times in my office?"

Dinger said, "We found twenty-six women's panties in your desk at work. Mrs. Dew said you kept the panties as trophies each time you assaulted her. I'm sure her DNA will be on the panties, giving me twenty-six pieces of evidence for each piece of ass you compelled her to give you."

"You've got this all wrong," I said, shocked.

Dinger said, "No. You took advantage of a woman half your age. You're a bigshot at a big company. You folks think you can fuck anyone you want, but no more. I'm taking you down, and you're going to stay locked up until they carry you out of prison in a casket."

I looked at Clint, and he said, "Connor, there's a lot happening right now, but after you get an attorney, they'll straighten everything out."

Dinger said, "There's nothing to straighten out. This is a slam dunk case. He's a sexual predator, and I'm putting him away."

Clint said to Dinger, "You're in charge of the investigation, but the deputies assigned to help you still report to me. We're going to make sure this is a fair and thorough investigation."

Dinger said to Clint, "Then get to work. Start bagging every item listed on the search warrant."

I said, "Search warrant?"

Dinger said, "Yes, we're going to gather the evidence we need to take you down."

The deputies started putting cushions from the couch in plastic bags. Other deputies took bags upstairs to gather more items.

Dinger said, "Let's get him in cuffs and chains so we can take him for a ride."

Clint said, "I'll take care of the cuffs and chains when we

get to Yellow River. I'll be driving him."

Dinger countered, "Standard procedure is to cuff and chain any prisoner being transported."

Clint said, "I'm in charge of transportation, so I'll make the decisions regarding cuffs and chains."

I asked, "Why can't I go to the Mantorville jail? Why do I have to go to Yellow River?"

Dinger said, "Because I want complete control of you, and besides, you have too many friends in Mantorville County."

It was time to call my big brother, so I picked up my phone from the table. Dinger said, "No phone calls!" and tried to grab my phone but didn't get it. Then he pushed me down over the table and pulled my hands behind my back so he could put handcuffs on me.

Zeus didn't like this, and he lunged for Dinger. Dinger reached for his gun, but Clint stepped between Zeus and Dinger. Clint grabbed Dinger's gun-hand away from his holster.

Clint commanded, "Don't pull your gun unless it's needed."

Dinger replied, "The dog was attacking me."

"You deserved to be attacked," Clint told him. "You don't start roughhousing a dog's human in front of the dog. It's only natural for a dog to protect its human."

Dinger said, "If we were in Yellow River, that mutt would be dead right now."

Clint looked at me, "Connor, we need you to pack up your medications to take with you."

I asked, "How long will I be gone?"

Dinger snarled, "The rest of your life."

Clint said, "Three nights. You should be able to post bail on Monday."

Clint had one of the deputies accompany me upstairs to

watch me pack my meds.

We came back downstairs, and Clint said to me, "Let's head over to Yellow River. I'll watch Zeus until you can post bail, and I'll make sure the house is locked up after this team is done."

I said, "I don't like the idea of leaving Zeus at home while Butch Cassidy is still here."

Dinger gave me an evil look, and Zeus started growling at Dinger again.

Clint said, "You're right, Connor, Zeus will come with us."

As I was getting in the car, Clint handed me my phone and said to make as many calls as I wanted. Dinger heard him and gave Clint a glare.

Clint then walked to the other side of the car and opened the door for Zeus. He was so happy to be able to jump in and lie down next to me. I was happy because I didn't have to worry about Zeus being shot.

The Yellow River County Jail is about an hour's drive from Mantorville. My first call was to Hank, who couldn't believe I was being charged with assault. Hank said he'd let Mom and Grandma know what happened. I told him Clint would take care of Zeus.

My next call was to Debra. She said she and Marvin had just met with the sheriff, who'd briefed them and explained Yellow River County would lead the investigation. Debra asked me about the panties found in my desk. I told her I'd explain the rest later but did tell her that the investigator believed each panty represented a sexual assault. I ended by letting her know the out-of-county investigator was determined to put me away for life.

I asked Clint if I'd be able to make calls from the jail. He said, "You won't have access to your cellphone, but there's a phone available to the prisoners. You'll have to call collect, and you can't make collect calls to cellphones."

"Okay," I said, deciding not to make any more calls until I got things straightened out. "Why did Dinger keep saying I was going away for life?"

"Because he's charging you with twenty-seven counts of sexual assault, and each count can have a prison term of up to twenty-five years."

"Oh God!"

Clint said, "Just make sure you get a good attorney."

"Right now, I can't afford a bad attorney."

"I'm sure your family will help you."

"I don't want their help. I've caused all this trouble, and I need to straighten it out myself."

The rest of the drive, I just sat quietly and prayed. Zeus lay quietly beside me, but every time we slowed down, he'd lift his head to see out the window. As we turned to the entrance leading to the jail, Zeus looked out, and then jumped up and started barking at another German Shepherd leaving the building with its officer. The officer and the dog got in their car and drove off. Zeus stopped barking but stayed alert.

As Clint slowly drove through the parking lot, he told me that the prisoners would be done with supper by the time I was processed. He said my first meal in the jail would be breakfast tomorrow morning.

Our car came to a stop in front of the jail building's doors. Clint said, "Before we go in, I need to get you chained up."

I nodded.

Clint got out of the car and started to walk around to my side. I tried to open my door for him, but I couldn't. It finally began to sink in: I was a prisoner; my door could only be opened from the outside. Clint opened the door, and I got out. Zeus wanted to follow me, but I told him to wait in the car for Clint. I stretched out my hands to Clint so he could handcuff me. Next, Clint dropped down on one knee and put a leg iron around each of my ankles, which were now connected by a chain, just like the handcuffs. He finished by connecting the two, ankle and cuff-chains, with yet another chain.

Clint stood, opened the front passenger door to grab my bag of meds, and then took my phone from me to add to the bag. "Let's go in," Clint said.

I started to walk but almost tripped over before I said, "It's not easy to walk like this."

"That's the idea."

The Jail

Chapter 33

We walked inside and turned left to go down a short hallway. We came to a closed door where Clint pushed a buzzer. An officer opened the door and said to come on in. Clint had some papers in his shirt pocket that he took out and gave to the officer.

Clint started removing the chains and cuffs he'd just put on me. Apparently, they were no longer necessary in this secure room. He gathered up all the hardware, then told me that if everything went as planned, he'd pick me up Monday morning for my court appearance in Mantorville. Clint said goodbye to both me and the officer who was now in charge of me.

The officer now turned to me, "Empty everything in your pockets onto the counter."

I had two quarters and my wallet. The officer asked, "Is that everything?"

"Yes."

He started emptying my wallet and filling out a form, listing each card and ID I had. Then, he looked at me and asked, "Any cash hidden in your wallet?"

"No. I seldom carry any cash with me."

He added my meds and phone to the list.

He slid the form over to me and told me to review it. The items listed were correct, so I signed the form and handed it back to him.

Next, he pointed to a corner of the room and said, "Go over there and take your clothes off."

I did as instructed. As I was undressing, I saw that what I'd thought was a closet had a drain in the floor. I must be going to take a shower. Once I was naked, he walked over and held open a plastic bag. "Place each item of clothing in the bag."

After all my clothes and my boots were in the bag, he set it on a chair and pulled two rubber gloves from his shirt pocket. He saw from my questioning look that I had no idea what was going to happen next. He put on each glove with a final tug, snapping each one just like they did in the movies. Then, he smiled before saying, "Cavity Search. Step forward and open your mouth."

I moved forward and opened my mouth wide. He stuck his gloved finger behind my lower lip and in front of my lower teeth, running his finger from one side of my mouth to the other. He repeated this behind my upper lip before having me hold my mouth wide open as he used a flashlight to look deeper into my mouth. Obviously, he found nothing behind my lips or anywhere in my mouth.

Next, he looked behind and in each of my ears.

Then he said, "Lift your arms up." There was nothing under my arms.

He knelt on one knee in front of me. He used his hand to move my balls from side to side, making sure I didn't have anything wedged between my balls and my leg.

He then checked between my toes, and I thought we were done, but I was wrong.

"Turn around and bend over," he said, "Use your hands to

pull your butt cheeks apart."

When he stuck his finger in my asshole, I was startled and let go of my butt cheeks. He didn't like that and yelled, "Keep those butt cheeks spread apart!" I felt his finger in my ass again. After a moment, he twisted his finger around, feeling for anything I shouldn't have in my ass. When he pulled his finger out, he said, "Stand up and turn around."

As I turned around, I could see that the pointer finger on his right hand had a brown stain on it. This was the same finger he'd put in my mouth. I was relieved that he did things in the order he did.

He pulled the gloves off his hands by grabbing the wrist end of the gloves, so they came off inside out. After throwing both gloves in the garbage, he said, "Get in the shower and be sure to use both the bar soap and the shampoo. I'll be watching to make sure you do."

I started to wonder if it'd be better if the officer were a woman. I hadn't showered with a man this close to me since my days of college hockey. I got in the shower, and he stood there, a couple feet from the shower opening. I shampooed my hair first, then I used the bar soap all over my body. I reached to shut off the water, but he said, "Use the bar soap on your body again."

"Again?"

"Yes," he said. "God only knows what you people bring into this jail."

Nobody had ever referred to me as "you people," and I didn't like it.

The officer said, "When you finish rinsing off, use the towel on the wall hook to dry off."

I finished drying off and wrapped the towel around my hips. The officer yelled, "Leave the towel on the hook and come on over here to get dressed."

I walked toward him, and he said, "Step to the side and stand on top of the mat on the floor."

I did as he said. He came out from behind the counter carrying a canister with a handle on it, like a flower sifter. He said, "Don't breathe while I disinfect you."

"What do you mean?" I said.

"I need to kill the lice on you and any other insects or germs you have," he replied.

He held the sifter above me and started squeezing the handle. White powder showered down on me. I kept my mouth and eyes shut, but I could feel the powder collecting on my skin. When he stopped squeezing the handle back and forth, I waited a while before opening my eyes. When I did open them, he was standing in front of me with a different device; it looked like the hand pump bellows I'd use to blow air on a fire.

He said, "Now we need to spray the areas I couldn't get to. Move your feet apart to spread your legs."

I did this, and he knelt and pointed the device toward my balls. He started pumping, and white powder sprayed out on to the bottom of my balls and back toward my asshole. Then he had me turn around and spread my butt cheeks apart. He sprayed my butt crack, then under my arms, and then told me to walk around on the mat so the white powder would get on the bottoms of my feet. I was absolutely covered with the white powder disinfectant; I felt like a steer being prepped for the county fair.

Then I heard someone in the hall punching the keypad to unlock the door. The door opened and in walked a female deputy. She glanced at my white naked body and was not impressed. She didn't even take a second look at me. She talked to the male officer for a little bit and then left.

The officer said, "Come over here."

I walked to the counter where he'd laid out jail clothes: gray socks, matching gray boxers, a gray T-shirt, an orange jumpsuit, and orange sandals. I got dressed and looked in the mirror. I'd never imagined anything like seeing myself in a prison uniform. I'd thought the deputy sticking his finger up my ass was bad, but seeing myself in an orange, jail-issued jumpsuit was worse than the finger. I should have listened to the angel.

The officer said, "I'm going to take you to your pod. Except for meals, your first twenty-four hours must be spent in your cell. After that, you'll be free to leave your cell and spend time in the dining area whenever you want during the day."

I asked, "Is there a phone I can use?"

"Pay phones for collect calls only are near the cells on both cell levels. No collect calls to cellphones."

I said, "How can I make calls if I'm locked in my cell for twenty-four hours?"

"During your first twenty-four hours, you can make short calls after your meals, on your way back to your cell."

"How about visitors?" I asked.

"You can have visitors between eight and five after your first twenty-four hours."

I remembered preregistering to visit Jim Rollins, so I asked, "Do my visitors have to pre-register?"

"No," he said. "This is a county jail, not a prison. Anyone can visit you if they pass through our security check. Now, enough questions. Let's go to your pod." He opened the door and we both walked into the long hall down to the cell area. "Stay to the left," he told me, "Always stay to the left when going down these halls."

We came to another intersection and turned right so we stood in front of a door. An officer on the other side of the

HR: Behind Closed Doors

door saw us through the window and buzzed us in. This wasn't like the doors at work that had a buzzer that made noise when the latch was released by an electric magnet. The buzz I heard in the jail was the sound of the deadbolt screwing back and forth into the doorframe itself.

We walked into the cell pod, a large room about the size of a basketball court. I looked around and saw doors to cells around the perimeter. The room was extremely high ceilinged to accommodate a second floor of cells above the ground-level cells. One side of the room had several tables with attached benches. I assumed they didn't use chairs because chairs could easily become a weapon.

The officer who let us in greeted the officer behind me, "Hello, George."

George replied, "Hi, Buddy."

Buddy said, "So, is this our rapist."

George confirmed, "Yes. This is inmate Stone. He's all yours." George turned and left the pod.

Buddy looked me over, "Well, you're our most violent prisoner. I'm warning you right now. You better not give me any shit, because I'll give it back much worse." Buddy was over six feet tall and probably weighed four hundred pounds. I didn't say anything. Then he pointed, "The guys sitting over at those tables are watching TV. The tables on the other side of the room are where you'll have your meals. For your first twenty-four hours, you'll stay in your cell except for meals. After that time, you can spend time in this room or in your cell. You're on the second level. Head over to the stairs across the room."

I started walking toward the stairs with Buddy walking behind me. As we crossed the room, we got the attention of the men watching TV. They all checked me out as I did the same to them. Except for one guy who looked over forty, no one else was even nearing thirty.

"Hey, Grandpa," one of younger guys hollered, "what'd you do?"

Another one yelled, "Yeah, Grandpa, why are you here?" I didn't respond.

Buddy said, "Looks like you have your jail name, Grandpa."

The young men, dressed in orange jumpsuits like me, watched as Buddy and I took the steps to the second level. The staircase and its top landing were both steel. The walkway around the top was open and circled the room so you could still see into all the cells from the bottom floor.

"Come on, Grandpa, what'd you do?" another one hollered.

We walked by several cells and I heard a buzz on a door up ahead. Buddy said, "Go into the cell that buzzed."

I pushed on the door and walked in. It wasn't like the jails in movies. There were no bars separating you from the other cells. All four walls were solid concrete blocks. There was only one small window, in the steel door. The cell was about eight feet wide and about twelve feet deep, smaller than my smallest bathroom at home. There were bunk beds against the back and a toilet and sink along the side wall.

"You'll be locked in here until breakfast tomorrow morning."

"Is someone else assigned to this cell with me?"

"Not yet," Buddy replied. "Right now, you have it all to yourself." He pointed to a toothbrush and toothpaste on top of the sink, "Those are for you. Do you take any meds before bed?"

"Yes."

"We'll unlock your door in about two hours. When you hear that, come down to the control counter in the middle of the room. We'll have your meds at the counter."

Buddy left the cell, and a few seconds later, I heard the deadbolt buzz into position. I looked through the little window and saw an officer standing behind the counter in the middle of the room. From my elevated position, I could see all kinds of buttons and switches on a board in front of the officer. I assumed that was where they locked and unlocked cell doors.

This was the first time in hours that I'd been alone. I lay down on my bunk bed and fell right to sleep.

The sound of the deadbolt woke me, and I went downstairs to the counter to get my meds. A deputy I hadn't yet seen was behind the counter. I asked his name, and he said Frank. He placed two cups on the counter; one had my name on it and contained all my nighttime meds. The other was water. I grabbed both and started walking away.

"Hold on, Grandpa," said the deputy. "Swallow all of them in front of me."

I set the water down and reached into the other cup to pick out the first pill. The deputy said, "Take them all at once."

"I'll probably choke," I told him. "I'm used to taking one at a time at home. Also, you have two big pills. My doctor changed the prescription to one of those at night, but I'm using the pills I have before I refill the prescription and get the new dosage label on the bottle."

"We go by the instructions on the bottle. Now, quit playing with the pills and take 'em all at once right now."

"I don't know if I can."

"Take them right now or Buddy will push them down your throat in the morning."

I didn't want to upset Buddy, so I poured all the pills into my mouth and took a big gulp of water. I didn't have any trouble and realized I could start taking them all at once.

Frank was still staring at me when he said, "Buddy talked to Dinger; he says you're going away for the rest of your life. He also said he's going to shoot your dog."

I just stared back at Frank, not saying anything. I was utterly helpless and now afraid for Zeus.

Frank said, "Get back to your cell, Grandpa."

I hid my face as I walked to the stairs; I didn't want anyone to see me crying. Zeus was going to be shot because he'd protected me.

On my way back to my cell, I saw a payphone on the wall up ahead and called directory assistance to get the number for Clint's landline. Shelly answered and accepted the collect call. I asked for Clint, and she said, "Clint's working, Connor, can I help you with anything?"

I told her, "One of the deputies at this jail just told me that Dinger is planning to shoot Zeus."

Shelly said, "Clint was worried about that, so he brought Zeus to your mother's place. Zeus will be with her until you get back home."

"I'm so glad to hear that."

"Get back to your cell, Grandpa," Frank yelled as he came toward me on the walkway.

I told Shelly, "I need to hang up. Thank you for taking care of Zeus." Then Frank grabbed the handset and hung it up.

I said, "I was told I could make calls on my way back to my cell."

"I don't give a shit what you were told. Get the fuck back in your cell."

I stood there silently, just looking at him.

Frank said, "Go ahead, take a swing at me. I'd love to finish you off right here."

HR: Behind Closed Doors

I turned around and went to my cell. Frank went down to the control counter and hit the button to lock my cell door.

I took off my jumpsuit and went to bed.

Once again, I woke to the sound of the deadbolt. I got up and brushed my teeth before peeing in the bedside toilet. Then I washed my hands, got dressed, and left my cell. All the inmates were sitting at the tables, waiting for breakfast. I asked one guy if breakfast was a buffet. He laughed before sitting down with some other guys. I walked over to a table with only two inmates and asked if I could join them. One replied, "We don't have reserved seating here."

Just then, a worker pushed a cart to the seating area and started handing trays to each person. Scrambled eggs, sausage, toast, and hash browns. It looked good and tasted good. I was halfway done with my eggs when a big inmate walked up behind me and put his hand on my shoulder. I turned around, looking up to see a familiar face. He said, "Do you remember me? I'm in here because you fired me."

I remembered firing him for threatening another employee with physical harm. I opened my mouth to reply when he interrupted me, "Just shut up and give me your breakfast. I'm a lot bigger than you, and they give us all the same breakfast."

I looked over at the counter and saw Buddy watching me, smiling. He knew what was happening, and he was going to let it happen.

I handed my tray to the big guy. He didn't say anything, just took my breakfast and ate it.

I looked back to see Buddy still smiling at the control board.

Since I didn't have anything to eat, I went back up to my cell, but on the way, I made a collect call to Hank's landline. He was home and answered. "How are you doing?" Hank asked.

I said, "I'm doing okay for being in jail. Did you know that Mom's taking care of Zeus?"

"Yeah, she called me after Clint dropped Zeus off at her place. They're both doing fine."

"Good. The Yellow River investigator is telling people he's going to shoot Zeus. Since he has no reason to go to Mom's place, Zeus should be okay."

Hank said, "I checked with the jail, and they said you could start having visitors tomorrow morning. Grandma and I are going to skip church so we can come visit you."

"I hate to put Grandma through the ordeal of visiting me in jail."

"You getting arrested really energized Grandma. She's interviewing attorneys right now. She wants to make sure you have a good one."

"I was going to look for an attorney after I post bail and get out of jail."

Hank replied, "Grandma is relying on advice she received from a friend who's a retired Rochester police officer. He told her that you should be represented by an attorney at your hearing."

"Are you sure I'm going to have a hearing on Monday? I was told by Clint that the judge recused himself, since the judge and I know each other."

"Yes, your hearing's scheduled for ten-thirty, Monday morning at the Mantorville courthouse. The hearing will be presided over by a judge from another county via video conference."

I said, "Hank, I don't know what I'm going to do. I only have access to a few thousand dollars, and I'm behind on my mortgage payments. My credit rating is terrible, so no attorney is going to work for me on credit."

Hank replied, "Grandma is taking care of the attorney, and I can help with the bail."

"I really screwed up this time. I'm accustomed to getting in trouble but not legal trouble. Now the whole family is being sucked into my problems. Dinger wants to shoot Zeus and put me away for life. I sinned, and I didn't listen to the angel. Everyone would be better off if I spent the rest of my life in prison."

"Have you repented and asked for forgiveness yet?"

"No. I just don't deserve it."

"Well, Grandma is going to ask you about it tomorrow, so please pray about it."

"I will. I need to go. I'm getting the evil eye from one of Dinger's buddies. In fact, the guard's name is Buddy. I have to hang up. See you tomorrow."

Buddy was still staring at me after I hung up. I went into my cell, and Buddy locked the door. I lay on my bed, praying and thinking for the next four hours.

Paul

Chapter 34

I HEARD THE DEADBOLT RETRACT and got up. I hurried down the stairs for lunch, hoping to get my tray fast and eat as much as I could.

My hopes were dashed when I saw they hadn't started serving yet. I sat down at one of the empty tables. The big guy I had terminated was already watching me. I just stared into the table.

"Can I join you?" I heard someone say.

I looked up to see it was the second-oldest guy I'd seen when I arrived last night. "Sure, have a seat," I told him.

"My name's Paul. What's yours?"

"Connor. Connor Stone."

"I've been here for two weeks; how long do you plan to be here?"

"I'm hoping to post bail on Monday, so two more nights."

"Why are you in here?"

"I had sex with a married woman. When her husband found out, she said that I raped her."

"Buddy's telling everyone you're going away for life."

"That's because Buddy's friend, Deputy Dinger, is charging me with twenty-seven counts of sexual assault."

"Twenty-seven?"

"Yes, because I had twenty-seven intimate encounters with the woman."

Paul asked, "Do you have a lawyer yet?"

"No, but I'll have one before my hearing. My family is finding an attorney for me."

"I hope they get you a good one. You have a lot at stake."

I asked, "Why are you in here?"

"I didn't pay the fine or comply with other requirements that were part of my sentence. I recently got my third DUI conviction."

"I'm sorry to hear that. I have friends and family who struggle with alcoholism. Do you have a plan for when you get out?"

"My wife is looking at different programs I can enter after my release."

I said, "A good program is just as important as a good attorney."

Just then, our lunch trays were placed in front of us. A few seconds later, the big guy was standing behind me, his hand on my shoulder. I turned to look up at him as he said, "Give me your lunch."

I started to lift my tray to him when Paul said, "Put the tray down, he's not taking your lunch."

The big guy looked at Paul and said, "You mind your own business, or I'll beat the shit out of you."

Paul responded, "I've killed three men with my bare hands. I'll be happy to make you my fourth."

The big guy said, "What the fuck! When did you kill three men?"

Paul said, "In the army when I was with a special forces' unit in Iraq. Now, get away from here so we can eat our lunch."

The big guy turned away and walked over to another table,

where he sat down with his own tray. I looked over at Buddy, who was staring at the big guy. Buddy had seen everything but didn't understand what had happened. I looked back at Paul and asked, "Three men?"

Paul said, "It was only one, but I find it to be more intimidating when I say three. I was with army special forces for three years."

While we ate our lunch, Buddy walked over to talk to the big guy. When they finished, Buddy stared at Paul for a while before returning to his control counter.

I told Paul, "Buddy doesn't like me, and now he doesn't like you."

"Buddy's not what I'd call a good cop," Paul sighed. "I'd stay out of his way and not challenge him on anything."

"I'm already careful around him. He seems to be focused on me. I think he's been talking to Dinger, the investigator assigned to my case."

"Why is this Dinger giving you trouble?"

"Dinger was rough when he tried to handcuff me in my kitchen, so my dog tried to protect me and lunged at Dinger. So, he wants to send me away for life, and he wants to kill my dog."

"Well, being in jail is a safe place for you. There are cameras everywhere, and Buddy knows it. He won't do anything to you unless you give him a reason to. Keep your distance from him."

Just then, Buddy came by and saw I'd finished eating. "Okay, Grandpa, time to go back to your cell."

I stood and asked him if I could get a pen and paper. He asked, "What are you going to write?"

"I plan to take one of the Bibles from the bookshelf to my cell, and I want to be able to make some notes."

"You can see Bill over at the control counter" Buddy told

me. "He can issue you some paper and a pencil. We don't hand out pens."

"Thanks." Then I looked at Paul and said, "See you at supper?"

Paul said, "Sure."

Looking at Paul, Buddy said, "Looks like Grandpa has a friend."

Paul just smiled before getting up and crossing the room to watch TV.

I got several sheets of paper and a short pencil from Bill at the control counter. On my way to the stairs, I picked out a Bible and then headed for my cell.

I entered my cell and closed the door. Bill immediately locked the deadbolt, the sound of which was starting to annoy me. I looked out my window and saw Bill looking up at me, so I waved to him. He didn't acknowledge my wave, so I sat on my bed and started reading.

After an hour of reading and not taking any notes, I decided to give my eyes a rest. To bookmark my place in the Bible, I picked up the paper, but noticed it was only blank on one side. The opposite side had printing I could see was a portion of a bank statement. Three of the four sheets Bill gave me were from the same bank statement. I didn't understand why a person's bank statement was being used as scratch-paper in a county jail.

I positioned the pieces together and was surprised to see it showed the owner's name, address, phone number, account number, routing number, and account balance—all details a criminal would love to have. This didn't make any sense. I placed the papers in the Bible and stood up to stretch before I began reading again. Eventually, I fell asleep until five thirty, the deadbolt screw woke me up. It was time for supper, so I headed downstairs and sat with Paul.

"Did you get some reading done?" Paul asked.

"Yes, but I'm still looking for answers."

"What are the questions?"

"Before I can talk about it with you, I need to know if you are a Christian."

"Yes, I'm a sinner and a Christian."

"Great, you'll understand where I'm coming from. I've been reading about repentance in the New Testament. Trying to determine what's expected of me. I've repented in the past for other sins, but when I committed the sin of adultery, I knew what I was doing before I sinned, intentionally. I accepted Jesus many years ago. I know He's the only way to heaven, but I realized today that in addition to accepting His salvation, Jesus expects us to repent from our sins. So, tonight, even though I feel I don't deserve forgiveness, I'm going to repent and ask him to forgive the sins I knowingly committed."

Paul said, "That's good. You'll be able to move on with your life."

"Well, that's part of what I must do to move on. While reading, I came across another important thing I need to do. At first, I skipped over the Lord's Prayer; I've prayed it thousands of times and have it memorized. However, after I skipped it, I felt an urge to go back. So, I read it slowly, thinking about each word. When I got to the part where Jesus talks about asking for forgiveness, it hit me hard: He follows our seeking forgiveness with 'as we forgive those who trespass against us,' and I'd completely ignored that part. I realize now I need to forgive the woman who falsely accused me."

"Are you going to?"

"I am, but when I forgive her, I have to be sincere. I can't just say the words. So, I have to pray for God to help me get to that place."

"Are you going to forgive her before or after your trial?"

"I don't know."

Our dinner was served. Paul and I were the only ones at our table. I asked him about his family and Paul reluctantly told me that he and his wife had three children: a daughter in grade school and two sons in middle school. I could tell he was uncomfortable talking about them, so I changed the subject and asked if he'd used the scratch-paper here. Paul said, "Yes."

"My scratch-paper was the back side of someone's bank statement. I don't understand why documents with sensitive information would be used for scratch-paper in a jail."

Paul said, "The papers I looked at were medical records from a clinic. I asked a few questions and learned that a shredding company contracts with the jail to have inmates shred the documents."

"My company uses a shredding service," I told him. "All the papers to be shredded are in heavy canvas bags with a lock on the bag. The shredding company claims they take the bags to a central shredding facility. I think their customers would be surprised to learn the central shredding facility is a county jail."

"That's for sure. I was assigned to shredding last week. The shred-company driver unloads all the bags, then unlocks the bags and dumps the paper into a large bin. We grab the papers from the bin to run through a big shredding machine. The deputies come in whenever they need more scratch-paper. They go through the bin and pull out any one-side-printed papers to cut into scraps for us to use."

"That's crazy," I said. "Can you imagine someone being arrested for identity theft and then being let loose in the shred room with all those documents?"

"I don't get it either."

Frank came to our table, "Well, Grandpa, you're at twenty-three hours. You need to go back to your cell for an hour, then you can come back down until bedtime."

Paul went to the TV area while I headed up to my cell, where I lay in bed and started speaking to God: "Dear Lord, I committed adultery and coveted. I knowingly did both and don't deserve forgiveness. Your word says to repent our sins and ask for forgiveness and that's what I want. Please forgive me. I committed terrible sins, and I am truly sorry. Please forgive me. I'm so grateful You died on the cross for me and all sinners. Lord, thank you for forgiving me. Please help me to be strong so I can face any temptations. Please help me get through all the trouble my sins have caused. And please take care of my family. I thank you so much for them. In Jesus's name I pray, amen."

After a bit, the deadbolt buzzed, and I went downstairs. It was eight p.m. so I walked to the control counter and took my meds. Everyone had to go to their cells at ten thirty, so I had some time to watch TV. I sat next to Paul as we watched two sitcoms. Neither of us found anything funny to laugh at. Halfway through the second show, after a commercial, my picture was on the screen. Everyone started yelling, "It's Grandpa, it's Grandpa!"

The announcer said, "Rochester businessman arrested for sexual assault. Connor Stone, an executive with Rochester-based Milk Trucks Inc., was arrested Friday and charged with twenty-seven counts of sexual assault. News at ten."

Everyone turned to stare at me. Then the questions started. "Did you rape twenty-seven different bitches?" "You're too old to fuck that many times!" "How many women did you rape?" "Were they hot?"

Paul told me, "Don't say anything."

I wanted to leave, but I just had to see the full story at ten. Every time a commercial came on, I received more questions, but I took Paul's advice and didn't answer. Finally, it was ten o'clock and the news started. I was the lead story.

My picture stayed on the screen as a reporter spoke: "After over two decades with Milk Trucks Inc., Connor Stone's employment was terminated after he was charged with twenty-seven counts of sexual assault. Most of the assaults allegedly occurred in Stone's office at MTI. Some of the assaults are alleged to have occurred at his house in Mantorville. All the assaults involved the same victim."

The screen changed to a video of a reporter talking to Dinger. "Officer Dinger, you're from Yellow River County. Why are you leading the investigation in the Connor Stone case?"

Dinger responded, "The Mantorville County sheriff requested that Yellow River County oversee the investigation because Mr. Stone has relationships with most officials and officers in Mantorville County. Officers from Mantorville will assist in the investigation, but I will be in charge."

"If Mr. Stone is convicted of all twenty-seven counts of sexual assault, what would his sentence be?"

"If found guilty, he would spend the rest of his life in prison," said Dinger.

The reporter said, "It's my understanding that most of the twenty-seven assaults took place in Mr. Stone's office at MTI. How could this have happened?"

"There were actually more assaults," Dinger said, "but Mr. Stone is only being charged for the assaults for which we have physical evidence."

"What is the physical evidence?"

Dinger replied, "The victim's underwear. You see, Mr. Stone required the victim to wear skirts or dresses to work most days. Each morning, she'd go to Stone's office, where he'd require her to remove her underwear before he'd assault her for his own gratification. When he finished, Stone kept her panties as trophies; he'd give her a thong to wear back to work."

"Oh my God, that's horrendous."

"The whole case is horrendous; I've never worked on anything so outrageous before."

The inmates all began glaring at me with disgust. Then the meal-stealing big guy spit, "You're fucked up!"

Paul repeated, "Don't say anything."

On-screen, the reporter asked, "Is it true that Connor Stone made his German Shepherd attack you?"

"Yes. During the arrest, Mr. Stone sicced his dog on me. If another officer hadn't stopped the dog, I would've put it down right there. The law enforcement team had to lock the dog in a squad car so they could complete the arrest and collect evidence."

The reporter asked, "Is the dog a danger to the public?"

"Yes. The dog has already attacked a law enforcement officer, and we have reason to believe the dog could attack anyone it's afraid of. We're in the process of getting custody of the dog so we can put it down."

"Thank you, Officer Dinger."

The station went to the next story while my heart started beating faster and faster. I had only twenty-five minutes before I had to be in my cell. I went upstairs to collect-call Hank.

"Hello, Connor," said Hank.

"Hank, I just saw Dinger on the news saying he's going to put down Zeus because he's a public danger!"

"Yes, Dinger tracked down Zeus to Mom's house, and he went there to take him."

"Oh no! Is Mom okay?"

"Yes, Mom's fine. It's a good thing that Dakotah was visiting Mom when Dinger arrived." Dakotah is my widowed sister in-law, James's wife. "The girls were all visiting Mom, too, so the girls took Zeus into the house when he started growling at Dinger. Dinger got all worked up, and tried telling Dakotah that Zeus would hurt the girls. Well, that was enough for her to order Dinger off the property; he had no legal right to be there in the first place, so he left. Then she got Sheriff Hanson on the phone and got him to promise he'd order Dinger to stand down regarding Zeus. But to play it safe, she, Mom, Zeus, and the girls went to Dakotah's farm to stay until you're out of jail. Dakotah took a few days off, so she'll be with Zeus twenty-four seven until you're home."

I sighed in relief, "Thank God Dakotah was there with Mom."

"Yes, that worked out well. Oh, I almost forgot to tell you about Grandma."

"Is Grandma okay?"

"Yes, she's fine. I told you she was really getting involved in your case. Now she, along with Dakotah, have basically declared war. She'd narrowed attorneys down to two but couldn't decide. Well, after hearing from Dakotah about Dinger, Grandma retained both attorneys."

"Two attorneys?"

"Yes. They're married to each other, and they usually work alone, but they told Grandma they'd work together on your case."

"Who are they?"

"John Sullivan and Emily Larson."

"I've heard their names before."

"Yes, they're in the news a lot. Grandma's police officer friend told her they're some of the best criminal defense attorneys in the country."

"This sounds expensive."

"Grandma doesn't care about the money. She knows Molly Dew is lying, and she is prepared to spend what it takes to prove it. She's selling some stock, so she'll have five hundred thousand dollars available later next week."

"Half a million!?"

"Yes, but she's only giving the attorneys one hundred thousand to start. And that's not all. Julia contacted Grandma to see how the attorney search was going. When Julia found out they wouldn't get paid until Thursday or Friday, she immediately wired fifty thousand to them, to arrive first thing Monday morning. Julia doesn't want the attorneys worrying about payment; she wants them to know you have plenty of money behind you."

"Oh, God! I'm causing so much trouble for my family and friends."

"It's good your family and friends are coming together to help you. You're giving everyone a common goal. The people who love you are going to take care of you."

"Are you and Grandma visiting me tomorrow morning?"

"Yes. We plan to be there at ten. Will we have a room where we can talk?"

"No, it's more like a booth where we're each on opposite sides of a glass wall."

It was almost ten thirty, and another inmate waited to use the phone. I said, "Hank, I have to go. I'll see you in the morning."

"Okay, bye."

I hung up and went to my cell. The door closed and the deadbolt slammed into place.

That night, I lay in my cell with my eyes open, thinking about Zeus, Dakotah, and Mom. I realized that despite my terrible behavior, God was still taking care of me. He'd made sure Dakotah, a strong woman not afraid to stand up to someone like Dinger, was at Mom's farm when Dinger had arrived.

I felt better now that I'd struggled through repentance and finally asked for forgiveness. But now I knew I faced another challenge. I needed to honor Jesus's instructions in the Lord's Prayer. I needed to genuinely forgive Molly Dew. I got out of bed and knelt down, leaning against the bed with my arms on top of it, just like at home.

"Dear Lord, I'm coming to you for help with this. I don't like forgiving Molly for what she's done to me, but I know you've already gone through so much more. You died on the cross for us, to save all humans from the consequences of our sins. You're asking so little of me compared to what you did willingly. Jesus, please grant Molly a good life. May she and her husband have a good marriage going forward. I loved Molly and she loved me, but I'm ready to move on. She totally betrayed me, and is still lying about the assault, but I forgive her for that. I truly do. I only want the best for her. Please give Molly a good life. In Jesus's name I pray, amen."

With that difficult task behind me, I felt better. And I was looking forward to seeing Hank and Grandma in the morning. This would be my second night in jail, and I still had one more to go. I fell asleep right away.

Cellmate

CHAPTER 35

THE DEADBOLT STARTLED ME AWAKE in the middle of the night. The door opened, the light came on, and in walked an officer I hadn't seen before. He said, "Just stay in bed, you're getting a cellmate." The officer told the new guy, "Go to bed. I'll get your toothbrush in the morning."

The officer left and I said hi to my cellmate.

He said hi back and started to undress. I rolled over so my back was to him as I closed my eyes to think how my life just changed for the worse again. I'd taken my private cell for granted. The toilet was right next to my bed. Last night, I got up to pee twice, and toward morning I took a shit. If I repeated that tonight, I'd be sitting on the toilet with my cellmate hovering above me. If he used the toilet, he'd be right next to me. When I heard him peeing in the toilet, I decided that going forward, I'd pee sitting down so I didn't make as much noise. Then I felt his urine splatter hitting the bald spot on the back of my head. I twisted around so my feet were at the end of the bed next to the toilet.

Two hours later, I had to pee. I rolled out of bed and sat on the toilet, peeing as quietly as I could. I decided not to flush because of the noise. I got back in bed with plans to flush the toilet if I heard my cellmate getting out of his bed.

The deadbolt woke me up at seven. I got out of bed, got dressed, and noticed my cellmate lying in bed with his eyes open. I asked him if he'd been in jail before and he said no. I told him, "Last night was my second night. When the door unlocks, it's time for breakfast. Just letting you know." I picked up my Bible with the scratch-paper and pencil, flushed the toilet, and headed downstairs. On the way, I passed a deputy delivering a toothbrush to my cell. After breakfast, I planned to watch TV until Grandma and Hank got here; I'd brought the paper and pencil so I could take notes when we met.

Paul sat down at an empty table, and I joined him. I said, "I got a cellmate last night."

"What's his story?"

"I don't know. We haven't talked much. I just know it's his first time in jail."

"Is he coming down for breakfast?"

"I don't know. I told him about it. When I left the cell, he was lying in bed with his eyes open, looking at the ceiling." My cell door opened, and I saw him emerge. "Here he comes."

Paul turned to look. "He's a big guy."

My cellmate was in his twenties, was about six foot two and roughly three hundred pounds. I said, "He doesn't have to worry about anyone taking his breakfast."

"Looks like he can take care of himself," Paul confirmed.

I waved at him, and he came over and sat down with Paul and me.

I said, "This is Paul. My name is Connor."

"My name's Cody."

Three breakfast trays were placed in front of us, and we started eating as I told Cody he'd have the cell to himself for a few hours. I was going to stay downstairs until my visitors arrived.

Cody said, "They told me I could only leave the cell for meals today."

I said, "Yes. Tomorrow you can stay down here after breakfast."

Paul asked Cody, "Why are you in here?"

Cody said, "I beat up a guy who was hitting on my girl. He went to the hospital, and they brought me here."

I asked, "When do you appear in court?"

"Tomorrow, so I should have only one more night here."

I said, "I appear in court tomorrow, too, so this should be my last night as well."

Cody asked Paul, "So what's your story?"

Paul replied, "I have a few weeks to go. I'm here because I've had too many DUIs."

Cody gave me a questioning look and I responded, "I had consensual sex with a married woman. When her husband found out, she said I raped her."

Cody replied, "So you have the most to lose."

I said, "Yes."

Buddy and Bill were both at the control counter, watching us. When Cody, Paul, and I finished breakfast, Buddy walked over and told Cody to get back to his cell. I told Cody I'd see him at lunch.

I walked to the TV area with Paul, who asked, "Have you learned any more about your dog?"

"I talked to my brother last night and learned that Dinger tried to take Zeus from my mom, but my sister-in-law was there and stopped him. Zeus and my mom will stay with my sister-in-law until I get back home."

Paul observed, "You keep saying sister-in-law. Where's your brother?"

"My brother, James, died in Afghanistan. He was in special forces like you, except James was a Navy Seal. He died in combat, but we don't know much more."

Paul and I sat down to watch Sunday morning sports shows. Two hours passed before it was almost ten o'clock. When I asked, the officer at the control counter told me an officer would get me when my visitors arrived.

At a few minutes to ten, an officer entered the pod and then took me to the visitor area. Hank and Grandma were already in the booth. I was locked into my side of the booth. Grandma and Hank looked good, and I could tell they were excited to talk to me.

"I'm sorry you have to visit me here."

Grandma said, "I'm just glad we can visit you. I thought I'd be able to hug you, but they told us this is as close as we can get."

"They have very strict rules here," I told her, "But at least we get to visit."

Grandma got right to business, "I don't see this so much as a visit. More like a meeting. We have a lot to go over."

"We can talk about anything, but we shouldn't discuss strategy here," I said. "And we shouldn't discuss Zeus. Our conversations are recorded, and we don't want Dinger or the prosecuting attorney to know our strategy or anything about Zeus."

"I understand. I'll be careful. Hank said he told you about the attorneys?"

"Yes. Hank said they're Larson and Sullivan, they're married, and they're good."

Grandma explained more. "They're married, and they make a good team. I can tell that he can be very intimidating when the time calls for it, and the people I spoke to all claim he's extremely thorough and never leaves anything to chance.

She's incredibly wise, and I believe she can read minds. She answered every question I had before I asked it."

"When will I get to meet them?"

"Emily will be with you in court in Mantorville tomorrow. John has a hearing with another client in Rochester then, but both he and Emily will meet with you on Tuesday morning."

"Do we know what's going to happen tomorrow?" I asked.

"I'll let Hank explain tomorrow's schedule."

Hank told me, "Clint picks you up at nine, so you'll get to the courthouse about twenty minutes before the ten-thirty hearing. Emily will meet with you beforehand and stay with you until Clint takes you back afterward."

Grandma said, "The hearing's where the judge sets the bail amount. The bail bondsman I retained will issue the bond to the court."

Hank told me, "When Clint takes you back, he can't wait for the bond to process, so I'll pick you up here in Yellow River after you're released. Debra wants us to go directly to your office so she can officially terminate your employment and you can pick up personal things from your office."

I said, "I don't want to run into Molly when I go to my office."

Hank replied, "Molly will not be there."

Grandma said, "There are more things we can discuss when we're not being recorded. But right now, I want to know what's most important—where you're at with God. Have you repented?"

"Yes, I repented last night and asked for forgiveness. I also realized I needed to forgive Molly Dew, and I did that as well."

Grandma was overjoyed. "That is such good news! I thought I'd need to preach to you all morning."

"I'm glad I repented," I told her. "I feel refreshed and renewed, ready to take on the world."

"That's good," said Hank, "because the world is coming after you. A Facebook group full of a bunch of Karens from Mantorville is saying terrible things about you, dragging you through the mud. They believe everything Dinger says about you and Zeus. I don't recognize any of their names, so I think it's just people who don't know you."

Grandma said to Hank, "Tell Connor about the graffiti."

"Oh yeah, when Clint got home from his night shift at three this morning, he saw someone spray painting your house. He chased them a couple blocks on foot and caught them. It was a thirty-five-year-old woman. I don't know her name, but she was arrested."

"What did she write?" I asked.

"It said 'A pervert lives here'."

"It sounds like things will be different for me in Mantorville."

"Don't let it get to you," said Hank. "Like I said, the only people doing this stuff are all people who don't know you."

At that moment, an officer knocked on the glass to let us know our time was up.

Grandma spoke, "I'm so glad you repented. I kept praying you would. Now I can concentrate my prayers on your trial."

"Thank you, Grandma." I told both of them, "See you tomorrow morning." The officer was waiting, so I waved goodbye to Grandma and Hank and started walking back to my pod, thinking about the graffiti and the negative Facebook group. I was looking forward to getting out of jail, but not to going back to a community that'd turned on me.

When I returned to the pod, everyone was heading to the lunch area. Paul asked about my visit, so I updated him on everything I'd learned from Grandma and Hank. Cody joined us. While we ate, Paul told Cody and me how things would go for us tomorrow. We'd be issued a razor and shaving cream. After we returned the razor, they'd issue us fresh clothes. I was surprised to learn I wouldn't wear my own clothes to court. Paul explained we'd go to court in jail-issued orange jumpsuits wearing all the chains we'd had before.

I spent the afternoon in bed reading, until about three, when I went downstairs to watch TV until dinner, which was uneventful. Buddy came over to tell me to be ready early the next day because I had a morning court date. Later that evening, I took my meds before going back to my cell, where Cody was already asleep. I lay in bed and prayed until I fell asleep, still praying.

Paul's Surprise

CHAPTER 36

MONDAY MORNING, CODY AND I quickly got dressed and joined Paul downstairs for breakfast. This being my last meal with them, I took time to say goodbye and wish them well. Then, Cody and I picked up our shaving supplies. I was anxious to get ready, so when I finished shaving and brushing my teeth, I returned the shaving supplies to the control counter and traded them for fresh clothes, shampoo, and a bar of soap. I hadn't taken a shower in the pod yet, so I asked where the shower was. The officer pointed to a door near the entrance to the pod, he grabbed a key, and walked with me to unlock the door, which he said wasn't connected to the main lock system.

The room was like my high-school locker-room, but without the lockers. There was a good-sized changing room and a smaller room with eight showerheads. I asked about a towel, and he pointed to a cart with a stack of clean towels. He said I was the only person scheduled to shower this morning, so he'd lock the door when he left, and I could just flip the knob on the deadbolt to get out.

The officer left, and I heard him lock the door. I walked to check that the back door was locked as well. I undressed and put my clothes on a bench before walking toward the showers. That's when I heard the deadbolt click on the back door. The door opened to reveal a grinning Buddy. He locked the door behind him before advancing toward me. Buddy said, "Hello, Grandpa, I'm here to give you a sample of what you can look forward to after your trial."

"What are you talking about?"

"Just stop talking, get on your knees, and give me a blow job." Buddy unbuckled his belt and dropped his pants and underwear to his ankles. He said again, "Get on your knees."

"No way am I doing that," I said. "I'll start screaming and the other officers will all run in here."

"You're not going to scream, but you are going to suck my dick because you don't want anything to happen to your mama and grandma."

"What are you talking about?"

"Yesterday, after work, I drove over to Mantorville, down that road they live on. I saw both their houses. I didn't see your mama, but your grandma was outside, working in her flower beds. I'd prefer a younger woman, but if you don't blow me now, I'm gonna visit your grandma after you're in prison. I'm going to stick my big cock in her mouth and fill her throat with my cum. Then I'm going to fuck her in her pussy until she dies, because I don't want a witness. I'll wait a few weeks and then do the same to your mother. Now, get on your knees."

I got on my knees, and Buddy moved closer to me. I lowered my head, looking into the floor, praying for God to help me. I couldn't help but think that I should've listened to the angel. I needed to protect Grandma and Mom; I was going to have to blow Buddy.

"Hurry up, get your mouth around me."

I looked up and saw Buddy was already hard. I kept my

teeth clenched as he pressed against my lips. He kept pushing against my mouth, his pre-cum smearing my lips and dripping onto the floor.

Buddy said, "Hurry up, Grandpa, suck me in or I'm going to do this to your grandma."

The thought of Buddy doing this to Grandma was too much for me to deal with. I was going to have to open my mouth and suck his dick. But before I did that, I leaned back and away and yelled, "Jesus, help me!"

Buddy started laughing. "Jesus doesn't give a fuck about you."

At that moment, we both heard the front door unlock. The door opened and in walked Paul.

"Connor, get up and get dressed," Paul said. I ran to my clothes on the bench.

Buddy shouted, "What the fuck!" as he pulled up his underwear and pants. He buttoned his pants but didn't take time to buckle his belt as he walked over to Paul and screamed, "Who the fuck do you think you are!?"

Paul said, "I'm the man stopping a sexual assault."

Buddy said, "I'm going to beat the shit out of both of you and then lock you up for assaulting a law officer."

Paul replied, "If you don't back down, you're going to get the shit beat out of you."

"Oh yeah? You think you can do that? You and what army?"

Then, we all heard the deadbolt at the back entrance and turned toward the back door. In walked six uniformed Minnesota State Troopers. Paul said, "This is my army."

"Hello, Paul," the trooper in charge greeted, removing his jacket and holding it out for Paul to slip into. "We want the other troopers to know you're one of the good guys."

Buddy had been speechless, but now demanded, "What the fuck is going on here!?"

Paul addressed Buddy, "My name is Special Agent Paul Saint Vincent with the Minnesota Bureau of Criminal Apprehension. The Yellow River County sheriff asked the bureau to investigate alleged corruption at this jail, so I've been here undercover, investigating the sheriff's suspicions. We also have two complaints from prior prisoners, claiming they were sexually assaulted in this room."

Buddy said, "You don't have any evidence. When you walked in here, Grandpa was begging me to let him suck my dick."

I said, "No I wasn't."

Buddy looked at Paul and said, "Who do you think a jury's gonna believe, a rapist or a law enforcement officer?"

Paul said, "Mr. Stone is not a rapist; he was framed. And you're no longer a law enforcement officer. You're under arrest. In fact, you're the one going away for the rest of your life."

The trooper in charge nodded to one of his men, who put Buddy in handcuffs. Then all six troopers walked Buddy out.

Only Paul and I remained in the room. "Did you say your last name was Saint Vincent?"

"Yes. I'm Debra's brother."

"Wow! How did this work out?"

"I was already in this jail when my wife gave me Debra's message," Paul said. "Debra knows I sometimes work undercover, but she has no idea I'm in jail with you. Her message said that you're innocent, and she wanted to know if there was anything I could do to help you."

"Paul, I'm so glad you were here!" I told him.

He explained, "Things worked out well this morning. I hadn't seen Buddy for a while, and I knew you were in here, where the assaults happened. I thought I'd check things, make sure you were okay."

"So, did you and the troopers have keys to this room?"

"The troopers had a key to the back door, but I didn't have any keys."

"Then how did you unlock the front door?"

Paul replied, "As I approached the door, I heard you yell 'Jesus help me.' Then the deadbolt retracted. I knew the troopers were taking over the jail this morning, so I figured one of them was at the controls and unlocked the door for me."

"The locks to this room are manual; they're not connected to the control system. You must have a key to unlock these doors."

Paul replied, "Then it was divine intervention."

"More specifically, I'm sure it was angelic intervention," I said.

Paul smiled, "We need to quit talking, and you need to shower. This is your big day, and your ride will be here soon. This room is now a crime scene, so you can't shower here. There's a private shower down the hall you can use."

"First, I'm going up to my cell to brush my teeth."

"I don't blame you." He looked at the floor where I'd been kneeling. "Are the drips on the floor Buddy's semen?"

"Yes," I told him.

"Okay," Paul said. "I'll secure this room until I get an evidence kit to collect the floor specimen."

We walked out into the pod, which now had troopers everywhere. All my fellow prisoners were in their cells. Paul walked me to the control counter, where he got an evidence kit from one of the troopers and swabbed samples from my lips and chin. Then he sent me up to my cell so I could brush my teeth.

I was quick and got to the private shower room in a few

minutes. Twenty minutes later, I was in my clean jumpsuit, waiting for an officer to escort me to Clint's squad car.

Clint, as always, arrived on time. I hated walking with the chains he'd put on me, but I made it to the car and got in the back seat. Once we were on the road, Clint asked, "Did Hank tell you about the graffiti on your house?"

"Yeah, but he didn't know who did it."

"Her name's Nelly Spiegel. Do you know her?"

"Yes. I fired her for theft of time."

"Theft of time?"

"Nelly worked alone, so she only saw her supervisor a few times a day. But she'd come to work, clock in, go out to the truck lot, get in one of the cabs, and sleep. She'd set her cellphone to wake her half an hour before lunch. Her supervisor was looking for her one day and happened to walk by the truck she was in when her alarm went off, so he found Nelly sleeping on the bench seat. The campus videos showed her doing this every day. The termination did not go well. She was terribly upset, claiming unfairness, saying she was going to get me back. I guess she has."

Clint said, "Now we know her motive."

"I hope it washes off easy."

"It did. Shelly took cleaning supplies over to your house and started scrubbing. Before long, a dozen different neighbors were helping her. They got it all off."

"That was really nice of Shelly and the neighbors to do that," I said. "I thought I'd come home to neighborhood protests."

"I think you're going to find that the only people negative toward you are those who don't know you. Those who know you will stand with you."

"I hope you're right."

We drove a few minutes in silence, and then I asked Clint, "What can you and I talk about?"

Clint said, "We can talk about anything that's public knowledge."

"So, can we talk about why there's so much interest in my couch? They put all the cushions in evidence bags, and Dinger asked me if I had sex with Molly on my couch."

"We can talk about that because it's in the police report, which you'll get a copy of. Molly claims you pulled her clothes off to perform oral sex on her while on the couch. The lab's looking for vaginal fluid on the cushions. She turned in the underwear she claims she was wearing; they're all stretched out because she said you stretched them when you yanked them off her. The lab will look for your DNA on the panties." Clint saw me start to speak and continued, "Before you say anything to me, remember that anything you tell me that I don't already know, I'm obligated to report when I'm interviewed by Dinger."

"That's fine," I responded. "If everything's out in the open, they may not even put me on trial. You already know she didn't have clothes on. You saw her nude in the garage, and you saw her walk into the house, still in the nude. When I walked in, she was already sitting on the couch, still naked. That's when she asked me to go get her G-string out of her car. So, there's most likely vaginal fluid on at least one of the cushions. I don't understand why she claims we had sex on the couch instead of on my bed. I also don't understand where the stretched-out panties came from."

Clint said, "Those are questions that your attorney will ask Molly."

We had several more minutes of silence, and then I said, "It's not going to feel good walking in there in my orange jumpsuit and chains."

"It will be humiliating," Clint agreed, "but it'll be short. The hearings go quickly. The prosecuting attorney recommends bail amount and conditions. Your attorney responds. And the judge sets the bail and conditions. It'll just be a couple minutes before you're out of there."

"Do you know anything about Larson and Sullivan?"

"Yes. They have a good reputation. They're known for playing hard and fair. They have the respect of law enforcement, because they treat the officers with respect. They're the best at getting juries to view evidence from a perspective that favors their clients. I've also seen them pull a rabbit out of a hat."

"What do you mean?"

"I was in the courtroom last year when Sullivan was questioning a witness. It was a slam dunk case for the prosecution; everyone thought the defendant was guilty. Then Sullivan asked a question no one saw coming. The witness broke down on the stand and said they'd lied earlier, said the defendant was innocent, and then named the real guilty person."

"Well, Grandma's very thorough, so I'm sure she picked the best attorneys."

Clint replied, "I've never seen a defendant retain two attorneys before, but you have a lot at stake, and your grandma's making sure you won't spend your life in prison."

My thoughts were on the hearing, but then I realized I hadn't told Clint about this morning's events. I told him how Buddy and Dinger were friends and how Buddy assaulted me. Clint was aghast, and shocked even further to hear an undercover MBCA agent had saved me and arrested Buddy.

I told Clint, "I'm concerned Dinger will really have it in for me now, since he and Buddy were friends."

"Dinger and this Buddy are two bad apples the Yellow River sheriff will have to deal with. Dinger seems determined to catch Zeus and put him down. It's a good thing Dakotah was able to take Zeus. Connor, you need to be incredibly careful. Make sure Zeus is in your sight whenever he's outside."

"I will. I sure hope my attorneys can exonerate both Zeus and me. I don't want to keep him locked up forever."

Clint turned onto Highway 57, which took us through downtown Mantorville and then up the hill to the courthouse.

We turned right onto Seventh Street and Clint said, "Oh shit." There were two TV news trucks parked on the street; I could see the cameramen by the entrance to the building. Clint pulled into a parking space reserved for law enforcement vehicles near the entrance. In addition to the newspeople, three sheriff's deputies stood by the entrance.

Clint said, "They're going to film you walking slow in the chains. They're also allowed to follow us into the building until we reach the elevator. The reporters will ask questions. My advice is that you don't say anything."

"Should I say, 'no comment'?"

"No, just hold your head up and say nothing."

"Should I cover my face with my hands like other people you see in the news?"

"No, just hold your head high and don't say a word. Covering your face makes you look guilty."

The car stopped and Clint got out as one of the other deputies opened my door and held out his hand to help me get out. The remaining deputies were keeping reporters away. As soon as I was out of the car, the questions started. "Was it really twenty-seven times?" "Did your dog really attack the deputy?" "Why'd you do it?" and so on.

We entered the building and walked to the elevator as reporters repeated their questions. Three of us got into the elevator: Clint, another deputy, and me. Clint pushed the button for the courtroom level and we went up. The doors opened to more cameras and reporters. I held my head up and walked as Clint led me to a private room. A dark-haired woman stepped forward and shook my hand, introducing herself as Emily Larson, my attorney.

Clint said, "I'll be just outside the door." To Emily, he said, "When it's time, I'll escort you to the courtroom."

She thanked him. Clint closed the door and Emily said to me, "He seems like a friendly officer."

"He is," I told her. "Actually, he's a close friend; he and his wife are my neighbors."

Emily asked, "Was the officer home the night that Molly Dew claims you raped her?"

"Yes. In fact, Clint talked to Molly that evening, when she was naked in my garage, rubbing her body against my groin. He also saw her walk into the house naked, leaving her clothes in her car. So, when she says I ripped her clothes off her, Clint knows she is lying; she never had any clothes to rip off."

Emily said, "We're not going to try the case today. We can start gathering details tomorrow. Today we need to concentrate on getting you reasonable conditions for bail." Emily's phone buzzed and she looked at a text message before saying, "The wire transfer from your friend Julia was just received by my bank."

"Good," I said.

"Your friends and family really care about you. They're making plenty of money available for your defense."

"I know. I hope I can repay them someday."

We stood on opposite sides of a conference table, so Emily said, "Have a chair. I want to go over some things with you."

As we sat down, I said, "There's something important I need to tell you."

Emily said, "You go first."

I told Emily about Buddy assaulting me and how an undercover agent saved me. I gave her all the details, and she was shocked to hear what I'd been through. I also told her how Buddy and Officer Dinger were friends, and that I was concerned Dinger would retaliate even more toward me and Zeus.

"Your grandmother, mother, and Dakotah met with me and told me about Dinger and your dog. I also talked to Sheriff Hanson, who assures me that Dinger's been told to leave Zeus alone."

I replied, "I believe that Dinger is a rogue cop that doesn't care what anybody says."

"We can deal with Dinger tomorrow. We'll be in court any minute, and I want to make sure you understand that I will speak for you. Don't say anything unless the judge speaks directly to you and asks you a question."

"Okay."

BAIL

CHAPTER 37

There was a knock on the door before Clint entered to say the judge was ready for us. Emily and I followed Clint into the courtroom. The setup was just like in the movies: Facing the front, Emily and I sat at a table on the left and the prosecuting attorney sat on the right. I'd never seen the prosecuting attorney before. His name was David Bower.

After I sat, I turned to see who was sitting on the pews behind me. Grandma, Mom, Hank, and Dakotah were directly behind Emily and me. Further back, I saw TV news crews and some newspaper reporters. There were several other people I didn't recognize. The judge was on a TV monitor placed on a table in front of Emily and me. The court clerk introduced the judge as the Honorable Jonathon B. Westbrook and then announced the case before the court: the State versus Connor Stone, charged with twenty-seven counts of sexual assault in the first degree.

The judge looked straight ahead at Emily and asked, "How does the defendant plead?"

Emily stood up and replied, "The defendant pleads not guilty."

The judge looked toward the prosecutor, "Mr. Bower?"

The prosecutor stood and addressed the judge, "Your Honor, the state asks for bail in the amount of five hundred thousand dollars for unconditional bail or two-hundred thousand dollars for conditional bail. The state also requests the following conditions: that the defendant be prohibited from traveling outside Minnesota, that he be required to surrender his passport, and that he be required to wear an electronic monitoring device."

Emily stood and replied, "Your Honor, the defendant grew up in Mantorville County and has strong ties to the local community. He's anxious for his day in court so that he can prove to the world that he's innocent. The bail and conditions being proposed are outrageous and not needed. The dollar amounts suggested by the prosecutor are ten times amounts considered reasonable. The defendant works in a profession that can require extensive travel; he needs to seek new employment and get a new job while we await trial, which could be an extended period of time. The defendant needs to have the ability to travel within the United States. As for the electronic monitoring device, I'm shocked at the suggestion that one is needed. These devices are normally required for individuals after they've been convicted. Requiring the defendant to wear a device at this time would imply a presumption of guilt. The defendant is entitled to a presumption of innocence."

The prosecutor and Emily were now both standing, waiting for the judge to respond.

After a moment, the judge looked toward the prosecutor and said, "I tend to agree with the statements just made by Ms. Larson. Do you have any reason to believe that the defendant would try to flee in order to avoid trial?"

The prosecutor said, "Yes. The defendant faces life in prison if convicted. The chief investigator on the case has expressed to me his concerns that the defendant may try to flee in order to avoid a life in prison. The defendant's family has the financial resources to enable him to flee the U.S. and escape to a different country."

Emily argued, "Your Honor, the chief investigator doesn't have a clue as to what's actually happened with this case. When the truth comes out, the defendant will be found not guilty. Further, the defendant is already confident that will happen, so he has no desire to leave. The chief investigator is from Yellow River County, which has a troublesome reputation concerning ethical law enforcement. In fact, a close associate of the chief investigator was arrested just this morning for sexually assaulting the defendant while he was still in custody in the Yellow River County Jail. The Mantorville County Sheriff's Department and the Minnesota Bureau of Criminal Apprehension have verified this. As a result of today's arrest of the chief investigator's buddy, we anticipate future problems with the chief investigator. I investigated my client before I took this case. He is not a man who avoids conflict; he meets conflict head-on. While he awaits trial, he needs to be able to earn a living. The proposed conditions will limit his ability to work."

Everyone was quiet for an extended moment. Then the judge said, "Unconditional bail will be set at fifty thousand dollars. Conditional bail will be twenty-five thousand dollars. The conditions will be that the defendant must surrender his passport to his attorney. All travel outside of Minnesota must be approved by his attorney in advance. No travel will be allowed outside the United States. There will be no electronic monitoring device."

The judge slammed his gavel on his table to end the remote hearing and the TV monitor went dark.

The prosecutor came over to our table and started asking Emily questions about my assault in Yellow River. Before she answered him, she said goodbye to me and gave me her business card. She reminded me that she and John would meet with me tomorrow at nine a.m. in their Rochester office. Clint took me toward the exit but allowed me to stop and explain this morning's events to my family.

Grandma was terribly upset. "It sounds like the man who assaulted you will be taken care of, but Officer Dinger could still be trouble. We need to trust that the Lord will take care of Officer Dinger."

"I agree," I told her.

Grandma said, "I'm going to go take care of the bail."

"I'm going to leave for Yellow River in half an hour," Hank told me.

Clint said, "We should get going so you're discharged when Hank arrives."

Everyone hugged me, and then Clint and I were on our way.

Clint was willing to take the chains and cuffs off for the ride back, but I chose to keep them on to save Clint the hassle; I'd need them back on to enter the jail. The ride was quick, and in no time at all, I was back in the secure room. There were still state troopers everywhere throughout the jail.

Clint removed the chains and cuffs and said he'd see me in Mantorville. The same officer who'd checked me in a few days ago brought out bags holding my clothes and other personal items. He re-checked everything against the list and then had me sign a receipt for the items. I took everything to the other side of the room and changed into my own clothes. The officer then escorted me to the visitors' room, to wait for Hank. I fell asleep in my chair and woke to "Connor!" being hollered by Hank."

This time, I walked out of the Yellow River County Jail in my own clothes and no chains. I hopped into Hank's pickup truck, and we headed to Rochester.

I asked, "Has Debra made arrangements to keep Molly away from my office during the termination?"

"Yes. Debra sent Molly home at noon. Oh, and Emily called me to say a restraining order was issued to prevent you going within three hundred feet of Molly or her husband. Emily will go over the details when she meets with you tomorrow."

"I hope that restraining order works both ways. I don't want Molly's husband coming after me."

"Do you think he will?"

"He thinks I raped his wife. I'm sure he wants to kill me."

Hank said, "You will be glad to know that Clint checked out your security system and all the sensors are working fine. He also checked your cameras and his. All cameras are working and are being recorded."

"I wish I had a camera in my bedroom. I never would have been charged if I had a recording of Molly in my bed, asking me to eat her out."

"She actually said that?"

"Yes, and she liked it."

"So, you did it?"

"Yes. It was my first time with her. I did a number of things with Molly that were first times for me. When I was married, my sex life was pretty basic. After my divorce, I only dated a few women, but they were modern women, and they showed me all kinds of new sexual things to do."

"Well, Connor, I guess I've lived a sheltered life."

"There's nothing wrong with that. When I was living

a sheltered life, I was happier than I am now. My divorce changed everything for the worse."

We spent the rest of the ride talking about the old days when things were simpler. Hank reaffirmed his belief that Faith was still alive and that she just needed to be found. I told him, "If the angel appears to me again, I'll ask if Faith is alive. You should do the same if it appears to you."

"I will, but you're the only one in the family the angel talks to."

"The angel only talks to me because I'm the only one in the family who makes bad decisions."

Hank asked, "Why do you think the angel is always with Grandma?"

I said, "I believe that Grandma has a very important mission, and the angel's here to protect her so she can complete the mission."

"I'm glad we have an angel to protect us, but it bothers me that Grandma's in such danger that she needs an angel's protection."

We neared MTI and both became quiet. I started thinking about my termination. Hank pulled up to my office building and I asked, "Are you coming in?"

Hank said, "Yes. Debra asked me to be the witness."

"That's good. So, it'll just be the three of us?"

"Yes."

We parked by the entrance and went into the building. Molly's office door was closed, and mine was open. Debra sat at the conference table and motioned for us to join her. I closed the door and sat down with Hank and Debra.

I looked lovingly at Debra, "Thank you for asking your brother to help me."

She was surprised, "You know about my brother!?"

"Yes. We were in jail together. Paul saved me this morning

when he arrested the bad cop assaulting me."

Hank said to me, "You didn't tell us the undercover agent was Debra's brother."

"Yep. Paul Saint Vincent is Debra's brother. He's a special agent with the Minnesota Bureau of Criminal Apprehension. He was investigating corruption there at the request of the Yellow River County sheriff." I told Debra, "Paul told me he got your message asking him to help me. He also said you didn't know he was working undercover in the same jail with me." I told Debra what happened, then said, "Let's get to the termination."

Debra slid an envelope across the table to me. "Those are the benefit documents. You know all about them." Then she slid a set of stapled papers to me and said, "This is the severance agreement. Everything in the agreement is standard except the severance amount."

"How much is it?" I asked.

"One hundred twenty thousand." Debra noticed Hank and I look at each other and said, "What did you guys do to Ronald?"

"What do you mean?"

She told me, "Originally, Ronald said no severance payment. Last week he called and asked what normal severance would be. I told him three thousand per year times twenty years, or sixty thousand. Ronald told me to double the amount because you've been a dedicated employee and because he thinks Molly is lying."

Hank said, "That was nice of Ronald."

Debra looked skeptical. "Nathan and Marvin agreed, so the amount is one hundred twenty thousand dollars. I don't know what changed Ronald's mind, but I'm sure you guys have something on him."

I asked Hank for a pen so I could sign the agreement.

Debra reminded me I had twenty-one days to review it before signing. Just like countless others before me, I said that I needed the money now.

"Hold on," said Debra. "Are there any notaries in this building?"

Then Hank left to get Peggy, Debra looked at me and sadly said, "If I'd married you, none of this would've happened. We'd be blissfully happy and never even known what we'd prevented."

"Don't try to blame this on your decision," I smiled kindly. "You made the correct choice, and you're with the right man. I'm the one who screwed things up."

Hank returned with Peggy, who notarized our signatures. Then, Debra and Hank helped me pack my personal items and haul them to Hank's truck. Debra confirmed someone would come get my company pickup tomorrow afternoon. She gave me a hug before Hank and I took off.

While Hank and I drove to my house, I received my first phone call since I got out of jail. It was Dakotah, who wanted to know when she should bring Zeus home. We agreed I'd pick him up tomorrow after my attorney meeting.

Hank dropped me off at my house, and I thanked him for everything. There were no cushions on the couch, and the sheets on my bed were fresh; everything else was clean and organized as usual. It was three o'clock, and I needed a nap. I set my alarm for five forty-five so I'd catch the news. I fell asleep alone, in my own bed.

The alarm woke me up, and I went downstairs to watch the six o'clock news. I was the lead story. The message was more professional than the newscasts I'd seen in jail, primarily because Dinger wasn't interviewed. They showed video of me entering the courthouse with a closeup of my chains. The news anchor simply stated what the charges and conditions of bail were. The story ended with people on the streets of Mantorville being interviewed.

People who didn't know me thought the charges were horrendous and said I deserved my day in court. People who knew me stood up for me and said there was no way I was guilty. Three of the women interviewed said they regularly walked by my house to pet Zeus; everyone said the charges against Zeus were ridiculous. All things considered; the news wasn't that bad. I still felt optimistic and was ready to dive head-on into this trial to exonerate myself.

After supper, the doorbell rang. It was Marjorie and Jim Rollins. They'd brought me a car to use. Jim said, "Connor, I know you only have the company pickup, so I thought I'd loan you this car until you get your own vehicle. I'd bought and fixed it up for my daughter, but she won't have her license for a few months."

"This is so great," I thanked them. "I'll need a month to find my own vehicle. I am so grateful to both of you!" I expected them to say something about the trial, but they just smiled at me encouragingly, without judgment.

Jim handed me the car keys, then he and Marjorie gave me hugs before they took off.

I went upstairs to my bedroom, but before I got into the bed, I knelt and leaned against the bed to pray. It felt odd without Zeus lying next to me as I thanked God and Jesus for everything—for Grandma's angel, for taking care of me in jail, for Jim and Marjorie and the car they brought me, for the ongoing support of my family and my friends. Then I made a request. I asked God to guide me and my attorneys and, if possible, to make the trial go away. I didn't know it as I prayed that night, but I would be making the same request every night for the next three years.

Three Years Later

Chapter 38

WE WAITED THREE YEARS FOR a trial date because we couldn't get a judge to do the trial in Mantorville County. The usual judge had recused himself because we were friends. Other judges in the state would only do the trial if we moved it to their counties. John and Emily insisted that the trial be held in Mantorville County because we wanted the jury to be local.

Many things happened to me, personally and professionally, during the subsequent three years' wait. But the only thing even slightly relating to the trial was Officer Dinger's discharge from his position for acting inappropriately and disobeying orders. At the time of his termination, he'd already completed his investigation of my case.

A lot happened to and in my life over those three years. Looking back, it was clear God used this period to humble me from my pride in my previous life. It was hard to live through the depression and anxiety of constantly having a trial hanging over my head. It wasn't as though I was on formal probation, but until a decision was made at trial, I was restricted from the typical freedoms I would've otherwise had in traveling, drinking and socializing, and otherwise having the flexibility to live an unencumbered life. I was forced to make many important changes not only to how I lived my life, but the restrictions and the waiting also forced me to reflect on why I'd been living the way I had.

My prior life had been spent pretty much doing whatever I wanted, with very few actual consequences; my wealth and position in life, my personality and intelligence, and my social and professional networks had always insulated me. God had to humble me to the very ground before He could build me back up again. I'd truly repented, and He'd forgiven me, but that was just the start. I know now that He wanted me becoming, a process He never wanted to end, a better person. And I see in retrospect that it took very hard times to trigger that process in me.

God knew me losing my job and getting criminally charged wouldn't be enough. It took those three, long years for him to work on me, while I worked on myself. This type of introspection was difficult for me, to put it mildly. Given my former preference for rushing to head-on confrontation, it was an incredible struggle for me to practice literal physical- and actual mental- and spiritual-patience. But God's grace was truly infinite.

Whenever I felt something was more than I could handle alone, He gave me the help I needed to keep growing. When I first lost my job and was crushed with embarrassment, it was Jim and Marjorie stepping up to loan me their car, freely given without judgment. When I struggled for months to find new employment and began to despair, it was old colleagues emerging with job offers, allowing me to remain in an industry I already knew well at this late stage in my career. When I lost my house in foreclosure and was literally homeless and alone, my fall into poverty was cushioned when Dakotah offered to let me move into the apartment above her garage. A hired hand had previously lived there, but as the girls grew older and started doing chores, there was no longer a need for a hired hand.

I'm positive God intended those three years to teach me how to grow into a righteous man; that it took such a difficult path to get me to a point of readiness was entirely my fault. Uncertainty and anxiety about my future freedom, personal shame and embarrassment for my family, loneliness and the solitude of "working on myself"—all still remained, because of my prior sinful choices, as a muck soiling my life. But God used it all.

His plan for me repurposed the filth I'd given him to work with. God used my shitty muck to fertilize the seeds of the man I'd grow into. And, far exceeding my own limited human expectations, God did it in the best way I could imagine: Dakotah and I fell in love.

The Eve of the Trial

CHAPTER 39

It was a sunny Monday morning in mid-April when my attorneys called to tell me we finally had a trial date in Mantorville County. The existing judge had retired and a new one, who didn't know me, had been appointed. My trial date was set to occur in four weeks. I began meeting with Emily and John twice a week, then every day in the week before the trial began. Trial-prep sped by. Nothing new came up; we just reviewed the same things we'd gone over for the last three years.

Sunday, the night before the trial began, I walked around and around the circular driveway, praying for God's help. After asking Him over a thousand times to spare me from the trial, I'd come to accept the waiting. I knew these years had been a time of humbling and growth. But I was still human; I had to plead one more time. "Dear Lord, please make the trial go away. I've repented. My family still suffers because of the embarrassment I caused, and we all still endure it. I know you've forgiven me, and you've blessed me in so many ways these last three years. So why? Why are you still putting me on trial?" Finally, I screamed, "Why!?" And then He answered.

At first, I thought it was the angel speaking, but I looked around and didn't see the angel. Then I realized the voice had spoken in first-person. It was God who had said: "I'M NOT PUTTING YOU ON TRIAL. I'M PUTTING HER ON TRIAL."

Day 1

Chapter 40

Monday morning was cloudy when I met Emily and John in the courthouse parking lot. There were no TV news trucks in sight. I figured they weren't interested in a picture of me in a business suit; orange jumpsuits and chains attracted more viewers. The three of us climbed the stairs to the courtroom, where we walked to the front and sat at the table on the left. This was where we'd be all week. John sat on the far right of our table, Emily next to him, and me on the left. The pew-seating behind us was already half full. I only saw one reporter; she was from the Mantorville Express.

In the pew directly behind me sat my family and friends: Hank, Grandma, Mom, Dakotah, Julia, and Debra. All eyes in the courtroom were on my supporters. Most people knew the four Thorsons, but they couldn't figure out who Julia and Debra were. The judge wasn't there, so the environment was relaxed. After a few more minutes, the court clerk walked in and said, "All rise for the Honorable Ronald Swenson, Judge of Mantorville County District Court." The courtroom was almost full by now, and everyone stood.

The judge motioned to us to take our seats, then instructed the clerk to bring in the potential jurors. They filled all the chairs in the jurors' box plus the two reserved pews next to the box. When they were seated, the judge pounded his gavel and the clerk said, "This is the trial of the State of Minnesota versus Connor Stone. Mr. Stone is charged with twenty-seven counts of sexual assault in the first degree." The judge declared that fourteen people would be selected: twelve jurors and two alternates.

For the rest of the day, John and the prosecutor, David Bower, questioned potential jurors. Some were MTI employees, who were immediately excused. Another person was excused because a relative of his was recently sexually assaulted and he thought people like me were disgusting. A number of people were excused because their answers showed they'd already formed an opinion. At the end of the day, thirty-one people had been questioned, and nine had been seated as jurors. That left only eleven people from whom we'd have to select five on Tuesday, so the judge ordered the clerk to bring an additional ten people tomorrow. Then he pounded his gavel, "Court is adjourned."

The clerk said, "All rise." We stood until the judge had left the courtroom.

Emily told me that she and John would meet me in the same place the next morning. They told me to not stay out late and to get plenty of sleep. They left, and I turned to my group, "This was a boring day. Are you coming back tomorrow for more of the same?"

Julia said, "I found it interesting. Especially the guy who already thought you were guilty."

Debra said, "I think he said that because he didn't want to serve on the jury."

"I agree," said Dakotah.

Grandma offered, "It's Monday, so Hubbell House is closed. Why don't you all come to my place for supper? I have two Crock-Pots full of venison steak." Everyone agreed to meet at Grandma's place.

Dakotah had gotten a ride with Mom this morning, and now she rode with me.

"Things went better than I expected today," Dakotah reassured me.

"It was just jury selection."

"No, I meant that things went better than I expected with Julia and Debra. I was concerned about how I'd feel after spending all day with two women you've slept with. I like both of them, and I can see why you were in love with them."

"I'm glad you feel that way," I said. "I still love them as friends, but you are the only woman I am in love with."

"I know. You always show it, which makes me feel good."

We smiled at each other as we got out of the car at Grandma's.

It was a good evening with friendly conversation. Julia and Debra were amazed to learn that the venison we ate was from deer that Dakotah and Grandma had hunted last season. All the women in my life were getting along fine.

Day 2

Chapter 41

After a good night's sleep, I was up at seven. I grabbed some toast and coffee, then drove to the courthouse alone to meet John and Emily.

On our way to the courtroom, we stepped into one of the available conference rooms so they could brief me on the presentation Emily had prepared. John said that if jury selection was completed early enough, the judge could start the trial today. The first thing would be the prosecutor's explanation of the charges against me. Then, Emily would present the biographical information about me. John emphasized that I need to look and actually be alert and attentive. He expected the jurors to watch me closely while Emily talked about me. I assured him I'd act accordingly.

When we entered the courtroom. Most of the pews were full; my support group was already seated. Emily checked with the clerk to verify the projector was working, then John and Emily smiled at each other before we all sat back to wait for the judge. I noticed something in the way John and Emily smiled at each other. John was normally profoundly serious and presented himself very professionally, but sometimes I caught him responding to Emily's smiles as if he was an excited teenage boy with the girl he had a crush on. It reminded me of how I felt whenever Dakotah smiled at me. I took another look at them and saw they'd already returned to their serious, ready-for-battle personas.

"All rise," said the clerk.

After everyone was seated, the judge said, "We need to select five more people today. The first three as jurors, the last two will be seated as alternates." He then instructed the clerk to begin the process. The first five people had already formed opinions favoring either Molly or me and were excused. The next person was accepted. The following two were rejected, one by my attorneys for saying I was the scum of the earth because I'd fired her husband, the other by the prosecutor for saying he appreciated me because I'd counseled his son through some tough times, saving his job, and getting him into tech school for a welding degree. We accepted another, then rejected two more. By lunch recess, we still needed one more juror and two alternates.

After lunch, the first two people were promptly accepted, so I began to hope that the trial may actually start, but the next five were rejected, and then we took another recess. Even though it was only Tuesday, John said that if we didn't get the last alternate out of the three remaining candidates, the trial wouldn't be completed this week. We had another recess, then returned and the first person questioned was rejected.

The next person took a long time to question, with both John and the prosecutor, Bower, asking her more questions than usual. I thought she'd make a good juror. Bower accepted her, but John took a minute to consult with me and Emily. Leaning over our table, he softly said, "She had exactly the right answers to all my questions."

"I agree," I told him. "Why didn't you accept her?"

"She had all the right answers, and I have this bad feeling in my gut."

I immediately said, "I always go with my gut."

Emily nodded in agreement.

John turned to face the judge, "Your Honor, we wish to pass on this candidate."

The woman became visibly disappointed at this decision.

Several months after the trial was over, I learned how that prior night she'd been at a local bar, telling everyone how she'd do whatever it took to get on the jury because she was sure I was guilty and felt I should be locked up for life. I was glad we went with John's gut.

We moved on to accept our fourteenth candidate.

After we ended for the day, Hank invited everyone to the Hubbell House. John and Emily declined because they wanted to concentrate on tomorrow's trial. The rest of us walked to the Hubbell House and received a warm welcome in the lobby. We requested one of the small, private dining rooms so our group of seven could talk freely in private.

As we all sat, Grandma asked me to close both doors to the room. Then, Grandma stood and prayed. She thanked the Lord for watching over the trial and asked him to bless the meal we were about to have. When she finished, we all said amen in unison.

We'd all eaten here before and debated which appetizers to order. We ended up with seafood melts, onion rings, and cheese curds. A couple bottles of wine were ordered for Grandma, Mom, Debra, and Julia. Hank had his strawberry lemonade while Dakotah and I had a bottle of non-alcohol wine. Dakotah had gotten me to stop drinking alcohol over two years ago.

We had good conversations but didn't talk about the trial. Grandma and Julia fought over who'd pick up the tab, and Julia won. Finally, we all headed home. Lately, Mom always drove Grandma wherever she needed to go and Julia was staying with Mom, so the three of them left together. Dakotah and I drove home in comfortable silence.

DAY 3

CHAPTER 42

THE NEXT MORNING INITIALLY MIRRORED the previous two. We all stood as the clerk announced, "All rise, Mantorville County District Court is now in session. Judge Ronald Swenson is presiding." We sat as the judge directed the clerk to bring in the jurors, who were sworn in. The clerk re-stated the charges and the judge began, "Mr. Bower, your opening statement please."

Prosecutor Bower walked in front of his table to address the judge, "Your Honor," then turned to the right, "Members of the jury, the defendant is charged with twenty-seven counts of sexual assault in the first degree. The state will prove beyond a reasonable doubt that Connor Stone committed these crimes. That he sexually assaulted Molly Dew, a woman who worked for him. That he did so twenty-six times over a period of months in his office at work and one time in his home. That Mr. Stone gave the victim a promotion and pay increase in exchange for sexual favors. And when she tried to stop the sexual assaults, Mr. Stone threatened to terminate her employment. On the night of the last assault, Mr. Stone demanded that Mrs. Dew leave her husband and move in with Mr. Stone.

"We will show that Mr. Stone was infatuated with Mrs. Dew's young body. That he constantly touched her inappropriately at work and he insisted that she wear thongs instead of panties to work. He also insisted that she wear skirts or dresses to make it easier for him to touch her private areas. The chief investigator in this case found twenty-six women's panties in Mr. Stone's desk drawer at work. The panties were trophies that Mr. Stone accumulated.

"Almost every day when Mrs. Dew came to work, she was required to lift her skirt or dress and pull down her underwear. Mr. Stone would then finger her until she had an orgasm. Many times, she had to pretend to have an orgasm in order to get Mr. Stone to stop. When he finished, Mr. Stone would check out her underwear. If she was wearing panties, he'd take them as his trophy and give her a thong to wear. If she'd been wearing a thong, she would be allowed to put it back on. Mr. Stone told Mrs. Dew this was to get all her panties so that she'd have to wear a thong every day. The state will show that Mr. Stone is a sexual predator who needs to be convicted and punished." Bower returned to the chair at his table.

The clerk began setting up the screen in the upper left corner of the room, where everyone could see the screen. The judge looked at Emily, "Mrs. Larson, your opening statement, please." Emily set up her laptop to project. The first slide popped up on the large screen as she said, "Your Honor and members of the jury, in the next few minutes, I'm going to tell you who Connor Stone is. He is not whoever the prosecutor just described. Connor Stone is a compassionate and caring man. I will start when Connor moved to Mantorville County at the age of eight."

Emily went on to talk about Mom adopting me, how active I was in the Mantorville schools,. She then talked about my hockey achievements. I was named to the All-State team as a hockey goalie when I was a senior in high school. I went to the University of North Dakota on a hockey scholarship and was the first freshman to start as a goalie for UND.

I received a bachelor's degree in accounting from UND, followed by an MBA degree from the Carlson School of Management at the University of Minnesota. That was followed by an Executive MBA degree from The Wharton School of the University of Pennsylvania.

I spent six years working in accounting and human resources for a farm implement dealer in Minnesota before going to work in human resources for Milk Trucks, Inc., where I worked for twenty years. The last three years I had operated my own HR consulting company.

She went on to list the numerous organizations I volunteered for and pointed out that I served as a member of the board of directors for most of those local organizations.

Emily began concluding: "Connor Stone is a good man. He will acknowledge that he made a mistake when he entered into an improper relationship with Molly Dew, a married woman who worked for him. The defense will explain how Molly Dew not only initiated, but also maintained the sexual activity over a period of months.

"Connor Stone was a mentor to Molly Dew and helped to advance her status at Milk Trucks, Inc. Connor did not assault Molly Dew. Connor did not want to continue an adulterous relationship; he wanted to marry Molly, so he told her to choose between him and her husband. Molly wanted to continue the adulterous relationship. That's why Connor gave Molly visible hickeys the last time they made love; he knew she'd have to explain the hickeys to her husband. Connor never imagined that Molly Dew would later lie and say that he'd raped her.

"The day after Connor gave Molly the hickeys, she came to work and told Connor that she'd chosen her husband. She even told Connor she planned to reveal their affair to her husband, who she was worried would reject her for it. Its obvious Molly feared losing her husband, and that is why she changed her story to say she was raped. She wanted to be a victim her husband would protect. Ladies and gentlemen of the jury, during the next few days, the defense will show you how everything I just talked about transpired. We will prove there is a victim in this case and that the victim is Connor Stone."

The judge called a fifteen-minute recess before pounding his gavel.

When we were back in session, Prosecutor Bower called his first witness to the stand. Deputy Arlon Grover entered the courtroom and was sworn in. Bower asked him a series of questions to establish the prosecution's story. Deputy Grover reported he'd been dispatched on a Thursday night to Mayo's Saint Mary's campus, where he'd questioned Molly Dew and her husband, who both reported Molly had been raped by her boss, Connor Stone. Deputy Grover continued, "She said the assault occurred at Connor Stone's home, in the living room on a couch. That Connor had pulled her clothes off before performing oral sex on her. That he used his fingers to penetrate her vagina and anus. After the assault, she escaped when Connor went to the bathroom." The prosecution rested, so John began his cross-examination.

John had the deputy reiterate that the alleged assault was said to have occurred on Monday night, but that Molly hadn't gone to the ER until Thursday night. The deputy told us, "Molly said she was afraid to go to the ER until her husband returned from his business trip on Thursday."

"Officer Grover," said John, "in addition to reading the

transcript of your interview with Molly Dew, I was able to listen to the interview's audio recording. When you asked her if she knew the person who assaulted her, she replied, 'Yes, Connor Stone.' You responded, 'Did you say Connor Stone?'. When you asked the question, your voice had a tone of surprise, as if you found it hard to believe that Connor Stone was the rapist. Officer Grover, were you surprised that she named Connor Stone as the rapist?"

Grover said, "Yes, I was surprised when she said Connor Stone."

"Why were you surprised?"

"I've known Connor for many years and worked with him on several community projects. Connor has a reputation for helping people, not hurting them."

John said, "Thank you, Officer Grover, no further questions."

The judge announced a lunch recess of one hour.

All nine of us walked to the Hubbell House for lunch. Emily, John, and I sat together in a corner of the dining room for privacy. The rest of the group sat apart from us.

John looked at me, "During our prep, you said that you never stuck anything into her anus. And you said over and over that you believe she ripped herself with her grinding in the garage."

"That's correct."

"I'm going to attempt to get the nurse to acknowledge that this is physically possible. Are you sure that in the heat of passion, you never touched her anus?"

"I'm sure. I've actually never stuck anything in her anus. I've held her butt cheeks in my hands, but that's it."

"How about her vagina, is there any chance you aggressively fingered her that night?"

I said, "No, the only body parts in her vagina that night were my lips and my tongue."

"Okay, those were good answers. I'll ask you the same questions when you testify."

"When do you think I'll testify?"

"Most likely tomorrow. This afternoon we'll hear from the nurse and from Molly and her husband. Tomorrow morning, we'll hear from Dinger, who's the last witness on the prosecution's list. We only have your two-character witnesses, followed by you and Clint. I may change my mind and have Clint go before you."

We ate our lunch, and all nine of us walked back together.

Back in court, the judge had Bower call his next witness.

Stephanie Holland, the nurse who'd examined Molly at the hospital, was sworn in at the stand.

Bower started asking questions to establish Holland had been a nurse for twenty-four years, the last seventeen of which she'd worked in the ER. During her tenure, Holland had examined hundreds of sexual assault victims. She had years of experience photographing victims and preparing reports for law enforcement. At this point, Bower entered into evidence the pictures Holland had taken during the exam of Molly's vagina and anus.

There were three pictures: two were closeups of Molly's vaginal area, the third was of Molly's anus, showing tears in two locations. Bower handed the pictures to the nurse and asked her to look at each picture to refresh her memory. As Holland finished looking at each picture, Bower handed them to be passed among the jury. Waiting until each juror had seen all pictures, Bower then asked, "Nurse Holland, why did you take a picture of Molly Dew's anus?"

"Because there were two tears or anal fissures on her anus."

"What could have caused the anal fissures?"

"They're typically caused by anal sex when a large, hard penis or when a large object is inserted in the anal cavity. If the penis or object has a diameter larger than the opening of the cavity, the skin around the opening to the cavity will tear, causing the anal fissures."

"Thank you, Nurse Holland. There are two other pictures. They're both of Mrs. Dew's vagina. Why were those pictures taken?"

"I took those pictures because she had some minor bruising, and her labia were very red."

"What caused the bruising and redness?"

"That's difficult to determine. It could be caused by rough sex, but Mrs. Dew told me that she and her husband have never had rough or aggressive sex. Mrs. Dew also told me that she had sex with her husband on Monday morning before he left on a business trip. Regular sex on Monday morning would not have caused the bruising and redness that I saw on Thursday."

"Could the tears on the anus and the bruises in the vagina been caused by a finger?"

"Not a single finger, but the injuries could have been caused by multiple fingers being thrust into the cavity of the anus or vagina."

"Thank you, Nurse Holland, I have no further questions for you."

The judge called on John, who began, "Nurse Holland, as part of your exam of Molly Dew, did you collect any specimens from Molly?"

"Yes, I collected specimens from her vagina, anus, rectum, and mouth."

"What did you do with the specimens?"

"They were all sent to the state crime laboratory for DNA

analysis."

"Did you receive a report with the results from the lab?"

"No, the results would have been sent to the sheriff's department."

John spoke to the jury, "Interestingly, I didn't receive a report either." Then, he looked back to the stand, "But I did see an email sent by the chief investigator, Officer Dinger, to the prosecutor, Mr. Bower. Officer Dinger's email said that he'd received the lab report and that Connor Stone's DNA was not found in any of the specimens taken from Molly Dew. Nurse Holland, does it surprise you that the specimens were negative for Connor Stone's DNA?"

"No, it doesn't surprise me because Mrs. Dew told me she'd taken four showers and two baths between Monday night and Thursday night. Any DNA on or in her as a result of sex on Monday would have washed away by Thursday night, when I collected the specimens."

John continued, "I'd like to learn more about the tears on Molly Dew's anus, but before I ask you any questions, I want to let you know that when the defendant testifies, he's going to explain how Molly Dew did sexual things to him that caused the rips or tears on her anus. My question to you is regarding the possible injuries that can occur when a woman violently 'twerks' or 'grinds' on a man. Can you begin by explaining to the jury what those actions physically involve?"

"To my knowledge, twerking is when a woman moves her butt cheeks from side to side and up and down in a sexually seductive way. Grinding is when she grinds her butt cheeks into a man's groin while moving the butt cheeks from side to side."

"That's a good description. Now tell us, would it be possible for a woman to rip her anus by vigorously moving her butt cheeks back and forth while at the same time thrusting and grinding her butt into a man's groin?"

"Yes. I actually examined a patient a few years ago who had a serious anal fissure. She claimed her anus tore while she was aggressively grinding her man."

"Thank you, Nurse Holland, no further questions."

John returned to his seat, and Bower stood to call Molly Dew.

Molly entered the courtroom, dressed conservatively in a very loose-fitting dress. She took her oath and sat down at the stand.

Bower began his questioning, "Mrs. Dew, how long have you known the defendant, Connor Stone?"

"I've known who he is for a little over four years. My first conversation with him was about three and a half years ago."

"What precipitated that first conversation?"

"Connor called me to his office to tell me he liked the way I looked when I wore jeans to work."

"Did Mr. Stone ever compliment you on your appearance subsequent to that first conversation?"

"Yes. A few months later, he moved his office to my building. That's when he changed the reporting structure of the department so that I reported directly to him. At that point, he complimented me daily and made comments about different parts of my body on a regular basis."

"When did the inappropriate behavior start?"

"The first day in his new office, which was right across the hall from my office."

"What did Mr. Stone do?"

"I'd mentioned that my husband and I were planning to go on a cruise. Connor said he'd like to help me pick some new bikinis for the cruise, but he needed to know more about my body type. He ordered me to close and lock both doors to his office. Then he told me to stand in front of his desk and undress. At first, I kept my panties and bra on, but he said that most cruise ships stop at islands with nude beaches, so he wanted to see what I looked like nude. I took off my panties and bra. That's when he told me my breasts were better than he'd expected. At this point, I was extremely uncomfortable and asked if I could put my clothes back on. He said I could, so I got dressed and returned to my office."

"When did Mr. Stone start touching you inappropriately?"

"Later that same day. At the end of the day, Connor and I were the last two people in the building. I stepped into his office to say goodbye on my way out and he asked me to come into his office and close the door behind me. I did as instructed, and Connor closed and locked the second door. He said he wanted to know how responsive I was to his touch and told me to take my panties off. He had me bend over the conference table and had me rest my arms on the table. Then, he lifted the back hem of my dress, exposing my whole butt. He said that he had ED and couldn't get hard; then he slid his hand in front of me and put a finger in my vagina. He fingered me until I had an orgasm. I didn't feel I had any choice, since he was my boss."

"Was this the only time that Mr. Stone fingered you at work?"

"No. He established a policy that every morning we'd have coffee together in his office. But before we had our coffee each morning, he'd finger me. After a few days, he received a package with a number of thongs he'd ordered, and he kept them in his desk. If I was wearing panties when I came into his office each morning, he'd keep the panties and give me a thong to put on. He did this until he had all my panties, and I only had thongs to wear. At the end of each day, if Connor and I were the only ones left in the building, we would do the 'conference table routine' until we both came. This would happen a couple times each week."

"Why did you consent to do everything that you have described?"

"I didn't consent. I had no choice but to comply with his requests. He made it clear that if I didn't comply with his desires, I'd have to find another job. After meeting his needs for a couple weeks, he promoted me and gave me a big pay increase. So, he rewarded me for the sexual favors, but also constantly reminded me that if I didn't comply, my employment would be terminated."

"Mrs. Dew, everything you have described so far took place in Mr. Stone's office. The statement you made to the deputy at the ER was that you were assaulted at Mr. Stone's home. Is that correct?"

"Yes, we were at his home the night he forced himself on me."

"Had you been to his home prior to the night in question?"

"No, that was the first and only time I've been to his home."

"Why did you go to his home?"

"He insisted. He was constantly asking me to move in with him, and he wanted me to see that he had a nice home. I agreed to look at the house, hoping that would satisfy him, but I was in no mood to have sex in his house."

"What happened when you entered the home?"

"As we walked into the house from the garage, my phone rang. It was my husband, and I let him know I was at Connor's. While I was talking to my husband, Connor used the bathroom."

"Did Mr. Stone ask you about your husband's call?"

"No, not at all."

"What happened next?"

"When we walked into the living room, he started to kiss

me, and I said no. Then he pushed me down on the couch and pulled my clothes off me. He wanted me to give him a blow job while I was naked, and I refused."

Bower walked back to his table and picked up a plastic bag. Then he said, "I am submitting into evidence one pair of women's panties." He removed them from the plastic bag and held them up to show how they were large and out of shape. Bower asked, "Mrs. Dew, are these the panties you were wearing the night you were assaulted?"

"Yes, Connor stretched them out of shape when he struggled to pull them off me."

"What happened after he removed your panties?"

"That's when he spread my legs apart and performed oral sex on me. No man, not even my husband, ever performed oral sex on me until Connor did it to me that night. After he finished, he started kissing me on my neck. I didn't realize until I got home that he'd given me a bunch of hickeys. While he was giving me the hickeys, I looked around the room for my phone. I wanted to call 911 because I thought he'd continue the assault all night, but I couldn't find my phone."

"How did you get away and get home?"

"He eventually needed to use the bathroom again and left me alone in the living room. That's when I gathered up my clothes and ran to my car. Thank God I'd left my keys in the car. I drove away still naked all the way home. I drove into my garage and then went straight to my shower and tried to wash all of Connor off me. When I got out of the shower, I looked in the mirror and saw all the hickeys."

"And what did you do next?"

"I cried myself to sleep. I couldn't call my husband because Connor had my phone. The next morning, I dressed to cover up the hickeys. I went to my eye appointment and then to work. When I walked into Connor's office, he tried to finger me again, but I told him I was done with that. Later in the morning, I went to HR and told them what Connor had done to me."

"Why didn't you call 911?"

"I wanted to wait until my husband got home."

"Thank you, Mrs. Dew, I have no further questions."

John walked to Molly and began, "Mrs. Dew, you just testified that your first conversation with Mr. Stone was when he called you to his office to tell you that he liked the way you looked in jeans. Is that correct?"

"Yes, that is correct."

"Mrs. Dew, I happen to know that when you had the conversation in Mr. Stone's office, that Debra Saint Vincent was present to witness the conversation. I have talked to Ms. Saint Vincent and Mr. Stone about the conversation. They both agree that what Mr. Stone actually said was that you were disrupting production in the shop because so many men spent too much time watching you in the shop. Mr. Stone told you the men watched you because you were very attractive. Isn't it true, Mrs. Dew, that you were called to Mr. Stone's office and were told to stay out of the shop? That you were told to do your work solely in the office and the classrooms?"

"Yes, he told me that."

"And isn't it true that Mr. Stone never actually said he liked the way you looked in jeans, but rather that he said that men in general find you attractive?"

"Well, that kind of means the same thing," Molly said.

"Mrs. Dew, when Connor Stone testifies, he will admit to having various sexual encounters with you in his office, but Mr. Stone will explain how you initiated each event. For example, you testified that on the first day in his new office, Mr. Stone had you take all your clothes off. Mr. Stone will claim that you walked into his office, closed, and locked both office doors. And that you then stood in front of his desk and asked for his advice on what type of bikinis you should buy for your cruise. That you then proceeded, on your own, to push your pants and panties down your body. He then told you to pull your pants up, to open the office doors, and to go back to your office. Mrs. Dew, isn't that what really happened?"

"No, he made me take my clothes off."

"Mrs. Dew, wasn't it the same for what you call the 'conference table routine'? It was your idea for Mr. Stone to finger you. Is that true?"

"No, it was all Connor's idea."

"Mrs. Dew, when Mr. Stone testifies, he will state that he spoke to you about the sin of adultery on many occasions. That you maintained that the two of you could have sex as often as you wanted, and it wouldn't be adultery unless one or both of you fell in love with the other. Is that true, Mrs. Dew?"

"Absolutely not. What Connor did to me was a sin."

"Mrs. Dew, you have testified that on the night you claim Mr. Stone assaulted you, that you were at Mr. Stone's home for the first and only time."

"That's correct."

"So, are you saying that you were never at Connor Stone's house prior to the night in question?"

"Yes."

"Mrs. Dew, do you recall meeting Connor's neighbor, Clint?"

"Yes, I met Clint."

"Mrs. Dew, in a day or two, when the defense presents its case, Clint will be called to this witness stand to testify about what he knows about this case. When he testifies, he is going to state that on the night in question, you were at Connor's home for the third time."

"That's not true."

"He is also going to state that on the first occasion, you spent the entire night at Connor's home."

"No."

"He will also state that almost every time he saw you at Connor Stone's home, you were naked and in a playful mood; that you even carried on conversations with him while you were in the nude."

"Clint is one of Connor's drinking buddies. He's going to say whatever Connor has told him to say."

"Mrs. Dew, do you know what Clint Schmitz does for a living?"

"No."

"Mrs. Dew, Clint Schmitz is the chief investigator for the Mantorville County Sheriff's Department."

Molly lowered her head before looking back up and staring past John. She was speechless, but every juror could see a small tear roll down her left cheek.

"Officer Schmitz will also testify that on the night in question, he walked into Connor Stone's garage and found you completely naked and aggressively grinding your bare butt cheeks into the groin of a fully clothed Connor Stone."

Molly maintained a blank stare and said nothing.

John went on, "Officer Schmitz will state that on the night in question, when you went from the garage and into the house, you were naked with no clothes on at all. Yet you claim that Connor Stone pulled your clothes off you in the living room."

Molly lowered her head but said nothing.

"Connor Stone will testify that when he entered the living room, you were naked and sitting on the coach. That you asked Connor to get your G-string from your car. After Connor retrieved the G-string, you wore it until later when you took it off in Connor's bedroom.

"Mrs. Dew, you never wore panties that night. You wore a G-string. The panties submitted into evidence were never in Connor Stone's home, were they Mrs. Dew?"

In a very weak voice, Molly said, "I was wearing panties that night."

John said, "Mrs. Dew, you testified that your husband called you while you were at Connor's house on the night in question. What did you say to your husband when he called you?"

"I told him I was with Connor."

"So, your husband knew that you were alone with Connor at Connor's house?"

"Yes."

"No further questions."

Molly left the stand and sat in one of the few empty areas in the courtroom.

The judge said, "Mr. Bower, your next witness."

"The state calls Samuel Dew."

Molly's husband entered the courtroom and walked to the witness stand to take his oath.

Bower asked a series of questions to establish that Molly and her husband had been married for over four years, that he was a salesman who traveled a lot and was away from home three or more nights a week. Then he asked, "When did you learn that Connor Stone had sexually assaulted your wife?"

Samuel replied, "When I returned home on a Thursday evening, Molly showed me the hickeys and said that Connor gave her the hickeys when he raped her."

"Did she say anything else?"

"Yes, she told me how Connor was obsessed with her and that he'd assaulted her many times in his office."

Bower asked, "Did she say why she went to Connor's house that night?"

"I asked her that question. She said that Connor insisted she see his house because she'd never been there, and he wanted her to see the house, so she'd leave me and move in with him."

"Thank you, Mr. Dew, no further questions."

The judge looked to John, "Mr. Sullivan, your witness."

John began, "Mr. Dew, the alleged assault took place on a Monday, and you just testified that you returned home from a business trip the following Thursday. Is that correct?"

"Yes."

"Mr. Dew, you also testified that on that Thursday, your wife told you she'd been assaulted the previous Monday, and she also told you that Mr. Stone assaulted her many times in his office in previous months. Is that correct?"

"Yes."

"Prior to the Thursday you arrived home, had your wife ever told you that Connor Stone was assaulting her at work?"

"No."

John asked, "Why didn't your wife tell you about her relations with Connor Stone prior to the Thursday when you returned home?"

"She said she didn't tell me earlier because she knew I'd make her quit her job, and she didn't want to lose her job."

"Mr. Dew, on the Monday night in question, did you make a phone call to your wife?"

"Yes, I did."

"What did your wife say to you?"

"She said she was at the Hubbell House with Connor and some friends from church."

At this point, every juror started writing on their notepad, which Samuel Dew noticed. He was visibly concerned.

John said, "So, your wife told you she was at the Hubbell House with friends from church?"

"Yes, they all had a bite to eat before she went to Connor's house."

"Mr. Dew, what would you say if I told you there were no friends from church and that your wife and Connor were never at the Hubbell House and definitely were not there at the time you called her on Thursday evening?"

"I would say that you were wrong."

All the jurors started writing again, which clearly bothered Molly's husband.

John said, "No further questions."

The judge pounded his gavel, said "Court is in recess until nine a.m. tomorrow," and left the courtroom.

John walked to our table, leaning to whisper to me and Emily, "If the trial ended right now, we'd have our verdict: not guilty."

I turned around to see all my supporters smiling. They hadn't heard what John said, but they were all thinking the same thing.

Day 4

Chapter 43

On Thursday morning, the courtroom was packed. This would be my day to testify. I'd had an early breakfast at the County Seat with John and Emily to go over my planned testimony. Everyone in the courtroom was waiting to hear what I'd say.

"Court is now in session," said the judge. "Mr. Bower, your next witness."

"The state calls Roy Dinger."

Dinger stepped into the stand and took his oath.

Bower only questioned Dinger for a few minutes to establish that Dinger was from Yellow River County and that he'd been appointed chief investigator because I had relationships with too many people in the Mantorville County Sheriff's office. Otherwise, Bower's questioning was just a summary of what prior witnesses had already presented.

When it was his turn, John walked up to the stand, "Mr. Dinger, do you know Clint Schmitz?"

"Yes, I do. Officer Schmitz is a deputy with the Mantorville County Sheriff's office. He is also the neighbor of Connor Stone."

"Clint Schmitz claims that you interviewed him."

"Yes, I did," Dinger replied.

"Then why didn't you submit an interview report?"

"I did. It was in the case file with all the other documents from this case at the time I left the Yellow River sheriff's office."

John asked, "What about the lab report? We have an email from you regarding the lab results, but we have not seen the actual lab report."

Dinger said, "The lab report and all of my other reports were in my case file in my desk."

John looked at the judge, who had an incredibly angry expression on his face. Then John looked back at Dinger, "No further questions."

As John walked back to our table, Dinger rose to leave, but the judge told him to stay seated.

The judge looked at the prosecution, "Mr. Bower, based on Mr. Dinger's testimony, we're missing critical evidence in this case. I want you and Mr. Dinger to immediately go to the Yellow River County Sheriff's office and locate the case file we just heard about. We will recess for four hours. When we reconvene, I want to see the case file in this courtroom."

Bower said, "Understood, Your Honor."

The judge asked, "Mr. Dinger, do you understand what I need you to do?"

"Yes, Your Honor."

The judge said, "Court is in recess until two this afternoon."

The judge pounded his gavel, harder than usual, then left.

There was a lot of noise in the courtroom as everybody left, talking about what had just happened.

Bower was packing in a rush and John approached him, speaking quietly for a minute before Bower and Dinger left the room together.

John let Emily and I know that Bower was furious with Yellow River County.

The courtroom was now almost empty, except for our group of nine standing around the table. Grandma asked John, "What happens next?"

"Emily and I will use one of the conference rooms here to do some research for the next four hours. I've never encountered a situation like this before, so Emily and I need to determine what our options are. All of you just need to make sure you're back here before two."

They left to find a conference room while the rest of us headed to the County Seat. As we entered the café, a hush came over the room. Most of the people there had been at the trial and were obviously talking about it when we walked in. Our group of seven placed our orders and then took a table in one of the corners. We sat down and everyone resumed talking again. We stayed at the County Seat until noon, then walked down to the park where we gathered around one of the picnic tables and Grandma said a group prayer. Then we broke out to different areas of the park for individual prayer. After we finished our individual prayers, we gathered back at the picnic table and visited.

Debra said, "It was good that the witnesses were sequestered. If Molly's husband would have heard her testimony, he may not have told the truth when he testified."

Mom said, "That's true. When he told the truth about the phone call, it exposed her lie."

I said, "I don't understand why she claims we had sex on the couch instead of in the bedroom?"

Dakotah said, "I don't think she wants her husband to know she was in your bedroom because it makes her look guilty."

Julia looked at me and asked, "Do you know what Clint

told Dinger?"

"Yes," I said. "Clint met with John, Emily, and me. He told us what he told Dinger. John plans to reveal everything when he questions Clint as a witness for the defense. That plan could change if they find the interview report in the case file."

Grandma asked, "Will the lab report help?"

I said, "If the lab report is found, it will verify the accuracy of the email but will not add anything to our defense."

Mom said, "It's one thirty."

We all stood up and started the fifteen-minute walk back to the courthouse. The courtroom was packed with more people than in the morning. Luckily, the bailiff had placed a reserved sign on the pew behind our table. John and Emily weren't in the room yet, but as we took our seats, John came through a side door and motioned for me to join him. He took me down the hall to the conference room with Emily. "I just finished talking with David Bower," John said. "He has the case file and read Clint's interview report. I asked him if seeing the report before the trial, would he still have gone to trial. David didn't answer me, but based on his face, I don't believe he would've proceeded with the trial."

I asked, "How is this going to affect the trial?"

John replied, "It all depends on what the judge does next."

"We need to get in the courtroom," said Emily.

The three of us entered the courtroom through the side door and took our seats. Bower was at his table, a box on the floor next to his chair. The clerk ordered all to rise, the judge walked in and sat. His gavel came down hard as he said "Court is now in session. I've asked the jurors to remain in the jury room until we resolve the issue of the missing case file. Mr. Bower, what do you have to report?"

David stood up and said, "Your Honor, Mr. Dinger and I

located the case file. It was in Mr. Dinger's old desk."

The judge asked, "Where is the file now?"

David reached into the box and pulled out a pile of papers about five inches high, "Your Honor, I have the file right here." He pulled out another pile, similar in height, and set it atop the first. "Your Honor, these papers make up the entire file we haven't seen yet, over two thousand pages."

The judge just stared at the pile of papers, then "Mr. Bower and Mr. Sullivan, take over a copy machine here in the courthouse to make a copy of the case file for the defense. Mr. Bower will keep the original. You have overnight to review the file. We'll determine how we go forward with this trial tomorrow. Court is in recess until then."

After the judge left, John turned so everyone in the pew behind us could hear him say, "Emily and I will be here until we have a copy of the file. Then we'll take it back to our office and start going through it." John looked at Dakotah, "Can you stay here for a little bit? We'll copy the lab report first and you're the most qualified person in this group to help us review it. It's twenty-eight pages long and I want you to see if there are any surprises in the results."

Dakotah nodded, "I'll stay as long as I'm needed." She smiled at me, encouragingly.

John got up to go coordinate with Bower, and Emily asked Dakotah to sit in John's chair while she went to help make copies. I said I'd wait with Dakotah, and the rest of our group headed out to Hank's place. Dakotah and I chatted closely for almost an hour before Emily returned to the courtroom with the lab report, "This is the twenty-eight-page report. Please read every detail to see if there's something we can use."

Dakotah asked, "Can I write notes on this copy?"

"Yes. Yours is a working copy. John and I are set up in the conference room next to the copy machine downstairs.

When you're finished, bring it down to me."

"Will do," said Dakotah.

Emily left and then Dakotah said to me, "Why don't you go for a walk?"

"Why?" I said.

"Because I need to concentrate on what I'm reading, and I can't do that if you're watching me."

I took a walk down the hill to the park, thanking God for bringing Dakotah into my life.

When I returned to the courtroom, Dakotah was seated at our table, but she wasn't reading.

"Are you done?" I asked.

"Yes, and I found something, but I want to tell everyone at the same time." She stood and said, "Let's go downstairs."

We left to find John and Emily. John was with Bower by the copy machine. Dakotah told John, "I found something."

"Let's go into the conference room," he said, leading us into the room where Emily was working.

John closed the door and Dakotah said, "Early in the report it states that Molly's DNA was found on a couch cushion. The report was pretty boring after that until I read page twenty-six."

Emily picked up her copy of the report and turned to page twenty-six.

Dakotah said, "Male DNA was found in the specimen taken from Molly's vagina. It was not a match to either Molly's husband or Connor. She obviously had sex with a third man between Monday and Thursday."

John said, "This could explain the bruising on her vagina."

I asked, "Are you going to tell Bower?"

"Yes, we're sharing everything we find," John confirmed.

Emily told him, "Get back to making copies. We're going

to be up all night the way it is."

John said, "Emily's right. Be back here with everyone tomorrow at eight so we can brief you all on what we found overnight."

Day 5

Chapter 44

Our group, including John and Emily, arrived at the courthouse together and went straight to the conference room. John and Emily both wore their same clothes from yesterday and John hadn't shaved. I asked, "Did you get any sleep?"

"We got a couple hours sleep at the office. We didn't have time to go home and change."

John addressed the group, "Does everyone know about the lab report?" Dakotah and I had filled everyone in, so they all nodded. Then John said, "Emily found something else last night."

Everyone looked expectantly at Emily, who said, "Three years ago, Connor had a neighbor who lived up the hill. He's an amateur photographer and likes to use a telephoto lens. This neighbor gave Dinger a photo of Molly Dew standing on Connor's deck with Connor and Clint. Molly's totally naked while the men are fully clothed. The photo is date-stamped over a month before the date that Molly claims she was at Connor's house for the first time."

"Oh, my Lord," said Grandma and Mom together. Everyone began getting excited.

John said, "At this point, I have no doubt that Connor

will get a not-guilty verdict, but I have no idea what direction the judge will take this trial."

I asked if Bower knew about the picture, and John said, "He most likely came across it last night. Nevertheless, Emily and I are meeting with David in a few minutes, and we'll make sure he's seen it."

Grandma asked, "Do you have any idea what's going to happen next?"

John said, "It's all up to the judge. He'll be terribly upset after David and I tell him what was in the case file. God only knows what he's going to do."

Emily said, "John and I have to meet with David."

The rest of us headed for the courtroom. On the stairs' first landing, we could see through the windows to Sixth Street, along which three different TV news trucks were parked close to the courthouse. We saw reporters and camera crews coming up the steps as Dakotah voiced everyone's thoughts, "They must expect something to happen today. They haven't been here all week."

Grandma voiced the same words Mom had told us boys every Sunday before church, "We better get in there before someone takes our pew!"

The room was so packed that the bailiff was setting up folding chairs in the empty space at the back. The room buzzed with the sounds of everyone, including our own group, talking nonstop in hushed tones. After several minutes, the attorneys entered. Some more time passed before the clerk's "All rise." We sat back down as the judge pounded his gavel and said, "Court is now in session. I've asked the jury to remain in the jury room until after we discuss the case file. Mr. Bower, do you have anything to report?"

"Yes, Your Honor. May counsel and I approach the bench?"

"You may approach the bench."

David and John walked to the bench and leaned toward the judge. The attorney's tables, where I sat, were close enough for me to just barely hear Bower explain, "Your Honor, after reviewing the case file, we found two significant things in addition to the Clint Schmitz interview report that will affect this trial."

"What are they?" asked the judge.

David said, "The lab report said that male DNA was found in the vagina specimen. The DNA did not match Connor Stone or Samuel Dew."

The judge said, "So she had sex with a third man?"

John said, "Yes, Your Honor. And that could explain the bruising on and in her vagina."

David said, "Your Honor, the other significant finding was a photograph. One of the defendant's neighbors lives up the hill overlooking Mr. Stone's backyard. The neighbor used a telephoto lens to take a picture of Molly Dew standing on Mr. Stone's deck, talking to Mr. Stone and Clint Schmitz. Mrs. Dew is totally naked while both men are fully clothed. The photo is date stamped over a month before Mrs. Dew claims she was at the house for the first time."

No one spoke for a few moments, and then the judge asked, "What about Dinger's report on his interview with Clint Schmitz?"

David said, "The entire report is there. It was actually more explicit than John was when he questioned Molly Dew."

"What do you mean?" asked the judge.

John replied, "The report describes how Clint Schmitz watched Molly Dew rub her naked body all over Connor Stone in very suggestive ways. That she was aggressively grinding her buttocks into Connor Stone's groin. This was the same night as the alleged rape."

David said, "The report states that Molly Dew was naked

at Mr. Stone's home most of the times Clint Schmitz saw her there."

The judge kept looking at David, then he briefly looked at John before slowly shaking his head. Then he told both of them to take their seats.

He issued a fifteen-minute recess, "I'll be in my chambers reviewing the options before us so I can return to announce the direction this trial will go. Have the jury return to the courtroom. This court is in recess." He pounded his gavel. We all rose as the judge left the room.

The second the door closed behind the judge, the former buzz turned into a dull roar, with people no longer whispering their conversations. I turned to see a surprising number of people packed into the room. Reporters were all in the back, with easy access to their camera people waiting outside the room. After only a few minutes, we heard the clerk, "All rise." The jury returned and as the last juror was seated, the crowd took their seats and started talking again.

John walked over to Bower. The two of them were always serious together, but it was apparent this conversation was more intense than usual. After a few minutes' discussion, they just stood there facing each other, not talking, but still communicating. And you could tell from their eyes that they were in agreement. Bower gave a small nod in the affirmative and John acknowledged it similarly before walking back to our table. He gave me a confident look before whispering something to Emily, who responded with a smile. I was just about to ask what was going on when— "All rise!"

As the judge entered and took his seat, the courtroom was uncomfortably quiet.

The judge spoke, "This court is back in session." He paused for a moment and then, "Throughout my long career, I've never encountered a case or trial like this one. We should've had a straightforward trial. All the witnesses were sequestered until they'd testified. The prosecution presented their case and their witnesses. All that remains is for the defense to present their case and witnesses.

"However, the prosecutor's last witness revealed that a significant amount of evidence had been lost. Now, what was lost has been found. After reviewing the newly found evidence, it is obvious that there are additional questions that should have been asked of the witnesses who have already given testimony. The new evidence is so significant that, had it been known before the trial, both the prosecution and the defense would have presented their cases in a much different manner. Knowing this, I cannot allow these proceedings to continue. I'm declaring a mistrial."

Collective gasps came from the courtroom as the judge spoke over them, "The state will have the opportunity to retry the case if they so wish. However, if the state does proceed with a new trial, I require the county to pay for Connor Stone's defense. Mr. Stone has incurred a considerable expense for this trial. Mantorville County subcontracted the investigation of the charges to Yellow River County, but Mantorville County remains responsible for the investigation and the mishandling of the evidence. If there is a new trial, Mantorville County will pay for Mr. Stone's defense."

The judge lifted his gavel high, ready to pound it for the last time and end the trial. But before he could lower his arm, Bower stood up and said, "Your Honor?"

The judge softly set his gavel down and responded, "Mr. Bower."

"Your Honor, I anticipated that this was a possibility, so I've already spoken to the county attorney and received direction from him regarding the mistrial. I can assure you that the state will not pursue a new trial."

Some people in the courtroom started to clap their hands. The judge pounded his gavel, "Order in the court." The room went silent. "Mr. Bower, is there anything else?"

"Yes, Your Honor. After reviewing the revelations of the last twenty-four hours, the state requests that in the interest of justice, all outstanding charges against Connor Stone be dropped."

The courtroom was deadly quiet as the judge considered this. Every person hung on the judge's next words: "The court rules that in the interest of justice, all outstanding charges against Connor Stone are hereby dropped. This court is adjourned." Bam. The judge pounded his gavel for the last time.

Cheers and clapping erupted as people jumped up happily. I was surprised to see almost everyone in the room was celebrating my favorable outcome. The judge stood there, waiting for the clerk to be able to audibly say "All rise." But the judge just looked at the joyous crowd, shook his head to the clerk, and went back to his chambers.

I Listened to the Angel

CHAPTER 45

E VERYONE WAS HUGGING EACH OTHER when Emily said, "We should leave now, or we'll never get out of here."

Hank said, "Follow me" and led us out.

John asked if I wanted to talk to the press. I told him to make a statement, but that I didn't have any comments today. I saw Molly and her husband making their way to the exit, but they were quite a way behind our group.

We got outside and were at the top of the steps when the media surrounded us. Newspaper reporters and TV crews all shouted questions at the same time and I kept repeating "No comment." When John started to speak, everyone moved toward him. Dakotah and I stood together, with the rest of our group, near John.

Then I looked back and saw Molly and Samuel walking toward me. They really had nowhere else to go on the narrow exit walkway where my group was standing. They got closer and she tried to hide her face. Not from me, but from all the reporters and cameras. As she neared, I realized I hadn't been this close to her since our last day at work. She approached and our eyes met for a moment before she abruptly turned to pull Samuel, so he'd walk faster. I also noted that, despite wearing a loose-fitting dress every day of the trial, today she wore very tight-fitting slacks. And as she walked by today, I felt nothing. For the first time in my life, I had zero desire to look at her body.

Dakotah stood in front of me with a big smile on her face. I'd already disclosed my entire past to Dakotah; she knew all my tendencies, habits, and struggles. And now, Dakotah was just as happy as me to learn that Molly no longer had any control over me.

"Guess what?" Dakotah said.

"What?"

"Molly turned around to see if you were checking her out. She looked incredibly disappointed when she saw the back of your head."

Dakotah and I just stood there, grinning at each other like teenagers in love.

Then suddenly, the angel stood between Dakotah and me. It told me, "Before you ask me Hank's question, the answer is yes. Faith is alive and will be rescued in a few more years. I'm here to tell you that if you marry Dakotah, she will alter the course of the rest of your life for the better." Then it was gone. Dakotah stood there rubbing her eyes.

Grandma tapped me on the back of my shoulder. I turned to face her, and she placed her wedding ring in my hand. "The Lord just told me that you needed this now," she said. I thanked her and turned back toward Dakotah.

Dakotah spoke, puzzled, "I had something in my eyes for a moment."

I said, "Your eyes are fine. The angel was standing between us for several seconds."

"What did the angel want?"

"The angel told me to marry you."

Dakotah smiled, "Really?"

I knelt down right there: "Dakotah, I love you and I want to spend the rest of my life with you. Will you marry me?"

As people saw me on my knees, everyone, including the media, were focused on Dakotah and me.

She said YES!

I held up the ring and Dakotah stretched out her hand. She recognized the ring as I slid it on her finger. Dakotah looked over at Grandma, who had a big smile on her face.

I stood and we embraced. We kissed the purest kiss I've ever felt. And then, we kissed some more.

When we'd stopped kissing, I still had Dakotah in my arms. I looked into my soulmate's eyes and told her, "I'm glad I listened to the angel."

About the Author

Terry Eckstein has spent fifty years as a career business manager with most of the years as a human resource professional. During that time, Terry had the opportunity to work for several different companies, ranging in size from twenty-person privately owned businesses to Fortune 500 companies with thousands of employees. While this story is a work of fiction, it is inspired from actual events that took place throughout Terry's career.

Raised in a little northern Minnesota community where he attended the same public school from kindergarten through high school, Terry was immersed in small-town values and small-town problems. Terry's family owned a small business where he worked since the age of ten. By the time he was a teenager Terry was interacting with customers, solving problems, and learning how to deal with different types of people. This proved to be the perfect environment to prepare him for a career in human resources. This all changed late in Terry's career when he succumbed to temptation and had an inappropriate relationship with a woman who worked for him. Terry not only lost his job and his standing in the community, but the woman filed erroneous charges, resulting in Terry's arrest, incarceration, and eventual trial.

The whole experience left an indelible mark on Terry but propelled him into writing this novel.

Made in the USA
Monee, IL
13 March 2024

54940810R00260